ONE SPARK

A Disparate Energy Novel

ONE SPARK

By Holly D. Morgan

Red Berry Press

Cover and dust jacket design by Benita Thompson of Kairos Book Design
Hardcover case laminate and interior illustrations design by EFA_finearts
Map of The Seven Republics by Vojin Kremic
Map of Stillfield by Jeremy Morgan
End paper design from Canva Pro
Publishing imprint by Christy Boughan

First Edition: 2024

Edited by Angela Morse of An Encouraging Thought
The text for this book was set in Garamond

Red Berry Press LLC

Red Berry Press

To Kimberleigh
Without you this book would not exist
Without you parenthood would be a lot lonelier
Thanks for being my BFF

The Seven Republics

Hastiet

Tesserin

Wuslick

Preen

Stillfield

Vasco

Vespher

THE FIVE ENERGIES

FEAR:
YELLOW PILL

ANGER:
RED PILL

DISGUST:
WHITE PILL

JOY:
PURPLE PILL

SADNESS:
GREEN PILL

NORTH
SECTOR

Hodgerton
Residence

Capital
Building

Energy Watch
Office

Public
Safety Building

Samay's
Restaurant

SOUTH
SECTOR

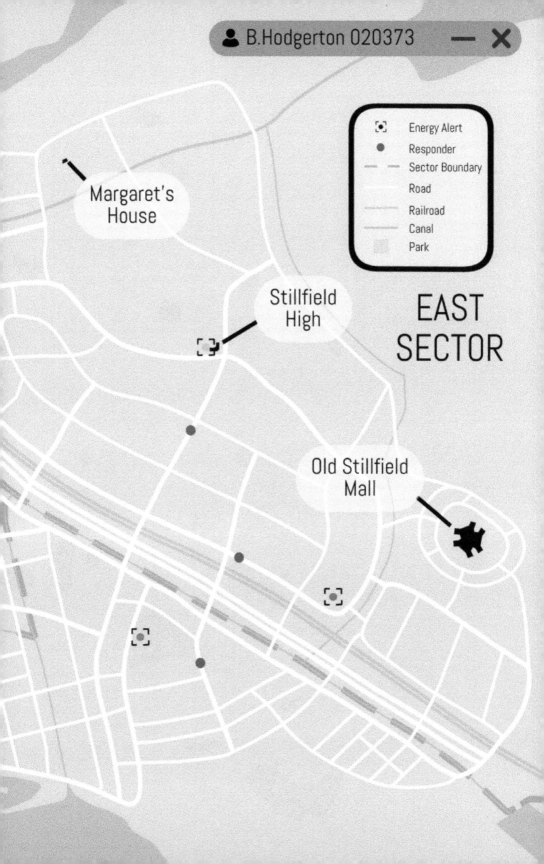

Margaret's House

Stillfield High

Old Stillfield Mall

EAST SECTOR

Energy Alert
Responder
Sector Boundary
Road
Railroad
Canal
Park

ONE

The computer alarm blared as lights flared across the screen. Safe in his cubicle at Energy Watch, Benjamin Hodgerton zoomed in on the alert, acutely aware of the time on the clock. Almost lunch time. His stomach clenched. He had ten minutes.

He turned his attention back to the screen. There, at the high school. A yellow circle flashed around the gym, quicker and quicker. On the side of his screen was the number seven. Looked like a teenager was nervous about his P.E. lesson.

Any alert seven or above required assistance, and the color signified the type of emotional energy. With his own nerves reeling, Ben pressed a button on the speaker next to him.

"Alert. Electric Disturbance. Stillfield High School gym. Immediate attention."

After a few moments, his call was answered.

"Unit Six, we're on our way."

A small blue dot on Ben's map closed in on the flashing circle. He imagined the scene when they arrived. A seven would result in a small burst of energy—not enough to hit anyone nearby but enough to see the lines of lightning arcing across their body. The Responders likely used a weighted grounding blanket to wrap the student, protecting them and others from the electricity becoming more dangerous.

But no, the alert wasn't lowered. Instead, it increased, the flashing escalating. The number crept up. Eight... Nine...

Ben's heart raced, worried for the unknown student. The numbers almost hit ten before slowly starting to lower, continuing until they hit zero. The threat had been neutralized. The slow decline of the numbers told Ben the student had been tranquilized, not killed. At least there was relief in that.

He jumped at a buzzing in his pocket. He hadn't realized how close to the edge of his seat he'd scooted. As his phone buzzed, he pulled it out. The lock screen glowed, notifying him of new messages from his wife, Jemma.

> MAYDAY!! HELP!!

> Everyone's okay, so don't freak out

> I'm just feeling a bit on edge

Three little bubbles moved at the bottom of the screen, not giving Ben time to process the previous calls for help.

> Another meltdown today. Literally.

Shoot, he thought. Ben's stress from the alert was replaced with worry for his family.

> What happened?

He turned back to his monitor, running fingers through his brown hair that was in need of a haircut. The other hand abandoned his phone on the desk in exchange for his computer mouse. Although he was assigned over the East Sector, and this shift was specifically over the school zone, he exited the screen and pulled up the North Sector. He zoomed in on the older ranch style house he called home. No new activity flashed. Well, none severe enough to need a Responder. They dodged a bullet—this time. There was no guarantee his six-year-old son Louie would be missed if his energy outbursts continued to grow.

As Ben relaxed into his seat, his side vision caught sight of his coworker, Buran, across the large walkway, looking toward him. His icy blue stare turned back to his own screen before Ben glanced at him fully. No matter. It was fine if Buran caught what he was doing. It wasn't like it was *wrong* for Ben to check another map sector.

A vibration caught Ben's attention once more. His racing heart slowed as he checked his phone.

The newest message was accompanied by a picture of a toy shark, the favorite of his four-year-old son, Mackie. The shark's tail now looked like dripping candle wax instead of a strong back fin.

> Boys fought over this, Louie lost some control. Bit chaotic, but finally the boys stopped yelling. Playing with trains now. Hope they don't get scorched.

Louie wasn't much older than Mackie, and yet their differences were like night and day. Where Mackie was sociable and outgoing, Louie was quiet and calm. Most of the time, anyway; today was one of the times he wasn't. And Mackie's shark toy, unfortunately, suffered the consequences.

> Checked the map. We're good. I'm glad everyone is okay. You still feeling on edge?

> Thank goodness. I was afraid Louie was going to hurt Mackie but he's okay. The shark is replace-able, Mackie is not. Teaching them both how to regulate their emotions is difficult when I'm not good at it either.

> I think you're pretty good! Nobody is perfect all the time. Believe me, I see it daily. You can take a bath when I get home.

He geared himself up to give the extra support he knew his wife would need after having a rough day. Of course, every day was rough when raising a child with superpowers.

His phone buzzed. Another message.

> Thanks. By the way, the playroom's lightbulb is burnt out again.

Ben sighed. *Something's gotta be wrong with that circuit; that's the third lightbulb this month.* One of the downsides to purchasing a home built before the Rain of Fire, but they couldn't afford a newer, luxury apartment downtown. Most of his home's interior had needed updating in the last hundred years, yet the same walls still stood. Ben saw it as a testament to his home's resilience. If it could survive the nuclear war that wiped out ninety-eight percent of the world's population, Ben could survive another work week at a job he despised.

He refocused on his work and glanced at the bottom right of his screen. 11:57 AM. Three minutes left.

Ben checked the map once more, making sure he was back over the East schooling zone before he locked the screen. He pulled his lunch bag out of a drawer, knowing the contents within were safely packaged. It was imperative they didn't end up in the wrong hands.

"Hey Ben! You coming to the break room today for lunch? After you take care of your bathroom 'business,' of course," his work buddy, Oliver, asked in his nasally voice. A smile spread on his round face as he peered over the divider that separated their desks. Oliver sat next to Ben but in a different row that matched his sector assignment. The silver frames of his glasses glinted in the light from the windows next to where Buran's desk was.

"You know it. Just gotta go real quick and I'll meet you there."

"Like clockwork. Maybe you should get that checked out." Oliver chuckled, like he did every day about Ben's bathroom routine.

"At least I can keep track of time." Ben raised an eyebrow.

"Hey," Oliver said. "I'm not always late when I drive the morning carpool."

"Not always, but every day this week."

Oliver scoffed, holding a hand to his chest. "It's only Thursday! I'll be on time tomorrow. Promise."

Ben wasn't sure he believed that, but he was grateful for Oliver—and glad he didn't sit next to Buran, the office outcast. Something wasn't quite right with him. Thankfully, they didn't have much interaction, considering Buran was an Intaker.

"Another sinkhole in those apartments downtown, Cavern Estates. Whoever named that place must have been a psychic," Torrie said as she pranced by on her way to the break room.

"Mr. Dogivan aggaaainn?" Oliver sniffled as he looked at Torrie.

"Yep. Whoever is on intake duty tomorrow's gonna have a heck of a time getting that stubborn mule to agree to treatment." Torrie's dirt-colored eyes rolled as she took a pump of the hand sanitizer Oliver kept on his desk. The strong scent filled the space, but Ben was used to it. Oliver was a stickler when it came to germs. Torrie continued, "How he can keep denying it's him when his bed is found at the bottom of the sinkhole every time is beyond me!"

"Need to ship him off to Lucky Island already," Oliver said with a smirk.

Ben cringed at the mention of Lucky Island. The place Disparates—the portion of the population whose emotions create physical energy—used to go to when they couldn't control their powers. The stories that came from there were ones of nightmares. But that was all they were, right? Just stories? No one in the government had confirmed what really happened there. They also hadn't denied any of it.

Thank goodness it was no longer in operation.

Ben stood, realizing the minutes were ticking by. "I'll meet you all in there." He rushed to the bathroom. Worry filled his soul when he entered and saw that the one bathroom stall was locked. Sweat formed across his palms; he didn't have much time. He checked his watch. It was already 11:59. He needed to get in the stall within the next minute. *I'm going to have to take it out here and hope no one walks in.*

He unzipped his lunch bag and reached inside. Smooth, round plastic met his grip, and he carefully untwisted the top, ensuring he didn't spill any of the last few small red capsules into his bag. He pulled out a water bottle with his fingers as he grasped one capsule in his other palm. He tried to pop it into his mouth, but the capsule stuck to his clammy palm a moment longer than ideal. The bathroom stall opened, and Buran walked out. He glanced at Ben as he walked to the sink, watching as Ben finally took a swig of his water.

Great, the last person in the office I'd want to know. Ben swallowed his water-encased capsule in one large gulp. Having accomplished the purpose of his bathroom trip, he washed his hands at the sink with Buran, hopeful he didn't realize what had just happened.

"You don't need to be ashamed, you know," Buran said as he pumped soap.

Ben turned red. "Ashamed of what?"

"I have the white ones." Buran winked as he dried his hands with a paper towel. He threw it in the trash and left the bathroom, leaving Ben behind.

Jemma turned the left faucet all the way on. A long, hot bubble bath was just what she needed. Steam started to rise out of the bathtub as she undressed. She liked her bath water piping hot, enough to feel burning without turning her skin red. When the water was a few inches from the top, she turned the faucet off.

Slowly, she inserted her feet, one after the other, and the bubbles on the water's surface swayed. Her bare body had been colder than she realized in the open bathroom air, the thawing of her feet forming goose-bumps across her skin. The sensation heightened her senses, focusing her on the moment she was in. The rest of her body followed her feet and submerged into the steaming bath. Water licked at the sand-colored hairs on the back of her neck that escaped her messy top bun, turning them a darker shade of brown.

As her body marinated in the bath, thoughts marinated in her brain. Worries, fears, desires. Her days were filled with conflict after conflict and snack after snack. She never imagined chasing around two boys would be this much work.

In the past, she was an analyst, helping the fifteen percent of the population who were Disparates get the treatment they needed. That job was tough, but she pondered if it'd be worth it to go back to work. She missed adult interactions, getting actual breaks to herself. The pay wasn't commensurate with the work, though. Plus, she knew if she went back, she'd be wondering each day if she should quit to be with her boys. The grass always seemed greener on the other side, but often, it was the same shade.

Bang! The wall shook from the impact of a little body. *That was probably Mackie,* Jemma thought. He loved running full speed down the hallway. He was an April Fools baby, his fifth birthday only six weeks away. Jemma was convinced that was the reason why he loved jokes so much.

She smiled as she recalled his joke of the day, remembering the laughter that escaped from both of them at the end.

"Knock Knock."

"Who's there?"

"Zoom."

"Zoom who?"

"Zoom did you think it was?"

Knock knock jokes were his favorite. Today's joke foreshadowed the zooming he'd been doing all day, running back and forth along the hallway between his room and the living room. Jemma had lost count of the number of times she had asked him to slow down. He was proud of how quickly his long legs moved him. Those long legs made him almost as tall as his older brother.

Louie was supposed to start Year One this upcoming school year. He had turned six last October, on the fifteenth, missing the cutoff to start sooner. This added extra stress to Jemma as she contemplated how the next school year might go.

He has such a hard time making friends. How are his teachers going to react to him? Maybe we should wait another year before sending him; he can't control his emotions enough to control his powers. What if something bad happens? Nowhere is truly safe.

Jemma's chest tightened under the pressure of the water. She tucked a wet strand of hair that escaped her bun behind her ear. As her fingertips connected with her head, she felt a small jolt of electricity. The surprise pulled her out of her thoughts as her lungs expanded with a deep breath.

No, his school is prepared for students like him. His teachers are trained. They'll know how to help him. Of course, he's pretty young for showing powers... perhaps his teachers won't have quite as much experience...

She pushed the thoughts out of her mind. Surely there had to be more children like Louie. He was different, but not that much.

And they had tools to help Disparates regulate their emotions. A safe room in each classroom, made of concrete and void of any objects, for the times other strategies didn't work. Safety was always the first priority. She was grateful for the advancements in understanding and treatment that had occurred in this last generation while fully aware of the mountain of work still ahead.

Have him come to my preschool class, Jemma recalled her friend Caty advising her one girls' night after she expressed her concerns. *Both your boys are old enough.* Jemma told her she would think about it, even though she knew she wouldn't. She wasn't ready yet.

Footsteps sounded on the other side of the door, and the knob turned. She froze, expecting one of her boys to barge in, attempting to escape bedtime.

"Mind if I join you?" Ben popped his head in the doorway and smiled at his naked wife. "The boys are both asleep now."

Jemma sighed, relieved to see his gray eyes watching her, surprised once again by the butterflies flickering in her chest. How he was able to make her feel this way after ten years, she didn't know, but she wouldn't want it any other way.

"The water is starting to get cold, but we can add some extra hot water to warm it."

"I'm sure I can get it hot in there," he winked, clearly aware of how cheesy he could be.

Jemma laughed as she scooted by the bathtub drain. She opened the plug to let some of the water out and turned the hot faucet on. Ben undressed and seated himself on the other side, sliding his legs around Jemma's waist and down the outline of her legs. She leaned against him and rested her head on his chest, right below his chin. They sat in silence, letting the sloshing water settle as they relaxed into each other.

Jemma closed her eyes, taking in the feelings of this moment. Ten years. He knew her better than anyone else, and yet she still felt like there was more she was hiding. A part lost, even to her.

Two

Ben leaned back, observing the screen in front of him from afar. He'd been put on intake duty as soon as he'd arrived at work that morning. Late again, thanks to Oliver. Buran had called out sick, and since Ben had previous experience as an Intaker, he was asked to sub in. Ben tried not to worry about their run-in yesterday, but he couldn't help but think it might be more than a coincidence that Buran was gone. Thank goodness it was finally Friday.

The thought had immediately filled him with dread. Not only that, but intakes were the worst part of his job. He didn't like to think about the time he'd been on the other side of the camera screen.

Thanks to his medication, he didn't dwell on that long. His anger washed away, like the water down the drain after last night's bath. If his anger had lasted much longer, he'd talk to an Analyst to get a higher dose of meds. At least, that was what he'd done in the past. Now that he was on the highest dose, he wasn't sure what the next step would be with an Analyst. With an Intaker, however, he knew what would happen.

Ben sat in an uncomfortable office chair, sipping water from a bottle, the video feed from Intake Room 3 on the screen in front of him. He sat straighter as an older man entered. A microphone rested on the desk, waiting to be switched on. Ben placed his water bottle to the right of the screen, catching it as it almost toppled onto a pile of folders. He screwed the lid tighter, his heart beat returning to normal after the close call. Redoing paperwork was not his idea of a good time.

Ben added a chocolate wrapper to the mountain that was forming on top of the trashcan under the desk. Intakes made him stressed, and stress made him eat. He knew it wasn't a healthy escape, but it was the best he could do in his current situation.

He had nibbled on the chocolate bar during his last intake, a Disparate who caused all of his employer's computers to short out while at work, feeling anxious and overwhelmed about the fast approaching deadline he was working on.

Then there was the bagel Ben barely finished this morning while intaking a young girl. She had caused her class to float to the ceiling when the teacher announced they had raised the most money for the school fundraiser and earned a pizza party.

Right before lunch, he ate an entire sleeve of crackers during an intake with a teenage boy. He had started a fire in his own home after a fight with his mom, who didn't want him going out with his new girlfriend. Ben wasn't surprised to see a teenager in the intake room; they were a common occurrence. Many times, Disparate energy didn't intensify until after puberty hit; as hormones raged, so did emotions. Ben understood that well, as that was when his own energy presented itself.

Each of these cases was an easy fix. An increase in the yellow pill would help with the work anxiety. A new school built and trained to handle Disparate children while they were still too young for medication would be a better fit for the girl; it was a shame about the pizza party she would miss.

And then there was the young teen who was scared and confused, insisting over and over again that he didn't mean to start a fire as tears fell from his eyes. Ben reassured him that he understood how he felt, that a little red pill would keep it from happening again, as long as he was diligent at taking it every day at exactly the same time.

He popped his own little red pill during this intake as the clock struck noon.

"Welcome back, Mr. Dogivan." The microphone squealed as Ben released the button, turning his attention to the last intake of the day. The Disparate on the screen winced.

"Welcome back? Who is this? You don't sound like Buran?" The wrinkles on the old man's face creased into tight lines.

"Nope, I'm Benjamin Hodgerton. Mr. Kuzmin is out sick today, so I'll be doing your intake. I know this isn't your first time, so hopefully we can get through everything quickly and make sure you get the best care possible."

"Buran's sick? Buran is never sick." Mr. Dogivan tilted his head to the side, his eyes narrowing.

Ben bent to the microphone. "I understand you've met with Buran in the past, but I can assure you that I am here to help. I only have a few questions to ask you. Before we start, I do need to let you know that our conversation is being recorded today. Can you state your full name please?"

"Charles Lee Dogivan, the third."

"Thank you Mr. Dogivan. Do you know why you are here?"

"Yes, I know why I'm here, but I didn't do it. It was my neighbor Carl, I swear. I ain't never had Disparate problems before! I'm sixty-eight years old. I think I'd know by now if I was!" The microphone screeched as Mr. Dogivan's voice rose at the end.

"I hear you." Ben tried to calm Mr. Dogivan. This conversation wouldn't get anywhere if he didn't. "It's hard to acknowledge what your energy can do. I see in your records that this is your third time being brought in by Responders."

Mr. Dogivan shook as he rose from the stool that was bolted to the ground. His eyes wandered around the room as if searching for the small round camera dot that was hidden in the corner, disguised as one of the bolts.

Intakes weren't supposed to know where the camera was; it needed to stay hidden so it was less likely for someone to break it. His gaze landed in the corner below the camera, his sad brown eyes sagging downward.

"It wasn't me. If my Eliza was here, she'd tell ya. Never once in our forty-seven years of marriage did I disparate. Energy? Pfth. What energy?" He sank onto the stool, then added in a quiet voice, "I can't believe I lost her."

Tears fell from his eyes. As they hit the ground, the spots where they landed shook. Thankfully, the room was covered in an insulated steel that resisted earth energy.

"I'm sorry for your loss, Mr. Dogivan," Ben offered a sincere apology. "Grief can open a lot of emotions. It can be a trigger. I understand this is new and scary for you. I'm here to help you find the best treatment to get you feeling like yourself again. I see last time you went home with red pills—no, sorry, green." Ben shook his head to clear his mind. He'd been thinking too much about his own pills today. Red for angry fire energy, green for depressing ground. "Is that correct? Have they been helping?"

"Have they been helping? Do you think I'd be here now if they were helping? I can't remember the joy she brought me when I take 'em. I don't care if it makes my heart ache more, I want to remember all of her. I want every part of her back."

A heaviness settled in Ben with Mr. Dogivan's words. There was only one place to send him, but he regretted being the one to give him his sentence.

Merrytime Clinic.

For dangerous Disparates, their safety, and that of the community, relied on having a place for them to go. The Clinic was supposed to be a place for healing but often became a prison cell.

"Mr. Dogivan." Ben sighed, weighing his next words carefully. "We want to keep you safe. Since this is your third infraction and previous treatments haven't worked, you'll need to have a short stay at Merrytime Clinic. The doctors and analysts there will be by your side every step of the way, finding the right combination of treatment for you. Do you have any questions?"

Mr. Dogivan's shoulders slumped as he stared directly at the small hidden camera. In a monotone voice, he answered, "No questions. I look forward to discovering the right path for me."

Ben leaned away from the brown irises on his computer screen. Even though a strong wall stood between the two men, the sorrow etched across Mr. Dogivan's face worried Ben.

"Goodbye, Mr. Dogivan," Ben said as he watched two Responders open the steel door to Intake Room 3 and escort him out, most likely to an armored van waiting with the words "Merrytime Clinic" plastered on the side.

Exhaustion filled Ben's bones as he arrived home from work. The burden of sending Mr. Dogivan away was still fresh on his mind. Especially after recounting the intake to Oliver on the ride home, who insisted on hearing every detail. It was a good thing it was Oliver's week to drive. Ben's guilt would've kept his attention away from the road.

Jemma rounded the kitchen corner. Her arms wrapped around him before he could shrug off his coat. He circled his arms around her, feeling her weight as she relaxed into him.

"He's figured out the handles in the laundry room." Jemma's tired hazel eyes found his. The yellow within her gaze was as captivating as the day they'd met.

"Wait, what happened?" The worry of the day shifted as he remembered installing those locks on the door when the boys were toddlers, after they found Mackie inside the dryer during a game of hide and seek. They had worked well the last couple of years.

"I was doing dishes when I heard a crash. Slipped on laundry detergent when I went to check on them." Jemma released Ben as she spoke, her hand lingering on his chest. Ben placed one of his on top before it could slip away. A smile twinkled across Jemma's face in response.

"I found the boys having the time of their lives slipping and sliding all over. Soap was everywhere."

Ben lifted a gobbed up section of her long hair. "I can see that."

"I haven't had a chance to shower yet," she said as she shot him *the look*. He knew it well. It was his warning to choose his next words carefully.

He couldn't help but chuckle. "The detergent is all the way on the top shelf. How did they even reach it?"

"I'm not sure," she said, shaking her head. "I must have left it lower after I started the last load."

"How long did it take to clean?"

"Well..." She paused. "The boys are all nice and clean after a bath, but you'll find towels laying all over the hallway. Tried to wipe some of it, but needed to help the boys pick a show to watch, and then Louie wanted to cuddle. I couldn't say no to that, now could I?" She shrugged with a half smile on her face.

He wasn't surprised she'd left some of the mess for him. She had enough on her hands being home all day. Plus, he couldn't be mad about it, even if he'd wanted to. His pills didn't allow it.

Thank goodness for that. Nobody needed torched laundry.

"No problem. I'll see what I can do." He glanced at his boys as they sat on the couch, still enthralled with the latest episode of a cartoon on the screen. Louie laughed as one of the dogs in the show landed in a pile of mud.

That helps explain his affinity for getting dirty, Ben thought as he went to get a mop.

J emma sat on the couch, her hair freshly wet, when Ben flopped down next to her. He laid his head in her lap, the news station playing on the TV in front of them.

"The courthouse on Second Street is still in flames since the fire broke out thirty minutes ago," the brunette newsman reported. "Firemen are on site…"

Jemma turned the volume lower as she ran her fingers through Ben's hair.

"Louie is finally asleep. Didn't take as long as usual—must have worn himself out today. Mackie, of course, was out as soon as I turned off the light." Ben yawned, like he usually did after lying with the boys to help them fall asleep.

"Thank you for getting them to bed. They both keep asking for Dad to help them at night. I don't mind the break." She smirked.

"Yeah, I don't mind either. Although, I almost fell asleep in Louie's bed laying with him. It's been a long day." Ben sighed as Jemma's fingers gently swept around his ear.

The television in front of them continued to show footage of firefighters with water hoses at the courthouse. Words at the bottom of the screen scrolled past, mentioning an unpredicted tornado hitting Preen. Looked like it'd be another year of low crops. One more thing to worry about.

The camera zoomed back to the newscaster. Grabbing the remote, Jemma adjusted the volume to hear the report.

"It appears this fire was not an accident," the reporter on the screen continued. "The Responders believe it was set deliberately, one amongst a trail of fires that have recently hit the city. The target looks to be government buildings. The motivation is unknown."

"Have you heard about this at work?" Jemma asked. Her insides churned as she thought about her husband's job. His government job. He didn't like to talk about work much at home, but this was important.

Ben eased himself off her lap. "A little. They don't believe my office would be a target, since we just send out Responders. We don't keep any confidential records or information they might be after—at least, not that I know of. Other than false alarms, the information we find is recorded in our watch program."

"But you *are* next door to the Responders' office. You go over there for intakes. It's all part of the same complex. What's to keep you from being in danger?" Jemma's speech quickened as she drummed her fingers across her lap. "What if my mom is in danger as well? They might attack the Public Safety Building."

The TV volume fluctuated with each tap of her fingers as images of other recent fires were displayed. Finding the remote was the last worry on Jemma's list. "What if he starts targeting families? Comes here? We need to teach the boys how to use the fire extinguishers. And we need to review our escape plan with them; do you think they'd remember it in an emergency? They can't even remember where they leave their shoes each day." Hot tears formed behind her eyes. "I can't lose you, or our boys, or my mom..." *They'll be taken from me, just like my dad. Gone like my brother, Asher.*

"Breathe with me. Breathe with me, Jemma." Ben took her hands in his. "We are safe, you hear me? We. Are. Safe. No one is after us. Your mom is safe in her bed. Breathe with me." Ben took a deep breath in, and Jemma copied him "One... two... three... four. And out... two... three... four... Again."

Ben placed a hand on Jemma's chest, over her heart. He moved her hand over his heart to match. Together they breathed, in and out, in and out, as Jemma's racing heart slowed to match the beating of Ben's.

They held eye contact. Ben's eyes were full of love and understanding as the fear in Jemma slowly dissipated. He moved his hand to wipe away her tears. "Feeling better? I know we can't know the future, but I know we can face it. Together. Everything will work out."

Jemma nodded, then turned her body and rested her head on his chest, listening to his heartbeat. She'd noticed the small spike his heart made at the beginning of their joint breathing exercise. Ben looked strong and stable on the outside, but she knew inside he was different.

The TV volume finally evened out. The newscaster on screen stood in front of the courthouse fire.

"Responders are asking anyone with information that may be helpful to contact them right away. The anonymous arsonist is still at large. If you know anything, please come forward. Back to you in the studio."

"Thank you, and this concludes our Friday evening news. Stay tuned for a word from our beloved Governor, Tobias Dunn."

A short moment later, Governor Dunn appeared on screen, the roots of his black hair turning white, showing his age. His bushy eyebrows raised as he smiled. Jemma's worries stepped aside for the grief that overcame her. A tickle on the side of her fingers alerted her to the warmth of Ben's hand on hers.

"Hey, you okay?" he asked. "You're thinking about your dad, aren't you?"

"It's been seventeen years and it still hits me. Governor Dunn used to come to our home for dinner sometimes. Of course, he wasn't Governor then."

"Yes, I know; your dad was." He squeezed her hand softly.

"He was a good man," Jemma said. "One time, Asher and I went to the capitol to visit. Before we went to Dad's office, Asher snuck behind Mr. Dunn's desk while he was at the copy machine and stole a handful of lollipops." She stopped to chuckle. "Mr. Dunn returned while Asher was back there, and I had to shout for him to run. Boy, did he look wide-eyed as he took off and ran into the girl's bathroom." Warmth filled her cheeks at the fond memories.

"You've never told me that story before. How old were you both?" Ben asked.

Jemma didn't bring up her brother often. Memories of him induced a deeper, more complicated grief.

"I must have been about ten at the time and Asher thirteen. He was always getting into trouble." Her smile turned down as she thought about the trouble he caused a few years after that memory.

Ben opened his mouth as if to say something but then squeezed Jemma's hand once more, the action more comforting to Jemma than any condolences he could say. She turned her attention back to the screen.

"Last but not least, I'm proud to announce tonight our quarterly improvements. Thanks to your support in implementing step one of Initiative 67, our crime rate has decreased by three, no"—Governor Dunn looked off screen—"five percent this quarter." The governor had always been a bit unorganized, but it hadn't kept him from being re-elected yet. "We will be continuing our efforts to prioritize and support our citizens' mental welfare and safety. I would like to urge each of you to become familiar with the warning signs of rising emotions and the strategies and resources that are available to help you keep them in control. Your safety, and the safety of our town, is in your hands."

Jemma wanted to believe Governor Dunn. He looked knowledgeable, with his well-fitted suit and freshly trimmed haircut. Plus, she knew him on a personal level. He was one of her mother's closest friends. But raising a Disparate was scary. Jemma wasn't convinced the world was a safe place for her son; she couldn't handle the thought of losing him. She couldn't lose another person she loved.

"In preparation for our special quarterly report in a few weeks, there is one more thing I'd like to announce," Governor Dunn continued. "For the next phase of Initiative 67, the age limit for Enertin will be cut in half. Young Disparates may now get the extra help they need at the age of six. This newly formulated, child-safe miracle pill will become available by the end of this week. I look forward to seeing the effect it has in making the Republics the safest place to ever live."

With her mouth wide, Jemma turned to Ben. "Louie can take the child pill. It's an answer to our prayers."

Ben was quiet. "I'm not sure..."

"What do you mean? You take Enertin. It's changed your life. Now it can change Louie's."

"He's just so young," Ben said. "I don't want to take his childhood from him. I don't want it to change him."

She tilted her head. "Do you feel it's changed you in a bad way?"

"Well... it's not that." Ben tightened his lips. "I want to do some more research before we decide if it's the right choice."

"Okay," Jemma said hesitantly. She understood wanting to make sure it truly was safe. But if it wasn't, why would they be announcing it?

And why wasn't her husband, the one who knew what it was like to live with emotional energy, thrilled by the idea?

Waiting at a worn, wooden door for her knock to be answered, Margaret held a clipboard in her hand as she tucked a strand of her white hair behind her ear. It'd only been three weeks since the Disparate she was investigating died. But investigate she must. She needed more information on whether this death was caused by Enertin. It'd still be fresh in the family's mind.

A young man, likely in his early thirties, opened the door.

"Hello," she said. "I'm Margaret Stillfield, your Public Safety Committee Member—"

"If you're here soliciting votes," he said in a gruff voice, "you can turn around. I don't vote."

Margaret's eyes widened. She restrained herself from going on a tirade about the importance of making your voice heard, even if it's only one amongst the thousands. "I'm here on official business. I'd like to talk about your mother's death." Although the first part wasn't fully the truth, he didn't need to know that.

There it was—the grief she was expecting to see in his eyes. Each family she visited after an outburst mirrored her own loss.

"Look, my parents and I are estranged," the man said. "If you want answers, talk to my dad."

"I understand that, but he refuses to speak with us."

"Sounds like him," he huffed.

"We could really use your help."

His head swiveled toward the inside of his house for a moment then returned to Margaret. "Fine. Anything to not be like *him*. What do you want to know?"

Margaret looked at her clipboard. *Cause of Death: Car Crash; Possible Earthquake by Disparate.* "Has your mother always been a ground Disparate?"

"As far as I know, she's never been one," he snapped, his voice steeped in hostility. "Like I said, I cut them off years ago."

"Your phone records show you called her before the accident occurred, is that correct?" Margaret asked.

His feet shuffled as he exited his house, joining her on the small front porch. He closed the door behind him. "I did call... I wanted to reconnect. You see, my wife's pregnant, and when you're about to become a parent, you start to think about how you were raised."

"I see. Congratulations." This poor woman passed away right before she was going to be a grandmother. Margaret's heart hurt for her as she thought of her own grandsons. The things she would have missed if she'd died before they were born. Things her husband did miss. He would have loved being a grandpa.

"So you wouldn't know about her history with Enertin, or anything else?"

"Nope. Growing up, she was normal. If anyone had struggled with unruly emotions, it'd be my dad." He paused for a moment, his face wrinkling. "What is it you believe happened? Last thing I heard on the call was her screaming and then she crashed into that radar pole. Are you saying a Disparate caused her crash?"

"The radar picked up energy activity before it was knocked over. We don't know exactly what happened, but it is a possibility."

His face hardened. "I don't know anything about that."

"What was your conversation that day?"

"It wasn't much of a conversation." He sighed. "I asked if Dad was near her, and when she said yes, I told her I'd call her later. That's when I heard the crash happen. Could it really have been Disparate energy that caused it?"

"I'm so sorry." Margaret knew she couldn't take away his pain. "There's not much more I can say, as we're still investigating."

"Do you have any other questions?" he asked.

Margaret shook her head. Enertin wasn't involved in *this* death. Even if she had more questions, it didn't feel right to continue asking. She'd delivered the news that there was more to his mother's death than they originally thought. That a Disparate might have been involved.

Just like one was involved in her own husband's death.

THREE

Sun rays pierced through the large windows of Energy Watch on Monday, creating panes of light across the floor next to Ben's desk. The calm day contrasted with his mood as he scanned the map on his computer. The announcement Friday night was the last thing he'd expected. Sure, he took Enertin. But that meant he knew firsthand how much it changed him. The last thing he wanted was to force Louie to change.

Thankfully, the morning had been quiet, giving him time to think. Only one small energy burst in his zone that Responders quickly resolved.

Ben didn't mind the lack of activity. In fact, it was what he hoped for each day as he walked in the door. He didn't like to be reminded of how unstable Disparates could be: how unstable he could've been. Perhaps that was a reason why Louie should take Enertin—make sure no more toys melted. That had been Jemma's argument over the weekend. "We don't know how strong Louie's energy will become, or when it'll turn into producing flames."

Still, it didn't feel right that a pill was needed for a person to be themselves. The government commercials touted how finding the right colored Enertin pill—yellow, purple, white, green, or red—would form you into the person you were meant to be.

Become your inner self with Enertin! the tagline went.

Buran said he had white pills. Without them, he'd cause quite the ice storm, making his cold stares literal. But if the pills kept him from feeling disgust, why did he still keep to himself and avoid joining everyone else for lunch in the breakroom? Maybe they weren't as effective as Ben's.

Ben rarely felt angry thanks to the red pills. And with less anger, he hadn't had an energy incident since he was a teenager.

Was it right to take away Louie's ability to feel upset so young?

"Any more action since Electrical Ellen?" Oliver looked above the side desk divider at Ben. He'd hit his boredom peak for the day already.

"Electrical Ellen?" Ben raised an eyebrow at Oliver. Electricity was controlled with yellow.

"Yeah, I've been thinking up ways to refer to the freaks. I've had some time on my hands, Electrical Ellen, Floating Featherman, Icy Isabella, Dirty Dogivan. You know, catchy names like that."

"I'm not sure Ellen's anxiety would appreciate that," Ben scolded. "It's not like she can help it."

"How else am I supposed to keep busy? I mean, that phrase 'floating on cloud nine'; people wouldn't be so happy if they knew it could literally cause them to float to the clouds!" Oliver was referring to Anthony Featherman, who had to have the fire department pull him, his new fiancée, and the contents of his apartment out of the sky after his proposal. He started taking purple pills right away to keep his joy in check, but Ben never did hear if they went through with the wedding.

"For the last..." Oliver said as he placed a finger on the side of his chin. "I'm thinking Arsonist Ana, you know, pay tribute to Stillfield's fire anarchist. Not sure what they're so mad about all the time." The corner of Oliver's lip raised.

Ben shook his head. He thought about the news segment, comforting his wife all while knowing that if things in his childhood had played out differently, he could have become that arsonist.

"Hey man, I'm just joking around." Oliver's face flattened. "I'm sorry. I forget how attached you get to people. That's something I admire about you. You're able to find the good in someone, even when they've frozen the freezer section, including the other shoppers in the aisle. Remember that one? You wanted to make sure the Responders went easy on the kid, especially after they got everyone defrosted. You bought her an ice cream cone while she was waiting for her intake."

Ben remembered that incident. It happened only two months ago. The girl, Isabella, was only a couple years older than Louie. It was surprising to see her energy so strong at such a young age.

"You would've been disgusted seeing a rat run across your groceries as well," Ben said. "These people aren't that far off from anyone else. Their brains just work differently. Our job is to help them, not make fun of them." Ben recalled the fear on the face of Isabella's father. It was all too familiar. "Especially if you become a Responder. Can't call them names then."

"That is the dream," Oliver said. "Alright, alright, I know. I said I'm sorry." His large mouth widened into a yawn.

"You need to get more sleep," Ben said.

"I would've had plenty of sleep if you didn't show up so early today." The sensor on Oliver's computer started to sound. "Duty calls," he said, his head disappearing behind the divider. "Looks like another grocery store incident downtown. What a coincidence."

Ben turned his attention to his own screen, a light flashing around the edges. *So much for a slow morning.* Ben sighed as he checked the map.

He found the small yellow dot, an electric disturbance, and zoomed in. His hand moved to his chin as he stared at the abandoned shopping mall. After double checking the roads, he confirmed the alert was coming from the building. This was the first time he'd seen or heard about an alert there in the five years he'd worked as a Watcher.

Old Stillfield Mall was in the older part of town, which expanded through the edges of both the East and North Sectors. It was built in the years before the Rain of Fire. After the end of what the world once was, survivors flocked to its full shelves, looting whatever they found.

The surviving world had turned to chaos and fear, years that were now referred to as The Crisis. Many tried to bring structure, but it wasn't found until twenty years later by children who had experienced the Rain of Fire and realized more needed to be done.

It was then Jemma's great grandfather, Fredrick Stillfield, banded together with six others to form the Republics. Learning from the failures of the old world, they realized they needed a system in which the different areas depended on each other. Allies had been important in the larger world, but with a world so small now, they needed to rely on each other even more.

Each Republic picked a specialty that focused on their strengths. Stillfield chose research and medicine. With the help of Vasco, the industrial Republic, the mall was restored. Its shelves were once more stocked with precious needs. And, over time, some frivolous wants. The survivors were still human, after all.

About fifteen years ago, a wing of the mall was destroyed by an earthquake. The media portrayed it as a targeted attack, instigated by an out-of-control Disparate. Since then, it'd been abandoned, the other wing boarded up and left to decay.

So the small yellow dot in the middle of the mall piqued Ben's curiosity.

Why would someone be there? Why would an Electric Disparate be there?

"Hey Oliver, got a minute?" Ben looked over the divider to see if his coworker was busy.

"Yeah, my alert was a false alarm. The Disparate calmed down pretty quick. Didn't need to call any Responders. What's up?"

"I need you to take a look at this." Ben turned his computer toward his friend. The map on his screen was calm, the abandoned shopping mall at its center.

"Oh yeah, Stillfield Mall. Sad what happened to it."

"No, there was an alert. It was coming from inside the mall. Do you think I should send someone to check it out?"

"Nah, it could've been the wind. Sometimes sensors pick it up and mistake it for an energy spike. My girlfriend mentioned a nasty storm coming through."

Oliver had been dating this girl long distance for the last several years. Why they hadn't made the decision to move in together already, Ben wasn't sure. His bet was on the girl, though. Oliver was like a lost puppy. Let him in and it would take a lot to get him to leave.

"She lives in Wuslick, right?" The Republic in charge of military and education training.

Oliver hesitated. "...Right."

"That's probably it then. The storm must be blowing south to us."

Oliver nodded in agreement.

Ben pretended to get back to work as Oliver turned to his own computer, covered by the divider between them. Something about the situation bothered Ben.

He glanced to the window on his left. The trees outside were still; no movement disturbed their branches. Lowering his eyes, he made contact with Buran's, who quickly glanced away. How long had he been watching him? Ben took an uneasy breath as he focused back on his work space, checking his map for any new activity. He hoped the weather a few miles away was windier than what he saw outside his office.

J emma's heart raced in her chest, feeling as if it would take off at
any moment. She had invited her friends to the park, needing adult
interaction and a distraction from the dark thoughts that cycled through
her mind. She couldn't shake the feeling that something bad was about
to happen.

The poster in the parking lot didn't help: *Embrace Your Emotions.
Disparates Deserve Deliverance. Dissentients are Watching.* She wasn't
sure where this new message came from, but it was clearly not put out
by the Republic Government. Not with being handwritten on crinkled
paper. The government had access to printers, where most citizens did
not. It wasn't high on the production list in Vasco.

"Did you see those posters?" Caty asked as they sat at the picnic table.
"I can't believe someone was brazen enough to tape those up."

"Disparates don't need to embrace their emotions." Haven shook
her head. "They need to control them. What kind of behavior are they
trying to encourage?"

"Hmm..." Jemma rubbed the back of her neck. These "Dissentients"
worried her, but something else bothered her more.

"Oh, you saw the news this weekend, didn't you?" Caty asked as she
brushed a perfect red curl out of her face. She sat next to Jemma at the
table, eating half a sandwich her daughter abandoned when the kids ran
off to play. Louie also left some lunch behind, but Jemma didn't feel
hungry.

Across from them sat Haven, whose attention was stuck on her
phone. She had unplugged the external charger and plugged it back in.

"This thing keeps dying," she muttered. "It's been plugged in!" She turned to Jemma. "Sorry, anyway, is that why we're here?"

Jemma nodded. These women were her best friends. It was hard to hide her emotions from them. When she texted that morning to meet for a playdate, she knew they'd understand why.

"The news of the age limit lowering surprised me," Caty said. "I wasn't expecting that. I'm sure it'll help a lot of families."

It should help my *family,* Jemma thought. She still didn't understand Ben's hesitation, but she didn't want to bring it up with her friends quite yet. "I hope it does." Jemma's leg shook. She glanced at the kids. Mackie was busy swinging next to Caty's daughter, Lily, who was the same age as him. Louie sat in the sand with Haven's three-year-old daughter, Addison, helping her dig a hole with the toy shovels they brought.

"What does Ben think about the fire anarchist?" Haven asked. "Does he have any insider knowledge from his job, you know, since he works for the government?"

Jemma had explained his job to her multiple times in the past, but Haven still didn't quite understand. Her questioning aligned more with him being a high government official rather than the simple Watcher that he was.

"Haven, he works for Energy Watch," Caty responded, relieving Jemma from having to explain again. She must have noticed the way Jemma's leg was shaking the entire picnic table. "Not as a captain for the R.E.I."

Jemma hadn't thought it was serious enough for the Republic Energy Investigators to be called in. But since the anarchist's targets were government buildings, it was likely they were working on the case.

She wasn't sure, though, if that brought her comfort. Her father had had a complicated relationship with the bureau before he died.

A soft hand landed on her leg, gently stopping her shaking. "Hey, are you feeling okay?" Caty's voice was almost a whisper. "You can tell us what's bothering you. Sometimes saying it out loud helps."

Haven nodded in agreement.

Jemma tried to muster the courage to share her fears, but the words weren't coming. The fire anarchist was one concern of many. He was a threat to Ben and her mother. But the root of her worries was deeper. She wasn't sure she was ready to unearth that wound.

"It's nothing," she said.

Caty raised an eyebrow.

Jemma avoided her skeptical gaze by turning toward Louie and Addison. The toddler laughed as she flung sand behind her, the way a dog does when digging a hole for its bone. Louie wasn't paying much attention as he created his own mountain next to him.

"Addi," Haven called out. "No throwing sand, sweetie."

Addison turned toward her mother's voice. The sand that spewed behind her landed on Louie. His body tightened as he leaned away, and Jemma's heart stopped.

He was angry. She didn't see smoke yet, but surely it was coming. He'd only melted toys at home, but she knew it was only a matter of time before his energy strengthened.

She sprang from the table and ran to Louie. In one swift motion, she scooped him into her arms and held him against her body. Sand rained onto the top of her head as she shielded him.

"Are you okay, Louie?" she asked once Addison finished her digging. "Did any sand get in your eyes?"

Louie pushed away from her chest and looked at her with furrowed brows. "I'm fine," he spat. "It's just sand. Watch out for my mountain."

Warmth radiated off Louie as she released him. Instead of intervening before a meltdown occurred, she'd almost caused one. He immediately went back to building his mound of sand higher, his body relaxing as he worked. Haven knelt next to Addison, showing her how to fill a bucket using a cup as a scoop. This new activity pleased the toddler, who quickly grabbed the cup and took over for her mother.

Jemma stood, wiping her sweaty palms onto her pants before walking back to the table with Haven.

"Everything okay?" Caty asked.

This time, Jemma only nodded.

"I'm sorry about Addi," Haven sighed. "It's like making messes is her life's mission right now."

"It's okay," Jemma reassured her friend as she kept an eye on her son. "He's alright. No sand in his eyes, thankfully. I just wanted to make sure he wasn't upset."

Jemma knew she looked like a helicopter mom, always hovering, waiting to rescue her child. However, her child wasn't the only one she was rescuing.

"Is he still having episodes?" Haven's voice piqued in surprise. "I thought he'd grown out of them."

"It's not really something you grow out of." Jemma took a deep breath, formulating the thoughts in her head. It was exhausting having to explain her child to others. "He's a Disparate. It will always be a part of him."

"Oh," Haven's voice was solemn. "I hadn't realized. I thought he was too young. Don't kids usually develop energy around thirteen?"

"Usually," Caty jumped in, "but it can happen sooner. I have a student in my school that's five and starting to show signs."

Haven's eyes widened. "Really? So it is more common."

"Yep." Caty nodded and turned toward Jemma. "I've taken training on how to work with Disparate children. I love Louie—and Mackie. My preschool offer still stands. And I'm a pretty good teacher, wouldn't you say so, Haven?"

"Yeah…" Haven's gaze drifted to Addison. "Addi likes preschool…"

"I'll think about it," Jemma repeated the same response she always gave.

Haven glanced at her phone, which was finally charged enough for the screen to turn on. Her eyes widened. "I didn't realize the time," she said. "We need to get going. Nap time."

She gathered her belongings and waved goodbye as she lifted Addison into her arms.

"That's strange," Caty said as Haven drove away. "I thought Addi's nap time was at two."

Jemma checked her own phone. The time read 12:30.

B en laid the bedtime book on the shelf once heavy breathing came from Louie's bed. The boy had fallen asleep before the end. Ben kissed his forehead goodnight before crossing the room to tuck in Mackie. As Ben pulled the blanket around his small body, Mackie's round, bright eyes met his. "Why don't I have magic like Louie, Dad?"

The question made Ben freeze. He wasn't sure what to say. How could he explain what his brother experienced—what he, personally, has experienced—wasn't magic, but rather a curse. How the thing he was most afraid of was himself. He was his own monster at the end of his book.

"Everyone is different. It's not actually magic. Your brother has different strengths and challenges, just like you do. Like,"—he paused trying to think of an example—"remember how good you are at soccer? You scored two goals in your last game!"

"Yeah!" A smile crossed Mackie's face. "Louie can't play soccer 'cause he'll melt the ball. I do like soccer."

Ben smiled back at him as he yawned. "Now, get some sleep, okay? You need energy if you're going to be a great soccer star. Goodnight, Mac N' Cheese."

"That's not my name!" Mackie shot him an irritated glare.

"Good night, Mackie. I love you always." He kissed Mackie's forehead as he snuggled into the bed.

"All ways?" Mackie laughed. "Even upside-down?"

Ben chuckled at his misinterpretation. "Yes, all ways. Especially upside-down."

"Good night, Daddy, love you upside-down too." Mackie yawned again as he rolled over, his eyes closing.

Ben scrolled through emails on his phone in bed as Jemma walked into the room. She'd taken a shower, and he was quick to notice her delay in getting dressed; only a white towel covered her, a slit open down the side revealing her naked skin. He perked up, wondering if she was trying to communicate her wishes for pleasure through this small act or if she had simply forgotten a piece of clothing.

"How was your shower? Did you get all the sand washed off?"

"I think so. Showering every day is getting old." She laughed. "Although I could've used your help to make sure." She winked at him as she sat on the edge of the bed, her towel inching higher on her thigh. Her stretch marks peeked out: a masterpiece created by a grand artist in parallel streaks of pink and white. His heart thumped in his chest. He wanted to see the rest of the canvas.

He moved over to join her, resting behind her back. "It's not too late for me to check." His hands found the top of her bare shoulders and massaged. Her body melted under his touch, her tension releasing as he worked on her knots. A deep moan escaped from her chest.

"Mmmm, make sure you don't miss any spots back there. Sand likes to hide, especially under my shoulder blades." His thumbs continued in small circles, easing to her front and releasing the towel that had become loose.

With the whole masterpiece revealed to him, he wasn't sure where to look first. Every spot he chose was beautiful, her worn skin a tribute to the life she had lived thus far. She turned toward him, her hand sliding behind his head, entangling in his hair and forcing his attention to her face.

"Is there anything else I can help you with?" he asked with a sly smile. "I think you know," she responded, her lips meeting his. He was intent on giving her exactly what she wanted.

Four

Ben skimmed the file that lay across his desk. It had taken him a couple of days to gather these reports. The papers inside were records of East Sector watch observations from the previous two months. Records of false alarms were only kept in the paper files. No need to waste hard drive space on a little wind.

The first page had a couple false alarms, noted by a light line crossing through the alert but keeping the words underneath legible.

~~Red. Fourth Street and West Avenue.~~ *Resolved by 020314*

A tapping sound diverted Ben's attention. Across the walkway, Buran worked at his computer, the tips of his blond hair extra sharp as he beat a pencil like a drumstick on the edge of his desk.

Of course *he* hadn't joined the rest of the group for lunch. At least Ben shouldn't have to worry about him wanting to socialize.

He turned his attention back to the files he'd grabbed out of storage as soon as his other coworkers left to try the new taco place around the corner. Thankfully, they'd accepted his excuse for not going. Technically, he *was* catching up on paperwork.

There. Ben's gaze paused on a blacked out line. The words were completely covered, unlike the false alarm from the first page. It wasn't ink from the workplace printer but rather drawn on with a thick marker. Ben narrowed his eyes and flipped through the next couple pages.

More crossed out false alarms.

More blacked out sections.

He lifted a page to the lamp light on his desk. It shined through, the words underneath barely visible.

Yellow: Old Town and Seventh. Resolved by 020128

The old mall. He held up another. And another. The alerts seemed to have begun three weeks ago. Same words. Same number resolving each.

The first two of the ID represented Stillfield, the second Republic formed after Wuslick. So whoever was resolving these false alarms worked here, at Energy Watch.

The second two numbers represented the map sector. Each Watcher and Intaker was assigned to a specific sector, so it could be someone from either position. All other false alarms in East Sector, Ben's area, were labeled correctly. This one, however, was done by someone who watched North—that could be any of a few dozen people over that sector. Why would they be marking a false alarm in East?

The last two numbers were uniquely assigned to each Watcher. Ben knew his own but was unfamiliar with the numbers of his coworkers. Their IDs weren't something he kept track of. He focused on his own map and alerts.

But there was a way to look up IDs in the map database online. He'd be able to see who was recording these false alarms and ask them why they marked out any signs of activity at the old mall.

Ben turned to his computer and sighed as he looked at the clock.

12:00

Pill time. He'd finish his search after.

He glanced around the office; Buran was no longer at his desk. Probably in the restroom taking his own pill. No matter; Ben could take his here.

He reached into his pill box and grimaced. He was on his last capsule. He had forgotten his new bottle at home.

He quickly popped it into his mouth and took a swig of water.

As he began to swallow, a loud bang came from behind, and he jumped. Water sprayed out of his mouth and through his nose, his nostrils burning from the unwelcomed shower. Unfortunately, his pill projected with the majority of the water. He coughed as he regained his composure, wiping his face on his sleeve.

Buran stood next to a box of intake files he had dropped on the floor. "Oh shoot, you okay?"

"No." Ben's reply was curt, but then he remembered what Buran had told him in the bathroom the other day: *I take the white ones.* "I lost my pill; do you see it? It's red." Time ticked away.

12:01

Ben hadn't been late since he was a teen. He needed to hurry.

He got on his hands and knees, feeling over the wet floor, hoping that if he couldn't spot it, he could at least feel it. Buran began to look as well, checking around nearby trash cans in case it had rolled.

12:02

It shouldn't have been hard to find, but perhaps the red of the pill blended in with the shadows under the desk. Ben hoped Buran, who was now checking around the cubicle in front of his, would have better luck.

12:03

Ben stretched his arm under the cabinet next to his desk, reaching for the back. The top of his wrist stopped him from going further. He grabbed a ruler and used it to resume his frantic search.

12:04

He swept it into the small space, pulling out old gum wrappers and dust balls. Still no sight of his pill. Hopelessness consumed him as he sat frozen on the floor. How had he been so stupid? What kind of person spits when they're caught off guard? He should've swallowed faster.

12:05

A strong scent permeated Ben's nostrils as he sat up. Hand sanitizer? Was Buran really cleaning his hands? This wasn't the time for that. He needed to find that pill.

His anger glared toward Buran, who was back in his sight. Why did he approach so abruptly? He knew better than to surprise a person, especially a Disparate. Buran lifted a trash can that sat at the edge of Ben's desk—one he'd already looked under.

Still no pill.

12:06

"You've already looked there!" Ben shouted.

Buran jumped, taken aback by the level of Ben's voice. His forehead creased as he looked toward his coworker, then his eyes widened suddenly.

"Fire!" His hand pointed at Ben's desk; a flame flickered across it, consuming the laid out files.

Where did that come from? Ben wondered. It had been over a decade since he'd last started a fire. It didn't feel the same; he hadn't noticed a release of energy. In fact, other than snapping at Buran, he felt in control of himself, despite it being a few minutes past pill time.

A high pitched siren reached their ears as water fell from the sprinklers. The fire wasn't that large yet. How did it set off the alarm already?

"Out of my way!" came a voice from behind them. Oliver ran from around the edge of the cubicles at the back of the room, a fire extinguisher in hand. He pulled the pin as he waved the extinguisher side to side. An avalanche of white exploded out of the bottle, covering Ben's entire desk area—including Ben, who hadn't had time to get off the floor.

Ben lowered the arm he had shielded his eyes with as he spat powder out of his mouth, the acidic taste still settled on his tongue. Tears welled in his eyes as he blinked to get rid of the sting. Water from above mixed with the powder and created a sludge that ran down his arm.

If he thought it was hard to find the red pill earlier, it was nearly impossible to find it now under the mountain of foam.

"Here it is!" Buran proclaimed as he pulled the little pill out from under the ledge of a filing cabinet.

"You guys okay?" Oliver shouted over the fire alarm. "Sorry about the makeover, buddy. It was for your own good. What was that?" He raised an eyebrow at Buran.

"Oh, um, just a piece of gum I dropped earlier." Buran pretended to put a piece of gum in his mouth and proceeded to chew said imaginary piece.

Ben grimaced at the thought.

"Well, I guess we should go let everyone know it's safe," Oliver called out as the siren overhead continued to blare.

Ben stood and ran a hand through his hair—water and white sludge squeezed onto his fingers. He grabbed a bunch of wet tissues off a nearby desk. It was better than nothing. He wiped the mess from his hands before following his coworker. Oliver led the way as Ben strolled next to Buran.

"Take a deep breath, stay in control," Buran said as he sneakily slipped the pill into Ben's hand. He popped it quickly into his mouth using the little saliva he had to swallow it with the sour taste of leftover fire extinguisher foam. As they left, he glanced at the receptionist's clock.

12:10

Ben squinted at his phone, the bright sun glaring across the middle.

Honey, are you okay? I heard there was a fire!

Everyone's alright, just a small one. It was put out quickly.

He'd give her more details at home that night. Better to tell her in person.

Buran and Oliver sat next to him on the curb, towels from the firefighters wrapped around their shoulders. It was standard protocol for the building to be inspected before reentry. Ben wiped off as much of the extinguisher sludge as he could.

He turned to Oliver. "Thanks again for saving us back there."

"Oh, no problem, buddy." His face dropped to the ground as he answered.

"I thought you'd gone to lunch; glad you were back in time." Ben meant what he said.

"I got my lunch to-go," Oliver explained, his eyes raising to meet Ben's. "I didn't want to leave you to eat alone at the office. Good thing too; your messy desk finally came back to bite you. Power cord probably shorted out."

Ben shuddered to think what would've happened without Oliver's quick response. Shock and confusion spread through him like the fire across his desk. How had it started? Oliver's half-hearted attempt at a joke about Ben's unkempt space was unusual, but it was a possibility.

However, Buran's eyes glanced in Ben's direction an unnerving amount of times, as if his suspicions were on Ben.

Maybe they were right.

It clearly began at his desk. The files laid haphazardly across the surface created a desirable kindling for it to spread.

The files.

How much was destroyed? The fire started on the observations for the past two months, the alerts for the old mall. He still wasn't sure if marking it as a false alarm was right. Especially after discovering someone else had marked false alarms there as well. That couldn't be a coincidence.

A group of Responders gathered outside, huddled in a circle as they talked in whispers. Ben recognized a few of them from his days of doing intakes. Two firefighters joined their circle and took over the conversation.

The Responders glanced Ben's way. Were they looking at him? It was hard to tell behind their dark sunglasses. Two he didn't recognize broke away from the group and headed to where he sat.

"Benjamin Hodgerton?" the taller one on the right asked, his sunglasses sliding down his nose as he looked at him. Buran and Oliver looked up, noticing the Responders.

"That's me."

"We're going to need you to come with us."

Ben was unsure, but not surprised; the fire had been at his desk.

"Um, sure. I'll help however I can." Ben felt each beat of his heart as he stood from the curb.

"Wait." Buran rose as well. "I was inside with Ben when the fire started, and Oliver, there, put it out. We'd like to leave our witness statements too."

"Yeah... yeah," Oliver stumbled as he stood. "I didn't see the fire start, but I knew what to do when I smelled smoke. Just saved some lives. Some might call me a hero, I prefer gifts as a form of thanks." He smiled.

The Responders were unmoved. "Very well. You can all follow us for questioning. The building has been cleared for reentry."

The three of them followed behind the two Responders, entering the familiar building. At the front desk, the shorter Responder motioned for Buran and Oliver to sit in the waiting chairs and directed Ben into the back. Buran's forehead wrinkled in worry as Ben followed alone. He looked back at him and shrugged, trying to comfort Buran even though Ben was the one most likely to be blamed.

The receptionist greeted Ben with a smile at first, until he noticed the Responders standing on either side of him. Ben was instructed to empty his own pockets. The receptionist placed his items inside a bag and labeled it with his full name. Ben wondered if he should've messaged Jemma again before he left his phone, but questioning shouldn't take too long. It was an accident, after all.

They walked past the hallway he was used to going down, the one that led to the interviewer's side of the intake rooms, and went down the next one. Doors lined the wall to his right; these doors entered the rooms he knew.

On his left were cell doors, at least twice as many compared to the number of intake rooms. The cell doors looked different. Bars covered in clear, heat-proof glass, the walls inside each room lined with different materials. One room with insulated steel, the next thick, white soundproofing foam. Instead of keeping sound from escaping, it kept Air Disparates from hurting themselves or the Responders that attended to them. Ben couldn't imagine it was actually needed. He didn't know who would feel joy while trapped in that tiny room.

They stopped in front of the next door. The shorter Responder pulled it open and gestured for Ben to enter the gray concrete cell. The room was long enough to fit Ben if he were to lay down. On the right wall was a concrete slab with a blanket, presumably meant for just that. A small metal toilet and sink that looked like it hadn't been cleaned in months stood to the left.

So they do think I'm to blame for the fire, Ben thought, his heart sinking as he entered the small room. He found it curious that they viewed him as a threat even though the fire was small and put out quickly.

He wasn't thrilled by that idea, but it was a misunderstanding. Certainly they would let him go soon.

"We need you to stay here while we examine the full situation. We'll take you in for questioning shortly." The tall responder closed the cell door and locked it from the outside.

Ben sat on the bed and ran his hands over the synthetic fabric of the blanket. A fire-resistant fabric for a Flame Disparate's jail cell. Scorch marks dirtied the walls, signs of past struggles and the damage anger left behind. As he waited for his questioning time, he imagined those same smudges marked the inside of him. His pills may be able to subdue his inner monster, but they couldn't destroy it for good.

Five

Ben sat in Intake Room 3. The cold steel seat permeated through his jeans.

The irony of this room was not lost on him. It was just days earlier he was on the other side of the camera, interviewing out of control Disparates. Now, it was his turn to be questioned.

It felt surreal, as if he were stranded on a deserted island. And after being kept in that small cell for hours, he was alone.

"State your name and energy," the voice on the other end was stern and unfamiliar. It wasn't an Intaker he recognized.

"Ben Hodgerton... uh..." Ben wasn't sure what to say. They weren't using a standard intake script.

"Your energy? State it for the record." Of course he was being recorded. They always recorded questioning in the intake room.

"Fire," Ben admitted.

"Can you tell me how the fire started on your desk? Have you been taking your medication correctly?"

Ben swallowed before he answered. "I'm not sure what started it. I take my medication every day."

"Every day? Always on time?" the voice quickly questioned. "It says here you medicate at noon. That's right before the fire started. Are you telling me you'd just taken your medicine when the fire began?"

"Um, well, today I was a little late. Accidently dropped my pill and had to find it."

"Did you or did you not have your medicine in your body when the fire started? Keep in mind we've already gathered statements from your coworkers."

Heat flushed Ben's cheeks as he realized he wouldn't be able to lie about what happened. He wasn't sure how much Oliver had heard, but he would fudge the truth for him if needed. Ben knew better than to trust that from Buran. If Buran had spoken to them already, he needed to have a matching story.

"I found it shortly after the fire started and took it then. It didn't feel like I started it. I can feel when energy escapes."

"And when was the last time that happened?"

Shoot. He shouldn't have given more information than was necessary. "When I was a kid, in high school. That was the last time."

"I see that incident here in your files. It says you started a fire in your history class. Is that the incident you are referring to?"

"Yes." Ben fidgeted in his seat as he recalled that outburst. They'd learned about the history of Disparates and were debating whether it was appropriate to ship them off to Lucky Island. Ben hadn't cared one way or the other. Apathy filled his emotions and felt out of place. He wanted to participate in the debate and refrained from taking his pill that day. The next morning, he was prepared for class and debated against sending the Disparates away to an isolated island, making the point that Disparates were like everyone else, only with more obvious struggles.

"*I deserve to be kept safe from these uncontrolled monsters,*" his classmate debated.

Needless to say, Ben did not win the debate that day. Not after his response was charring the hair off his classmate's head and burning down History Hall.

"You were moved to the highest dose after that. I'm surprised you've done so well since," the interviewer said with a hint of disbelief. "Where were you last Friday night?"

The sudden topic change caught Ben off guard. "Friday night? I got off work at five and went home." And watched the news—the next step of Initiative 67 had been announced. He had a feeling this had more to do with the story before the announcement. The one about the Fire Anarchist.

"If you are taking late doses now, you pose a threat to society. I'm referring you to the Merrytime Clinic for observation."

The microphone clicked off. Ben sat open-mouthed at the small table, processing what he'd been told as two Responders entered the room and led him outside to a waiting van. The thought that he could run entered his mind but was quickly shaken off. He knew better than to try fighting his fate. Many Disparates had tried before and ended up with a tranquilizer shot in their arm. He wanted to be alert for the journey.

"Can I call my wife and kids first?" he asked as he stepped into the van.

The Responders ignored his question as the van door closed.

The car squealed as Jemma rounded the corner. *Calm down, Jemma. Everything will be fine.* Laughter emerged from behind as both Louie and Mackie straightened their heads in their car seats. They were on their way to Jemma's mother's house.

Ben hadn't arrived home on time, and her phone calls went straight to his voicemail. She'd done enough waiting. She would find him herself.

The car jolted as she sped over the bump in the road. She hadn't realized how close she was to the bridge that stretched over the canal behind her mother's house. The boys laughed in the rear-view mirror. At least they were having fun. Her gaze wandered to the side, into the darkness swallowing the canal and toward the treehouse she knew she would find if she turned down the dirt path next to the water. Asher's and her childhood hideout. The place where they would play for hours, making up stories and practicing Asher's art skills.

Asher, who disappeared mysteriously.

She took a deep breath. This wasn't what was happening with Ben. No.

"Wait, Mom, I have soccer practice tonight!" Mackie announced with sudden realization.

"I know. You'll go next week." Jemma sighed. She'd hoped he wouldn't have noticed. "Grandma's house will be fun."

"But she doesn't have any games," he whined.

Jemma pulled up to her mother's house prepared. She handed over the boys' tablets as she dropped them off at her door.

"You know, too many video games will fry their brains." Her mother stared her down with a critical eye. Jemma was used to her unsolicited opinions and ignored her remark as she hugged her boys goodbye.

Leaving them at grandma's without their tablets would guarantee an energy episode from Louie, and that was not something she wanted to leave her mother in charge of handling.

"You boys be good for grandma, okay? You can have game time after you eat dinner." Jemma turned to her mother. "Call me immediately if there are any problems. I shouldn't be too long."

"I don't understand why you want to go down there anyway," her mother whispered, checking to make sure the boys were safely in the house and out of ear shot.

They'd found the container of blocks she kept in her TV stand and were busy playing. Jemma had bought the blocks as a special toy for grandma's house when they were toddlers. It was a way to get their energy out safely during monthly dinners. She didn't want them breaking the trinkets and decor her mother kept in arms reach.

It worked, for the most part. Only a few casualties over the years. Including the ceramic teapot that featured a hodge-podge of cows and chickens drawn in an abstract style. Jemma wasn't too upset to see that one go.

"I'm sure Ben will be out soon," her mother continued. "Responders don't hold people for no reason. I can give the sergeant a call. I'm sure he would hurry up his Responders. Although, I do believe he's on vacation in the mountains right now."

Margaret was a force of a woman. She'd been elected to the Public Safety Committee of Stillfield ten years in a row, providing her a close connection with top government and safety officials. Marrying into the historic Stillfield family and being the widow of former Governor Skyler Stillfield definitely gave her the upper hand during election time.

"That's true. He's just been there awhile, and I can't get a hold of him by phone. I tried calling the office on my way here, but the receptionist said he couldn't share details of a pending investigation with me. Even though I'm his wife." She sighed. "I'm sure everything is fine, I just want to pop in and check how much longer he'll be."

It was almost dusk by the time Jemma's car pulled into the mostly empty parking lot of Energy Watch and the Responders' Office next door. Her car door slammed shut behind her as she hurried to the double glass doors that stood between her and information.

The doors jiggled and fought back as she pulled on the handles, refusing to surrender their secure position. The lights inside the building were dark. Jemma pounded on the bullet proof glass, knowing there were Responders on duty at this time even when the reception desk was closed. The fact that Ben must still be inside gave her confidence that someone would respond to her drumming.

A light turned on, and the figure of a female Responder emerged from the back room. "Hold on! We're closed. Unless you're in immediate danger, you'll have to stop by tomorrow." Her voice had a certain drawl to it, tending to hold onto the "o" sound longer than necessary.

"I'm here to pick up my husband," Jemma yelled through the glass. "He's been in for questioning. Ben Hodgerton?"

"Oh no, ma'am. He's not here. No one's called you yet? He was taken over to Merrytime Clinic for the night."

Merrytime Clinic?

Jemma's hands sank to her sides, followed by the sinking in her chest. The hole she'd plugged inside expanded, swallowing her hope and releasing the dread that'd been hiding behind it. Her body began to shake uncontrollably. Fear took control, leaving her a spectator watching the event unfold.

They took Ben from me.

The lights inside flickered and went out. "Shoot, we changed that lightbulb last week." The Responder eyed Jemma suspiciously, who stood shaking in her spot. "Looks like another power outage," the Responder continued slowly as she backed away. "I need to check the fuse box. I'll be back."

The woman walked backward into the room she'd come from. She kept her gaze on Jemma until she slipped through the doorway.

The street lights out front flickered on. The sun had begun its descent for the day, casting an orange haze across the sky and long shadows on the ground. Jemma didn't notice the beauty above her. She was trapped in her own skin, held captive by her despair.

Ben had been caught. They deemed him a danger to society. Her chest tightened. He'd be kept at Merrytime Clinic for who knows how long. The hair on her arms rose. He was already at the highest dose. No way they would let him out knowing his energy could no longer be controlled by his medicine. Her shaking intensified. She'd be alone, raising her boys. She wasn't strong enough for that.

The street light behind her burst, sending shards of glass splattering to the ground.

"Jemma!" She heard a voice shout but couldn't place where it came from. Arms wrapped around her body and pulled her to the side of the building. "Jemma! Can you hear me?" A face shouted inches from hers, blurry from the tears in her eyes. She couldn't recall when she started crying.

She blinked, and the world around her cleared. The gaping hole shrank just enough for distraction to momentarily plug it up.

"Buran?" A groggy word escaped her mouth. She recognized him, with his head full of blond hair, from the work holiday party a few months earlier.

His strong jaw relaxed slightly. "Yeah, yeah, it's Buran. Good. Keep talking."

She pursed her lips as she fought the hole that now fought back. "What happened?"

"You're okay. Just having a panic attack—I think. Have you ever done that before? Wait, don't answer that yet. Can you count how many fingers I'm holding up?"

Confusion stayed parked in its spot as she looked at his upheld hand. "Two?" She raised an eyebrow.

"Good. Do you see that soda can over there? What color is it?"

Jemma wasn't sure why Buran asked her random questions, but the intensity of her body loosened. "Red... no, orange? It's a little far to tell."

"Close enough." Buran shrugged as he dug his hand into his pocket. "Here, hold these." He handed Jemma four ration coins.

"What are these for?" she questioned as she rubbed the metal circles in her outstretched hand.

"Exactly that." Buran smiled. "Now tell me, and I need you to focus. What noises do you hear around you?"

"Why does that matter?" Jemma challenged. This all felt pointless. Her husband was missing.

"Just listen. What noises do you hear?" Buran insisted. He reached a hand out to touch her arm, then immediately withdrew it when a small shock jolted.

Jemma felt the electricity come off her body, but it didn't hurt her. As Buran rubbed his hand, she decided to do as she was told. Her attention focused on the breeze rustling the ash tree they stood under. "Wind...." she said as she gestured above them.

"Leaves...." She pointed at the leaves that crunched under Buran's feet as he rocked back and forth on his legs.

"Oh," Buran said with a nervous smile. He steadied himself.

The last noise she noticed was the sound of electricity in the air. A quiet sizzling omitted from the broken light behind her. She turned around to see glass littering the sidewalk. Her eyes grew wide.

"Wh—what happened?" she asked while she stared at the scene.

"Don't mind that right now. It happens to the best of us. I saw the energy alert and ran downstairs as fast as I could. I don't think the Responders have realized this is Disparate work yet, but it won't be long. We've got to go."

Energy alert? Disparate work? Why would they need to leave before the Responders came? The string of clues met all at once as realization dawned on her.

Me. It's me. I'm a Disparate.

Six

The first time Margaret babysat her grandsons was, well, tonight. She'd offered in the past, but her busy schedule always seemed to get in the way. At least, that was the excuse she told herself to explain her daughter's hesitancy to accept her help. Deep down, she knew the real reason, but it hurt too much to acknowledge.

She was determined not to mess up tonight.

"Hey! That's mine!" Mackie shouted.

Margaret checked on the boys, leaving behind the pot of water she'd been filling to make dinner. Mackie's golden eyes glared at Louie, who held a blue block in his hand, other blocks scattered around the floor. Louie's eyebrows furrowed as he scowled back at his brother.

This was not going well.

"Boys, there's plenty of blocks for both of you." Margaret picked an identical one off the floor in front of her. "Here Mac, is this the block you're wanting?"

"My name is Mackie! And Louie has the block I want!" Mackie reached for Louie's hands.

"I was gonna grab it!" Louie said as he twisted away and lifted the block above his head to keep his little brother from reaching it. "You only want it because I was gonna get it."

Margaret sighed, annoyed by their childish fight. *Although*, she reminded herself, *they are children.*

"Mac*kie*, this block is the same one. Just use it instead." Her voice was stern, conveying an air of control.

It didn't work.

With all his little might, Mackie jumped and grabbed hold of the block in question, ripping it out of Louie's hand before he quickly dropped it to the floor. A wail escaped Mackie's lips; his fingertips were bright red, a small part of the blue plastic melted onto his pointer finger as if it'd been dipped in candle wax.

Louie used flame energy.

Margaret's heart quickened. She hadn't expected an incident. Jemma had told her he was a Flame Disparate, but she'd seen him get mad without causing any heat. Tonight though, he obviously had.

Louie's whole body tensed. His hands fell to his side, each clenched into a fist. Smoke floated out between his fingers like a snake escaping his grasp, his eyes fixated on Mackie.

"What were you thinking, Louie?" Margaret chastised her elder grandson as she grabbed the younger. The smell of smoke made her want to run, but she couldn't abandon her family.

Not again.

Her voice was raised, but she tried to hide her fear. She didn't want to provoke him further. "You could've started a fire! Do you want to burn down the house?"

Without waiting for an answer, she carried Mackie to the sink, turning on cool water to soothe his burn. The melted block remnant easily rinsed off, circled around the drain, and disappeared. As Mackie's crying settled to quiet sobs, she kept an eye on Louie. He stayed glued to the spot where she left him.

Her hands shook as she held Mackie. Louie could've started a fire, and he still might. Although... maybe not. As far as Margaret knew, he was only able to melt objects.

But there was smoke. Smoke always came before the flame.

She grabbed the pot of water from earlier. The thought crossed her mind to dump it on Louie. *No Margaret, that will not help; it'll only make things worse. It'd evaporate too quickly.*

Instead, she handed it to Mackie, encouraging him to put his fingers inside if they still burned. She would get a new one to make dinner. He nodded as he sat at the kitchen table.

Margaret approached Louie slowly, not wanting to startle him. She tried to think of what her daughter would do, how she'd seen her calm him down in the past. His frozen demeanor worried her. He stood with his hands in fists at his side; however, they no longer smoked. She looked into his gray eyes and saw tears.

Her heart shattered in that moment, no longer worried about her home. All her worry went to the tiny boy in front of her.

"Louie." Her voice was soft. Her hands settled on his arms as his fists relaxed. His shirt warmed her palms, but she didn't mind.

"I don't want to burn your house," he said as tears streamed down his cheeks.

"I know, honey. You need to be careful when you're mad. You hurt your brother."

"He stole my block!" Louie's face scrunched.

"No," Mackie quickly interrupted. "I had it first!"

Margaret tensed, watching to make sure Mackie's response didn't trigger more smoke. Thankfully, it didn't.

"I know you were mad, Louie. However, it is not okay to hurt others. Do you understand?"

Louie's eyes fell to the floor, his eyebrows tight together. "I know. I didn't mean to hurt him."

"That's good," Margaret said. "You have to be extra careful because of your energy power. Not everyone has to worry about that, but you do."

She wrapped her arms around Louie and pulled him close. His small body relaxed in her arms, and its warmth brought attention to the knot that had formed in her stomach. She no longer felt hungry.

"Why don't we play on your tablets for a bit?" Margaret tried to keep her voice from shaking as she released Louie. He nodded enthusiastically.

"Yes!" Mackie jumped off the chair with a smile on his face. The pot of water crashed to the floor, soaking the kitchen rug. Great—another mess to clean.

"My finger feels better, I wanna play."

Margaret glanced at his finger, and sure enough, it was no longer red.

"Mine is the blue one." Louie grabbed his tablet and sat in the plush rocking chair. Mackie sighed as he took his green tablet, gazing longingly at the chair as he sat on the couch. He must not have wanted to cause more anger either.

"Just don't let your mother know you played before dinner." Jemma would see right through this decision. She didn't want to worry her daughter for no reason. Margaret handled the situation, and everything was fine.

But then, why is my stomach in knots? she thought as she placed her arm across her waist.

The wall of the van was cold on Ben's skin as his arm bounced against the side. The driver seemed unconcerned by the rigid terrain he powered over. The location of Merrytime Clinic was confidential, revealed only to those deemed necessary.

The van lurched to a stop. Ben's body rocked forward, his hands reaching out to keep from colliding with the seat in front of him. They had arrived at their destination.

As Ben exited the van, his eyebrows furrowed. Where he expected to see a building instead stood a dock. In front of him was an expanse of ocean, the reflection of the full moon rocking across the small waves.

Two new Responders in black uniforms stood on either side of Ben, both armed with a tranquilizer gun on one hip and a real gun on the other. One wore dark sunglasses, even though the sun had fully set, while the other carried a ring of keys strapped to his side. The way they stood, rigid with their hands at their sides, told Ben they wouldn't hesitate to shoot if given a reason. The moonlight reflected across the badges on their right arms: a silver clover with five leaves.

"I'm supposed to be going to Merrytime Clinic," Ben said.

The shaded Responder released a laugh. "Yeah, that's where you're going. That's where they all go." His voice sounded low and gruff, like the warning growl a dog makes before it strikes. He motioned Ben forward, toward the end of the dock where a ferry floated, a small enclosed room in the middle of the boat destined for him.

"No, this isn't right." Ben stood his ground. If he let them take him to Lucky Island, how would he get back? The betrayal caused his muscles to clench, and heat rose through his body. "Call the Responders Office. They'll tell you I'm supposed to go to Merrytime Clinic."

"I know exactly where you're going," the Responder said as he grabbed one of Ben's arms and pulled.

"It's not there." Ben motioned to the dock and the ocean beyond it as his feet stayed put. He wasn't going to leave his wife, his sons. This was not the sentence he was given. How would Jemma know where he was? How would he get back home?

The other guard grabbed his free arm, and together, they dragged Ben toward the boat. He struggled and tried to pull away. To no avail.

But there was heat. A familiar inkling. The one from his childhood. However, it was small. Not enough to shoot bright flames. Not quite yet.

But maybe it could grow. He leaned into his heat, willing for it to become more. If ever there was a time he needed his energy, it was now. He stopped his physical fighting and focused only on his anger. They were almost to the boat.

"Good," the guard on his right remarked, the keys on his side clanking together. "No point in fighting us. We'll get you there one way or another."

They reached the end of the dock. Ben's anger flared, stronger than it'd been in years. They wouldn't take him from his family. From his home. This wasn't right, and Ben needed to fix it. He pinned his feet against the boat platform, refusing to be carried on. A loud roar escaped his lips as he fought back once more, his head facing the sky.

Nothing happened.

The medicine in his system was doing its job. Keeping him controlled.

"Let's go!" the guard shouted.

Hands pushed against Ben as a foot kicked into the back of his knee. The force caused him to fall. His head banged against the metal walkway. The guards pulled his body upright, now too weak to fight back. Blood streamed down the right side of his face, boiling hot, searing his skin as it seeped from the cut. In his vision, a concrete door flashed before everything went black.

Jemma found herself in the back room of a local Indian restaurant, still shaken and surprised by the new knowledge she had of herself. She wasn't sure what to think as she glanced at a poster similar to the one she saw in the park. *Embrace your emotions.*

This wasn't her. She wasn't a Disparate. She helped Disparates. That was what she went to school for. That was what she did as an Analyst for four years after college, before Louie's energy explosions began. She didn't know this new person that came into existence an hour ago.

And yet... she did. Technology always stopped working around her. *Just bad luck,* she often thought.

The high cost of our lightbulb budget must be due to bad wiring, but the electrician noted the wiring was newer than the house itself. *Our car was getting old and needed a checkup,* but there was never anything consistent about when the engine would struggle turning over, except it did so at the worst possible times. She recalled burnt out computers while in the middle of an important deadline, a phone battery dying in the middle of a call she had been dreading to make.

Deep down, Jemma knew something was different. She never wanted to dig to find out what, and now, the truth could no longer stay hidden.

"Have you asked her about the files?" a tall Indian man in a red apron whispered to Buran. He looked to be in his forties, salt sprinkled through his dark beard. The wavy hair on his head, however, was the shade of charcoal.

Jemma overheard them from where she sat, at a table covered in spice packets and surrounded by boxes of supplies. A wooden doorway decorated with an ornate arch was in front of her, a small television hanging on the wall next to it. It must have led to the main restaurant, as the door they entered at the back was a plain utility door. She wasn't told where they were going on the drive over, only that Buran had some friends that would keep her safe. He didn't want her to risk going home until they made sure the Responders didn't realize she had caused the power outage.

She wasn't sure what to think of that, but she'd been too shaken up to protest. It was now occurring to her that she barely knew this man. Let alone his *friends*.

"Not yet, she's had a bit of a rough night as is, Samay." Buran looked over at Jemma. Her elbows rested on the table as her hands supported her head.

She straightened herself as she spoke. "What files?"

"We can talk about that in a bit—"

"The files Ben removed from the archives," Samay interrupted Buran's response. "The ones he was studying. The ones that were burned in the fire. We need to know what information was on them." He was straight to the point.

Jemma didn't know what they were talking about, but it made her curious. It seemed Buran's true reason for bringing her here wasn't to keep her safe.

"You don't have to answer yet. It's okay if you need a moment," Buran said. The look on Samay's face was hot as an iron.

"I don't know anything about any files. I need to get home."

She was worried about their intentions. What if they wouldn't let her leave?

The light above the table flickered. Her eyes once again found the words on the poster, which prompted her to take a deep breath.

No. She shook her head. The times she'd met Buran at work functions, he was friendly, despite Ben calling him a bit strange. Plus, he let her keep her phone. If this was a kidnapping, he'd have taken it. Unless he was a really bad kidnapper.

"I need to get back to work." Samay's bluntness was something to get used to. She watched as he turned around and went out the ornate door at the front of the room. The sounds of metal clanking and meat sizzling escaped as the door swung open.

It must have been the end of the dinner rush. Jemma's stomach rumbled, reminding her that she hadn't eaten, but the thought of food made her queasy. Or perhaps it was the fact that only she and Buran were in the room.

"I understand you want to go home. I've got a friend making sure the coast is clear." Buran sat in the empty chair next to her and swiped some chili pepper packets to the side to give himself more space. "It's okay if you don't know about the files. We were just *hoping* you might know something. It's a shame Ben burned them before I got a chance to look."

Jemma's head swarmed. Ben was taken away for starting a fire in his office. How was that even possible?

Before the question formed on her lips, the television shone the red and blue banner across the screen with the words "Breaking News."

"The fire anarchist has been caught! Benjamin Hodgerton, an employee at Energy Watch, has been taken into custody after an arson attempt on his own office failed thanks to the quick thinking of a coworker who jumped into action with a fire extinguisher. We can all be grateful for his service and help in apprehending this dangerous criminal! And remember, always keep emergency supplies nearby. You never know when a Disparate outburst may occur."

The news disappeared and returned to the Bollywood dancers that were on before.

Jemma bent over, her stomach queasy. This couldn't be happening.

"So, it's true," Buran said. "Ben's the anarchist." His face fell in disappointment.

"No…" Jemma shook her head, recalling what she knew about the anarchist. "That's not possible. He can't be. The last time the anarchist hit, on Friday, he was home with me."

"You're sure?" Buran asked. "There's no way he could've snuck out?"

"He was cleaning up laundry detergent when the strike happened. Trust me, it wasn't him."

"So…" Buran paused, his brows narrowing in thought, "you're saying he was framed?"

Jemma was quiet, staring wide eyed at Buran. This all felt unreal. She heard a soft ringing come from Buran's side pocket. Her heart skipped a beat. Maybe the coast was clear for her to head home.

"Just a sec," Buran said as he pulled out his phone and stood to pace. "Hey hon… yeah, I'm okay… No, not yet. Looks like I'm gonna be home later than expected… Yep, at Samay's now. I'll let you know when I'm headed out… Love you too."

That didn't sound hopeful. Jemma would be stuck here longer. Her thoughts went to her boys; hopefully everything was going well at Grandma's.

Her mother—had she seen the broadcast?

The lights in the room flickered as Jemma's breathing became shallow.

"Jemma…" Buran's voice sounded clouded.

It was happening again. Jemma took a deep breath through her nose, closing her eyes to focus on calming her nerves. The lights steadied.

She checked her phone. Her mother had sent a picture of the boys, smiling as they ate spaghetti. Sauce lined their lips. Relief washed over Jemma. Nothing about the news. Her mother must not have seen it.

"Sorry 'bout that," Buran said. "The wife checking in, you know how that is. You okay?" He put his phone away.

Jemma nodded. She couldn't help but wish she could have that conversation with her own husband as she stared at the phone in her hand. She sent a quick text to him just in case before setting it in her lap.

Buran sat. "Are you sure Ben didn't mention anything out of the ordinary?"

Jemma tried to remember, but the last few days had been a bit hectic with family life and her own worries the recent news had brought. Perhaps that was why Ben hadn't mentioned anything wrong at work; he didn't want to add to her fears. Guilt settled on her chest as she realized she'd been so distracted with her own problems she hadn't noticed his.

Buran's eyebrows moved together as the side of his mouth lifted slightly. "I'm sorry this is happening," he said in a soft voice. "We want to help you, and Ben. We just know whatever it was he found would help us too."

Jemma wasn't convinced. There had to be another way out of this situation than trusting a stranger. But who else could she trust? She studied the ring on her finger, its small gem shimmering in the dim light.

There was Governor Dunn. But she wasn't sure how much power he had over Merrytime Clinic. He might be able to advocate for Ben, but he didn't have the power to let him go. Her mother wouldn't be much help, not once the news about Ben reached her and triggered another depression episode. The only reason she'd grown to accept Ben as a son-in-law was because his energy was well contained, as if he wasn't a Disparate.

And here was Buran, offering his help. Jemma needed to trust someone, and maybe Buran was it. But she wanted to make sure she wasn't following blindly.

"Don't you work with Ben? You'd be more likely to know what he was working on than I would."

"I work as an Intaker and Ben is a Watcher. We don't get to chat much."

Jemma sat quietly for a moment, a question on her mind. "So, if you're an Intaker, were you the one that sent Ben away?"

Buran's eyes widened as he shook his head. "No, they brought in someone new... I've never seen them before."

"Someone new? I thought they always used someone from your office."

"This was the first time I'd seen an Intaker from somewhere else doing it." Buran said. "But it's also the first time someone from our office has had an intake done." He fell quiet after his answer, looking at his fingers that drummed on the table.

"I feel like there's more you aren't telling me."

Buran sighed. "The Intaker was part of R.E.I."

Jemma clutched a fist to her chest as she drew in a sharp breath. "Because they believe he's the fire anarchist..." Her voice fell off.

"Yep. This will be harder than we thought."

Jemma nodded softly. "Is there anything else you haven't told me?"

He looked at her, one eyebrow slightly raised. "What do you want to know?"

Jemma thought about that question. There was much she wanted to ask. Much she didn't understand. But she didn't know this man in front of her. Didn't know if his intentions were good. "Why *do* you want to know?"

Buran reclined into his chair and let out a low whistle as he stretched his neck back and forth. "That's quite a long story."

"Well, if you want to help, as you say, then I need to know," she challenged.

Buran smiled with a glint in his blue eyes. "You make a fair point. Better get comfortable."

SEVEN

B en's head throbbed as he awoke, his cheek cold from the concrete. He lifted a hand toward his face but was stopped by a pair
of handcuffs cutting into his wrists. He braced his back on the wall
behind him as he sat up, noticing the small pool of blood that now
stained the porous surface. Its dark red color was barely illuminated
by a dim light bulb that hung from the ceiling. As he stretched his
long legs, his feet bumped into the door that had briefly flashed across
his vision before he'd passed out.

Where am I? He wasn't sure if it was him or the room that was
swaying.

The skin on the right side of his face burned, no longer cooled
by the ground. Metal chains across his hands clinked as his fingers
gently brushed against blisters, causing him to wince. The heat from
his blood had left its mark.

That's right. The boat.

Salty air from a vent above the door floated into his small prison.
The air became heavy, he imagined with the same weight he carried,
and billowed across the floor. He stomped his foot and watched the
mist run away. Afraid of his blue sneakers.

He should be home putting the boys to bed right now. Warm tears formed in his eyes as he thought about his family. Jemma would not take the news of him going away to Merrytime Clinic well, and she definitely wouldn't handle knowing he was actually on his way to Lucky Island. He knew the way her mind worked and the conclusions it would jump to. He could hear her voice in his head. *You won't come back.*

She might've been right.

But he wasn't ready to accept that.

Ben tried to muster the anger he'd felt earlier, when his blood was boiling. His energy power was inside him. His medicine had worked and kept him contained, but even that had its limits, and Ben was at the ceiling.

The rocking of the boat swelled, disrupting Ben's focus. He reached his arms out together, and the metal of his cuff clanged against the side walls as the rocking slowed. He no longer felt a forward momentum. The boat had stopped. He heard shouting and clanking outside, then the turning of a key.

As the door opened, the full moon illuminated his prison. He hadn't been out more than a few hours. The keyring guard stood in the doorway, and the other behind him held his gun at the ready.

The guards ushered Ben out. Once in front of them, he hesitated for a moment. The guard in the glasses noticed right away, the barrel of his real gun pressing into Ben's back.

"You only get one redo. I suggest you use it wisely," he whispered. Ben swallowed the bile he felt rising and stepped forward off the boat.

Stars glared upon the new arrival, giving enough light to illuminate the forest in the distance. The strong scent churned his empty stomach: a mix of musty pine and fire smoke.

A layer of leaves covered the worn trail they walked. No, not leaves. There were no trees in this area. Ashes. Burnt logs splayed out around the pathway. At least, Ben hoped they were just logs.

At the edge of the trees that were still standing, two new Responders waited, outfitted in the same uniform as the others—including weapons. One man and one woman. The latter's squinting stare at Ben relaxed as they approached. It was almost as if she'd been expecting someone else.

"So this is the fire anarchist that's been causing so much trouble on the mainland?" the male guard said.

There it was. Confirmation. One small fire at his office and he became an easy target to blame for the rest of them. "But I'm not," Ben growled.

The gun pressed harder into his back.

The glasses-wearing Responder nodded. "Your problem now."

Ben was shoved forward, the pressure on his back finally removed. He was relieved to have it gone, but that relief quickly turned to anger that it'd been put there in the first place. He was no criminal. The new guards took their spots on either side of Ben.

"This is a misunderstanding. I'm innocent."

"Of course you are..." the male guard muttered and rolled his eyes.

"It's very early, or rather, late for you," the high-pitched woman said, talking to Ben as if he mattered. "I doubt you've gotten much sleep on your journey here. I'm sure you're ready for some rest. I know I am." The bags under her eyes were visible even in the shadow of the trees. They seemed more defined than what one early morning rising would create.

"It's part of the job, Colleen," the man on his right mumbled, clearly not happy to be there either.

At least we all have something in common, Ben thought as they marched forward. *But I* don't *belong here.*

"Of course I know that, Markus."

A noise from the woods caused Colleen to jump. "What was that?"

"Probably just a bird." Markus sounded exasperated.

"Maybe we should walk a little faster." Colleen placed a hand on Ben's upper arm as she increased her pace. Her hand quickly disappeared and found her mouth as a critter scurried across their path. Colleen's short gasp seemed to annoy Markus more, yet something about it didn't feel genuine to Ben. He wasn't sure she was truly scared by a small animal.

"It was just a squirrel. Did you think it was another Disparate? Come on now."

Colleen shook her head. "No... I didn't. But—if one escaped, maybe another could too?"

This perked Ben's attention. Maybe there was hope for him to get off the island.

"No one's getting out again. Are you serious? We're locked down tighter than that pickle jar yesterday."

Colleen chuckled nervously. "We did get it open eventually. Just had to smash it against the counter and break the glass." Ben wasn't sure if the side eye she gave him was hinting at a possibility of escape, or a warning.

Likely the latter.

Heat rose within Ben's body. These guards were missing the injustice in front of them. Or rather, they were part of the injustice.

"Just like the one that escaped." Markus smirked. "Try not to give this new recruit hope. That guy that escaped? You saw what came of him. Burnt himself to a crisp before he reached the dock."

The smugness triggered a spark inside Ben. Talking about a life as if it meant nothing. He thought about what brought him here. The fire at his office, his intake, the white van, the island, being pulled away from his family:

Mackie.

Louie.

Jemma.

It wasn't right. The thought fueled his emotions, the ceiling they'd been sitting at threatening to burst.

"Do you feel that?" Colleen looked at Markus, concern etched on her face.

Markus returned her concern as he lifted his tranquilizer gun. "Heat."

The flame came quickly, trying to catch onto the leaves around them. But just as fast as it came, it was smothered out. The sharp prick of a needle shot into Ben's arm.

"I thought this Disparate was drugged," Markus stated, lowering his now unloaded weapon. A drop of sweat rolled down his forehead.

Ben's body gave out on him as he crashed to the ground. The edge of scorched leaves blurred in his vision before everything, for the second time that night, went dark.

"You work at Energy Watch so you can recruit Disparates?" Jemma's mouth was agape, staring at Buran. She knew her face showed her disbelief, but her jaw stayed dropped. "How do you not get caught? Isn't everything recorded?"

"That's the tricky part. It took a bit to figure it out. If we can get the Disparate to calm fast enough, the computer will register it as a false alarm and we're in the clear. Have to calm them down within two minutes, though, or manually mark it as one. Some cases are too far gone to be potential recruits."

"And that's why you have members on standby all over the Republics?"

"Well, ideally. That's what we'd like to have. Currently having some growing pains, but we'll get there. The ones we are able to get to fast enough tend to be luck. Kind of like tonight: I got lucky. That electrical surge could've fried me instead of the street light."

Jemma's cheeks flushed as she thought about the damage she caused. Her potential ability scared her. She didn't understand why someone would want to learn to use it, to control it. It was too unpredictable, too dangerous. "Wouldn't it be safer for everyone to be medicated? It's helped Ben pretty well. I've seen the damage energy causes."

Buran stared at her, wrinkles forming on his forehead. "That's the thing though. The medication doesn't work the way everyone thinks it does. It actually puts the Disparate at a higher risk. It doesn't fix what causes the ability to release energy, it just suppresses the emotions that lead to energy release. They keep the user apathetic. Have you ever seen Ben get mad?"

Jemma tried to think, but it didn't take much for her to know the answer. "No, never. He's usually so calm, he keeps me calm."

"I know it looks good on the outside, but trust me, the inside is empty. One day it will catch up to him. It always does. I see it daily at Energy Watch. The medication may help for years, but then one day, something triggers past it and you end up with a sinkhole swallowing the highway."

She recalled that event a few years ago. The Disparate had recently lost his mom to cancer, and on the way home from the funeral, a gaping sinkhole developed. He crashed inside it, leaving his body to join his mother. It was a devastating story that increased the government's campaign for the importance of taking your medication.

"But I thought he wasn't taking his pills anymore?"

"Oh, he was; that's why the crash was so deadly. If he had been able to feel his grief before it got to such an extreme, he could've controlled the energy that accompanied it. Or at least, had smaller, warning potholes and I could've helped him." Buran's eyelids drooped, his inner eyebrows slanting together.

Jemma recognized the expression on his face. It was one she had worn numerous times throughout the past seventeen years. "You knew him, didn't you?"

"He was my brother. I do what I do every day because of him. There's got to be a better way to handle Disparates than what the government wants. Better than just suppressing and hiding away." His voice raised and became more pointed.

"I'm sorry for your loss." Jemma felt his pain as if it were her own, thoughts of Asher popping into her mind. She no longer doubted that Buran only wanted to help. "What is your full plan? To get to Disparates before the government does, and then what? Keep them from taking the pills?"

"There's more to it than that. People need to be taught how to control their emotions and their energy." Buran's eyes brightened as he talked. "I'd like to have a place to teach Disparates how, but that's a ways off. It's difficult enough convincing people the pills are dangerous, let alone asking them to stop taking them. But it is possible. There are Disparates walking around, free of the medication they were once forced to take, able to use their energy at will."

Jemma couldn't imagine such a thing was possible. Surely someone would slip up. But then if they caught their slip before it got extreme, they wouldn't be caught.

Samay walked through the door. "Dinner rush is over. Have you found anything out?" He addressed Buran directly.

"Why don't you ask her? She's in the room, you know." Buran gestured toward Jemma.

"Sorry 'bout the attitude." Samay shrugged. "It takes me a bit to relax after a busy night. Can't find better fire-grilled curry in all of Stillfield, though. I make it fresh and cooked to perfection." Samay winked at Buran.

"Yeah." Buran smirked. "He never burns it since he's learned to control how much energy he releases at a time."

Samay seemed pleased with the praise.

Jemma stared at him in surprise. Buran had said there were Disparates able to use their energy when they wanted, but she hadn't quite believed him. Now, one stood in front of her.

"Ha, thanks for giving away my secret. Time to freeze the leftovers. They always defrost fresher when you do it."

Buran rose from the table and headed to the kitchen, leaving Jemma alone with Samay, who untied the string of the apron around his round waist.

She wanted to say something to break the silence in the room, but she couldn't get the words to move from her mind to her mouth. She didn't know Samay, and he hadn't sounded very friendly in the short conversations he held with Buran. Instead she looked at the poster. No wonder he had it in his backroom. It was a reminder to tap into his own emotions.

"So, what did my friend there tell you while I was gone?" Samay asked as he draped his apron across his arm. "He's always been one to say too much too quickly." He kept his face straight as he talked, looking down upon Jemma.

"Um, well, he explained what you're trying to do. You know, with teaching Disparates."

"That's all he's shared so far? Surprised he hasn't convinced you to help overthrow the government yet, starting with the governor. I'm not saying we shouldn't, just that we need to go about it more rationally."

Jemma froze. She wasn't sure what she'd gotten involved in. She understood Buran had a different idea than the government on what would help people, but overthrowing it? Starting with the governor, her family friend? That didn't seem like the right route to go. Governor Dunn, while a bit spacey, was a decent person.

Buran returned from his duty, wiping his hands on his pants. Flakes of ice fell to the floor.

Jemma's eyes widened. Buran was an Ice Disparate. An unmedicated one.

"Gotta warm up after an energy release," he said as he looked at Jemma's pale face. "Whoa, what did he say while I was out? I was gone maybe two minutes. What have you done to her, Samay?"

"I just, I don't know about all of this." Jemma gathered the courage to speak. "It feels like a lot. I need help getting Ben back. I'm not looking to overthrow anything."

"You threw that at her, Samay?" Buran ran his fingers through his light hair as he sighed. "Look, I'm not asking you to help us with that. It is part of why we need to know what Ben found, though. I know you said you don't know what it was. Which means *we* need to get Ben out as well. Samay, can you schedule a meeting for tomorrow?"

Samay nodded in approval as he pulled out his phone and started typing.

"Now Jemma, it looks like the coast is clear for you. No one caught on it was you that blew the power. They're thinking it was caused by the street light shorting out. You can head home. We'll work on getting Ben off the island."

"Island? You mean Merrytime Clinic," Jemma corrected, her limbs turning stiff.

Buran's eyebrows once again slanted together as the side of his mouth raised. Softly, he explained, "I meant island. They didn't take Ben to Merrytime Clinic. They took him where they take everyone that knows information they don't want to get out. They took him to Lucky Island."

Jemma's heart raced. "That isn't possible. The island was shut down decades ago." That was her father's most prized accomplishment. Opening Merrytime Clinic and closing the island associated with so much

Disparate hate and harm. He'd been adamant about treating everyone with dignity.

"I wish that was true." Buran's face fell. "We believe it's been in operation for the last several years. Too many Disparates have gone missing from 'Merrytime Clinic' for it to be the only place for treatment. If it's even a real place."

Missing Disparates? She knew many died, others ran away from their families. Disparates tended to be unstable. Unable to participate safely in society. Yet, that had been changing. Enertin had changed that—hadn't it?

"And you don't believe Ben is at the clinic?" she asked.

"Well, no." Buran took a deep breath. "They think he's the anarchist. Pretty sure that's a high enough threat for the island."

Jemma covered her mouth. If this were true, he was in deeper trouble than she'd thought. Perhaps she should reach out to Governor Dunn, regardless of the fact this "group" didn't like him. "How would they keep something like that hidden? Surely the governor would shut it down."

"The governor doesn't care," Samay spit out. "I've tried talking sense into him, and he doesn't believe us."

"You've met with him, then?" Jemma asked.

"He's gotta be involved in this mess," Buran said, placing his palms on the table.

Jemma didn't want to push these Disparates too far. They were dangerous.

So are you, she reminded herself, a tingling spreading under her skin.

Regardless, her plan to get Ben home as quickly as possible still stood. Whether he was at Merrytime Clinic or Lucky Island didn't change that. Just made things a bit trickier. And if the governor truly couldn't be of help, she'd need someone to trust. "You're not getting him out without me. I can help."

"You don't have to, we can figure—"

"How can you help?" Samay interrupted Buran before he could finish. He raised one questionable eyebrow toward Jemma.

"I was an Analyst. My communications degree taught me how to talk to Disparates. My family also has a history with the government. If there's information you need, I can find a way to get it." She didn't want to go into too much detail about what her family connection was. Not yet.

Samay looked at Buran and nodded.

Buran sighed dramatically. "Okay, you're in. Meet us tomorrow at noon. I'll send you the address. Just be warned, you'll have to convince everyone on the committee to trust you."

Jemma didn't know what committee he spoke of, but she felt a warmth in her chest that she hadn't felt all night. She wasn't in this alone.

It was late by the time Jemma pulled into her garage, the empty space next to her vacant. She needed to figure out how to get Ben's car back home; perhaps his coworker, Oliver, could help. But that was a problem for another day. Her boys were passed out in the backseat. It was well past their bedtime. Her mother understood when Jemma didn't want to stay and chat.

After the night she had, Jemma wasn't sure she could handle being a parent on top of it all. But for her boys, she would be brave. She adjusted the rear view mirror until the peaceful faces of Louie and Mackie were reflected, just in time to see Mackie's eyes flutter open.

"Are we home yet?" he asked as he yawned.

Jemma nodded. "Yes, we are. Ready to go inside?"

"Carry me?" Mackie requested. Jemma smiled softly. His little body was tired, but she was exhausted. An energy release was no joke. Regardless, she fulfilled his request.

After carrying Mackie to his bed, she returned quickly to the car to retrieve Louie. He was fast asleep when she released his seat buckle and scooped up his small, but heavy, frame. He'd grown so much, too much, since the last time she held him in her arms.

As she lowered him onto his bed, his eyes slid open.

"I want Dad," he said in a groggy, slurred voice.

The phrase stabbed Jemma directly in her chest. She, too, wanted his dad.

"I know, sweetie. He'll be back later," Jemma reassured him. "But right now it's time to go to sleep."

"No." Louie lifted his body. "I want Dad to put me to bed." His voice raised. "I'll wait for him."

In his sleepiness, he struggled to understand why his request couldn't be answered. Jemma felt helpless, her mind racing for the answer that would appease him.

"Dad won't be back tonight. He had to leave on a work trip." It felt wrong to make up an excuse, but she realized it was a lie she needed to tell. "Your body needs rest so it can have energy tomorrow. Don't you want to have energy to play?" Her words dripped with desperation.

"I want Dad!" Louie's face tightened, and Jemma's heart raced. Frustration was building in his little body, and nothing she said calmed it.

"Dad puts me to bed!" Louie shouted louder.

"Well, Dad's not here, and you're stuck with me tonight," Jemma snapped back. Her patience was wearing thin, and her own frustration slipped out.

Mackie sat in his bed, rubbing his eyes as he turned to watch his brother.

The dark room lit up in a flicker of flames.

Jemma gasped as she jumped back. Smoke rose off Louie's body as the curtain next to him danced under the fire that burned it. This was the first time he'd created flames. She froze for a second. Her mind focused on what needed to happen next. She'd always been good under pressure.

The closet.

She ran to it and grabbed the fire extinguisher hidden inside.

Once a thick layer of foam covered the curtain, dresser, and Louie's bed, Jemma was able to step back and assess the damage. The rest of the light blue curtain had turned black. About a foot remained, barely holding onto the metal rod. Behind the layer of foam, slightly visible scorch marks decorated the wall.

The room would be repaired, but she wasn't sure about the emotional damage that was done.

Louie had pulled his blanket over his head and curled under it.

Mackie stood in the corner of the room, his small body shaking with tears on his face.

Jemma sat the extinguisher down. The metal clanged as it fell over onto a pile of toys.

"It's okay, the fire is out." Jemma looked at Mackie first, who ran and crashed into her side. She put an arm around him as she glanced at Louie.

He slowly peeked out from under the covers, tears marking his cheeks and foam speckling his hair. "Did I burn the house down?"

"No, honey. I put the fire out." His question had pierced her chest. He was only six. Burning a house down should not be on his list of worries.

Yet it was one of many at the top of hers.

He looked at what was left of the curtains. "I could have," his voice was shaky. "I'm not safe."

Jemma thought about Buran's mission, his goal to teach Disparates to control their energy. If that was truly possible, maybe he could help Louie.

Louie, who was still wrapped in his blanket. She waddled over with Mackie and stretched out a hand.

"How about we sleep in mom's bed tonight?" she suggested. Mackie expressed his agreement as he squeezed tighter to Jemma's legs.

"I don't want to hurt you." Louie hid himself back under his covers.

"Don't worry." Jemma kept her voice soft. "You won't. I'll make sure of that. You're safe with me." She kept her hand accessible, waiting for it to be filled with his.

Finally, Louie's little fingers reached out and accepted his mom's help, allowing her to pull him out of the covers he was stuck in.

Jemma lay sandwiched between her boys minutes later, both of them once again fast asleep.

She pulled out her phone and opened the response Caty had sent her earlier, after she'd realized the boys needed somewhere safe to go in the morning.

> Of course they can start preschool tomorrow. I look forward to having them. And I'm so sorry about Ben.

Jemma allowed herself to crumble. Her body shook with tears as she thought of her husband, her boys, and the danger she posed.

It was too much to bear.

But there was no one to pull her out of this mess but herself.

Eight

That night, Margaret tossed and turned in her bed. Each time her eyelids closed, her mind betrayed her, keeping her from drifting to sleep. The nightmare had returned: the one she'd experienced in real life. The one she couldn't keep from dreaming once again, triggered by the events with the boys earlier in the evening.

As her eyes closed, she stood with her arms wrapped around a child. Louie? No, this child in her mind was older, a teenager. He was already taller than his mother. Ashes fell from his brown hair.

She opened her eyes to the darkness in her room, wanting to confirm she was still in the present. She tried to keep her eyes open, to make her mind focus on something else, but the events from that evening had triggered her fear. It wasn't going away until she faced it. Her eyelids were heavy as they closed.

In her dreams, she pulled her child close as they watched the flames burn. The contrast of the night sky caused the fire to appear brighter. The firemen ran inside, looking for the two members who were still trapped in the inferno. Margaret wanted to go with them but was stopped by a hand on her arm.

"You won't help, Mom; you'll get in the way. They'll get them out. They have to." Asher's face was worn. Smoke settled on his shoulders.

She knew he was right. Hope was the only feeling she could allow right now. She needed it and so did her son.

A fireman burst through the front door, flames glowing behind him. In his arms was a body, small and frail. Margaret ran to her daughter. Relief spread through her as Jemma's chest swelled and a cough exited her mouth.

"Her breathing's rough," the fireman said as he laid Jemma on a stretcher. "She'll need to be monitored in the hospital for a couple days."

Margaret's chest tightened. She woke with a gasp, as if it were her lungs fighting for air. She grabbed her phone from her bedside table and squinted against the light as she opened her photos.

There. A picture of Jemma with her family replaced the image of her frail twelve year old daughter. She hoped the confirmation that Jemma was well would appease her nightmare. She couldn't keep her eyes from closing and taking her back to that time.

Asher stood a few feet away, his face wrinkled with worry, eyes locked on his sister.

"Ma'am," the fireman addressed Margaret. "We weren't able to get to him."

Margaret's face wrinkled with confusion. "Keep trying, he was in his office."

"We tried, but we were too late," the fireman's voice was soft. "He's gone, ma'am. Skylar Stillfield is dead."

Margaret's eyes flew open again, not wanting to relive the horror of her past. She rolled over in bed and stared at the spot next to her. The spot that had lain empty for the last seventeen years. Her hand rested on the sheet next to her as her body relaxed once more.

Her dream world turned cloudy. The sound muffled. This was the moment Margaret's heart had shattered.

She looked at her sweet daughter as she struggled through a coughing fit on the stretcher below her. With the sound muted, the pain on her face was more pronounced. Margaret looked over her shoulder to see her son—

Except, he wasn't there. Her head twisted around the scene, searching for the hair speckled with fire dust. A voice from behind stopped her search.

"Maggie? Are you alright?" She turned to see Tobias Dunn standing beside her, concern written across his face.

"Have you seen Asher? He was here a moment ago. He heard that Skylar..." Emotion blocked her throat from confirming the truth.

"I know." Tobias rested his hand on her arm. "We'll find him. You're not the only one looking for him." His voice sounded bleak.

"Mrs. Stillfield, will you be riding with Jemma?" A firefighter disrupted her thoughts. Jemma's stretcher now sat in the back of an ambulance.

Margaret was conflicted. Torn between her two children. Go with Jemma, or stay and search for her lost boy? The boy that may have just killed his father.

"You go," Tobias answered for her. "I'll keep looking for Asher."

The sirens blared as the ambulance headed to the hospital—mother and daughter safe inside.

The same sirens continued as Margaret began to rouse from her sleep. When she realized the sound was in her real world, she sat straight in her bed. Her heartbeat quickened.

It was then she registered it was coming from her phone.

As she canceled the alarm, she noticed an unread message from Tobias.

> Are you still available for coffee today?

Margaret felt a weight on her chest. The mention of coffee caused her stomach to churn.

> Not feeling well today. Taking a sick day.

Margaret lay back in bed, pulling the covers over her head as tears soaked her pillow.

A sliding sound caused Ben to jump. His head hit the small light hanging from the ceiling of his cell. Flickering shadows were cast across the small room, which was eerily similar to his last. The main difference being that, minus the lightbulb, this one didn't sway.

He looked toward the door. A small slit exposed the narrow view on the other side.

He didn't see much before a metal plate was pushed through the hole. It fell clattering to the ground, spraying the contents across the floor.

"Damn it, Newbie, you're supposed to have your tray up!" a deep voice shouted from the other side. "Read your welcome packet!" The slit slammed shut.

Ben's hand clutched his head; it hadn't stopped throbbing since he'd woken. He noticed a metal rectangle hanging under the door's opening. That must be the *tray* the voice on the other end was referring to. As for a welcome packet, he didn't see anything.

"Wait, come back," Ben's voice croaked, barely above a whisper. He took three large steps to the door, avoiding the spilled food on the ground. His fingers lay across the food slit and pushed, trying to pry it open. It wouldn't budge.

Ben examined the breakfast that now littered the floor. Plain brown oatmeal and toast. *The breakfast of prisoners,* he thought, any hint of appetite now fully gone.

His attention moved to the marks on the walls. Scratches etched into the concrete. Likely done by someone in pain, trying to claw their way out. At the foot of his concrete bed were long, precise lines. They were carved in groups of four with a fifth slashed across. Someone had been keeping track of time.

Ben counted each group of five but was stopped by a large burn mark that covered the endless counting.

It stretched toward the ceiling, covering a small window on the back wall. Ben climbed onto the toilet below. His muscles ached with the movement. Between metal bars, he saw a dense forest. A tall fence covered in spikes led through the trees. On the other side of the barrier was another building, a good ten feet away. Above, the clouds were as gray as Louie's eyes—and, well, his own. They looked as if they would release their tears at any moment. Seagulls flew in spirals before plunging out of view.

He returned his attention to the room. It'd been used for a Flame Disparate in the past. Were they held here before or after the Enertin pills were made? The island was supposed to have been closed after the medicine's discovery, but clearly it was still in use.

As a Watcher, Ben knew the medicine didn't always work as intended. But the island?

His chest tensed. It was a feeling he wasn't used to. A dangerous feeling.

Ben recalled the night before. His flame energy was there. He'd felt it pulsing through his body even though he'd taken his medicine the previous afternoon. It shouldn't have been possible for him to create energy. But he'd seen the burnt leaves. It had to have been him.

Had he also started the fire in his office? No, he would have felt the same energy as last night. It wasn't him that started the fire he'd been carted away for. Something, or someone else, had started it.

Buran was the only one there with him at the time. He knew Ben was a Flame Disparate. He had an opportunity while Ben was distracted looking for his lost pill. He seemed a likely suspect. The question left was why?

But Oliver was there as well. He'd come pretty quickly after the fire had started, armed with an extinguisher. It was lucky that he'd returned from lunch on time—wasn't it?

The files showed the false alerts from the East Sector. Someone had been changing the alerts coming from the old mall. If only Ben knew if the number he saw was for a Watcher or an Intaker. Then perhaps he'd have a better idea of who framed him, or if this all were an accident to begin with.

Ben knew he should be angry, but curiosity filled that void. If he could create flame energy, he may still be able to get away.

After what felt like hours sitting in his cell as thoughts smoldered in his mind, a bell rang. His door clicked then swung open, causing the metal breakfast plate on the ground to crash against the opposing wall.

Ben stood back from the doorway. A guard blocked his view of a room behind him.

"Lunch time!" His voice matched the one from breakfast.

"What? I thought the food came through the slot," Ben said as he pointed toward the mess on the floor.

"It does for newbies." He threw a red jumpsuit at Ben with the number 1232 on it. "Here, put this on. And no funny business, I heard about the trouble you caused last night." A red haired man in a Responder's uniform rested a hand on the weapon perched delicately on his right side: the tranquilizer. Thick black frames covered his brown eyes, and freckles dotted his tan face. The small metal rectangle on his right chest read "S. Flannan." Ben stared blankly at the guard.

"It took us a while to find a jumpsuit that was still intact. Most of them get burnt up. You have to be in your coordinating color in order to socialize." Flannan narrowed his eyes.

Ben turned his back to the guard as he removed his old clothes. Flecks of mud fell to the floor as he changed. He didn't mind the new clothes, however, he wished for a shower... in his own home. He left dirt marks on his jumpsuit as he stepped into it.

Once dressed, he followed Flannan out of the cell. They were in a large warehouse. The ceiling was covered in steel beams and fluorescent lights. Concrete doors that matched the one to his cell lined the edges of an open room. Clusters of furniture were arranged in small sitting areas throughout. The mismatched patterns and sizes read "junk yard" more than a welcoming home. Of course, this was far from a welcoming home, anyway.

They continued walking, entering through a large door and into a cafeteria. There were tables scattered around the room in no particular order. Other people were dispersed at the tables, in yellow or red jumpsuits like his own. There was a whole operation going on here, and somehow no one on the mainland had noticed. Ben pursed his lips. *How many Disparates did* I *unknowingly send here?* he wondered.

His guard parted with him at the line of other islanders waiting for food. He went to the only empty corner of the room, the other three corners already taken by other guards. One he recognized as Markus, the guard that escorted him to his room last night. He saw no sign of Colleen.

Ben wasn't the only one in a red jumpsuit. He looked around, count-ing the islanders. About twenty-three altogether. A fairly even ratio be-tween those in yellow and red.

Everyone ate quietly. No friendly greetings or whispered conversa-tions. There was nothing lucky about this place. It truly was a prison.

"Oh, sorry." He bumped into the woman in front of him. Her blond hair blended into the yellow jumpsuit she wore.

Without responding, she picked up a metal tray that matched the plate his breakfast was served on. Her eyes stared off into the distance as she took a deep, slow breath. She continued forward to receive a helping of mashed potatoes from a hair-netted guard on the other side of the cafeteria line.

Ben copied her, last in line. He got his own serving of mashed pota-toes, a roll, and a main dish that looked to be some kind of flat, breaded meat. At the end, he was given a small, clear cup with a red pill sitting inside. He'd noticed the girl in front of him received a yellow pill.

"Do you know what time it is?" he asked the woman passing out medication. She wore a blue lab coat and white gloves. A clipboard sat on her lap.

"Time to take your medication like a good little Disparate," she said with a condescending smile. She lifted her clipboard and began to write as Ben walked away.

He found a table to the side of the room, closest to the door that he entered from. A fellow red jumpsuit wearer sat next to him, a white streak in his jet black hair. He was undisturbed by Ben's presence as he chewed on the white meat in front of him.

"Hey," a quiet voice whispered from the other side of the table. The woman he'd bumped in line sat hunched over her tray. Her blond hair fell to the sides, creating her own little hideout. "Are you going to take that?"

Ben's eyebrows drew together as he glanced at her. "Take what?"

She leaned in slightly. "Shhh, don't talk so loud. And don't look at me." Her hair swayed just above her shoulders as she glanced at the guards around the room to make sure they hadn't heard.

Ben quickly looked at his tray, embarrassed that he didn't understand the order of this new place.

"You know he can't give it to you," the black haired boy next to him said. The youthful tone of his voice made Ben uneasy. He glanced sideways at him and noticed his pimpled skin. He couldn't be older than sixteen.

"You don't have to ruin it, 1227," she hissed, her voice still a whisper.

"You should probably take your pill already, 1198," the boy snapped back. "You seem to be getting cranky."

The woman picked up a yellow pill from her own cup container. She plopped it in her mouth then took a swallow of water.

"There, that should help you feel much calmer."

Without missing a beat, the woman's shoulders relaxed and her breathing became as slow and deep as it'd been in line.

"What were you wanting?" Ben whispered, still thinking maybe she wanted some extra mashed potatoes. He would've shared with her. They were too bland and thick for his taste.

"Oh, she's out now. Won't get much from her for the next twenty-four hours. That yellow pill mellows 'em out faster than lightning. Get it? Lightning? That's what they'd be making without it," he chuckled lightly into his lunch roll. "She wanted your happy pill. The yellow pills aren't as fun. Supposed to keep 'em calm, but ends up doing more than that."

Ben glanced at 1198 once more. Her hazel eyes were glossy as she slowly spooned her meal into her mouth. She seemed unaware of the conversation that continued on the other side of the table.

"So, our suits correlate to our energy type, and therefore our pill color then?" Ben asked.

"Yeah." The boy nodded. "Obviously, you're new here. What you in for? Did you burn down your gym? Maybe torch your jerk of a cousin at Thanksgiving dinner?" The corner of his smile twitched as he continued. "No, you must have done something bigger to get you here. You look roughed up. Bet you're one of 'em that overheard something you shouldn't've." He chuckled again.

Ben felt the dull burn on the side of his face. He could only imagine the scar it would leave once healed.

This boy intrigued him, sitting there smiling to himself as his leg shook the entire table. The clear cup on his tray was empty.

"I don't know why I'm here." Ben wasn't sure he could trust him. "I just want to get back home."

The boy's chuckling turned into howling, his laugh unrestrained. Markus looked in their direction.

"No one gets home!" the boy cried. Tears from laughing too hard streaming down his cheeks. "No one—no one gets home! You're stuck here! Everyone's stuck here! Isn't it great?"

Markus headed toward their table. The other guards watched to see if the rest of the room reacted.

"We get happy pills here. We're so lucky!" The boy was grabbed from behind and hoisted to his feet. Markus's cheeks turned red as he dragged the boy away.

"No one ever goes home! If you try, you'll die! Just like the last one! Burnt to a crisp!" The boy continued his laughing shout as he was taken through the sitting room doors. "NO ONE GOES HOME!"

Ben sat still through the whole ordeal, unsure how to react. He glanced carefully around the room. The other yellow suiters wore the same glossy look as 1198, unchanged by the commotion. The red suits, however, didn't stop moving. Their shoulders raised as their legs bounced. The other three guards on watch duty were stiff, their hands at the ready in case of further disturbances.

These pills clearly didn't work the same as the one he was used to.

The woman in the blue lab coat sat in her spot. Her hand moved quickly across the clipboard. As he watched her, she glanced up, meeting his eyes. She smiled as she lifted a small, empty cup. She mimicked raising the cup to her mouth and pouring the contents into it. She wanted him to take the pill. Her eyes stayed glued to him, waiting for him to submit.

He picked up his cup. The red pill looked similar to the one he was used to, yet he knew it wouldn't have the same effect, not if it did the same to him as it seemed to be doing to the other islanders. Taking their emotions to the extreme opposite.

He weighed his options in his mind. Give in and allow the drug access to his mind and body, or reject it.

The guard, Flannan, stared at Ben. His hand rested on his gun, not his tranquilizer. Refusing the drug would have its consequences.

The pill felt heavy on his tongue. He raised his water cup to his mouth, pushing the pill to his cheek as he swallowed. The lab coat woman nodded as she scrawled across her clipboard once more. Flannan relaxed his weapon and smiled.

Ben's thumb moved slightly between his chin and the cup before he lowered it. His hand balled into a fist, a small, combustible capsule held in the middle. His lips curled upward as his leg began to shake, matching the movement of his identical uniform wearers.

Inside, however, he began to heat up.

NINE

The old bowling alley was the last place Jemma would have guessed as a secret meeting spot. Neon lights flickered as old music videos played on staticky televisions. Empty lanes lined the walls on either side of her.

Round divots littered the pine floors, evidence of a Disparate incident. The reason the alley had closed. One league win, and a gravity Disparate was so happy bowling balls floated in the air. Until they had to come back down, causing irreparable damage to the floor—and multiple league members.

She sat at a small table covered in old papers—informative flyers put out by the government about Enertin. Why would they need those here? A thick marker laid in the middle of the mess.

Three other seats at the table were filled while one stood empty. Across from Jemma sat a young woman with dark hair, her arms crossed as she spoke to Buran.

"She hasn't received any training. I don't understand why she's here." Her booming voice carried through the empty building.

Jemma checked her phone, pretending the exclamation didn't bother her. There was a message from Caty. The boys were doing great at their first day of preschool.

"She has analyst training, Aniyah." Buran defended Jemma. "She knows how to talk to people. I'm confident she can get him to help us."

Jemma leaned forward as she put her phone in her pocket. "Get who to help you?"

"She doesn't know why she's here, does she?" Aniyah narrowed her copper eyes.

Not really, Jemma thought. She'd surprised herself by even showing up, but she had to give this group a chance. She had to get Ben home.

"That's enough," Samay jumped in. "She needs our help, and we need hers. We'll explain more once Calum is here."

As if on cue, the front doors opened. In walked a tall, broad-shouldered man, possibly in his early twenties. He flipped his jet black hair out of his eyes as he took his spot.

"I got another letter." He slapped a worn piece of paper onto the table, causing some of the flyers already there to disperse onto the floor.

The handwriting on Calum's letter was scribbled, as if it had been written quickly. Jemma couldn't read it.

"'Whirlwind month at the clinic,'" Calum read for the group. "'Lots of traffic in and out. Grilled a steak just the way you like it. Love you, Bro. Chayse.'" He folded the letter back up. "Isn't that amazing?"

Samay's and Jemma's faces stayed blank as Aniyah wrinkled her forehead. Buran, however, grimaced.

"Well, go on. Translate," Samay said as he kept his eyes on Calum.

"Hold on." Calum turned to look at Jemma. "I forgot my manners. I'm Calum. Nice to meet you." He held out his hand.

Jemma accepted it, feeling out of place among the group. "Nice to meet you as well. Now, can someone explain what's happening?"

"This letter is from his brother." Aniyah spoke quickly, trying to catch Jemma up to speed. "He's not at the clinic. That's what they want his family to think. He's on Lucky Island. It's how we get news about what is happening there."

A cookout didn't seem like much news. But...

"His brother is on Lucky Island?" Jemma asked, sitting upright. "And he can send letters?" A crumb of hope built in her chest. She could write to Ben. Send word that she was going to get him home.

"Since he's a teenager, he gets to write letters," Buran's voice was sympathetic. "It's heavily monitored, and he has to write in code. Calum's the only one who can translate."

Jemma's heart sank along with her body. Teenager. How could someone so young be taken there? And he might not be the youngest. She fought to keep her thoughts away from Louie, but it was difficult. What if he was taken to join his father? *No. Focus Jemma.*

"What do your parents think of that?" Jemma couldn't keep herself from asking.

Calum's almond eyes tightened. "Not much. They're... not around."

Jemma wanted to melt into her seat. Did he mean they were dead?

"But that's okay," Calum said quickly. "At least they left us this building and pay the power bill."

No. Still alive, but it didn't sound like that was much better. She couldn't imagine ever abandoning her children.

"So, what does he mean?" Aniyah turned to Calum.

"They've been experiencing 'whirlwind' storms, but that's not the most intriguing part," Calum said. Storms in the ocean weren't uncommon. The weather was unpredictable and often rough. "Someone tried to get out, but it didn't work. Burnt up. Well done. Just like how I like my steaks."

Both Samay and Aniyah winced. Jemma wasn't sure if it was for the poor Disparate who wasn't so lucky or the way Calum ordered his steaks.

"But get this," Calum continued. "Chayse says he didn't escape, but I overheard some council women gossiping the other day. Said they think the fire anarchist is the escapee! Can you believe it? What if it's true?"

Jemma must have looked confused again.

"He works at the Capitol as a janitor," Aniyah said. "The fire anarchist is the one who's been burning government buildings."

"I know about the fire anarchist." Jemma didn't like the condescending tone Aniyah used. "Supposedly, the government, and the rest of the Republics, think it's my husband."

"Oh," Aniyah softened her voice. "Buran left that piece of information out."

Buran raised his hands in defense. "I was waiting for everyone to arrive so I didn't have to repeat the details multiple times."

"Well," Calum said, "people at the Capitol are pretty split on the anarchist actually being caught. They aren't buying that he'd attack his own work place in the middle of the day."

"He didn't," Jemma said. "He's being framed."

Samay nodded. "We need to continue with our plan. Find the real fire anarchist and get him to join our cause."

Their *cause*. The one to overthrow the government? Jemma was still unsure of what she'd gotten involved in. "If we find the anarchist..." Jemma spoke slowly, attention turning to her. "Then we can prove that Ben is innocent. Get him released." Her hope swelled. This could work.

"That would never work," Aniyah said. "He's on Lucky Island; they aren't gonna let him off that easily."

Buran turned to Jemma. "I agree. He found something in those files, and they won't let him walk free."

Her face fell to the floor, her hope crushed. The pages from the table littered the ground. The one stating the dangers of unmedicated energy was now flipped on the back, words written across it.

"Wait..." Jemma said as she picked it up and read it: *Embrace your emotions. Disparates deserve deliverance. Dissentients are watching.* "Are you the ones putting these posters around town?"

Jemma looked at Buran. He pursed his lips. "Yeah," he said, "we need to get the word out somehow that the medication isn't safe."

"And that's why you want Ben," Jemma said, each word coming out slowly. "Because... he's one of you?" The thought caused her airways to constrict. Had her husband been working with this group? Was that the real reason why he was taken away? Why he hadn't wanted Louie to take the medication when it was announced?

But then, why did he still take Enertin himself? It wasn't adding up.

"No, no!" Buran waved his hands in front of him, as if wiping away that idea. "He's not. He doesn't know anything about us. As I said before, we're looking for something to help us expose the dangers of Enertin. And the look on Ben's face as he flipped through those files... there has to be something important there."

But there's no way to know if what he found was really important, Jemma thought. And yet, it was the one thing they were betting on to make rescuing him a priority.

This group, these Dissentients, were really grasping at straws. Jemma bit her lip. "The fire anarchist can help us get to Ben?" she asked.

"If what I heard was true," Calum said, his face wide with hope. "We could find out where Lucky Island is."

Jemma nodded. If the rumors were true, they had a shot at saving her husband. "Responders have been trying to catch him for weeks; how are we going to do it?" She wanted to know more before agreeing to the risk. She couldn't leave her boys without their father *and* their mother.

"Well." Buran shifted in his seat. "He's a Disparate. We're Disparates. If we can catch him at his next target, approach him to talk, I'm sure we can convince him to join us."

"That's the plan?" Jemma was uneasy. It didn't feel like much of a plan to her.

"More or less." Samay shrugged. "We won't have a chance if we don't try."

Samay hadn't seemed like much of an optimist, but even he was willing to risk the fire anarchist turning on them.

"Look," Aniyah spoke, her voice vulnerable. "If we can figure out what he wants, we can use that to bargain. Status quo. We help him, he helps us. He clearly has a goal with his break-ins and attacks. There's something the government has that he's looking for."

She was right, but what would they have to risk to give it to him? Whatever it was, if it led to getting Ben back, Jemma was in.

"Okay." She took a steadying breath. "When are we doing this?"

"Tonight." Buran smiled. "We're going to catch him tonight."

After lunch, Ben was escorted out a door past the kitchens with the rest of the prisoners. He followed the crowd, doing his best to remain inconspicuous. His counterparts in red jumpsuits continued to smile, giggles escaping in occasional bursts. He followed their lead as the group stepped through the door. Sunlight cascaded through the trees, causing him to squint. As his eyes adjusted, he got his first look at the island in the daytime.

Trees towered over the edge of what looked to be three warehouses. The other two were next to his, one after the other. The space they exited to was surrounded by a large metal fence. A soft buzz told Ben it was armed. It extended between each warehouse, keeping the inhabitants apart. Not that there were other inhabitants out.

Throughout the yard, people were scattered. Their blue coats matched the sky above. Each with a clipboard, matching the pill-giver from lunch time. They watched the group as they exited, their hands moving to scribble notes.

Ben heard a clicking sound behind him.

"Contents of Wing One out for recreation time," Flannan spoke into a walkie-talkie.

Wing? Ben didn't like the sound of that. Like they were at a hospital recovering instead of this isolated prison. There was nothing healing about this place.

The line of people in front of Ben spread out. Those in yellow suits, including 1198, meandered over to a circle of a dozen stools. Art easels stood in front of each. Paint palettes were claimed as the prisoners arrived. Ben glanced at the canvases as he walked by. Each painting consisted of straight brush strokes, not much more.

Those in red suits walked, skipped, and galloped to different destinations. A basketball hoop stood in the middle of the yard, at which a group of six now took turns throwing a ball into the basket. Except, right when each was about to throw, their body would jerk and the ball would miss their target. Instead of the player being upset at the miss, they smiled and clapped.

The other four red suits ran around the edge of the fence.

Ben joined them.

His pulse increased as sweat formed on his brow. He kept his face to the ground as his eyes glanced to the side, taking in his surroundings. Each time he passed near a blue coat, he made sure to giggle, hoping to blend in with the others around him.

It was hard to keep his thoughts away from where they wanted to go, but he couldn't think about the unfairness of this place. Not if he didn't want to get caught skipping the lunch pill.

He was here on the island now. A fact he didn't plan to keep true for long. He completed a run around the perimeter of the fence. It didn't take long. No noticeable weak spots. They were truly caged in. Like wild animals. Captured and drugged.

Ben's chest tightened. A new wave of heat cascaded over him. Not from the sun above, but from within.

The heat threatened to surface, and Ben took a deep breath, his legs growing unsteady as he ran. A loud mechanical sound interrupted his flow. He stopped, and the feeling in his blood cooled, saving his secret. A garage door on the warehouse next to them opened, revealing a group of guards with uniformed prisoners waiting behind them. Green, purple, and white. Each marked with the threat they posed on the mainland. Here, while drugged, they weren't much of a threat at all.

Ben watched as the tenants exited. Only three were in purple: Air Disparates. The once uncontrollably happy people now walked with hunched-over shoulders. One turned her face toward him. The sun glared off the tears that streamed down her cheeks as she walked to a stone bench and sat.

There were over a dozen dressed in green: Earth Disparates. The ones plagued with a deep, dark sadness. Of course there would be so many here. It was easier to avoid what made you happy in life than it was to avoid what brought you down. They, however, had smiles on their faces. They weren't quite as giggly as Ben's fellow red suits, but they looked happy and serene. The effect of whatever drug was used on them here.

Then there were those dressed in white: Ice Disparates. Thoughts of Buran and how easily he was disgusted by others jumped into his mind, which he quickly shook off. He couldn't risk the anger he associated with that name.

Ben counted seven. They each looked rather pleasant, chatting with the guards and other Disparates around them. Not much seemed to bother them.

A pair of Disparates chatted close to the fence. No guards or blue coats nearby. Ben approached slowly, curious what they were talking about.

"Did you sleep well last night?" the one in white asked his companion.

The side of a green suit was directly in front of Ben. The whirring of the fence stood between them. The wearer had lifted his face to the sky, soaking in the sunlight. "Not the greatest sleep, but also not the worst," his voice was lighthearted. As he lowered his head, he noticed Ben.

When they made eye contact, Ben's heart stopped. He knew this man. The wrinkles and aged skin. Those brown eyes. This was Mr. Dogivan.

"Oh, hello there!" The white suit waved at Ben. "You look new here. 1231 is new too. Only been here about a week. He seems to be getting the hang of it. I'm sure you will too!"

"Yes, welcome," Mr. Dogivan said. "It's not so bad here. I'm happier than ever."

Ben couldn't believe what he was hearing. *Happier than ever*? He remembered this man's intake. The pain in his eyes every time he thought about his wife.

This wasn't right.

"What's your name?" White Suit prompted.

"Ben," he answered instinctively, not even thinking about giving his number.

At his answer, Mr. Dogivan raised an eyebrow.

"Or, actually, 1232," he quickly corrected.

"Ben, huh? Sounds familiar..." Mr. Dogivan's face looked strained. "Maybe a friend from college."

"Don't worry." White Suit placed a hand on Mr. Dogivan's back. "Just one of the effects of the island. Can make it hard to remember things from your past life. Especially if it's something sad. Let yourself forget. It'll be easier."

"Like his old life never happened?" Ben questioned, incredulous. A drip of sweat rolled down his forehead. "We're locked behind a fence."

"Exactly!" White Suit nodded. "Forget the things that troubled you. Everything is in harmony here. We're on a tropical island. A cool breeze. The whirring of the fence just adds to the aesthetic."

Ben's body shook, but now it wasn't fake. He focused on slowing his breathing. It wasn't this man speaking. It was the medicine he was forced to take.

A woman also in white approached the small group.

"Guess what I found—a dead snake," she said. "The fence burned it in two!" Her eyebrows raised while she smiled.

"Really? That's amazing!" The original white suit responded as the two rushed off together.

"I, uh. I guess that's exciting." In truth, his stomach churned. Ben wasn't sure what to say now that the others were gone. The Mr. Dogivan in front of him was not the same man he spoke to last week.

Mr. Dogivan shrugged. "I guess so. I don't care much for snakes, but I'm glad they enjoy it. Where are you from? You sound familiar."

"I'm from Stillfield." Ben swallowed. It was his fault this man was stuck here.

"That's where I'm from too!" He smiled. Ben noticed the dimples in his cheeks for the first time. Although they brightened his face, they looked artificial. This wasn't his true smile.

"My wife and kids are back home." Ben watched to see if Mr. Dogivan reacted to his words. Could he take this sense of joy away from him? Even if it wasn't real?

"Those are the days. They sure go by fast." Mr. Dogivan's dimples deepened. They began to look more natural before they shallowed once more. "At least, that's what I'm told."

"Were you married? Any kids of your own?" Ben didn't want him to stop remembering. An idea was forming in his mind. A risky idea.

"I... I don't remember. But I do remember my wife liked to be the fun aunt." His true smile was back for a second before it fell again.

"Your wife sounds like a great woman."

"She was. I think." The old man's face wrinkled together in frustration. "Oh bother, I can't remember her face. Has this happened to you yet?"

"No, I haven't forgotten," Ben said. "I'll do anything not to."

Mr. Dogivan looked at him, his artificial happiness gone. "What can you do? We're stuck here."

"There might be something." Ben watched Mr. Dogivan as he spoke. "But it's risky. And you won't feel this happy anymore."

Mr. Dogivan's face softened. "I don't care. I want her. I want to remember all of her."

The words from his intake echoed in Ben's head.

I don't care if it makes my heart ache more. I want to remember all of her.

A bell rang from the warehouses. Recreation time was over, but Ben had been given the confirmation he needed.

He moved his face as close to the fence as he could without getting shocked.

"Find a way to hide your pill," he whispered. "Don't take it. But only if you really want to remember Eliza. Including the pain of losing her."

Mr. Dogivan's eyes widened at the mention of his wife's name. Ben would let him decide if he wanted to fight. With a quick nod, Mr. Dogivan turned and walked away, back toward the walls of his prison.

As Ben turned to do the same, he reared back. Fabric on his arm sizzled as it hit the fence.

1198 stood a few feet away. The sun was blindly bright across her yellow jumpsuit. She watched him with narrowed eyes.

Ben plastered a smile to his face, waving shakily as he jogged back to the warehouse door. A scorched line darkened across his sleeve. She followed more slowly, her eyes glued to him as he disappeared inside the building.

TEN

As the sun set, Jemma's nerves rose.

She sat in the passenger seat of Buran's truck as they headed to the Public Safety Building. The buzzing from under the hood was deafening. Calum was in the back seat, tapping a finger against his knee.

Over and over again. Buzzing and tapping. Tapping and buzzing.

The noise unsettled Jemma. Or maybe it was the thoughts of what they were about to do. She replayed the plan over and over again in her head. This needed to go right.

The fire anarchist had been operating for the last couple of weeks, which made the list of possible targeted government buildings quite small. The most likely two options left were the Public Safety Building or the Capitol.

They decided to split into two groups. Since Calum worked undercover at the Capitol, the group didn't want to risk him getting caught. Samay and Aniyah volunteered to go there.

Jemma joined Buran and Calum. Although she had some knowledge of the layout of the Capitol, she knew the Public Safety Building better, having been in it more recently thanks to her mother's job.

Her mother. She had laid on the couch when Jemma dropped the boys off, claiming she had a long day at work. Even let the boys pull out their tablets without making a remark. Jemma was grateful for her fatigue. She couldn't handle a Margaret line of questioning. Not yet.

"Jemma," Buran said as he kept his hands on the wheel. "You're gonna need to calm down before our car stops completely in the middle of the freeway."

She hadn't noticed their slowing speed. Taking a deep breath in, she counted to four in her head as she released it. The speedometer crept up once more.

Burnt curtains popped into her mind. If only she could find out how Buran taught Disparates to stay in control. Maybe he could help Louie. But—

"Have I told you about the time I got detention in high school?" Calum leaned between the two front seats as the car started to slow once more. "It's a pretty good story. Although I don't care much for the ending."

Jemma shook her head. She was grateful for the distraction, her body calming. She smiled as Calum wove his tale about high school pranks and the lengths he was willing to go to for a girl's attention. It sounded like something out of a teenage drama.

"The worst part? She didn't even get detention with me! Even though it was her idea to paint the principal's car." He shook his head as the truck turned a corner.

After the story finished, there was silence once again. The memory of last night's fire flared into Jemma's mind again.

"Buran," Jemma said. "You teach Disparates to control their energy."

He nodded, even though Jemma didn't mean it as a question.

"Well," she continued. "Do you teach children?"

Buran glanced briefly away from the road to look at her. She kept her eyes forward. She didn't want him to see the tears that were threatening to fall.

"Sometimes. Usually teenagers. I've learned the best way to teach the little ones is through their parents."

Jemma wrinkled her face in confusion. Calum stayed quiet in the back, as if he was pretending not to listen in.

"You see," Buran continued. "Parents are their kids' best teachers, and they often learn through example. You don't have to be perfect, but as you learn to control your energy, you can teach him."

Jemma pondered that. She had a natural sense of control, considering she only just learned she had electric energy. Although, it'd been triggered to a higher degree. If she could learn to control it without medication, so could Louie.

Buran pulled into the parking lot of the library next to the Public Safety Building and hid his truck behind some trees. Security at government buildings had been increased from one guard to two since the fire anarchist began his reign. Stillfield didn't have the resources for more than that, not without requesting more help from Wuslick.

However, it'd still be best to avoid any guards, and they would if they got to their target before he entered.

Calum was to set up in some bushes about twenty feet from the front doors with a pair of pink children's binoculars. "Don't knock them till you try them," he had said with a smile, his chest puffed with confidence as he left to his lookout spot.

Buran stayed in his car; he had a good view through the trees of the side receiving doors that led to the storage area.

The lights of his car shut off as Jemma headed to the back of the building. She positioned herself behind a half-wall, peering through a small hole in the bricks. Branches from the tree above gave her enough coverage to remain unseen from a distance.

She watched for signs of movement while keeping herself still. Every twitch caused the leaves underneath her to crunch. If she scared the fire anarchist away, she wasn't sure how much longer it would take to bring

Ben home. Her boys would only accept that he was away on a work trip for so long.

And her hope that she'd get him back would only last so long before she broke. Like her mother did after losing her father and brother. Leaving a fragile Jemma to take care of them both.

"Any unusual signs?" A staticky Buran came through the two-way radio Jemma held in her hand, interrupting her thoughts.

It was then she noticed she was sweating despite the temperature outside being cold. She wished she had brought her jacket. It had been warmer that day, but she should have known better. Weather was unpredictable. Any moment a storm could brew or a heat wave could strike. Weatherologists of the past were able to predict three, five, even ten days in advance. Now, they were lucky to get an hour's warning. Hopefully the cool weather tonight wasn't a sign of an incoming storm.

"Nothing here. A guard just finished their outside patrol, so keep an eye out. Might be a good opportunity for the anarchist to strike," Calum responded, his voice quiet on the other end.

A light breeze blew, feeling like shards of ice against Jemma's sweaty skin. Her body trembled. She lifted her radio to her mouth, took a deep breath, and clicked the button.

"Other than a raccoon rummaging through the trash can for the last hour, nothing suspicious here." She'd been watching the animal sift through tissues and empty pill bottles until it finally scored a half-eaten apple, held it between its sharp claws and chowed down.

The raccoon perked up. Sitting back on its hind legs, its alert eyes looked toward where Jemma hid. *It must have heard me talking,* she thought. But no, the animal's glowing eyes weren't looking at her, but past her.

Footsteps sounded on the path close to her hiding spot. Her heart raced as the raccoon scurried away, the apple rolling close to her. *Okay, fine. Abandon me now.*

Jemma turned her head to the right, her breathing slow and shallow, afraid of what she might see. Through the branches was the faint outline of a man wearing all black.

This had to be the man her husband was mistaken for.

Jemma turned the volume dial on her radio all the way down. She sat frozen, physically and emotionally. *This is why I'm here. I need to confront him. But—he's dangerous.* The hair on her arms lifted. She couldn't move.

The man continued forward, seemingly unaware of the woman watching him behind the trees. He climbed gracefully over the half-wall a few feet away from her, landing quietly on the other side. At the door he pulled out a small tool; Jemma couldn't make out what it was from her distance. She knew what she was expected to do, but she couldn't get her feet to comply.

How am I supposed to teach Louie to be in control when I can't control myself?

The light above the door flickered as her anxiety rose. The man paused what he was doing for a moment and looked around, his face fully covered by dark cloth. Had he heard her heart beating?

When he saw the coast was clear, he proceeded. His shoulders hunched as his small tool worked inside the doorknob.

I can't just sit here. I'll miss our chance. I can do this for Louie. I can do this for Ben.

The man stood tall as the entrance budged open. He slipped inside, the door slowly closing behind him.

Suddenly, it stopped, a chunk of mutilated apple stuck in the crack. Jemma stood in front of the door, still sweaty, still cold, and still anxious.

The outside light flickered again and went dark as Jemma entered the Public Safety Building feeling anything but safe.

A knock at the door caused Margaret to jump. Both boys turned their heads away from their tablets to look as the tapping continued.

Margaret didn't want to move from her spot on the couch, wrapped in a blanket made of Skylar's old shirts. His smell had disappeared from them years ago, but their fabric still brought her some closeness.

She never should have agreed to watch her grandsons tonight, but she couldn't tell her daughter no. Plus, she'd told herself she'd be over this by now.

She was wrong.

"Maggie, it's me." Tobias Dunn's voice boomed through the wooden door.

Of course it'd be him. She'd missed their coffee date earlier that day and Tobias knew her too well to let her get away with that. He'd been good friends with Skylar before the fire, and after he'd kept in touch with Margaret to make sure she had everything she and Jemma needed. He was the one who encouraged her to run for the Public Safety Committee, and ever since, their friendship had grown closer. He was like a brother to her.

"Come in. Use your spare key." Margaret tried to project her answer, but it came out small and hoarse. Nevertheless, a minute later she heard a key turning in her lock.

Margaret's view was blocked by the back of the couch, but she heard the door close as Tobias's footsteps hastened near.

"Maggie." His salt and pepper hair appeared as he stood behind her spot on the couch, looking around at her living room.

The boys had dumped out the blocks, leaving them spread out. Snack wrappers and food smears decorated the mess. They now played once more on their tablets, although there couldn't be much battery power left.

"You can't ignore my calls. I know you're probably mad, but I had nothing to do with it..." His roaming gaze stopped at her blanket. "Oh, we're at Skylar's shirts level depressed." Tobias knew her too well.

Sometimes Margaret resented that fact. Especially when he wouldn't allow her to wallow in her misery. The nightmare was brought on by Louie's energy burst... but what Tobias said didn't make any sense. Why would she be mad at him? Her lack of sleep last night made it hard for her to register what was happening.

"Grandma isn't feeling well," Mackie said as a crashing sound came from his game. Louie kept his eyes on his own screen, uncaring about the conversation going on next to him.

The boys knew Tobias from family events as "Grandma's friend" and couldn't comprehend that he was actually the governor.

Tobias looked at Margaret. His eyebrows knitted together in concern. "Alright boys, time to take a break. We need to get this place cleaned."

Mackie groaned as Louie growled.

"Once we get it clean, we can have ice cream," Tobias bargained. It seemed to do the trick. The boys placed their tablets on the couch and started to gather the blocks.

Margaret sat up, her heart protesting, wanting her to lay back down. She felt empty. Nothing left to give.

"Maggie." Tobias sat next to her, taking her hands into his. "It's been awhile since you've shut down like this." He moved one arm to wrap around her shoulders, enfolding her into a half-hug. "It's okay. I get it.

It's hard to believe when something like this happens and it's so close to home."

She laid her head onto his open shoulder. "Thank you," her voice squeaked out. She didn't have the energy to say much more, although her curiosity was piqued. What happened so close to home?

Margaret shot up, her eyes wide. "Is Jemma okay?"

"I was going to ask you that question. How is she doing?"

"I haven't seen her since she dropped the boys off to go to a girl's night." Margaret's heart raced. Had something happened to Jemma?

Tobias gave a soft smile. "Spending time with friends, that's good. I'm sure that'll bring some comfort."

So, Jemma was okay. Margaret clutched her waist. Something still felt off.

"Have you had anything to eat today?"

Margaret paused; she couldn't remember.

"I'm going to take your silence as a 'no.' Wait here. I'll see what I can do."

Margaret listened to the sound of blocks being dropped into a bin as she resisted her urge to lay back down. She knew Tobias would get after her if she did. She'd allowed herself to feel sad long enough.

Time to stop this, Margaret. You have responsibilities.

She lied to herself if she truly thought that would work.

"Ew, I stepped in applesauce." Mackie plopped on the couch next to her, showing off his foot.

"Careful!" she said as she jerked her blanket out of reach, not wanting the applesauce to contaminate it. She'd never laundered it once in the past seventeen years and hoped she'd never have to. She didn't want Skylar's presence to be washed away.

"Don't worry." Tobias's voice came from the kitchen. "I've got a towel."

He stepped in to save the day, carrying a plate of food with him as well. Once Mackie's foot was cleaned, he sent the boys to the table, where two bowls of ice cream waited for them. They had done a decent job picking up.

"I got more than you!" Mackie teased his brother.

Louie's face scrunched as he held his bowl. Smoke rose around the edges, and Margaret smelled burnt plastic.

Tobias straightened. His eyes went wide. Margaret, having no strength to step in, watched to see how he would respond to Louie's energy use.

"You both have the same," Tobias said. He looked into Louie's bowl. "Although, yours does look a bit melted now. How about I get you another scoop?"

Louie's face beamed, pleased with the solution. The smoke stopped.

Margaret sighed, relieved the situation didn't escalate. Louie looked at her with his angelic smile as he headed to the dining room. She saw so much of Asher in his narrow face—especially his shaggy, dusty hair.

Tobias handed her the plate—her own little charcuterie board filled with crackers, cheese, meat, and fruit, plus some chocolates and cookies. They were not arranged neatly but tossed on to fit. Tobias wasn't one for organization.

"I wasn't sure what you'd be in the mood for, so I thought I'd bring you options." He positioned himself back in his spot on the couch. "Now, would you like to talk about it?"

"About how well you reacted to Louie just now?" Maybe she could take the attention off herself.

"No, you know what I mean." He looked at the boys munching away at the table. "He did remind me of my daughter for a moment. In a good way. She used to use her energy on food as well. There's just something about kids and sweets."

Margaret nodded as she picked up a strawberry and took a small bite. Its sweetness was too much for her, but she continued to chew, slowly.

"Do you have plans to visit her soon?"

Tobias stared off for a moment, as if in a daze. "I'm sorry. What did you ask?"

Margaret placed the half eaten strawberry onto her plate. "Do you have plans to visit your daughter soon? I've heard she's doing well at her new place."

"Yes." Tobias nodded. "She is doing well. I'm hoping to visit her soon. Now, enough about me. Your turn."

Margaret hoped talking about his daughter would buy her more time, but that time was up. "I had the dream again last night. I'm not sure what's going on. Ben seems to be gone, and Jemma won't explain it to me. Just says he's gone on a work trip." Margaret checked to make sure the boys weren't listening before she continued. "But that doesn't make sense. Not after how terrified she was last night."

"Hmm..." Tobias bit his lip.

Margaret knew that look. Jemma wasn't the only one keeping secrets from her. "What do you know?" she asked.

"You haven't seen the news? Of course not. You've disconnected yourself."

So something had happened to Jemma. "Tell me."

Tobias rested a hand on top of her knee. He kept his voice low so the boys wouldn't hear. "Ben isn't on a work trip. He's the Fire Anarchist."

"No." Margaret couldn't muster much else. "That can't be it. That's ridiculous." Then again, Ben was a Flame Disparate.

But he took Enertin. It was contained.

But... Margaret gasped. "Did he have an outburst?" She raised her hand to her mouth. "Is he... gone?"

"Oh no, he's okay. At least, he hasn't overdosed on Enertin like the Disparates we've been researching. Just taken for treatment at Merrytime."

"Then, why is he believed to be the anarchist?"

"He started a fire at his office," Tobias said.

A government building.

"And that was enough to think it was him?" The hole in Margaret's chest filled with desire for justice.

"They found matching fingerprints from the other fires."

Her eyes widened. That was definitive proof. Margaret set her plate on the couch next to her, no other food touched. "I can't believe Jemma didn't tell me all this. I know I'm a burden to her. Ever since Skylar died, she's had to take care of me. No wonder she doesn't want to talk. I've been a terrible mom."

Tobias rubbed her knee. It was meant to comfort her, but it didn't. "You've been through a hard life together. I'm sure she'll talk with you when she's ready. In the meantime, it seems you are helping her out, watching your grandsons. That takes a lot of trust. Maybe you aren't as far apart as you think."

Margaret's heart ached. She wanted to believe her friend, but she couldn't muster the hope. Instead, she nodded quietly.

"All done!" Mackie's high pitched voice came from the table.

"I'll stay and help you tonight," Tobias said. "At least until Jemma gets back. Would you be okay with that?"

Margaret was reluctant. She didn't want to be a burden. "She's going to be late. The boys are sleeping over."

"That's okay," he said. "I can sleep on the couch. Or perhaps a pillow fort is in order?" He raised his voice with the last question.

"Pillow fort?" Mackie's dishes clanged into the sink as he ran over to join the construction crew. Louie left his own bowl at the table.

Wasn't much else to do but accept his help now. An extra hand *was* what she needed. She'd be over this slump soon. It never lasted long in the past. And hopefully Jemma would have more to share in the morning.

"I'd appreciate that. Thank you."

ELEVEN

B efore Jemma entered through the back door, she'd felt her energy release. It was small, yet it was enough to cause the power to go out. Her increased energy would take some getting used to.

Her skin defrosted as she entered the building, her insides twisting at the fact she hadn't called for backup. She didn't have time. Following the anarchist inside wasn't the plan, but she had to do it, for Ben's sake. She couldn't let the anarchist out of her sight. Although her heart raced, her mind cleared. She was in control of her choices, not her fear. It was still there, but she allowed it to coexist with her determination.

Even in the dark, Jemma knew where she stood. Her mother's office was down this hallway. The darkness didn't change her surroundings, only made it difficult to see.

She saw no sign of the fire anarchist. Proceeding forward, she kept her steps soft in hopes of not alerting anyone to her presence.

"Go check the generator," a voice echoed from the front of the building, where the security office was. "Then check the back for intruders. I'll circle the front."

"Yep. I got it," another responded.

Jemma grabbed the handle of the door next to her. Locked. She thought about where she was in relation to the back door. Her mother's office should be the next one. The door was slightly ajar.

Her pulse raced, but she didn't have time to question it; footsteps were coming. She quickly entered, hiding just before the security guard passed. A flash of light shined briefly through the window next to her, missing her spot against the door. Her mother had left the blinds open. The back entrance clicked closed. He was on his way to fix the electricity.

A buzz flowed through Jemma. Instead of holding her back, it propelled her forward. She didn't have much time before the guard turned the power back on and the cameras with it. Which meant, neither did the fire anarchist. She needed to find him, but doing so in this blackness would be difficult.

A wavering light cast a glow on the office desk in front of her. She froze as she processed the source. A small flame burned atop a palm as it slowly moved back and forth, as if looking for something. Above the flame was a face.

No. She pressed her hand to her mouth.

It couldn't be, but the resemblance was uncanny. She blinked once. Twice. *It's a trick of the light. There's no way.*

The face turned sideways as it searched the file cabinet next to the desk. His movement was frantic, unaware of his audience.

Jemma had a better view of his profile, and there, on the side of his neck, a small scar was illuminated, shaped like a tree branch with sprouts protruding from the middle. A gasp escaped her lips.

Asher.

The flame extinguished, plunging them into darkness. A moment later, safety lights from the hall turned on and streamed through the window. The soft whirring of the heater brought attention to how quiet the building had been moments before.

Jemma searched near the desk but quickly shifted to the movement on her right. There, exposed by the dim hall light, stood her older brother.

This time, he froze as he realized he'd been caught. She could tell he was thinking, his eyes darting to the edges like they did when they were kids. He was preparing to run, only Jemma blocked his path to the door. He held his hands to the side, but smoke rose toward the ceiling.

"No, wait, don't go. The cameras in the hallway will see you." She hoped that'd be enough for him to know she was on his side, but she prepared herself to jump out of the way, just in case.

His brows furrowed as he took into account the new information. He seemed unaware of who she was. Jemma ran a hand through her hair, leaves and twigs tangled inside her waves. She was a mess after crouching under a tree all night. It would be difficult for him to recognize this woman as his twelve year old sister. Especially as the light shined behind her, keeping her face hidden in the shadows.

"You're not a guard," he stated, although his voice sounded unsure.

"I'm not," she confirmed.

The back door creaked as it opened fully, causing Jemma's heart to spike. She had forgotten about the actual guard who was now returning to his desk.

Asher jumped to the side, flattening against the wall to escape being seen through the window, now fully emerged in the shadows. Jemma followed suit, standing only feet away from him.

Escaping detection with Asher felt familiar and yet surreal. She used to imagine the trouble they would cause together when he came home, but as she grew older, her daydreaming stopped as she resigned herself to the fact that he was gone.

But now, here he was. Hiding with her in their mother's office.

In her imagination, Asher was the loyal big brother, always going along with her plans. But the Asher a few feet away was foreign to her. He was taller and thinner, and his hands looked more worn than the Asher in her mind.

"Who are you?" he whispered, his voice deep, changed from the fifteen year old tone Jemma remembered. Another reminder that this Asher was not the same as the one she once knew.

"I'm here to help you." She didn't want to confess who she was yet. She couldn't predict how he'd react. "I have friends watching outside. They want to work with you."

Asher was quiet. The guard's footsteps trudged past the office door. Jemma wondered if he was quiet because the guard was close, or because he realized who she was.

Once the footsteps faded, Asher scraped himself off the wall and headed to the office door. He pulled a hood over his head, the front covering his face with a loose black mesh.

He was ready to leave. She wasn't sure what he was thinking. His face was covered, but the rest of him would be in full view of the security camera. The guards weren't far away. If they arrested him now, her brother would be gone again, and with him, her hope for saving her husband.

Who was stuck on Lucky Island.

Which was why they needed the fire anarchist to take them there.

If that was Asher... if he was the escapee then...

"Stop!" Jemma yelled, her hand reaching toward Asher as he opened the door and stepped into the hallway.

Electricity escaped from her fingertips, striking past Asher into the hall. A black line blurred in her vision, marking the path her energy had taken. An alarm sounded as noises came from the front.

"Shoot," Asher expressed, his voice irate. He took off running toward the back door. Jemma knew what to do in an Asher escape. Follow him and keep up. He wouldn't hesitate to leave her behind to take the blame.

She pulled her shirt over the back of her head as she ran, hoping it would give her enough coverage to not be recognized on the security recording. She didn't care that her midriff was exposed. Glass crunched under her feet as she exited her mother's office.

Asher burst through the back door, Jemma close on his heels. "Move!" he yelled as he turned around. His arms stretched out as a bellow of flames escaped, assaulting the back door of the office and spreading outward. A spare ember flew into the ransacked trash can, bolstering the fire.

Asher turned around and continued to run. His hood blew off from the speed.

Jemma wasn't about to lose him. Behind her, she heard swearing. The guards found the present Asher had left for them, the fire too large to be put out with a simple fire extinguisher.

The fire department would be called. They'd know the fire anarchist was still attacking. She hoped Buran was wrong about the government keeping Ben locked up, even after learning there was no way he was the anarchist.

As they ran, Jemma became woozy, regretting her inconsistent exercise schedule now. The sprint through the forest didn't seem to phase Asher. His long legs gave him the advantage. Yet, somehow, Jemma's adrenaline helped her keep pace until they ran out of the woods and into a back alleyway where a fence blocked their path.

"Why are you following me?" Asher huffed as he caught his breath.

"I just..." Jemma's breathing was quick and shallow. She focused on slowing it down, holding up one finger as she bent over and counted her breathing in and out. As it calmed, she continued, "I need your help. Please. My husband is stuck on Lucky Island. I have to get him off." The meaning of her own words fell into place once more. If Asher were the fire anarchist that escaped the island, that meant all along...

"I don't know anything about Lucky Island."

His declaration crushed her hope for her husband, leaving it as flat as his voice sounded. However, Jemma noticed the fingers on his right hand twitch. He was lying.

She wasn't sure if she was relieved. The thought of her brother suffering all this time tugged at her heart.

"Asher, please. I need your help," she begged. He was here now, and her husband wasn't. They could worry about the past later.

Asher stared at Jemma. The hostility behind his eyes burned into her. The look reminded her again that this wasn't the same Asher she once knew.

"How do you know my name?"

He still hadn't figured out who she was. She tried not to let that hurt, but somehow, her already damaged heart found a way to break a little more.

"Jemma!" A call from the bushes next to them diverted Asher's attention. Jemma however, kept her gaze on her brother. She didn't need to look away to recognize the voice as Buran's. Plus, if she did, she might lose Asher. He disappeared in the blink of an eye last time. She didn't want to risk it happening again.

In the corner of her vision, she watched Buran trip while exiting the woods.

He cursed, wiped his hands off, and righted himself. "Thank goodness I found you both. I'm Buran," he said as he outstretched his hand toward Asher.

Asher didn't move. Instead, he turned his attention back to Jemma. The rage behind his eyes now softened. "Jemma?" he said, a question and statement all in one.

Jemma saw her Asher once again in those green eyes. The color of the salads he used to hate. She nodded.

"Right. I seem to have interrupted something here." Buran's hand lowered to his side.

"Jemma." Asher smiled. "Jemma!" He walked swiftly to where his sister stood and embraced her. His arms wrapped securely around her shoulders.

She rested her face on his chest, tears wetting his black shirt. Hopefully he wouldn't mind; she couldn't hold them back. Years of worries and wonders wrapped together in this embrace. Asher squeezed her tighter before he loosened his grip and stepped back, keeping his hands on her arms as he looked at her.

"You're a full blown adult! I tried to picture you all grown up, but I never could." Asher's head shook back and forth slightly as he examined her.

"Me? What about you?" Jemma laughed, relieved by her brother's reaction to figuring out who she was.

Asher's face dropped as his hands fell to his sides. "Yeah, I guess I'm an adult now too," he said solemnly.

Jemma's heart tugged. She couldn't stand seeing him this way, but then again, she hadn't seen him for over seventeen years. She didn't know what he'd been through. She wasn't sure if she was ready to know.

"Buran, everything okay? Did you find Jemma?" a staticky voice on Buran's side interrupted the reunion.

"If y'all will excuse me a sec," Buran said as he pulled out his two-way radio. Jemma had forgotten about hers, still attached to her side, the volume turned off. "I found Jemma. She's alright. We also found our target." He glanced at Asher, an apologetic look to his eyes. "We'll meet you at headquarters in an hour." Buran clicked his radio off.

"Who are you people?" Asher's slightly squinted eyes glanced between Jemma and Buran.

"We're friends of Jemma's," Buran answered. "Dissentients. It looks like you two already know each other pretty well. You'll have to tell me the story on the way over." Buran smiled as if he'd just won the lottery. "I can't believe you know each other."

"On the way over to where? I'm not planning on going anywhere with you." Asher's voice was flat again, assured of his decision. Buran's smile quickly dissolved as he looked at Jemma. His eyes called out for help.

"Asher, please, don't leave yet. Just hear what he has to say, then you can decide if you want to go," Jemma pleaded, but tried to be understanding. "I've always wished I'd be able to find you and now here you are. Please don't leave again. Not yet."

Asher's eyes narrowed as they looked at Jemma. "I don't really know you. Not anymore." His right fingers twitched again; he didn't truly mean what he said. Regardless, a pang in her heart almost took her to her knees.

"We can meet on your terms. Just me and you." Jemma hoped this proposal would work. "I'll tell you about my life, about Ben, and about our two beautiful boys."

Buran looked as if he wanted to interject, but he seemed to change his mind once he saw Asher.

Asher's face softened. Not completely, but enough that Jemma no longer worried about being barbecued.

"I'm an uncle?" he asked.

"Yeah. They're four and six and know all about their Uncle Asher and the trouble he used to get me in."

He scoffed, a smile playing on the edge of his lips. "*I* got *you* in? You got us both in plenty of trouble as well."

"Did not." Jemma laughed, hoping to lighten the mood. "Mom is watching them right now. If you're up for it, you could meet them, and see Mom again."

The air around them thickened as Asher tensed. His smile dropped, and his brows creased together, his forehead wrinkled in worry.

Jemma hadn't expected this reaction at the mention of their mother. She wasn't sure where it came from.

"No. You can't tell anyone I'm here. Especially not *that woman*."
The scorn in his voice surprised Jemma.

"Okay," she hastily agreed. She felt as if she were approaching an
injured animal, walking cautiously and speaking calmly to not scare him
away. "I won't tell anyone, I promise. But please, let's talk. You don't have
to say much if you don't want to. I'll tell you about my life, and you can
ask me whatever questions you want." She knew she sounded desperate.
"We can meet at our old hideout tomorrow night."

"The treehouse?" Asher said, his face still undecided.

"Yes."

The last time Jemma had been to the one room wooden structure
was after her release from the hospital when she was twelve. After her
lungs had recovered from the fire. It was the first and only time she'd
ever gone alone. She wasn't even sure it was still standing. "I haven't been
there in a while, but it would be a good place to meet. Do you remember
where it is?"

Asher nodded then turned toward the fence behind him. He
grabbed the top and hoisted himself over, disappearing to the other side.

Buran placed a hand on her shoulder, a gesture of comfort for Jemma.

She wasn't sure if Asher's nod was to signify he remembered where
it was or him agreeing to meet her there tomorrow.

She hoped it was both.

TWELVE

"**I** want in—" 1198's eyes were filled with urgency. A direct contrast to their glossed over look from earlier.

Ben sat across from her in the area between their cell rooms. The islanders were allowed an hour of social time after dinner each night.

"I want in," she leaned closer. "Whatever you're planning, I want to be part of it."

Despite her eyes looking alive, the rest of her face was serene. He wasn't sure he could trust her.

"I don't know what you're talking about." His leg bounced up and down on the old sofa, joining the blurs of red around him. He lowered his eyes, tracing the outline of dark pink roses on the chair 1198 occupied.

"Don't play dumb. I heard you outside." 1198 glanced toward the blue coat across the room.

On one hand, having an Electric Disparate could be helpful. A blast from her would shut down the fence. However, it might also do the opposite and burn him to a crisp.

If Mr. Dogivan took his advice and found a way to skip his pill tomorrow, his earth energy would be enough to create a tunnel for them to escape through. Of course, that would be assuming the energy could be controlled.

He'd seen the posters around town, urging Disparates to embrace their emotions, but that was often shrugged off, the posters torn up and pieces left to flutter in the breeze. People didn't like to be reminded of the power Disparates could unleash at any moment. They saw it as a threat.

And they were right. Emotions led to danger for Disparates and those around them. But even though it was unlikely, *perhaps* uncontrolled emotions could lead to beneficial energy bursts. They just needed a sinkhole to form in the right place.

Then what? They were on an island surrounded by water. His fire energy would keep guards away, but it couldn't carry them across the ocean.

Neither could electric energy. Gravity, on the other hand—

"I know where a boat is," 1198 whispered, as if reading his mind.

A boat? Now we're talking.

"Where?"

"Where what?" She looked directly in his eyes as she sat straighter, her shoulders back. Challenging him. "I don't know what you're talking about."

Ben chuckled out loud, making sure to keep his cover as he looked at her with narrow eyes. "Why should I trust you?"

"Because," she leaned forward, her eyebrows raised, "I'm tired of peace. I want to feel *alive*."

That night, a white booklet waited for Ben on his makeshift bed.

Welcome to Lucky Island! Where all your ailments can heal.

About time he got his "Welcome Packet." He flipped through the black and white pages, past the daily schedule and *Rules of Civility*. It seemed at one point, this island pretended to be more of a hospital than a prison. So much for that outlook now.

He glanced around his cell. He was familiar with hidden cameras and the sensors they used to detect energy bursts. There didn't appear to be any in his room.

Safe in his cage, he allowed his feelings to increase. The paper in his hands began to smoke. The edge raveled as a small flame devoured the offensive pamphlet. As the last of it turned to ash in his hands, he closed his eyes, focused on his breathing, and tried to subdue his energy release.

It worked.

He'd been holding his energy back all day, and now, he controlled a small burst. He embraced his emotions. It was amazing what motivation could do.

He smirked as he climbed to the small window and dumped the ashes outside for the natural ecosystem to dispose of. When he brought his hand back in, flashes of lightning drew his attention.

Each bolt worked together. A jarring fight across the cloudless sky. This was not from the weather. With each strike, the intensity heightened, building to a climactic finish when the lightning ruled the heavens.

But it stopped as quickly as it began. The island returned, once again, to its darkness.

Ben felt a wave of heat wash over him. This wasn't fair. For him or anyone else on the island. They didn't deserve this treatment.

He wasn't the only one suffering here.

An uncontainable flame developed in Ben's chest. The cement walls greeted it as it exploded outward through his palms. His hands faced out, filling the space in front of him. He grunted as he shut his eyes tight, blocking out the brightness of his own feelings.

He didn't mean for that to happen.

As the fire dispersed, Ben hunched over, his breathing heavy. Sweat pools dotted his skin, causing his jumpsuit to stick. The burn on his face throbbed. His wound from falling onto the boat platform had reopened, the color of his blood matching the color of his clothes as it dripped onto the surface.

His body shook.

Hopefully no one heard him.

Footsteps sounded outside his cell. There had to be more than one set. How many guards came to restrain him?

He waited for the sound of keys. Straightening, he tried to summon his anger once more—only his fear was stronger.

As the footsteps neared, he heard moaning. The keys came, but instead of turning in his lock, the cell door next to him creaked open. A loud thump was followed by a groan before the door slammed shut. Heavy silence settled as the footsteps slowly disappeared.

Luck was on Ben's side tonight. He couldn't say the same about the Disparate next door.

Morning took its time to arrive. As light poured through the small window, silence finally came from the cell next to him. It didn't last long. It only took a few minutes before a loud wailing rose, breaking through the sound barrier between their rooms. The opening from the window only increased the volume. Then, the pounding began.

Over and over again, inconsistent beats echoed through the prison warehouse. No guards came. Whoever was next door and whatever pain they were in didn't matter. The rising sun had been a relief. Sooner to breakfast. Ben's stomach growled, though he was unsure of the time.

Breakfast meant the cafeteria. Which meant a brief release from this cage. Ben hoped to catch a glimpse of the pained Disparate. Maybe, just maybe, there was something he could do to help.

Finally, the pounding stopped. Silence once again settled. But it was too late for Ben to get any sleep.

Being awake gave Ben time to think.

He'd been trying to control his flame energy.

He failed.

His fire burst was contained by the concrete walls around him. But what was used for Earth Disparate cells? Steel.

Ben looked through the bars of his window at the other warehouse. He couldn't help but notice the sun was near the middle of the sky. How late did they eat here?

He tried not to think about his empty stomach. The walls on the warehouse looked thick, but would that be enough if Mr. Dogivan faltered?

It would need to be.

He'd warn Mr. Dogivan. Remind him to stay in control. Keep his mind off any thoughts that would sadden him.

His mind swam with the new knowledge he'd accumulated over the past thirty-six hours. Dreamless sleep enveloped him for some time until the clanking of his cell door opened. Red hair greeted him. The guard didn't even bother to meet Ben's eyes before moving on, skipping the next cell.

"Lunch time," Flannan shouted. Not just to Ben, but to the other Disparates filing into the large seating room. "Get in line."

Ben followed the instructions, wondering if he'd missed breakfast. Or, perhaps they didn't feed the prisoners regularly in this place. Lunch time, however, couldn't be skipped. That was when the pills were handed out.

His attention turned to the cell next to him. The door was closed. No clues as to who was trapped inside.

"He keep you up all night? Heard he was thrashin' about. We scared him good." Flannan let out a chuckle as they passed. "Had to sleep in a bit this morning, hope you didn't miss breakfast too much. Be good and you won't have to worry about that happening too often. Well, actually, I can't make that promise."

Ben didn't like this guy. He didn't like any of the guards here. He focused on his breathing. The last thing he needed was for his energy to escape now.

"Huh, not amused, are you?" Flannan examined Ben. "Good thing it's almost time for your pill."

Ben looked at him; the guard's fiery red hair burned into his vision. His lack of sleep combined with the indecent treatment of the individual next to him made it almost impossible to continue his game of pretend.

A flame burst out of his palm and singed the red hair right off.

At least, that was what Ben let himself imagine. If it weren't for the line of Disparates in front of him, he may have done it. He barely kept it contained.

His palm was hot as he formed a fist. Instead of releasing it, he laughed in the guard's face.

The guard narrowed his eyes as he wiped spit off his cheek. "Stupid Disparates," he snarled under his breath before marching toward the front of the line.

A red suit walked directly in front of Ben. His gait was uneven, swaying side to side, as if coming back from a late night out with friends that he'd regret in the morning. Ben matched him as they entered the cafeteria. The guards moved back to keep an eye on the two dozen or so *patients*. The process followed the same as yesterday: grab a tray, get unappetizing muck placed onto it, then receive a pill in a plastic cup.

He headed to the same table as before. 1198 was at the back of the line, again. She must be in one of the farthest cells. Once she collected her items, she sat across from him, her blond hair cascading around the sides of her face.

Ben needed to warn her about what happened to him last night. It could happen to any Disparate that he advised to follow his plan. He needed to make sure she knew the risk.

"Hey," he whispered. "Are you sure about this?"

1198 kept her face to her tray but tilted her head slightly. She stabbed a piece of broccoli with her fork. "More people will be more risk," her voice was calm and even.

"No, not that." Yesterday he had expressed that he wanted to help more people. But he understood now wasn't the time to do it. He needed to get himself off the island first. Then he could work to get everyone else freed, one way or another.

He took a deep breath. "I created a *flame* last night."

"That's good."

"No." She wasn't understanding. "I didn't mean to."

At his confession, she glanced up, but only for a moment. "You're still here. Not sure what the problem is."

Her yellow pill sat in its clear cup. No other Disparates were sitting near them. Including 1227, who was still gone from yesterday.

Could he be the Disparate next door? Ben wasn't sure, but if he was, at least he wasn't dead. Not yet anyway.

"Do you know where 1227 is?" Ben asked. He didn't know how long she'd been at the island, but it was long enough to have seen more than he had.

"Special experimentation. When the pills no longer work, they get taken."

"Taken? Where?" Ben didn't like the sound of that.

"Not sure. No one's returned." Although her voice stayed calm, Ben noticed a slight static to her hair. It was time for her to take her med, but the plan was for her to skip it. Would she be able to keep her energy contained?

No one's returned.

The risk was worth it.

1198 lifted her pill cup, pouring it into her mouth before grabbing her drink. The unsuspecting eye would have missed the way she pushed the pill out of her mouth into her water. As the guards lined up the group, she'd sneak her hand in to grab the pill once more, slipping it into her sleeve to dispose of outside. The way Ben had told her to.

Thankfully, the guards here were incompetent enough not to notice.

As the sun scorched his skin, he ran around the outskirts of the buzzing fence. The circle of yellow jumpsuits painted their same straight lines. This time, the paint color was black.

Once next to 1198, he stopped and bent over to breathe, his hands on his knees. Hopefully it wouldn't draw too much attention.

"You need to be careful," he panted.

Out of the corner of his vision, he saw a small nod of her head.

"I'm"—he took a deep breath—"serious. No accidents. Try not to even think until tomorrow."

His hands were still on his knees, but this time, Ben looked up. The canvas in front of 1198 didn't match the ones around her. Instead of straight brush strokes of black covering the white surface, she focused on the edges. The middle she left untouched, creating a V shape with the paint around it.

No. Creating a pit.

1198 was ready. She understood what needed to be done.

The second warehouse doors squealed open. Out walked the flood of purple, green, and white. Ben's eyes scanned for Mr. Dogivan's wrinkled face as he started his run once more.

Seeming to know what he wanted, Mr. Dogivan made a slow walk to the fence. On his way, he diverted slightly to drop something small onto the ground between some bushes. Ben glanced at the blue coats. There were two on his side and three on the other. None of them were observing Mr. Dogivan at the time. Thankfully.

Mr. Dogivan had followed Ben's direction. They were going to do this.

They'd all be home by tomorrow night.

As Ben approached the fencing, his speed increased. The best way to look out of breath was to make it true. Once he closed in on Mr. Dogivan, he slowed to a stop.

"You did it," Ben huffed out, a space between each word.

Mr. Dogivan nodded, a smile on his face. His true smile.

"I'm remembering more already. She had blue eyes. They shined so bright compared to mine."

A feeling of warmth flushed over Ben, but not the kind he'd been used to on the island. He was genuinely happy for Mr. Dogivan. His plan was working.

"You should remember more and more as time goes on. I'm hoping by tomorrow we'll be ready to attempt our escape."

At Ben's words, Mr. Dogivan's eyebrows furrowed. Only then did Ben realize he'd never told him the plan. His goal of stopping the medicine was to remember his wife. She was already gone. Did he have anyone to go home to?

"Look," Ben said, finally breathing normally. "I'm sorry if I caught you off guard. I really need to get home to my wife and kids. This isn't a good place."

"But it keeps us safe." Mr. Dogivan seemed to believe that. "Disparates are dangerous on the mainland. Here, doctors are keeping them medicated and in control."

Ben's warmth changed. His breath began to get heavy once more. How could this old man believe these things, even though he was a victim? "I'm supposed to be at Merrytime Clinic, and so are you. Not caged on this island."

"They may be wrong about me." Mr. Dogivan looked Ben in the eye, the buzzing fence between them. "Doesn't mean they are about everyone here."

Ben wasn't sure how to respond. Mr. Dogivan was a crucial part of his escape. And now he wasn't going along with it—didn't agree with it.

Maybe he could appease his concerns. "I'm not trying to get everyone off the island. You may be right." Ben swallowed, the next words hard for him to say. "Some of these people are dangerous and may need to stay here. My plan only involves you, me, and one other."

"Who?" Mr. Dogivan's eyes narrowed.

"Someone on my side. They know where a boat is." Ben wasn't sure he wanted to point 1198 out in case Mr. Dogivan turned them in. Although, if he did, he'd have to admit to skipping his pill. Surely that was enough of a threat to keep him from doing so. Right?

Mr. Dogivan paused. "Only us three, no one else?"

Ben nodded.

"Before I agree, I have a question for you," Mr. Dogivan said as his eyes sized Ben up. "How do you know I'm supposed to be at the clinic?"

Ben's heart skipped. This was the second time he'd let a piece of information slip out to this man. However, something about him made him seem trustworthy. Ben was only now realizing that looks could be deceiving. But he'd see through him if he lied.

"I know because... I was the one that sent you there. I was your Intaker." Ben waited for a response, but Mr. Dogivan's expression stayed the same. He couldn't read his face.

"You worked for the government. And now you're here? Interesting how quickly the tables can turn, isn't it?" His words were ominous.

"I'm sorry. I had no idea they would bring you here," Ben said.

Their conversation had been going on for a while. Some blue coats glanced in their direction before writing notes on their clipboard. They needed to wrap this up quickly.

"Please, help us. I've been done wrong by the government now too. Without your help, I can't set things right. They'll make you take those pills and forget again if you stay here."

"You want to get back to your family?" Mr. Dogivan asked.

Ben nodded.

"What's your wife's name?"

"Jemma." Saying her name made his heart ache. It wanted to be back near her. "And my boys are Mackie and Louie. They aren't even old enough for school yet."

"I have a son." Mr. Dogivan softened. "Haven't talked to him since the funeral. Didn't talk to him much before that either."

"Maybe it's not too late to reconcile," Ben said. Mr. Dogivan's vulnerability was a good sign.

"I'll think about it." The ground shook slightly as Mr. Dogivan turned away from the gate and headed toward a bench on his side of the fence.

Ben braced himself, looking around to see if others felt what he had. The shaking was tiny and seemed to only affect his area. As he watched Mr. Dogivan walk away, he tried to assess if the man would help. He hoped that he would.

THIRTEEN

Jemma's heart jumped as she pulled into the driveway of her mother's house, next to a black sports car she recognized. The rising sun cast dark shadows across the ground. Governor Dunn was here.

Her mother knew about Ben. He must have told her. But what about her boys? Would they know too?

Her chest tightened, thinking of the way they'd respond if they heard their father was a criminal. He wasn't, but how did you explain that to a child? They believed Responders were heroes. They saw their dad as a hero. One of those bubbles would pop, and Jemma wasn't ready for that. She needed to keep them protected.

Plus, Louie had his flames now. If the news upset him and he had an outburst, he could be taken away—just like his father. Just as it turned out, Asher had been.

Expectant doom propelled her forward. She jumped out of the car, leaving the door ajar behind her. With each footstep, her very soul quickened. Dark thoughts assaulted her. With hands that shook, she put her key into the lock.

Before she could turn it, the door opened.

"Mom! I saw you from the window." The smiling face of Mackie greeted her, pulling her into a hug. He was dressed in the pajamas she'd packed for him the night before. A yawn escaped his lips, but he was in one piece.

"Hi, sweetie." Jemma held him, relief washing over her. Inside the house, a makeshift fort had been constructed in the middle of the room, half of which had fallen. Under the pile of blankets lay Louie, fast asleep. Another wave of relief. He was safe.

"Where's Grandma?" Jemma asked.

"She's on the couch."

Her mother stirred, pulling down the edge of her quilt. A lump formed in Jemma's throat.

Her father's blanket.

Did her mother have it yesterday, or had the news of Ben triggered her need for it? She couldn't recall. Jemma's mind had been so preoccupied with everything going on with Ben and Buran that she hadn't paid attention to her own mother.

She was having another episode. Of course. That explained why the sports car was still here.

"Where is Governor Dunn?" Jemma asked quietly, not wanting to wake Louie.

"Mornin'," her mother yawned. She ignored the question.

"Mom..." Jemma expected a lecture about Ben. Surely it was coming. Tobias was her mother's closest friend, and she often wondered if there was more between them. But her mother always denied anything more than friendship.

After some of the things she'd learned from Buran, Jemma was grateful for that. It'd be even more awkward around his group if the governor was her step-father. Considering they wanted to take him out.

But perhaps he wasn't as awful as they said. Maybe he could help her.

"He slept in the guest room," her mother whispered. "Just stopped by and was helping get dinner ready. When the boys fell asleep out here, it was too late for him to head home. He insisted on staying the night."

Jemma watched her closely. She didn't say anything about Ben. And although she had the blanket, she sounded okay. Confident. Sure. Ready to put up a fight if Jemma tried to push the topic of Governor Dunn.

That was okay. Jemma wasn't ready to talk about Ben yet either.

"How did the boys do?"

"I was great!" Mackie answered.

Jemma shushed him as her mother nodded her head. A smile on her soft lips illuminated the wrinkles across her cheeks. They made the bags under her eyes more prominent. She may have been feeling better this morning, but just barely.

It'd been over a year since the last time her mother had gone to that dark place. Right after she'd learned about Louie being a Disparate.

Jemma couldn't really blame her. She'd wanted to go there too. Ben helped keep her out of it.

Governor Dunn had become that comfort for her mother once Jemma moved out. And Jemma would be forever grateful that he'd taken her role. She only wished he'd been able to do it sooner.

As if on cue, Governor Dunn emerged from the hallway. "Good morning, everyone."

At the same time, Jemma and her mother both put a finger to their lips.

A tingling lifted the hair on Jemma's arms. Governor Dunn. She'd never felt uncomfortable in his presence before, but now? She wasn't sure how to feel about him. The Dissentients didn't like him much, but they also didn't know him like she did.

Governor Dunn noticed Louie sleeping on the floor. This time, he whispered, "Good morning, everyone. I've got to leave for an early meeting. Glad to see you made it back safely, Jemma. Hope you had a good time with your *friends.*"

Jemma's forehead wrinkled. Why was he acting so carefree? Surely he knew about Ben. The governor wouldn't have that information kept from him, would he? Besides, the news had announced it.

The governor didn't seem to catch her confusion. He grabbed his wallet and keys off the dining room table and headed for the door.

"Thank you, Tobias." Her mother had risen, leaving a dent behind on the couch. She walked to the door to give a hug goodbye.

Jemma headed to the kitchen with Mackie to keep him from waking his brother. Plus, she heard her stomach rumble. Her nerves yesterday had kept her from eating all day. And an excuse to keep busy would help keep her mind off the brother who'd just walked—or rather broke—into her life. The one who didn't want their mother to know about him. She wasn't sure why, but she wasn't about to break his trust right after getting him back.

Moments later, her mother joined them. She eyed Jemma as she searched through the cabinets.

"Jemma, what are you looking for?"

"Your griddle." She opened another cabinet. "Mackie asked for pancakes for breakfast."

"Yeah." Mackie perked. "Can they be chocolate chip?"

"Umm..." Jemma wasn't sure what her mother had on hand. While she glanced around the kitchen, a yawn escaped.

"Why don't you go lay down? I can make breakfast for my daughter and grandsons."

Jemma wanted to protest. Sometimes it was hard to accept her mother's help. Her teenage years had been spent keeping her mother taken care of, not the other way around. This change of pace was nice.

She conceded and headed to the couch. The blanket made of her father's shirts was left in a lump, which was out of character. Jemma must have truly startled her by arriving so early.

As she folded the blanket, a red t-shirt stood out. An image of her father crossed her mind, sitting across from her at breakfast on her ninth birthday, wearing this shirt that Jemma had picked out for him that morning. He chastised twelve year old Asher for stealing her jam covered toast.

"Not on her birthday. Give that back to Jam—Jem," he'd mistakenly said, cementing a new nickname for her brother to tease her with.

She'd been a bit embarrassed about it back then. Now, she wondered what life would've been like if their family hadn't been torn apart.

That image was impossible to conjure. Not after she'd spent so long keeping her thoughts from going there. Tears welled in her eyes as she hugged her father's blanket.

If only he were here to give her advice.

"Are you crying?"

Jemma hadn't heard Louie wake. He sat on the floor, watching her.

"I am." She didn't want to hide her emotions from Louie. To teach him to use his own, she needed to be the example. That was what Buran had said. "Do you know what this blanket is?" Jemma asked.

"That's grandma's special blanket. We have to be careful around it."

"That's right." Jemma sniffled, trying to gain control of her crying before she broke into sobs. "It's special because it's made of Grandpa Stillfield's old shirts. Do you remember me telling you about him?"

Louie nodded.

"He was a great man. And he was a lot like you."

"Did he make fire?"

The question made Jemma pause. She never knew her father to be a Disparate, but then where did her energy come from? And Asher's?

They were either the first of their line, which was rare nowadays, or they inherited it.

And it seemed unlikely that it came from their mother.

"Well, he had strong beliefs about what was right and wrong. Like you."

Her answer seemed to satisfy him.

But she wondered if she had inherited her father's sense of right. Was it right for her to help Buran with their mission? To keep Asher secret from her mother?

She wasn't sure.

But she did know it was right to save her husband. The other questions she'd figure out once that was done.

Louie sniffed the air. "Is that pancakes?" he asked, his eyes wide in anticipation.

"Chocolate chip pancakes." She touched a finger to the tip of his nose as a wide smile spread across his face. He bounded toward the kitchen, Jemma close behind. The blanket, folded neatly, left behind on the couch.

"You're supposed to be resting." Margaret flipped a pancake on top of a stack on the kitchen island. The bags under her daughter's eyes worried her, but she understood why they were there.

"I can't sleep. Besides, Mackie has a soccer game this morning," Jemma explained. "I don't want to sleep through it."

"Mmm hmm." Margaret wanted to send her daughter back to rest, but she knew there was no point. Jemma might take some time making up her mind, but once she did, she stuck to it.

Besides, she needed to talk to her about Ben. It'd be nice if Jemma offered up the information herself, but if not, Margaret didn't mind confronting her.

"Breakfast is ready! Boys, let's go eat in the dining room. Jemma, can you watch the ones cooking?"

Jemma nodded, grabbing the spatula.

The boys followed Margaret as she placed two full plates on the table. With the pancakes covered in butter and syrup, the boys looked pleased.

"Thanks, Grandma!" Mackie shouted as he stabbed a pancake with his fork and lifted it to his mouth.

"I can cut that for you if you'd like."

Mackie nodded. Once Margaret finished cutting his, she moved to Louie's. Now both ready for eating, she headed back into the kitchen.

"Did you burn the last batch?" Margaret asked as she shriveled her nose. She hadn't noticed the smoke smell while she was cooking.

Jemma turned the griddle off. "Must be some leftover food on here. I'll make sure to scrub it off once it cools." She crossed her arms, her hands moving up and down. She seemed nervous.

No wonder. Margaret had missed the signs the last couple days. Clearly Jemma was struggling, her eyes were red, likely from crying.

"That's nice of you to offer, but you don't have to do that. Leave the griddle and I'll take care of it later. You need to get some food." Margaret sat on a stool on the other side of the island as Jemma slowly grabbed herself a plate, clearly doing so because she was told to. She didn't seem to have much of an appetite as she chose the smallest pancake. Perhaps Margaret could ease some of her burden. "Why don't you eat here? I believe we have some things to talk about."

Jemma stiffened. Her syrup pouring paused as her eyes twitched slightly. "Um... sure. What about, exactly?"

"Why didn't you tell me about Ben!" Margaret didn't care to beat around the bush. She needed answers. She'd been in a dark place the last twenty-four hours, and knowledge would help keep her out of it.

Jemma sighed, a hint of tears gathering under her eyes. "He's... well... remember the fire at his office two nights ago?"

Margaret nodded. The first night she watched the boys. She knew where this was going.

"They think Ben started it." Jemma fidgeted with her fork as she spoke the next words. "He's at Merrytime Clinic. I'm trying to get him out."

Just as Tobias had said.

Margaret wasn't too surprised. Jemma held the fork in her hand, her fingers twitching across the metal. It seemed her daughter was hiding more, but at least she was opening up.

"I'm so sorry to hear that," Margaret said. "I imagine it's hard on the boys as well."

Jemma put the fork down. "That's why I told them he was on a work trip. I don't want them to worry."

"How long do you expect them to believe that?" Margaret regretted her question as soon as Jemma's face fell. It was too direct. She'd only meant to try and understand. Perhaps help Jemma break the news to the boys. But it was too soon.

"I'm hoping he'll be home before they start to wonder. At least, I'm working to get him back home."

Margaret's brows furrowed. "How? If he's at Merrytime Clinic, it'll take some time for him to be treated."

"I have my ways..." Jemma bit her bottom lip. "Do you think Governor Dunn could help?"

"He really doesn't have authority over the clinic," Margaret explained. "Or the Responders. But I suppose he could put in a good word for Ben. Not sure it will do much."

Tears welled in Jemma's eyes. Margaret wished there was more she could do.

Louie walked into the kitchen, an empty plate in his hands. "More, please!" he squealed.

"Of course," Jemma said, taking his plate. After she filled it, she took a step with him toward the dining room.

Margaret placed a hand on her shoulder. "If you need more, just let me know," she said as she slipped a paper ration sheet into Jemma's hand.

Ben could be at Merrytime Clinic for weeks. That was a lot to put on her daughter. Leaving her to take care of the boys on her own. And not just the boys, but the financial responsibilities as well. Margaret didn't know what their situation looked like. It didn't feel right to pry, but maybe that was an area where she could help.

Jemma raised an eyebrow but then stopped and sighed. "Thanks, Mom. We should be okay for a while. I'll let you know if we need anything."

Margaret didn't mind the sighing. The smile that accompanied it looked appreciative. Most mothers had to deal with that type of behavior in adolescence, but Margaret never had. She was grateful Jemma now showed her signs of what she was truly thinking inside.

Jemma placed the ration sheet into her pocket as she entered the dining room. Their conversation was over.

FOURTEEN

A barrage of messages popped onto Margaret's screen. Multiple coworkers checked in on her, asking if she'd seen the recent news.

The headline read: *Fire at the Public Safety Building.*

Margaret's eyes grew wide as she opened the website. Her heart encompassed the mass of her chest as she scrolled through the article, each beat threatening to break through her rib cage.

Middle of the night... Break in... Started in the back... Two guards on duty, firefighters discharged right away...

She went to her recent calls and clicked on the last one she'd missed.

"Maggie, did you hear?" Tobias's voice was strained.

"Just saw. Is the fire still burning?"

"No—" He was hesitant. "It was put out before it passed the break room. I'm here now. It looks like your office was the target."

The weight Margaret had shrugged off returned full blast. Not quite the same as the night before. This time it was accompanied by fear.

"Who did this?" she asked, her thoughts going to Ben. "This looks like the work of the Fire Anarchist... how is that possible?"

"Looks like a copycat. Or perhaps he wasn't working alone. There were at least two people at this break in."

That was different. But why? "I'm coming down," she said as she grabbed her purse. She didn't care that she was still dressed in yesterday's clothing.

"Don't come yet." Tobias's words caused her to pause. "The building's not cleared for entry. Firefighters need more time to check the structure and allow the smoke to dissipate. In twenty-four hours, it'll be safe to enter."

Twenty-four hours. A lot could happen in that amount of time. And if someone stole her letter from Tobias...

No. She needed to keep her thoughts from spiraling. There was no proof anything was found. However, the pit in her stomach deepened.

That afternoon, Jemma headed for home. Both the boys needed baths after Mackie's soccer game and the celebratory ice cream they devoured. A little bit of joy in the messiness that surrounded her lately. They'd used the ration bill her mother had given her to celebrate. It was important to keep the tradition for the boys, even without Ben.

However, it did leave her needing to clean them up before taking them over to Caty's later that night. She could use a shower herself after last night's espionage. The water had the added benefit of soothing her nerves that came with thinking about meeting with Asher tonight.

"Daddy, Daddy!" Mackie's high-pitched squeals echoed through the car as the driveway came into view. Ben's silver car sat on the cement. Oliver must've dropped it off.

"Oh, no honey," Jemma said. Of course the boys would recognize their father's car. "He's not home yet. His car was just brought back."

In the rear view mirror, she saw his little face melt. Any joy the ice cream had brought was now gone. Louie stared out the side window.

"Where is he?" Mackie asked as they pulled in next to Ben's car. Jemma didn't bother with opening the garage.

"Remember, he's on a work trip?" She hated lying to them. She exited the car and opened Mackie's door, ready to get him out of his car seat as Louie got himself out on his own.

His eyes filled with tears, and he crumbled into sobs. "But I wanted him here for my birthday!"

His birthday wasn't for another month, but he was already obsessed with it. Jemma couldn't promise him he'd be back in time. Her own tears escaped as she scooped up her baby boy. "I'm sorry. I'm so sorry. I wish your daddy was home too. He's..." She wanted to tell them the truth, but how could she put that on her children who were so little? "Daddy's getting some help. I don't know when he'll be back. Hopefully soon."

Mackie's breathing soon shallowed and his tears stopped. "Can I watch my show?"

Jemma smiled. "Yes, that sounds like the perfect plan. Let's head inside." She didn't care any longer about giving them baths. She sat Mackie on the ground. "Louie?" She looked around but didn't see where he'd gone. "Louie!" she called once more.

Just as she was about to head toward the front door to search the house, the sunlight glinted across the windshield of Ben's car. A small movement in the backseat drew her attention.

"Of course." Jemma's heart threatened to break more as she grabbed Mackie's hand and headed to Louie's favorite hiding spot.

She took a deep breath as she opened the back door to her husband's car and slid into the seat next to Louie, Mackie following her inside. "Are you okay?" she asked.

Louie remained quiet.

"Did you hear what I told Mackie?"

This time he nodded. "What kind of help?"

Jemma let out a long breath. "Help with his fire." She was done lying to them. "I'm not sure if it's really helping though."

"I miss him. Why can't he come home?" Louie sniffled. "I could use help too."

"I know, buddy." She brought him in for a side hug. "You do love your dad's help, but I can help you! And you can help me too. What do you think of heading inside and getting cleaned up?"

"I thought we were gonna watch my show!" Mackie crossed his arms.

"What if I add bubbles?" Both Mackie and Louie straightened. Her bargaining was working. "And let you go to Lily's house tonight?"

"Yes!" Mackie shouted.

Louie gave a half smile and nodded.

The stars in the sky reflected Jemma's hope as she made her way to the old treehouse. The day had dragged on as she waited for this moment.

She kept her headlights off as she passed near the edge of the canal. She didn't want to attract attention.

The moon lit her path. The same moon that shined on her husband. Wherever the island was located, that was one thing she was sure of—they were underneath the same sky.

Her phone buzzed on the middle console, causing her to jump. With it, her headlights flashed on for a moment before returning to the darkness of the night. At least the surge of energy she released hadn't stopped her car.

The message might be something important. From Buran or Caty, who was watching her boys. She drove slow enough to risk a peek.

> Just started the movie and Louie is already sleeping. He was one tired boy! Lily and Mackie are cuddling under the same blanket. It's pretty cute, you're missing out.

Jemma relaxed, but only slightly. She waited until she arrived at the old tree to respond.

> You bet I am!

> Hope your mom is feeling better.

Jemma paused. She didn't like lying to her best friend, but she wasn't ready to explain everything. Not yet. She knew when that time came, she'd have to come clean about being a Disparate herself.

But she wasn't ready to admit it yet.

There was no sign of Asher outside. That didn't worry her. Well, maybe slightly. He could be waiting above. She closed her car door slowly as she looked at the remains of their old hideout.

The wooden structure was still there, but it hadn't been maintained. Planks were missing; a hole was broken through the window pane. The blocks nailed on the side of the tree as a ladder were tilted and loose.

Butterflies assaulted her stomach as she stood at the trunk of the tree. Her eyes followed the old stairs to the floor opening. It was higher than she remembered. As a young girl, the height never fazed her, but now as an adult, her fearlessness was gone, replaced with an understanding of how fragile human life was.

"Asher?" she whispered to the space above her. No one answered. If he wasn't there then no reason to risk her life on the worn and possibly unstable structure above her.

Then again... he could be. *Maybe he didn't hear me, or maybe he doesn't want to answer me. As he said, we don't really know each other anymore.*

The last time she'd stood in this spot, she'd whispered the same name. When she had climbed up after no answer, her heart was ripped into two at the sight of an empty room.

This moment brought back that broken feeling. The gurgling of the canal water matched the beating of her chest as goosebumps ran across her arms. Her brother had abandoned her once again.

"Hey, you coming up?" Asher's voice came from above, startling Jemma just as she was about to turn around and head back to her car. She jumped, and a bolt of lightning struck into the trunk of the tree, causing one of the good steps to fall sideways.

"Shoot, Jem Jam, you alright?" Asher asked.

Jemma's fear settled as it registered her brother's presence. "Don't scare me like that!" she scolded her brother just as she had years ago.

"Sorry." His laugh caused the shadowed outline of the scar on his neck to squirm.

The sound warmed her insides, settling her doubt. Like heat to a hot air balloon, her chest filled with courage to climb up and join him.

At the top, she looked around. The small room was arranged the way they'd left it, preserving their childhood. Reminders of a different lifetime. Jemma's heart both swelled and crushed with each surfacing memory.

In the corner was a small table; two round stools on each side. An old Persian rug covered in dust lay in the middle of the room. The day she found it, she roped Asher into helping her carry it up the ladder. She'd wanted to abandon it after they dropped it on the first try, but Asher wasn't a quitter.

As she passed their old bookshelf, she noticed a rolled out sleeping bag. This was where he'd been staying.

Their art wall was in the opposite corner. Many of their portraits were still displayed, hanging on by old nails. She wondered if Asher still loved art the way he did back then. His painted murals covered the walls of the treehouse. Granted, they'd deteriorated over the years, but the mountain landscape on one side and the ocean on the other were still there.

She moved closer to their gallery, examining the drawing she'd made of Asher when she was eleven. She'd captured the wave of his mid-length hair just right, then added horns and dragon wings.

"That's my favorite one." Asher stood behind Jemma, smiling.

"I totally thought I would annoy you by drawing you like a dragon. You surprised me when you hung it up."

"Yeah, at fourteen, I used to think my fire energy was a curse. Seeing you compare me to a mighty dragon made me realize I could do something that was once only heard about in myths and legends." He shrugged. "I thought that was cool."

Used to. Jemma caught those words. "Do you not think your energy is a curse now?"

Asher's eyes shifted. "Well, not a curse. Obviously not always the easiest to live with, but not a curse." He tilted his head to the side, looking like he had more to say but wasn't sure how to say it.

"It sure seems like one to me," Jemma said more to herself than to Asher. Emotional energy had only ever brought her and her family trauma and pain. There were many days she wished everyone around her was normal, that they didn't need to fear an outburst or meltdown. It was exhausting living on edge. She was surprised she hadn't had an electric outburst sooner.

"That's because it's described as one," Asher spat out, his eyebrows furrowed. "Everyone says it's such a problem that it became one. Instead of learning how to embrace our emotions, we've been told to hide and lock them away. That's how it's been marketed all these years. Pushing pills down people's throats to control them."

Jemma's eyes widened at Asher's passion. She kept hearing about Disparates being treated wrongly. First Buran and now Asher. Maybe there was more to emotional energy than she thought.

"But the pills can help, can't they? Isn't it better than letting people run wild with nothing? The world tried that, and people were dying."

Asher's face smoothed. "People are still dying, Jemma. The medicine doesn't help the way they say it does. That's why they keep testing new ones and making them stronger."

"Testing new ones? What do you mean?" Jemma hadn't heard about new medicine being developed. If so, it hadn't made it to the Analyst field while she was there.

"What do you think they do with the Disparates at Lucky Island? It's not some tropical vacation. The strongest Disparates end up there for a reason." Asher's eyebrows furrowed together, a sharpness reflected in his eyes. "They want to make new drugs that will control even the strongest energy. And they want to have fun doing it."

"So you do know about Lucky Island." She wasn't sure how much to ask, but she had to save Ben. He was her priority. She needed to get him home.

Asher sighed. "Yes, Jem Jam. I do." His eyes fell, casting a sullenness over his features. "So, what do your friends, these *Dissentients*, want with me?"

Time for small talk was over. Asher wasn't wasting any time. "Well," Jemma said, "they're hoping you can lead us to the island."

"To save Ben?"

Jemma nodded.

"Why do they care to save him?" Asher's voice was sharp, cutting into her like a knife.

"They believe he has information that would help them..."

"Help them with what?" Asher asked. "I'm not sure I'm following. There has to be more in this for them to go to this risk. The island isn't a tourist attraction."

"Well, I'm not sure..." She trailed off. It was evident she didn't really know that much about this group that she'd put her trust in. "But we could go ask them about it."

"Shoot," Asher cursed under his breath. "Do you see a light out there?"

Jemma turned to check and saw a small light shining through the woods on the opposite bank of the canal. It wavered as it moved, likely from a small flashlight.

"We need to get going, and fast, before whoever that is makes it out here." Asher was already headed for the exit.

"We can take my car."

The two siblings descended the tree. Jemma's foot slipped on one of the loose steps halfway down. Asher caught her before she fell.

"Thanks."

"Let's just go," Asher said.

She started the ignition before her door fully closed. Her pulse quickened. Electricity flowed through her veins like the water in the canal. There was no time to worry about people hearing her tires on the rocky dirt road. The light was getting closer.

Asher drew his eyebrows together in the seat next to her, wrinkles crumpling across his forehead. If he was caught, what would happen to him? He was an island escapee—and the arsonist.

Jemma needed to be strong. She buried her fears as she switched the gear into reverse and backed out of the narrow canal road. A breath escaped her lips.

She was grateful the car worked.

FIFTEEN

Ben's eyelids flashed open, a trembling throughout his cell jostling him awake. Cracks broke across the outer concrete wall. Not deep enough to break through to the other side, but enough to leave an impression. They crawled their way across the ceiling above his head. As he shot up, bits of rock rained upon where he had laid.

He leapt to the window, searching through the bars for the building next door. Dust and smoke assaulted his lungs, blocking fresh air from coming in. He turned away, covering his face as he coughed to clear his airways. Tears formed in his eyes as a defense against the debris. When the shaking stopped and the world stilled, an eerie silence settled.

But not for long. An alarm rang. Wiping his eyes, Ben looked out once more. Warehouse Two was still standing, having been made and reinforced with strong steel. However, not all of it. Ben tilted his head to see further, noticing the fencing had fallen. He followed it to a caved in spot at the end of the building.

He wondered if the collapsed cell was Mr. Dogivan's. The wake of destruction mirrored his own grief for losing his family.

Ben's heart stopped. There was no way Mr. Dogivan survived the cave in.

A figure emerged from under the rubble, tossing rocks to the side as he clawed his way out of the hole. As soon as Ben saw the wrinkled, battered face, shocked relief swept over him.

"Over here!" he yelled. Mr. Dogivan looked at the hand Ben pushed between his bars. They needed to move fast, before guards arrived.

Mr. Dogivan seemed to understand. A trembling began to murmur under Ben's feet. He jumped back from the window and onto his concrete bed as more rocky debris fell. The earth where he'd just stood opened its dark mouth, swallowing the sink, toilet, and at last, the wall.

Ben didn't stop to see how far the fissure expanded. He burst through the cold water that now sprayed from his broken pipes. The metallic taste was bitter on his lips.

As he headed to Mr. Dogivan, he noticed the crumbled wall exposed the cell next to him. He hadn't heard the Disparate's moaning since that morning.

It was empty.

Ben arrived at Mr. Dogivan's side as the old man collapsed. His face was wet, but it wasn't from water.

Tears.

"S-She's," he stuttered, "gone."

With the destruction that surrounded them, he must have meant his wife. His memory had returned.

"I know. I know," Ben said. "Are you okay?"

Mr. Dogivan didn't acknowledge Ben's presence. He held his knees as he muttered under his breath. "It was me... my fault..."

"Come on. We've got to move."

Mr. Dogivan stayed frozen. Ben wondered how badly he'd been injured.

From the front of the warehouses, shouts rose above the ringing alarm. "Code Green." The guards were closing in. They were running out of time.

Ben pulled Mr. Dogivan's arm around him. He was heavy, but Ben wasn't going to leave him behind.

Carrying most of Mr. Dogivan's weight, Ben hustled toward the back recreation area. Although the timing of their plan was disrupted, maybe it would still work. They at least needed to find a place to hide and assess Mr. Dogivan's wounds.

As they passed the end of the warehouse, Ben stepped back into the shadows. The field was already covered in guards.

No. Not guards.

Other Disparates. Covered in dust and running. Howls of fear filled the air.

Ben glanced behind him. His eyes widened at the sight. A crevice spread across the ground, creating a gaping pit down the middle of Warehouse One. The two sides fought to keep from falling inside.

Mr. Dogivan's energy hadn't stopped after Ben's cell. It kept growing. Following them.

"Don't stop now!" 1198 approached them from the back of the warehouse, out of breath. She cradled her right arm. The shoulder was lower than normal. "We've got to get to the fence! To the boat!"

She was right. She threw Mr. Dogivan's other arm over her good shoulder, wincing as she released her injured one. Her arm fell to her side—limp.

As they pressed forward, the gash in the earth followed. It swerved in their direction. A predator chasing its prey.

Ben examined Mr. Dogivan. His eyes stared down, glossy. Ben held his body, but his mind was elsewhere.

"Make it stop," Ben pleaded.

"I did it," Mr. Dogivan's voice cracked. Similar to the ground that continued to break apart.

The opening was gaining speed as the three of them hobbled forward. Ben tried to gauge how deep it went, but he couldn't see the bottom. He wasn't sure they'd make it to the fence before the hole devoured them.

Only a few more yards...

The blur of a yellow jumpsuit passed across the side of Ben's vision. 1198 tripped, creating an instant domino effect. Mr. Dogivan went with her, dragging Ben down until he slipped out of his grip. His frail body crumbled to the ground.

1198 stood as Ben steadied himself just in time to lose his footing from the chasm at his heels. He stumbled forward as he fell, thankfully out of reach of the hole. A shooting pain radiated through his ankle.

Mr. Dogivan was still down, right in the cavity's path. 1198 noticed first, leaping forward to grab hold of his arm with her one usable hand.

"I killed her," Mr. Dogivan murmured as his body slipped into the ravine. 1198 wasn't strong enough.

Ben was close behind her. He grabbed Mr. Dogivan's other arm before his shoulders joined the rest of his body. Ben's ankle screamed out in protest. He dropped to his knees as he held on.

Mr. Dogivan's eyes locked with Ben's. "I killed her. She's dead because of me. I deserve to die." His voice was soft, filled with emotion.

"No," Ben shouted. He wasn't letting him go.

With each heave, the hole widened, keeping Mr. Dogivan's body from gaining ground. Ben shuffled backward as he pulled, his ankle scraping across the rough dirt.

1198 held on with one arm, but pain flickered across her face. She wouldn't last much longer.

They were almost to the fence. The soft buzz of electricity could barely be heard over the sound of screaming. Soon it would block their path. The three of them sacrificed to the pit, or fried.

"Dogivan, you need to control your emotions!" Ben tugged, bringing the old man's shoulders back on solid ground. But only for a moment before they were swallowed once more.

"I made the dip in the road."

Ben strained to hear what Mr. Dogivan said.

"The dip that caused her car to veer to the side." His frail body shook as he continued. "She crashed into the light post. Because of me."

His wife. That was why he had never accepted he was a Disparate. To accept was to admit he had caused her death.

Mr. Dogivan's body shuddered once more as the hole surged wider. His wrinkled face disappeared inside of the chasm.

1198 had lost hold of him. But Ben hadn't.

His body lurched forward, grasping an arm as his face smashed into the side of the crevice. He breathed in dirt as his grip slid to Mr. Dogivan's hand. He tightened his own around it, his other hand clenching the grass on the surface. One shoulder above and one stretched into the abyss. Ben wasn't ready to give up.

"Tell my son I'm sorry," Mr. Dogivan's voice echoed off the canyon walls.

"You can tell him yourself." Ben's muscles tightened as he pulled skyward, but he made no progress.

1198 grabbed onto Ben's waist. "Let go!" she yelled. "Or you'll go with him!"

Ben tightened his grip, but the full weight was too much. He was afraid, but as he looked at Mr. Dogivan's face, he saw peace.

"It's time for me to be with her," he said, a smile spreading on his face. "She's here, I can feel her."

The earth rumbled once more beneath Ben, pushing against his chest. He didn't want to let go, but sweat pooled around their grasp. As he strengthened his hold, Mr. Dogivan's grip relaxed. There was nothing left to do. The old, weathered hand slid through his fingers, leaving Ben's clutch empty.

Mr. Dogivan's eyes closed as he fell into the pit, engulfed inside its shadows.

"No!" Ben grabbed at the open air, desperate to catch Mr. Dogivan. If it weren't for 1198's hold on him, he'd have fallen as well.

A thud echoed through the trench. Ben froze, his arm extended. Mr. Dogivan was gone.

1198 tugged on his waist, pulling him back to reality. Alarms rang out as drugged Disparates ran with no sense of direction or place to go. Their maniacal screams resembled a child on a roller coaster—scared of the impending drop but excited for the thrill of falling.

Ben couldn't be sure in the faint light, but the jumpsuits all seemed to be the same crimson shade of his own.

Guards encircled the panicked Disparates, their guns at the ready as they tried to usher their charges into some sort of order. It wasn't working well. The giant hole in the middle of the yard fueled the chaos.

Back at the end of the broken warehouse stood a circle of figures. Their golden suits reflected the starlight as they stood watching the events unfold. Even in this mayhem, their medicine kept them composed.

Unhuman.

Inhumane.

A shudder ran through Ben. He was grateful the island drug never crossed his lips. He was intent on keeping it that way.

Ben caught sight of Flannan at the same time the guard seemed to spot him. His red face matched the jumpsuit of the Disparate he held onto as he shouted at Ben and 1198, warning them not to move.

That was not a command Ben planned to follow. Just past them, the fissure had ended. Breaking through the fence.

Mr. Dogivan had left them a gift.

Ben heard no buzzing as he headed toward the gap. The breakage must have stopped the electricity. 1198 was right behind him.

Sharp wires from the fence cut through the fabric of his jumpsuit. He turned around to watch 1198 shimmy through. Her cheek grazed across the sharp steel. Blood dripped from the wound.

Flannan stayed rooted to his spot. In his free hand, he held a two-way radio. His mouth moved furiously.

"Which way?" Ben asked.

"What?" 1198 wiped the side of her face, smearing red across it.

"The boat, which way is it?"

"Follow me." 1198 ran along the fence line.

Ben followed, trying to keep pace with her. The urgency dampened the pain from his ankle.

They were headed toward the front of Warehouse One. Ben worried they ran too close to the chaos they'd left behind. Surely that would increase their chances of being caught.

1198 veered to the side and into an opening in the thick brush. Finally, more cover. They pressed forward, jumping over logs and dodging bushes until they arrived at a small clearing. Trees around the edges provided some protection.

1198 bent over, breathing hard. "Just... catching my breath."

"We have to keep going." Ben understood her need for rest. However, the adrenaline coursing through his body begged him to keep moving. The longer they stopped, the more likely they were to be caught. He couldn't let that happen. Not now that he was so close to getting back to Jemma.

"Where?" She took another deep breath.

"To the boat—"

"No." She paused, her face contorted. "Where do we go if we make it back?"

"We go home." Ben knew where he was going. To Jemma, and Louie, and Mackie. That was why he needed to escape in the first place. They *were* the plan.

1198 gazed at Ben. He wasn't sure if her expression showed pain or confusion.

"Do you have a home to go back to?" he asked slowly, unsure if he was getting too personal.

"We're gonna need a place to hide on the mainland." 1198 straightened and looked at Ben. "They're not going to stop looking for us."

She was right. Once they made it off the island, they would be fugitives.

Wanted.

His heart sank. He wouldn't be able to go back to life the way it was before.

"I know Governor Dunn," Ben said, trying to find some hope. "He may be able to help me. Us."

"The governor is in charge of all this." 1198 spit on the ground. "He'd want us back the most."

Ben knew Governor Dunn to be a good person. Being a close friend of Margaret's, he'd spent holidays with their family. Surely he didn't know of everything happening on the island.

"Anyone else?" 1198 waited, her eyes glued to Ben.

He tried to think of anyone that would help. He couldn't.

"I'm not sure," he answered her, but his confidence started to return. "We can figure that out once we're off. People are good. If we tell them what's happening here, they'd want it to stop."

She continued to stare at him, her brows knit together. She shook her head as she raised a hand to her forehead. A moment later, a sound shot through the air. 1198's eyes turned glossy as her body slumped forward and crashed to the ground. He wasn't sure if she was breathing.

Ben rolled to the side as a projectile flew by. He couldn't tell in the dark if it was a bullet or a needle.

"1232." Flannan emerged from behind a tree, his gun pointed toward Ben. "We're gonna need you to stop."

Two more guards emerged, standing on either side of Flannan. One Ben recognized: Markus, the guard who'd escorted him his first night. The memory caused heat to swirl within his chest.

Ben didn't give them time to shoot again. He raised his hands above his head.

"Oh good, he's giving up." Markus smirked. He spoke just as carelessly as he had that first night.

Ben let himself release, yelling as his energy exploded out of his arms. A ball of flames passed over the limp body of 1198 and blasted the trio. They stumbled back, falling to the ground as their uniforms were set ablaze.

While they smothered the evidence, the flames illuminated 1198's body. She'd rolled onto her side, a sign she had enough energy at least for that.

Flannan had already regained his stance, bits of uniform hanging off his left arm. The red skin glowed under the light of the waning moon. He raised a gun.

Ben didn't wait to find out which kind—death or sleep. He took off running into the patch of trees behind him, following the route 1198 had been headed in. He didn't want to leave her behind, but he didn't see any other choice.

Flannan followed.

Ben dodged to the side as he lifted his arms, pointing them at the guard.

Except—nothing came out. Adrenaline pumped through his veins, replacing the anger that had been there.

Crap.

Ben fell to the ground and rolled. A bullet pierced the spot he'd left. Getting onto his hands and knees, he crawled into nearby bushes just as another bullet whizzed past.

He scrambled to his feet and ran. Shouts erupted behind him. From more than one person. The other guards must have gotten up and joined the chase.

He'd abandoned 1198, but it sounded like the guards had too. If the guards were now on his trail, did that mean she was left alone? Possibly bleeding to death on the ground? Or perhaps someone had been called to cart her off. But there may have still been time to save her...

He wasn't sure if the risk was worth it. His life and freedom... for hers.

There was still the matter of the boat. If he kept running forward, he'd make it to the ocean. He could follow the shore in hopes of finding it or possibly another way off the island.

However, if he circled back for 1198, she could still be alive. She'd rolled over. If she were only tranquilized, she'd wake up in an hour or two. But if she were shot and already dead, he'd be putting his own life on the line.

His heart tightened within his chest. Everything his medicine had been suppressing since he was a teenager came to the surface. It wasn't just anger at his circumstances that fueled his flames, but also anger at injustice. Wrongs done to others. 1198 needed him.

But first, he needed to get his anger built up.

He thought about 1198's body, lying on the ground covered in sticks and leaves.

Mr. Dogivan's death. Swallowed by his own pit of sorrow.

The Fire Disparate, missing since that first day.

The time he should be with his family, ripped from them with no regard and no plan for reunion. Not even the opportunity to communicate.

Ben jumped to the side. His bad ankle caused his knee to buckle slightly as he hid behind a tree, touching the bark for balance.

A flame escaped. Not behind him toward the guards, but to his left. He'd caught sight of an old, dead log and hit it perfectly. As the fire caught, he heard the guards switch direction and head toward the distraction. He shot a couple more fireballs down a path he may have taken. Hopefully that would buy enough time.

He circled back, searching for anyone that may have stayed behind. There was no one in the forest, but as he neared the clearing, he heard voices.

"I told you I'm alright," a female hissed. It sounded like 1198 except for the sharp edge. She shouldn't be awake yet. "It's Flannan and his crew you should be worried about if they don't bring that *fugitive* back here."

Surely this was someone else speaking. They'd beaten him to her body. He started to turn until he heard a second nasally male voice—

"Ben?"

He startled, stopping in his tracks. The voice accusing him of being a fugitive was familiar to one he was used to hearing daily at work.

"Who else?" the first snapped back.

"About that..." the man said before taking a deep breath.

He should've left while he still could. He'd figure out another way off the island. Yet the voices drew him in. He couldn't leave without knowing.

The second person let out his breath as Ben inched closer to the edge of the trees. "I didn't think he was going to be blamed."

Ben hid himself behind a thick trunk and peered through a branch. He saw 1198 standing, as if she hadn't been tranqed minutes before. She had been the one talking about him. Ben's head throbbed as the pieces came together. She wasn't shot. She spoke of Ben as if *he* were a prisoner, not her.

Had she been lying to him the whole time?

And the face of the man next to her, illuminated by the moon, was one Ben knew well.

Oliver.

Sixteen

B en rubbed his eyes, almost hard enough to gouge them out. They were deceiving him.

There was no way Oliver would be here—now.

Yet the proof stood a few feet in front of him.

Next to the woman he thought was helping him escape but had instead announced she wanted him caught. Probably to receive some kind of reward. He regretted turning back to save her, but his shock kept him rooted in place.

"I thought the fire anarchist was going to be framed," Oliver said. "Or maybe Buran. Not Ben. I would have waited to start the fire until after he'd left."

Ben's face wrinkled, waiting for Oliver's words to register. Was he talking about the office fire?

"You needed to do it," 1198 said. "And before he figured out why you've been manipulating the alert files."

It was Oliver. All this time, Ben had wanted to give him the benefit of the doubt. But why would he do it? What was he hiding?

"I know," Oliver said with a shrug, "but I didn't mean for him to get hurt."

Ben had been framed by his closest friend. Flames grew within his chest, the heat rising through his neck and to his face. He slowed his breath to keep it from escaping. He needed to stay hidden.

1198 swiped dirt off the legs of her yellow jumpsuit with her good arm. "You did what you were told, and you did it well. She is very proud of you." She faced Oliver, placing her dirt covered palm on his cheek. "And now you are here, and we are together. Isn't that what you wanted?"

He was working for someone. Ben thought back to their conversation about Oliver's long distance girlfriend. Was that 1198? That didn't seem right. If she'd been locked away on the island all this time, wouldn't Oliver had said something? Especially when it came to the way he spoke about Disparates, and yet, here he was dating one the entire time.

"Of course it's what I want..." Oliver paused and swiped blood off 1198's cheek. "But Ben is my friend. He has a family that's missing him. There's got to be a way to get him home."

Oliver wore a uniform adorned with a silver five leaf clover. He'd finally achieved his dream of becoming a Responder—at Ben's expense.

His chest flared, but pain radiated from his ankle, and his leg buckled. He gripped the tree trunk next to him, biting his tongue to keep from screaming.

"Did you hear that?" Oliver's hand went to his side, where a gun rested.

1198 glanced in Ben's direction. He shifted back, hiding his full body behind the tree.

"Sounded like wind to me," she said. Ben released his breath, peeking through the leaves once more. His ankle throbbed, as if barbed wire were wrapped around it, slowly constricting. "I understand Ben was your friend," she continued, "but you can't blame yourself for what happened."

"What do you mean?" Oliver asked the question Ben had been thinking. Although, he wouldn't have asked so nicely.

"You didn't know he was a Flame Disparate." She placed the hand of her good arm on her opposite shoulder and winced as she popped it back into place. At least her injury wasn't fake. "There was no way to know he would be blamed."

"That's true." Oliver raised his head. "I can't believe he never told me. I thought we were friends."

Hearing Oliver speak in such a way caused Ben's blood to boil, smoke rising from his skin. It seemed as if they were putting the blame on Ben for what happened. As if him not sharing something about himself was truly what caused all of this.

He wasn't falling for it. Oliver played the hero, when all along he was the villain.

"And don't forget your plan," 1198 said hastily.

Ben perked up. What other plans were they making?

"You promise it'll work?" Oliver said.

"It was your idea, darling. I know it will. We just need to find our friend and tell him we are going to get him off the island. Escaping isn't the way. EnertinX is." Her voice was sweet, but her words were opposite to the ones she'd used only hours before. When she was convincing Ben to run.

Then there was the fact that Ben had never known Oliver to be a planner. In fact, he was often the opposite. Going along with what everyone else wanted. Ben knew he couldn't trust these two. Let alone EnertinX. If that was what they call the pills on the island, he didn't want them.

"You're right," Oliver said.

"And it shouldn't take too long to find him. Almost all Responders have been called into action. At least those that aren't dealing with the mess at the warehouses right now. They're scouring the island as we speak."

Ben twisted his back against the tree trunk as noise sounded in the distance. The sound of footsteps. He wasn't sure how many Responders were looking for him. If he headed into the woods now, his odds of being caught were much higher.

He had no other choice. He stumbled forward, desperate to leave despite his ankle's resistance. Following 1198's path was a bad idea after she'd deceived him.

Instead, he headed in a direction he believed would lead to the ocean.

He didn't make it far before a figure stepped into his path. Markus pointed a gun at Ben.

"Stop right there, scum," Markus said.

The anger that'd been brewing inside spread through Ben's limbs. He'd been framed. Abused. Lied to. Flames burst forward, encompassing Markus. A shot rang out from the guard, the smoke from his barrel joining in the dance of Ben's fire as he screamed.

A bullet pierced Ben's left shoulder, throwing him to the dirt as a new burning of pain replaced his anger. He gripped the fresh, warm blood with his hand as he raised his head toward the fire in front of him.

Within its flames, a body lay. A putrid smell within the smoke caused Ben to hold his breath.

"Is that Ben?" Oliver emerged through the trees, 1198 close behind. He knelt next to Ben. "You idiot, you weren't supposed to get shot!" It was then his gaze moved to the fire and the body being consumed. Oliver's eyes widened as he shuffled slightly away.

"We need help over here!" 1198 yelled into a two-way radio. Ben wasn't sure when she'd gotten one of those. He became lightheaded. A combination of the heat, pain, and loss of blood.

There was no time to build another fire burst, and there was no way his wound would let him continue to run. This was it.

He was caught.

"Look, I know you didn't mean to kill him, right?" Oliver said, as if trying to reassure himself that Ben wouldn't target him next. "That was only self defense. We're friends, remember? I'll get you out of this. I promise."

The Oliver Ben knew never kept his promises.

J emma's heart raced as her car sped down the road. In her rear view mirror, a white truck followed them. She made a last minute turn—so did they. She made a U-turn, thinking she would lose them, but a few moments later, there they were. At least, she thought it was the same white truck until it turned right at the next light that she proceeded straight through.

A sigh of relief escaped her lips as she relaxed. She hadn't realized how tense her body had been. Color flowed back into the creases of her knuckles.

Asher stared forward. Now that the truck was gone, he spoke. "I think we're okay. Doesn't look like we were being followed after all. The light was probably some teenagers exploring the woods."

"Yeah," Jemma agreed, her hands shaking.

Asher sat with darting eyes, tilting his head side to side. "Those friends of yours. Are they really trustworthy?"

Jemma thought for a moment. "I trust Buran. I'm not sure if I understand everything they want to do, but they are trying to help me. We share a common goal when it comes to Ben. We both want him back."

Jemma glanced at Asher's face. It was smooth and untelling. She wasn't sure how much to give away. She didn't want to spook him, but it was important he understood what they were getting into.

"They say the pills the government pushes are not actually helping," she continued. "That they cause larger and more dangerous energy releases. I guess once the energy inside a Disparate builds past what the medicine can suppress, it gets worse."

Asher sat quiet for a moment. "They're right. The pills are dangerous. They need to be stopped."

Jemma came to a red light. "But there are so many people they *do* help," she said slowly. She was still convinced they helped Ben. He'd only ever spoken positively about them.

"Any help is outweighed by the side effects. Look, Jemma, I was used as a test subject on the island." He paused for a moment, his face darkening as he seemed to debate how much to tell her. "I saw firsthand what the new medicine can do to people. Enertin seemed to work well, at the beginning. Each new dosage seemed to give more and more control... until it didn't." Asher's head fell.

"Because it doesn't fully take away a Disparate's energy, right?" This was sounding exactly as Buran had explained. The drug appeared safer. More effective. But it wasn't.

"Exactly," Asher confirmed. "The energy is still there. Growing. Brewing. Waiting for the person's breaking point."

A car horn blared. Jemma jumped. She hadn't noticed the light turned green. She stepped on her gas and took a deep breath.

"People need to know about this, Asher. Are you ready to speak?"

In her peripheral vision, Jemma noticed the corner of Asher's mouth lift. "More than ready," he said.

"Alright." Jemma turned at the next street and headed to where Buran would be waiting.

"How did you know I was craving Indian food?" Asher laughed as she parked next to Buran's truck. The words "Blazing Biryani" flashed on a neon sign. She caught a glimpse of Aniyah's dark hair entering through the back. The group had planned to gather after her meeting, whether Asher was there or not.

"Listen. If at any moment you decide this is too much for you, let me know," Jemma said as she turned the ignition off. A sense of protection for her older brother burned in her heart. "I don't want you to feel forced into anything." She also didn't want to spook him.

"No worries, Jem Jam. I can handle more than you know." The deep lines on his face were a testament to that.

The back door opened wide as Jemma and Asher entered. The smell of turmeric and ginger caused her stomach to growl.

"Come and sit. Your tikka masala's getting cold." Samay placed two bowls full of meat onto the small table. A plate of naan rested in the middle. "A full belly makes for better plotting."

Asher didn't seem fazed by Samay's curtness and lack of greeting. The food likely helped with that. He immediately took the open seat next to Aniyah, nodding at her as he took a piece of naan and scooped up some of the well-sauced meat.

"You sure know how to make an impression," he said with a full mouth. "Not gonna lie, I haven't eaten all day."

"I'm glad to hear you don't plan on lying." Buran sat across the table.

Asher paused as he lifted another bite to his mouth. "You're Buran, right? Glad to see you're sitting down already. For your own safety."

Jemma suppressed a laugh, remembering the way Buran had tripped during their first meeting.

Buran didn't look as amused, his strong jaw clenched.

"Like we would even know if he was telling the truth." Aniyah watched Asher with narrow eyes. She was the most skeptical of the group.

"You're right to be wary," Asher said, licking sauce from his lips. "Everyone should be."

"Where's Calum?" Jemma asked as she looked around.

"Finishing the night clean at the Capital," Buran said. "He'll stop by after. Asher, we're glad you joined us."

Asher nodded. His whole demeanor was opposite of what it was last night. Instead of guarded and defensive, he looked almost eager.

Maybe Aniyah was right in questioning his motives.

"Sorry about last night," Asher started. "I wasn't too sure who I could trust. After talking with Jemma, it seems we could work together."

Buran smiled. "I'm hoping we can."

"You escaped off the island?" Samay asked. Instead of sitting at the table with everyone else, he leaned against the kitchen wall.

"Jumpin' right into it, I see." Asher swallowed a bite then wiped his hands on the side of the chair. "I did. It wasn't easy."

"How do we do it?" Jemma spoke up. She was grateful to have her brother back and even more grateful that he was going to help them.

"Well…" Asher pursed his lips. "Not sure if it could be done again. Not without being caught—or rather, killed."

With each word, Jemma's heart sank more. This wasn't the response she'd expected. "There has to be a way."

Asher shrugged. "I don't think there is."

"You did it. You're proof it's possible." A shiver ran across her arms, the hair rising. She fought the feeling of betrayal.

"I was in very different circumstances." Asher leaned forward. "I almost didn't make it off."

"Yet, here you are," Jemma countered. She needed him to agree.

"Not without help," he said.

"You have help right here." Jemma motioned around the room, which was silently watching this exchange between siblings. "Ben needs *our* help."

"You don't get it." His eyes darkened. "I wasn't the only one that should have made it off."

The room was heavy. Jemma had no response. She'd let her fear of losing her husband replace her fear of losing her brother. She'd almost forgotten the risks Asher had taken to be here now.

The silence in the room was interrupted by the sound of the door sliding open.

"Should I come back later?" Calum asked as he glanced at the faces around the room.

Buran cleared his throat. "You came just in time. Asher, I'd like to introduce you to Calum. He has a brother on the island."

Asher's face softened as his gaze fell on the college boy who'd entered.

"You're actually helping us." Calum smiled, his voice eager. "Guess I owe you an apology for startling you in the woods."

"What?" Jemma and Asher spoke at the same time.

"I didn't mean to scare you," Calum continued. He turned to Jemma. "When I heard you were meeting with him one-on-one, I couldn't stop thinking about it. How going by yourself was kind of dangerous. But also, he may have known Chayse. So I followed you."

"You did what?" Buran's mouth fell open. Jemma matched his surprise. She'd learned Calum was impulsive, but that... that was risky.

Calum continued, "I think my flashlight might've startled you. Before I knew it, you were taking off."

"What's his number?" Asher asked.

Calum's face wrinkled. "Number? What do you mean? Like for his phone?"

"No," Asher said. "They number us like cattle. What did he look like?"

"Uh... it's hard to say. I haven't seen him in two years. He's only seventeen, dark hair like me but with a white streak. He shouldn't be there in the first place... it was an accident. He didn't mean to burn our dad's arm. He was just so angry about him abandoning us. It's not like Chayse had any choice in developing flame energy. But the fact that he did scared our parents away. I refused to go with them."

Two years. That meant that Calum's brother was sent away when he was only fifteen years old. The same age Asher was when he was taken.

Asher nodded. "I think I might've seen him around."

Another insight into the treatment of Disparates on the island. Jemma sank in her chair, her heart grieved for her brother while worry for her husband dug in its claws.

"I knew it!" Calum exclaimed, his countenance changed from depressed to excited. "You were there. You did escape!" Calum glanced around the room. "Did I miss how we're gonna save Ben? I know he's our main target, but maybe we'll have a chance to grab Chayse as we—"

"He can't help us," Samay said.

"Oh..." Calum's shoulders fell. "Is that what I interrupted?"

Jemma nodded. She understood his disappointment. His distress. "I don't think we should give up on it. Asher, you said you were ready to come here. I thought that meant you were ready to help." She held her breath, holding onto the hope that he was still the loyal brother he'd been as children.

Asher sighed. "I'm not able to lead a suicide mission to an island I was locked up on for over a decade and a half, but I may still be of help. I mean"—he turned to face Buran—"depending on what your true goal is."

Buran rubbed the bottom of his chin. "What are you implying?"

"We both know you aren't wanting to save Ben for the sake of doing a good deed," Asher said.

Jemma balled her hands into fists. *What was Asher doing?*

Buran stuttered, "Well... uh... we do want to—"

Samay cleared his throat. "You're right. Our goal is to create safety for everyone to live their lives. Including Disparates."

"That's good." Asher smirked. "There's a reason why I escaped Lucky Island. There's a plan I have to stop."

A plan that didn't involve saving Ben. All coming from her "loyal brother." The loyal brother that ran away before he got caught.

The loyal brother that was quick to point the finger at someone else.

The loyal brother that stole her breakfast on her most important day of the year.

The film her brain had placed over her view of Asher when he disappeared started to peel. She'd glorified those memories.

But the person that sat next to her did not match that image.

"You have information?" Aniyah's eyes widened.

"What plan?" Buran perked in his seat. This was exactly what he'd been after. Information. If Asher could provide it, he, too, would have no need to save Ben.

Calum, who had joined the rest at the table, kept his gaze on Jemma. Could he see the storm that was raging in her head?

"Initiative 67," Asher shared, "is more dangerous than the others in the past. The government wants to push a new form of Enertin. One that doesn't keep energy under control..."

Always the one for flair, Jemma thought.

"Go on." Samay stood straight.

"It takes energy powers away."

"Why is that a problem?" Jemma's voice was sharp. A buzzing crinkled in her mind.

Calum placed a hand on her arm. Static immediately made him move it off.

At that moment, Asher made eye contact with her.

"Not everyone survives it." His green pupils were filled with pain, the death of a forest seen within their depths. However, a hint of brighter, newer growth lined the edges.

Jemma's mind quieted.

She was being unfair.

It wasn't selfishness that kept Asher from being loyal. It was understanding. He knew how harsh the world was. He lived it. And he was going to stop it.

"They call it EnertinX and plan on rolling it out to the masses in a few weeks," Asher said. "A half a dozen shots in the arm and all your problems go away. Sounds like the perfect drug. They did it. They cure Disparates and kill half of them in the process."

"Half?" Aniyah questioned. "Surely with such a high rate of failure it wouldn't be approved."

Buran laughed. "That's the thing with this government. The Disparates are the enemy. If they have to kill them to protect everyone else, so be it."

Governor Dunn popped into Jemma's head once more. The new treatment would have to go through him. Certainly he wouldn't approve of it. Although, he had already been promoting Initiative 67.

Each of her fellow rebels nodded, Ben long forgotten.

"What about my husband?" All eyes turned to her.

Buran spoke. "I promised you we would rescue Ben. I don't intend to go back on that promise. But this..." He shook his head. "This is worse than I thought. I understand if this is too much for you."

The new threat took precedent, and as much as she didn't want to agree, she did. Her husband and children were *her* world but they weren't to the people around her. For all she knew, Ben might already be gone.

No. She didn't want to think that way.

But if they didn't stop EnertinX, there was a strong likelihood he'd be forced to be injected. Him. And Louie. And according to the odds, only one was likely to survive it.

Her stomach tightened. "How do we stop it?"

"I found something at the Public Safety Building." Asher pulled a folded sheet of paper out of his pocket. "A letter, written by the Governor himself and addressed to the widow of Governor Stillfield." He was talking about their mother like she was a stranger. "If we can find a way to expose the information here that would be taken seriously, it might cause enough public dismay to shake things up."

"Is this what you were looking for in all the break ins?" Jemma asked.

"I was looking for anything I could use to expose corruption," Asher explained. "Figured I'd start with the less secure government buildings first. Besides, catching things on fire is kinda fun." He smirked.

Buran reached for the letter, his face brightening with each word he read. "Aniyah, you're still interning at Stillfield News, correct?"

She smirked. "Absolutely I am."

SEVENTEEN

Twenty-four hours. It'd been twenty-four hours since the fire was reported.

"Calm down, Maggie." Tobias placed a hand on her bouncing knee. "I'm sure they'll be done soon."

"I don't understand what is taking so long."

"Well, considering the back wall is only posts, the structural engineers are doing their due diligence. Have some patience. They've been extra busy lately with the increase in fires."

Margaret's chest tightened. A flier blew in front of where they stood. Margaret caught sight of something handwritten across it.

She rushed a few feet forward and snatched it before the wind continued its journey. It was partially burnt, the words "Embrace your emotions. Dispar—" the last readable bits.

"What about this group?" she said, walking to Tobias.

Tobias eyed the poster. "Dissentients. They believe the pills are dangerous and have been trying to get me to stop production for the past couple years. Obviously, that's not something that happens quickly."

"They're the reason we've started investigating the deaths of Disparates, correct?" Margaret would never forget the wary look on Tobias's face as he received letter after letter from this anonymous group. Margaret had insisted then they start researching their claims. So far, they'd been proving true, but they were just getting started. "Do you think they could be involved?"

"I wouldn't put it past them. Their letters are always... strongly worded. Only a matter of time before they began to take more drastic measures to get their point across."

Which, if they were the ones who broke into her office... if they found what she desperately hoped they didn't... she and Tobias could be in danger. If word got out they were conducting their own investigation behind the backs of the other Republics, that would be cause for direct removal and rehabilitation time... the nice "new world" way to say prison.

"I need to get into my office." She lowered her voice as a firefighter walked past. "I need to check our files."

Tobias's knowing eyes met hers. "You kept everything well hidden, correct?"

"I think so. With the amount of paperwork I sift through, surely no one would be able to find the right folder. Like a needle in a haystack."

"Except it wasn't, was it?" Tobias asked. "You have a system for everything."

His statement rang true. After years of allowing her life to go into disarray, she thrived off order. The more she controlled, the better.

"No one knows this system," she reassured him. Although the sinking pit in her stomach cast its doubt. Someone close to her may have figured it out. Was Ben truly the anarchist? Had he revealed information about her before he was taken away? Something about that still didn't make sense. Ben wasn't one to put others at risk.

Margaret shook the thought from her mind. This wasn't the time to be entertaining conspiracies. Not until she had more evidence.

"All clear," a firefighter said as he approached. "Just avoid the back half that's missing. If you want to clear valuables from what's left of your office, you are welcome to do so."

Margaret needed to hear no more. She entered through the front of the Public Safety Building. Instead of the glass doors sliding open, they were left ajar. The electricity no longer worked. Light from open windows guided her to the offices.

The view of the back of the building was strange. As if she'd walked into the wrong place, yet reminders that this was her office were still there. The sign on the staff door laid on the ground, the words *Notice: Staff* still visible, but the *Only* black and burnt. The plastic bobblehead from the office next door was melted on the ground. Everything was covered in a layer of ash.

Margaret fought the urge to liken the destruction in front of her to the home she lost many years ago. Yet, this was not the same. This fire was put out. No one was killed.

She pulled her gaze away and focused on her office door. Crunching from under her foot distracted her. Glass from the light fixture above. She examined one of the shards. Instead of being consumed in black smut, only the edges were scorched. This wasn't done by fire.

She stepped over the glass and rushed to her filing cabinets. The urgency she'd been holding at bay consumed her as she flipped through the files in the top drawer. One... two... three... four for April. The fourth folder from the back. The month she fell in love with Skylar Stillfield.

She pulled out the entirety of the yellow folder and took it to her desk. Dried water drops the sprinklers had left behind were hidden by papers as Margaret sprawled out the stack, searching for the coded envelope.

It wasn't there.

Margaret shouted as her head crashed into her palms. The papers were missing. She hadn't realized Tobias had followed her until his hand rested on her shoulder.

"We'll figure this out," he said. "We can't jump to conclusions. We don't know who found it."

"You don't understand." Margaret lifted her face to his. "Only some-one close to me could've found it."

Tobias's face paled.

"We have barbecue chips at home," Jemma snapped at Mackie as she grabbed hold of the bag he'd removed from the shelf. They were running low on food, and her boys needed to eat. However, her patience was at an all time low. Crying and energy releases took a lot out of her. The impending news segment did not help.

Neither did the fact her brother refused to rescue Ben. Instead of bringing her a step closer to being reunited with her love, he hurt it. She understood why, but that didn't heal the sting.

Mackie pulled at the bag. The air inside puffed, threatening to es-cape. Jemma let go as a woman passed by, an amused grin under her freckled cheeks.

"I love chips!" Mackie exclaimed. He threw the bag into the cart. It crunched as it landed on top of juice bottles and the bag of purple balloons he insisted on buying for his birthday, even though it was a few weeks away.

Jemma glanced at the front of the cart, expecting to see Louie standing there. But he wasn't. Her breathing quickened as her eyes darted down the aisle.

There, toward the end, was Louie. Still walking. He didn't seem to notice, nor care, that his family had stopped.

He was too far away. What if someone grabbed him? What if something angered him?

"Louie!" Jemma shouted. He turned to the side, but before he finished his rotation, he stopped. Something on the shelf had caught his attention. His eyes widened as a slow gasp inflated his lungs. Jemma wanted to yell at him again, but she saw the gleam of joy beam off his face. This was the first time he'd smiled all week.

The realization hit her, distracting her from the incident that was unfolding. As if in slow motion, her brain processed every sight and sound. Popping chip bags mimicked the end of a firework show. Waves of crispy potatoes flew into the sky, hovering like a swarm of bees waiting to attack their prey.

A Disparate was in the store, having an outburst.

And she was alone with her boys. One of which was yards away.

Jemma swept Mackie into her arms as she sprinted to Louie. Feeling as though she was being dragged by a quarterback, she pushed through the hive of grease in the air. Crumbs found a new home within her hair, but her eyes were set on protecting her boys.

The freckled woman who'd passed by a few minutes before matched Louie's wide-eyed stare, though her palpable fear contrasted with the joyfulness underlying his expression.

Fear of him.

The boy with a smile across his face.

The Disparate.

The threat.

Why would she be staring at him as if he were the one causing this display of power? Unless… Jemma didn't have time to process the information her brain was receiving. The clues that floated around her head. Once she reached Louie, she sat Mackie on the ground.

Her arms wrapped around Louie's small body, pulling him into a hug. His breath released and with it a shower of potato chips, covering the entire aisle—and the people nearby—in a thick layer of crumbs.

Her mind raced. Floating. The chips had been floating.

"Mom, can I have it? Please?" Louie pointed at the shelf. On it sat a stuffed Dalmatian dog, a character from his favorite TV show, standing atop a giant red fire engine.

The source of his excitement. His joy. His energy.

Louie looked at Jemma expectantly, oblivious to the clean-up in aisle seven waiting behind him. Jemma hugged him tighter as she felt his little body pulsing, as if it, too, would float to the ceiling if she were to let go.

She couldn't deny it. Louie had used air energy. Thoughts of what that meant swirled in her mind. Louie had flame energy. But he'd used air. How was that possible? Disparates only had one.

A crowd started to form, curious to see what the commotion was. A pair of workers pushed a trash can toward the mess as if this were an everyday occurrence. Just part of the job.

Mackie stood next to them, snacking on barbecue chips that had fallen on him as he wiped orange dust off his clothes. His face gave an air of indifference—this was part of being Louie's brother. Jemma wondered if he already knew about his brother's second ability. The laundry soap on the top shelf popped into her mind. The clues had been there.

Guilt in Jemma's eyes stung as she looked again at her eldest son. Not only did he have flame energy, but air as well. Whether he was happy or mad, he'd have to be careful.

She regretted she couldn't shield him from the consequences of his emotions. But at this very moment, she could. And hopefully before any Responders arrived.

She grabbed the Dalmatian dog and handed it to Louie. The last thing they needed was a meltdown. People in the crowd whispered as the three of them walked toward the self-checkout, the sound of crunching heard with each step.

"I've never seen anything like this before. Only on TV."

"This is why they lowered the age for Enertin. Irresponsible not to have him medicated."

"Kids like that should be left at home, not brought out in public."

"Has anyone called the Responders? Are they on their way?"

Jemma held the tears in and stood confidently as she scanned Louie's prize. Chip crumbs fell around them with each movement. She scanned the half empty bag Mackie had somehow held on to. She didn't have enough ration credits to pay for the hundreds of bags Louie ruined, but she could pay for this one.

Jemma quickly left with their few items. She no longer cared about the rest of her shopping. They needed to get home.

"Wait!" a woman's voice shouted to her in the parking lot.

So close. Jemma turned around and saw the woman from the chip aisle coming toward her, grocery bags swinging in her hands. *Is she going to yell at us? Call my child a freak? Say he needs to be sent away?* Jemma's body tensed as the woman approached. Instead of yelling, a soft smile appeared on the stranger's freckled face.

"Don't worry about what happened back there; raising kids is tough, even when they don't have such strong emotions." The stranger spoke in a kind voice. "You're doing a great job. Plus, they have insurance for incidents like this." She reached into one of her grocery bags and pulled out a bouquet of carnations, shades of yellow and purple mixed together into a beautiful dome. She handed them to Jemma and walked in the opposite direction to her car.

The threatening tears finally fell as the woman walked away. There was conflict and confusion in this world, but there was also good. This woman was proof of that.

And Jemma was going to join her. Be a part of the good.

She hoped the world would listen.

EIGHTEEN

B en stirred awake. His vision squinted against the white walls and bright lights as he regained consciousness bit by bit. Heaviness hung over his body, limp on the thin hospital bed. He wanted to fall back asleep.

A strong chemical smell increased his awareness. He wasn't alone. Two blue coats wearing medical masks surrounded him, busy blurs going about their respective tasks.

One stood next to a large machine, typing on a computer. Try as he might, Ben's eyes wouldn't focus on the screen to see what was being inputted. The man in the blue coat moved to a desk, checked files, and then continued typing away.

The other, a woman, held a syringe filled with a blue substance and fitted with a needle. She took a seat next to Ben. "Do you think she'll notice if we take an extra break today?"

Her question confused Ben—but she hadn't been talking to him.

"She's off the island; how would she know?" the other blue coat said, his voice deep but muffled through the mask.

"That's a good point. But you know she has her ways to find out."

"Like that sister of hers back in the lab? Always knowing what's in my mind?"

They both laughed at some inside joke. Ben wasn't sure what was going on, but he knew he couldn't let that liquid enter his body.

The syringe lowered toward his arm. No, it lowered toward an IV port that was already inserted into his veins.

He pulled away but was met with resistance. His arms and legs were restrained. He tried to see his bindings as he fought against their grip. Blinding pain erupted from his shoulder, reminding him of the bullet Markus had shot.

"We've got a live one." The female moved the needle away. "Quick, get the mask on him."

"Wa…" Ben tried to speak, but his voice wouldn't work. The drugs they had used on him still had some effect. "Sto…" he pleaded as the man placed a clear mask over his mouth and nose. Vapor rose through the gaps.

He struggled harder against the restraints, resisting breathing, which he couldn't do for long.

The mist slithered into his airways, gliding through his muscles as each relaxed. His mind became flat as haze enveloped his every thought.

Maybe his flame energy would help, but as much as he tried to change his fear to anger, it didn't work.

His heartbeat slowed as the blue coat smiled at him. "There, that seems to have done the trick."

She lifted the syringe once more, tapping it twice before lowering it to the IV port. "This is going to help you. Trust me. You'll want to get all of it."

Ben watched, helpless. The blue solution seeped through the IV and into his body as the woman flushed the line with saline.

The liquid was ice cold as it entered his veins. It spread to his torso. Ben screamed, his body writhing as his chest condensed. Caving in on itself as if it were shrinking, no—freezing.

The glacial cold moved north. Ben's neck turned to ice. His scream froze in place. Crystals formed across his lashes.

He wanted to fight. He needed warmth. He needed his heat. His fire. But there was nothing he could do. The pain was sharp as his brain was consumed by this winter. His head throbbed as it froze, encapsulated in ice. Even his ability to think was dwindling.

"That was your last dose, Benjamin," the female blue coat said as his vision blacked out. "I promise this pain will be worth it once you're no longer a Disparate."

Fire. Air. Fire. Air. Thoughts stormed through Jemma's mind as she walked the boys to preschool.

"Good morning," Caty greeted as she opened the front door. Mackie and Louie headed inside, needing no further promptings. They'd adjusted well to their new routine.

Caty's brows lowered as she looked at Jemma. "How are you doing today? Have you heard any news about Ben? I still don't believe he's the Fire Anarchist."

Jemma wanted to say more. To confide in someone who wasn't involved in the mess her life had become.

Caty was her best friend. They'd known each other since Ninth Year. Had gone away to college in Wuslick together. If there was anyone she could trust, it was her.

"I'm not sure when Ben is coming back."

Caty's mouth widened. "I can't believe it," Caty said. "I thought for sure they'd have him cleared by now. There's no way he'd do something like that... right? Like, why would they keep him away from his family if he weren't truly the anarchist?"

Jemma paused. Of course Caty would start to question if Ben were innocent. It was hard to believe he'd be falsely accused. "The government has their reasons."

"What do you mean?" Caty's face was a mixture of worry and confusion. A scream from inside the house reminded the pair that children were waiting.

"I'll explain more later," Jemma said as she glanced in the front room Caty had converted into a classroom. Her chest raced as she looked for the disturbance. A little girl was crying next to Lily, who was holding a baby doll. Jemma took a breath of relief. Louie was on the floor, happily playing with cars.

"Okay," Caty agreed. "But I expect a full explanation." She placed her hand on Jemma's arm, keeping her from leaving. A small shock jolted at the touch, but Caty didn't pull away. "If you need any help with the boys, let me know. I'm happy to watch them anytime."

The gesture warmed Jemma's raging heart. "Having a safe place for them to be right now means the world. Thank you." Her thoughts from earlier spattered into her mind. "And keep an eye on Louie. His energies seem to be growing."

"Energies?" Caty questioned. "His fire?"

Jemma nodded. If Caty was watching him, it was important she knew. "And air."

Caty's eyebrows shot skyward. She turned to look at Louie. "Wow," she said, as if in awe. "Two energies? I've never heard of that happening. I'll watch him, don't worry."

As Jemma sat in the driver's seat of her car, she calmed her breathing. Her boys were safe in Caty's watch, and she had an important mission to attend to. The special quarterly news would air live in under an hour, and she would be there. Sitting opposite of someone who may be able to help them.

And, in turn, help Ben.

Jemma arrived at the news station, her nerves on high alert. She focused her attention on three things within her vision, the way she'd practiced previously with Buran.

Green stitching on her sweater caught her eye first. A strand was loose. She tucked it between stitches as she opened the car door. The white back of the building contrasted with the dark door. Aniyah's head popped out from behind it, ushering her inside.

Electricity tingled at her fingertips. Jemma counted the squealing door as the first sound she heard. She focused on finding two others.

The studio was near a busy street. The sound of wheels rolling across asphalt created background noise she wouldn't have noticed without intent. Behind her, two birds chirped. She imagined they were bickering rivals, fighting over the worm they'd spotted at the same time.

Lastly, it was time for movement. Jemma headed toward Aniyah, each footstep heavy on the asphalt. She wiggled her fingers, stretching them out as she walked. As she approached the door, she rolled her shoulders, imagining her fears and worries flowing out of her body with the movement.

I am safe and in control, she affirmed. *I can be here now, in this moment. I can handle this.* She took a deep breath, feeling the electricity calm inside her veins as she inhaled peace and exhaled her worries.

"Are you okay?" Aniyah asked once they were inside the studio. Aniyah's dark brows slanted together as she examined her.

Jemma took another deep breath in and exhaled. "Yes, I've got this," she said with confidence. Aniyah's face relaxed.

The back door opened into a wide hallway. Old lights and boxes were stacked along the walls.

"You said you know how to talk to Disparates," Aniyah said, stopping at a door labeled *Guest Dressing Room E.* "I hope that applies to non-Disparates as well."

"Of course." Jemma nodded. The discussion techniques she learned as an Analyst should apply to any conversation. She swallowed as the door swung open.

Buran was inside, sitting in an old folding director's chair. A dark screen hung in front of him, and a standing microphone was nearby. He was ready for his part of this. He glanced up from his twiddling thumbs to greet them. "You look great Jemma! A star if I've ever seen one."

She certainly didn't feel like one, but Buran's confidence gave rise to her own. She would follow through on her end of the bargain. Keep whoever was coming to promote the new drugs talking. Long enough for the Dissentients to hack into the broadcast and cast Buran on the screen to inform the Republics of their plan. Try to convince more Disparates to trust in themselves.

Embrace their emotions.

"You two wait here," Aniyah said. "I'll come get you when it's time for the segment." She turned to Jemma. "Do you have your question cards?"

Jemma reached in her pocket and felt the folded paper and small note cards stored there. Her lifelines for when she sat on stage. She nodded.

"Good," Aniyah said. "The teleprompter will keep the conversation short, as this announcement is only scheduled to last a few minutes. It'll take at least ten minutes to get everything connected to the feed, and that's assuming everything goes to plan."

"Last I heard," Buran started, "Calum and Samay were ready. Asher's waiting outside, in case we need back up. Don't want him anywhere close to keep him from being seen. But if things do get hot, it'll be good to have him around."

Jemma pursed her lips. She focused her eyes on the carpet at her feet to keep from thinking of the repercussions of what they were about to do. Silver and gray stripes. Reminders that not everything was black and white.

"Hey," Buran said, directing her attention to him, "I really think we can pull this off."

Jemma nodded and lowered into the chair next to Buran as Aniyah left the room. She took deep breaths to keep her nerves calm.

"Are you sure you're ready for this?" Buran asked. "You only learned about your energy a week ago."

A week ago yesterday, she thought. That was how long Ben had been gone. And she wasn't sure how many more weeks she'd be without him. "I'm ready," she said.

"And remember, stick to the prompts on those cards. No one will suspect you're with us *and* you'll be able to buy us enough time."

Jemma placed a hand over her pocket. These questions would keep the cameras rolling. "I'll make you proud."

"That's the spirit!" Buran grabbed a two-way radio off the vanity desk behind them. "The emerald is in the house," he spoke into it.

"Emerald?"

"Wouldn't want to use your name in case they've been caught. I thought emerald was quite fitting considering your name means 'precious gem.'"

"Smart," Jemma said.

"Thanks again for volunteering to do this." Buran shook out his hands. Clearly the nerves were getting to him. "Now, I just hope this thing works." He tapped on the special voice changing microphone. It was time for the Dissentients to make themselves seen. Hacking into the broadcast was the way to do that.

Now that she was alone with him, her thoughts went to Louie. There was something she wanted to ask. "Have you had time to learn anything more about..."

Buran shrugged. "Not much. My source wasn't very forthcoming. Said he hadn't heard of someone having two energies, but I'm not sure we can fully trust him."

So Louie may be one of, if not *the* first, to show such power. The thought of what that meant brought unease to her stomach.

"I'll let you know if I hear anything more," Buran continued. Worry flowed from his eyes as he met her gaze. "But one energy or two doesn't matter. He'll learn to manage both emotions and, in turn, manage his power."

"Thank you," she said. She wasn't feeling as sure, but she needed to return her attention to the task at hand.

She pulled the folded paper from her pocket. She had insisted on having the letter. She needed to read it for herself, looking for some other meaning in the words. For what was likely the hundredth time, she read it again:

Dearest Maggie,

You were right. We can't let this get out.

The drugs aren't safe. I don't believe Enertin is becoming more effective, but quite the opposite.

We need to keep this secret.

Something feels strange when I'm around her.

Yours,
T.D.

Jemma couldn't wrap her mind around how her own mother was working to hide that the medicine was dangerous. This plan needed to work. The citizens of Stillfield needed to listen.

Unlike her mother—she believed they had a right to know.

Nineteen

Fifteen minutes later, Aniyah returned and waved for Jemma to follow.

"I'll be waiting for my turn. You sure this screen will silhouette me?" Aniyah nodded.

"You've got this Emerald." He gave her a thumbs up as she left the room.

"Dr. Paxton is on stage," Aniyah said. They walked farther down the hallway from earlier, crowded with television equipment and people busily darting from point A to point B. "I told the crew you were a guest anchor from Wuslick. They didn't question it. No one questions Wuslick."

"Dr. Paxton." Jemma repeated the name to herself. One of the doctor's from Merrytime Clinic, here to give the quarterly update. As expected. Everything was already going smoothly.

They stopped on the edge of the stage. Past Aniyah's shoulder, Jemma saw Dr. Paxton, sitting in an armchair in the middle of the stage. Something about her reminded Jemma of her high school principal, Ms. Hays. Perhaps it was the way her shoulder length blond hair fell across her face, highlighting her sharp nose as she adjusted the sleeves of her blue blazer over her wrists.

"Now's your moment. Wait for my cue when we'll switch the feed to Buran. You've got this." Aniyah patted Jemma's back and nudged her forward. Jemma fixed the hem of her own sweater as she trod onto the stage toward the seat opposite Dr. Paxton.

As Jemma approached, the doctor stood and smiled. Jemma's head spun, worried the woman in front of her would see right through her act. She was educated. Seemed to truly care about the Disparates in her care. If anyone would listen to the truth that Lucky Island was still in operation and be able to change that, Jemma hoped it would be her.

But that wasn't what they were exposing right now. Their focus was on Enertin. Making sure the world knew first that it was becoming more and more dangerous. And that there was something they could do about it—learn to control their emotions themselves without the help of Enertin.

Exposing Lucky Island would come next.

"Hello, I'm Dr. Elizabeth Paxton. And you are?" The doctor stretched out her hand.

Jemma breathed in through her nose, calming herself as she accepted the handshake. She released her breath as their hands connected without a shock. "I'm... Jennifer, from Wuslick. It's nice to meet you. I'm looking forward to our conversation today."

Dr. Paxton didn't seem to catch her hesitation as she lowered herself into her seat. Jemma followed her example and sat in her own chair.

A man with a headset shouted for everyone to take their places. Lights dimmed around the studio, except for center stage. The camera operator turned the lens to focus on his targets. A computer screen underneath lit up with words of welcome.

Very quickly, everything became real to Jemma. She stared at the screen as she processed what she was about to do. If she was successful, she would be one step closer to getting Ben back.

If she failed—it would be a giant leap backward.

A cough somewhere behind the camera reminded Jemma that it was her time to lead. She smiled directly at the camera as she read the words on the screen.

"Hello, and welcome to our special segment tonight. I'm Jennifer…" Jemma paused. It felt wrong to lie, but necessary. "Hays. A guest interviewer here for tonight's quarterly update. I'll be talking with Dr. Elizabeth Paxton about the new rollout of Initiative 67. What differences have been seen, and what the next steps are." Jemma turned toward her guest. "Dr. Paxton, thank you for being here with us."

"Thank you for having me. I'm happy to talk about the new initiative. As head of Merrytime Clinic, I've been able to see firsthand the good that lowering the age for treatment has done for our community. Over the past couple weeks, the average age of energy emergence has lowered from twelve to six. The Clinic has been able to send its young patients home to their parents quicker than ever."

This news surprised Jemma. Dr. Paxton wasn't someone random who worked at Merrytime Clinic as Aniyah described; she was in charge of it all. This wasn't what they expected. Why would the head of the clinic be here tonight? She never gave public appearances—too busy for that.

But it sounded like she actually cared about the Disparates in her clinic. Perhaps she would be able to see their side.

Although, if she was seeing success treating Disparates with Enertin, she may be difficult to convince.

Across from Jemma, Aniyah pressed her ear, or rather the hidden earphone that let her communicate with the rest of the group. Her brows furrowed in distress. Jemma needed to buy them some more time.

She thought about the notecards in her pocket, but she knew she didn't need them. She had some questions of her own. Perhaps ones that would better set up what the Dissentients were wanting to do.

She'd have to be careful to keep herself safe. But she had questions she needed to know the answers to.

"I'm glad they were able to go home," Jemma responded truthfully. "Now to get every Disparate home. That's the goal, correct?" This also wasn't on the teleprompter, which increased Jemma's nerves. In the darkness behind the cameras, a throat cleared. The words on the screen flashed.

"That would be the greatest hope. However, it is important to make sure that each Disparate is in their right state of mind and no longer a threat to the rest of society. The first concern of Stillfield's leaders is safety."

Jemma nodded. "Are you aware that the current medication can fail when a Disparate's brain makes more energy than the pill can suppress? Often resulting in traumatic outbursts that do more damage than if they never took the pill?" The sound on set was silent. This question was bold, but she was playing the part of an investigative journalist. Might as well embrace it. Any bit of doubt she could place in the minds of viewers before Buran took over the broadcast the better. And if she played her cards right, perhaps she could do more to get Ben home than the Dissentients wanted her to.

Dr. Paxton's smile softened into a small grimace. "I'm afraid the data we've compiled shows those outbursts occur when the medication is not being taken as prescribed. Some Disparates forget or even choose to not take their pill. There have indeed been some disastrous incidents that have occurred, and with each one, you feel the heart of the world break. That is why Initiative 67 is so important. This new medicine plan was put in place to address the increasing threat energy outbursts have become as more and more citizens are affected by this disease."

Disease.

Jemma never thought of Disparates being diseased. She thought about Ben, about Louie, about Buran and the Dissentients, about herself. She cleared her throat and focused on the now.

Of course Dr. Paxton wasn't willing to believe the treatment her job revolved around was flawed. Changing a person's mind was never easy.

Jemma smiled, unfazed. "It's not happening because Disparates are misusing or forgetting their medication. It is caused by the medication itself. Increasing the dose will only increase the strength of the future disaster, causing larger sinkholes, more severe lightning storms, wilder fires, extreme blizzards, and floating to higher heights. I don't believe the administration is being forthcoming with their data. Instead, they're choosing to bury the truth. Their plan is more harmful than good."

On the teleprompter, the word *Ready* appeared. Dr. Paxton rubbed the side of her face with her hand, one finger pointing out from the rest.

"I understand," Jemma continued, "the immediate effects look promising. But if we continue down this road, life as we know it will become more dangerous."

Jemma waited, hoping the men were successful in their part of the plan. Waiting for Buran's silhouette to shine through with truth. The silence was deafening when no gasps or reactions came from anywhere in the studio.

The message from Calum disappeared from the teleprompter. To the side of the camera, Jemma barely made out Aniyah's figure. She shook her head, her face downcast. The men hadn't been able to project their truth.

Jemma was on her own, but she wasn't giving up hope.

"I'd like to show you proof in a communication current Governor Dunn recently wrote referring to his concerns about Enertin." Jemma knew she needed to do something more. She'd already taken a risk in breaching the subject of Enertin, now time to follow through.

Dr. Paxton's face was smooth. Without the evidence, any claims Jemma made would be written off as lies and conspiracies.

"Well," Dr. Paxton responded, "I would very much like to see that communication."

Jemma retrieved the letter from her pocket, her hands shaking. She needed to read it out loud. If they weren't able to take over the broadcast, at least she could share this with the world. As she unfolded the page, the doctor reached over and snatched it out of Jemma's hands.

No... Jemma lifted her hand slightly, then thought better of it. Assaulting the director of Merrytime Clinic would for sure be too risky of a move. Responders would be on her faster than a fly on moldy toast. Jemma took a breath to steady her emotions.

The doctor's eyes narrowed as she read the letter. Perhaps she would agree the world needed to hear it as well. Then, she folded it and put it in her own pocket. Guess not.

"If what I read in this letter is true, I will make it my top priority to verify and remedy," Dr. Paxton said. "I truly do not wish for any harm to come upon my patients or anyone around them. I want them to live happy and healthy lives. I thank you for bringing these concerns to my attention."

The doctor didn't look particularly concerned. Jemma immediately regretted letting her grab it. Now there was no proof to show the Republics. Not unless Jemma jumped across the space between her and Dr. Paxton and pulled the letter from her jacket.

The cameras certainly would be turned off at that point. It was already nearing the end of the segment as the lights dimmed. Dr. Paxton raised one finger into the air. The lights obliged, brightening once more.

"Before we leave for the night, I have a question for you." Dr. Paxton glared at Jemma. "Is it true your husband is a Disparate currently under treatment?"

Jemma stiffened. How did she know who her husband was? "Yes," she said slowly. Perhaps it wasn't too late to draw the public's suspicions in another way. "My husband was supposed to be receiving care at Merrytime Clinic. However, he was lied to and taken to Lucky Island." Jemma tried to keep the anger out of her voice.

Dr. Paxton clutched her chest. "Lucky Island? That is quite the accusation. It's been decommissioned for over two decades. What led you to believe he was being treated there?"

Heat rose to her cheeks. Jemma had as much evidence that Ben was there as Dr. Paxton had belief in her. The lights in the room flickered with her confidence. Jemma regretted mentioning the island.

Dr. Paxton's face softened at her silence. "I know it's hard when a loved one needs to go away for treatment. I promise you, he is under the best care, and we are working on getting him home as quickly as it is safe to do. It is for the good of the person, as well as those around them, that uncontrollable Disparates receive treatment at an isolated facility. We wouldn't want any buildings to be burned down... Well, not any *more*."

She was referring to Ben being the Fire Anarchist. "He would never cause harm," Jemma responded. "He never burned anything down." She couldn't help herself from defending her husband.

"Interesting..." Dr. Paxton rubbed her chin. "If that was proved, I'm sure his treatment could be hastened."

Jemma narrowed her eyes. Was the doctor playing games with her? "The Fire Anarchist is still out there," she said. "He hit another building after Ben was 'arrested' for arson. Isn't that proof enough that someone could be falsely committed?"

"Oh, the Public Safety Building?"

Jemma nodded.

"That was found to be faulty wiring," Dr. Paxton said. "Seems the power box shorted out and the spark caught onto the overfilled trash can."

The electricity shorting out was her doing, but she couldn't explain that. Anger flashed through her. "My husband was taken to be silenced."

"How long did he take Enertin for?"

"Why is that—"

"How long?"

"He's taken it since he was twelve. Never missed a day." Jemma couldn't see where the doctor was going with her questioning. She wasn't sure if she was giving away too much.

"That is a long time to be taking Enertin without incident. Well, until his recent one that brought him to Merrytime Clinic. It seems more logical that something changed in his routine versus Enertin suddenly not working."

"No," Jemma shook her head. "He was very strict about taking his pills on time."

"He was fifteen minutes late the day of the fire."

Once again, Jemma wrinkled her forehead. New information no one bothered to tell her.

The doctor continued, "I understand your concern about Enertin. It's not perfect and has to be taken correctly and on time each day. However, can you imagine the damage a Disparate like him would cause without it? Medication worked for him without incident for so long. We are working to make sure another lapse in judgment will not occur again. I assure you"—Dr. Paxton leaned in—"he will be well and home again *very* soon. A cure is in development that will change the lives of many Disparates. EnertinX, our expectant cure, is in its final stages of development and will be the focus of the next phase of initiatives."

Murmurs exploded throughout the newsroom; however, Jemma was speechless. Asher had warned her about the new cure. But Dr.

Paxton told her exactly what she wanted—her husband would be home with her soon.

Maybe they were wrong about the medication. Dr. Paxton worked with patients daily that relied on pills. Or maybe their fear was no longer needed. EnertinX was a new medication. If it did what the doctor said—cured Disparates—the world would never be the same.

A cure was what she wanted. What she dreamed of. Yet Asher had said they were dangerous. "And this new 'EnertinX' is safe?" Jemma asked. "Half of the Disparates it was tested on didn't die?"

The doctor's eyes widened. "Certainly not. It's had its kinks in development, as all medical miracles do. But with each test, success becomes greater, and people certainly weren't put at such a risk. We will make sure the benefits outweigh any side effects before it becomes fully available to the public. I thank you for your concerns, and assure you—we know what we are doing." The doctor faced the camera and smiled. "Thank you to the seven Republics for tuning in tonight. More information will be available in the coming weeks."

Could Asher be mistaken? Or did the doctor believe it was safe? Surely there would be extensive testing before mass production. The drugs would be safe, at least by then. Jemma wanted, no, *needed* it to be true.

The spotlights dimmed once more, this time cascading to black before the producer yelled "Cut!" Ceiling lights turned on as the crew busied themselves taking down sets and readjusting cameras.

"Well, *Jennifer,* that was quite the interview," Dr. Paxton stood and removed her microphone.

"Does it work...." Jemma started her question but was unsure of how to finish.

"EnertinX? Well, we certainly believe so."

"No. Does it work for all energies?" Jemma couldn't stop her hope of a cure for Louie. That he wouldn't have to live his life afraid of being himself.

"Each cure does have a slight variance in how it is created, but we have worked out the formulas for each of the five types."

"Does it work for someone who has *two* energies?" The question slipped out. Jemma held her breath. Dr. Paxton had dismissed their concerns about the pills. She'd claimed Ben wasn't on the island. Everything Buran and the Dissentients had told her the past few days, the doctor had information against.

Truth was, Jemma wasn't sure who she believed.

"More than one energy type?" Dr. Paxton tilted her head curiously. "Well, that would be something to explore. It is rare for such a Disparate to be found. Why do you ask?"

"I'm... an Analyst," Jemma tried to cover her tracks. "I've heard of it and was curious."

Dr. Paxton nodded. "It is rare, but there have been a few Disparates showing more than one energy. Please inform your colleagues to report any such Disparates so they can get the specialized care they need."

Jemma caught her wording. *More than one energy,* not just two.

"Now," Dr. Paxton continued, "I must be going. Lots to prepare. I promise your husband will be home soon."

As the doctor stepped off the stage, two people dressed in blue coats flocked to her sides. Jemma resisted the urge to follow her.

Aniyah waved at Jemma, catching her attention. People were waiting for her.

People she still didn't fully trust.

TWENTY

The news played on Margaret's television as she filtered through paperwork at home. Her office burning down wasn't enough to keep her from meeting deadlines.

Today's special guest was the elusive Dr. Paxton. Her short blond hair framed her face. An uneasy feeling crept over her. Although the woman on screen was in the field of social work, a dark aura seemed to follow her. Not to mention the change in Tobias's personality after each meeting with her. Thankfully, they didn't happen as often as they once did. And Margaret hoped to keep it that way—as long as the doctor wasn't behind the missing information from her office.

The anchor started talking, and with her voice, Margaret's focus transferred to the screen. A small gasp escaped her lips. Jemma sat opposite the doctor. Her hands folded together in her lap. Worry creased Margaret's brow as she scooted close to the television.

"Hello, and welcome to our special segment tonight..." Jemma began.

Margaret wasn't fully comprehending her words. She picked up her phone ready to dial Jemma's number, but she knew she wouldn't answer. She thought about calling Tobias, but he was in a virtual cabinet meeting watching this segment with the other Republic Governors.

It was for the best. She didn't want to miss a word of this interview.

The conversation sounded on script, for the most part. That was until Jemma started questioning the validity of the Enertin pills. *She knows*, Margaret thought. *How does she know about the pills? How much does she know?*

When a letter was mentioned her heart almost stopped. Then when Jemma claimed Ben was on Lucky Island, it felt as if it did. Dropping her into the hollows of her soul. Ben couldn't be on Lucky Island. It wasn't in operation. Yet her daughter had spoken with such anger, such confidence.

Although she had many questions, pride swelled in her chest. Her daughter was displaying the strength Margaret always knew she had. Strength she wished she had herself.

As the segment wrapped up, the letter Dr. Paxton had gently tucked in her pocket wouldn't leave Margaret's mind. She'd been told two figures were caught on the security tape during her office break in: a man and... a woman. The Responders investigating the break in wouldn't say anything more than that.

If Ben was involved with these *Dissentients,* was Jemma as well?

Margaret needed to see that video.

She jumped in her car and rushed to the office. It was Monday, and even though the building was closed, she knew the security guard would let her in.

When she arrived, Jerry looked surprised to see her. "Good afternoon, Mrs. Stillfield," he greeted her at the door. "Did you leave some items in your office?"

"Hi Jerry, yes and no. There's actually something I need your help with." Margaret was hopeful the friendly relationship they had developed over the last seven years would be enough for him to let her watch the security footage.

"Happy to help," he said as he held the door open for her.

"How are Sarah and little Lucas doing?" Margaret asked as they headed toward the station. Jerry's wife had given birth to their first baby six months ago. He had taken six months paid family leave to help care for his wife and new child, returning in time for the fire anarchist attack. Thankfully, he wasn't hurt.

"They are doing great. Sarah's excited for spring break. She's ready to spend all her time snuggling Lucas. He's growing up too fast—started crawling a few days ago! Here, I got a video."

Like a proud father, Jerry pulled out his phone and played a video of a chubby little Lucas rocking back and forth on his knees before taking a small tread forward. Jerry's face beamed with joy.

When they arrived at the security desk, another guard sat behind it. There used to be only one on duty, but since increasing the surveillance at all times, temp guards had to be hired to fill the spots. Margaret didn't recognize him. He leaned back in a black office chair, his bushy mustache visible above a book of puzzles in his hand. He placed a sudoku onto the desk in front of him.

"You can sign in here," he said as he pushed a binder toward her. She noticed she was the first and only to sign in. Since the attack last week, people were extra wary about spending time at the office. At least, what was left of it.

"You can head back, just make sure you sign out when you leave," Jerry smiled at her.

"Actually, I was wondering if I could speak to you in private."

"Sure, let's go to your office." Jerry's eyes narrowed, but he still smiled as he spoke.

"Actually, mine's still a bit of a mess. I was hoping we could talk in yours." Margaret needed to get into the security office if she was going to find the footage. She had a feeling Jerry might risk his job to let her watch them, but she didn't want to put him in that position. He had a family to feed.

"Um, sure. I guess that wouldn't be a problem. Are you good manning the front out here, Bristles?"

"Ha, only my second time here and you've already got a nickname for me," Bristles chuckled. "Of course, I've got this. I've been here all day."

Margaret followed Jerry into the security office. Inside, screens displayed feeds from multiple cameras around the building. Margaret rubbed the small chip in her pocket, making sure it was still there.

Jerry pulled a chair for Margaret to sit in as he sat in the other. "What's going on?" Jerry questioned.

"It's been a week since the break in. I'm still a bit shaken by it," Margaret began, trying to pick her words carefully. "You were here that night, weren't you?"

"I was. I tried to stop the intruders, but if I'm being honest, they caught me by surprise. Knocking the electricity out was smart. I'm still not sure how they were able to shut off the back up generator as well. Likely one of those Disparates. One of them definitely was. It wouldn't surprise me if they've been working together to break into these places."

The Dissentients. So it could be them.

"Did you get a good look at either one?"

"No... one had a hood covering his face. The other, I only got a good look at her back, but she had long brown hair." He paused. "They were both wearing black."

Margaret's suspicions needed to be confirmed. She glanced around the room, noticing the computers. That was where the footage would be stored. She coughed, lightly at first but growing into a coughing fit. The back of Margaret's throat stung by the pressure; she needed to make it look convincing.

"You okay? Need me to get you some water?" Jerry asked exactly what Margaret had hoped for. If he left her alone in the room, even for just a few moments, she could download the footage. It was risky, especially if she was discovered, but she had to know the truth.

Jerry's furrowed brows lifted as he followed her gaze. He glanced at the computer behind him and then at Margaret. "That ain't gonna help you."

"What do you mean?" Margaret moved her gaze to Jerry.

"The night of the fire was pretty hectic. In fact, some of our servers were damaged."

"But the Responders said there was security footage from that night." She narrowed her eyes. Was Jerry lying to her?

"Oh, there is. However, it's been moved off these computers to a secure server at the capitol. Won't find anything here."

"Why would they do that?" Margaret muttered.

Jerry shrugged. "Those R.E.I. folks don't mess around."

"R.E.I. Of course." The Republic Energy Investigators were on the fire anarchist case. They would have seized any evidence related to the perpetrator. Seeing this footage would take more work than she thought.

Her heart raced, thinking of the implications if Jemma was on that tape. She needed to hack into the R.E.I. servers. But how? An idea popped into her mind. Good thing she was on the Public Safety Committee. And, not to forget, the widow of a previous governor.

She had her connections.

Long faces and hopeless eyes filled the back room of Samay's restaurant. Not only had they failed to provide evidence to convince the Republics that Enertin wasn't safe, they had ushered in the announcement of the next phase of the rollout. The one Asher had escaped the island and risked his life to stop.

The nerves in Jemma's stomach quivered as Asher angrily paced. She clutched her waist as she waited for someone to say the first word. Dr. Paxton's interview had messed with her mind. A strong, well-educated woman who worked firsthand in the field surely understood how Enertin worked. Who were they to question it?

"Paxton!" Asher screamed. "If I had known it was *her*, we never would've gone through with this."

"What do you mean?" Aniyah asked.

Asher was quiet for a moment, softly shaking his head. A pained expression painted across his face. "She can't be trusted. She's involved in everything that's gone wrong. You guys have to trust me on this."

No one said anything. Jemma couldn't help but feel confused. What Dr. Paxton had said made sense to her, so she wasn't sure why Asher was so adamant. But then her gaze fell on Buran.

The pained expression on his face was as deep as the color red within his bloodshot blue eyes. With a hard sigh, he spoke. "She announced the cure." He shook his head. "We gave her the perfect platform to do it."

"I don't believe they've made it any more effective in the last few weeks since I've been gone," Asher said, crumpling up a paper menu.

"I'm sorry I let Dr. Paxton take the letter," Jemma said. "I should've held it tighter or gotten it back from her."

"It's not your fault," Samay's matter-of-fact voice stated. "She had an answer to everything. It was our job to get Buran projected."

"Yeah," Calum joined in, "If anyone failed, it was me. We got into the projection room and were ready to go, but when it was time, the computer shut down. I don't know what happened; there was a pop and the screen went black."

Jemma couldn't shake the feeling she knew what that popping was. "Before I realized I was a Disparate, I thought I was really bad at buying good computers. But a popping sound? It might be electric energy." All eyes turned to her, their stares creating a burning sensation that spread to her cheeks. "I don't think it was me. At least, I didn't feel my energy escape. There could've been another Disparate."

"I don't know of any at the news station…" Aniyah said, "but it could still be possible. Might be someone I don't know about. But only that computer was affected."

"That sounds like it was purposeful, controlled energy," Samay said.

"Well, we're gonna have to be better prepared next time." Asher straightened his back.

"Next time?" Jemma questioned.

"You aren't giving up already, are you? Just because today didn't work out like we wanted doesn't mean next time won't." Her brother's stubbornness wasn't always a bad trait.

"You're exactly right. There are no quitters here." Buran latched onto Asher's pep talk. "I'm thinking we need to know what Ben knows. We need to get him off that island."

Jemma's heart leapt. She thought everyone had given up on the idea of rescuing Ben, thinking it was an impossible task.

"Speaking of the island," Aniyah turned to Calum. "Wasn't yesterday letter day?"

Calum's face fell. "Haven't gotten anything."

Any hope Asher's talk had given vanished, the air heavier than it'd been when they first gathered. Aniyah placed a hand on Calum's back, as if comforting him for a loss.

"Perhaps it'll arrive late?" Jemma said.

"For the first time since he's been gone?" Calum shook his head. "I was warned this would happen. I just didn't expect it so soon."

Jemma's chest tightened. "What does it mean?"

"We don't know for sure," Samay said. "But when communication stops coming, it doesn't resume."

"So people just disappear?" Jemma's body tensed. "They get sent to the island and never return? Even children?" How was the government able to get away with this? All in the name of safety? This was the opposite of that.

Calum's eyes widened. He set his pleading stare on Buran. "If we're going to the island—"

"Don't say it." Buran winced, as if an arrow were aimed at his chest. "You know we can't."

"But we can. We can find him. We can save Chayse too."

The silence in the room settled like a dark mist. Calum narrowed his gaze.

"We can't save everyone," Buran said. "We have a mission, and we can't risk it."

Calum looked as if he wanted to say more. Instead, he wiped under his eyes. "Fine," he finally said, his voice shaky. "We'll focus on Ben."

Guilt wrapped around Jemma's heart. The fact the person she loved was the focus of the rescue meant more than she'd realized. What they were planning to do was dangerous.

"You'll be staying here," Buran said. "We need a contact on the mainland in case anything goes wrong."

Although he didn't say it, Jemma could tell he didn't trust bringing Calum with them. She knew if he had the chance to save his brother, he'd take the risk. She'd do the same for Ben if she were in his shoes.

Pain shadowed Calum's face. "Are you serious?"

"I need you here." Buran's voice was stern.

"I can't believe this!" Calum huffed.

"We can't risk the mission. And after what you pulled following Jemma to the treehouse—"

Calum stood from his seat next to Jemma and slammed his hands on the table top. "You can't, or you won't?"

Buran raised to meet him at eye level. "If you want to be part of this group, you will stay here and do what you are told."

The vitriol on Calum's face was clear. "Perhaps I don't want to be part of a group that only cares about how they can use you."

"Calum…" Aniyah said as he turned and stomped toward the exit. He didn't stop. The door slammed as he left. The impact rattled Jemma's teeth, or perhaps it was just her nerves.

"You didn't have to be so hard on him," Samay spoke first.

"You're one to talk." Buran ran a hand through his hair, ice flaking off as it passed through. "He needed to hear it. We can't risk the mission."

"He's right," Asher said. "We won't have time for anyone else. Ben has information we need. He is our focus."

Jemma's stomach churned. As much as she was ready to get her husband back, the contention amongst the group heightened her anxiety. They'd need to work together to pull this off.

"So," Aniyah said, taking a deep breath. "What's the plan?"

Before she finished speaking, the door creaked open. It seemed a bit soon for Calum to return. However, Buran's face paled before Jemma turned to see the intruder.

A woman with dark hair stood by the closing door. Disbelief painted across her face as her eyes darted around the room, finally landing on Buran.

"Keesha, what are you doing here?"

"I was going to ask you the same thing." Her arms folded across her chest. "Indian food was *not* the plan for lunch."

"Oh crap. That was today?"

"Of course it was!" Keesha shook her head. "You're just like my father."

"I bet he's furious I wasn't there." Buran sank in his seat.

"*I'm* furious you weren't there. He doesn't even know, considering 'urgent business' caused him to cancel. I looked like a fool sitting at a table for three. Stood up by *two* men. Worst of all, my own husband!"

Buran stood and walked to his wife. "How did you even find me?" he asked.

"I have my ways."

Jemma squirmed in her seat.

"Shall we give you some privacy?" Samay asked, rising from his own.

"Please don't," Keesha said. "I'd like to know exactly what's going on here."

Buran looked as uncomfortable as Jemma felt. She stayed quiet in her spot. Her eyes locked with Asher's for a moment. His widened as he pressed his lips together.

"How much does she know?" Samay looked at Buran.

"This is the group of people that are helping me teach Disparates about emotion control." Buran gestured to the room. "I know I missed lunch. We scheduled this meeting at the last minute, and I totally forgot."

"Then explain why the man I passed going out the door was muttering something about 'Lucky Island'? How does this play into teaching people how to breathe properly?" The anger in her eyes was deep. It was clear Buran hadn't explained everything to her. The thought unsettled Jemma. Why would he keep something he was so passionate about from the woman he loved?

Noises from the kitchen floated into the back room. "My prep crew has arrived to prepare our dinner menu," Samay said. "This conversation will need to move elsewhere."

"We can talk about this at home." Buran placed a hand on Keesha's arm. She pulled away, her eyes roaming around the room once more. They settled on Jemma for a moment before continuing on.

"Fine," Keesha said. "I'll meet you there." She turned and threw the door wide open as she left.

Buran was as still as a statue.

"What was all that about?" Aniyah asked what Jemma was thinking.

"I haven't exactly told her about everything we're doing." Buran sighed. "I'll need to come up with something."

"Perhaps the truth?" Jemma said.

"I can't put that on her." Buran turned to face the group. "The responsibility would be too great. She didn't sign up for all of this."

"She's your wife," Jemma protested. "You should tell her everything. She loves you; she'll understand."

"You might be right. However, I'd be asking her to choose between me or her family."

"What do you mean?" Samay asked, still in the back room with the group.

"Her dad is the head of R.E.I. If word got back to him about what we're doing..." Buran shook his head.

That was why he was keeping secrets. Although Jemma didn't agree with his choice, she couldn't keep her own nerves down thinking about his wife exposing them. She didn't know Keesha, but if her own husband thought it was a possibility, Jemma had to believe it was.

Asher laughed, breaking the tension. "This is the type of drama I missed while on the island." He shrugged at Buran. "You should probably get going. You've got some excuses to make up."

"Yes." Buran's shoulders sagged. "We'll resume our discussion later." He looked defeated as he left through the back door.

Jemma felt for Keesha; however, she was more worried about her own husband. They'd finally started talking about rescuing Ben again. Hopefully this disturbance wouldn't alter the plan.

TWENTY-ONE

Jemma walked down the flower lined path to Caty's door. She'd arrived fifteen minutes late, which meant there'd be no other children to distract their conversation.

She wasn't sure how it'd go. The way the Dissentient meeting ended left her with little confidence. How would they come together to rescue Ben when the group had internal problems to address? And now, she needed to explain things to her best friend.

It didn't take long for the door to swing open. "There you are!" Caty shouted, her red curls resettling around her face.

Jemma winced at the volume.

"Sorry," Caty said, her voice at a reasonable level. "I've been waiting for you. I've got the kids watching a movie with popcorn. They should be entertained for a bit. It's time for you to come clean."

The look she gave Jemma confirmed she wouldn't let her leave easily. Tears welled in her eyes, and she hadn't even started.

Caty put her arm around Jemma's shoulders and ushered her to the couch in her preschool room. She heard laughter from the room next door.

"Spill," Caty said.

"No time for small talk?" Jemma said with a light smile.

"Nope. What's happening with Ben? Why isn't he home yet?"

The stress of the day washed over Jemma. She'd expected Caty to have seen the news before she arrived and already know. She forgot the handful of kids would have made that difficult.

"He's on Lucky Island."

Caty gasped, covering her mouth with her hand. "How? What? Why would he be there? Is it even a place anymore?"

"Oh, it's still a place," Jemma said. Caty knew about the fire at Ben's office, his false accusation, and that he was taken away. But Jemma came clean about the details of that night and the Dissentients helping her. She left out any mention of Asher, her mama bear instincts kicking in once more. She continued with her story. The whole story.

"The entire street light burst?" Caty exclaimed. "Wow. This explains so much."

"What do you mean?"

"Do you remember our tenth year ball? When Mr. Hot-Stuff-Computer-Club asked for a dance? The DJ had 'electrical issues' right after."

"That might not have been me."

"But it could've been. Same thing with our train ride to Wuslick when we started Uni."

"No," Jemma protested, but the dark start to their college years came to mind. They traveled through the train cart by the light of the windows. At the time, they blamed the old wiring, but Jemma always found it odd it had only affected their cabin.

"So, someone came to your rescue?" Caty raised an eyebrow.

"I hope you understand why I can't give you more details."

"I do. And I promise I won't tell anyone what's going on." Caty picked up her phone. Her eyes widened as she scrolled through the screen. "Jemma, did you seriously go on the news today?"

There it was. The surprise. The disgust. The disappointment.

"We thought it'd work to stop the new initiative."

"You interviewing a doctor? It sounds like you just joined this group; couldn't someone else do it? Almost sounds like they're using you."

"Well... everyone else had their reasons to stay off screen." Jemma wasn't sure how to explain her own doubts about the Dissentients. How she wasn't fully convinced the medication was dangerous. But she didn't have much choice. "And I volunteered."

"And that's going to help you get Ben back?" Caty questioned.

"Not right away. But the hope was that it would eventually." Jemma sighed. "Truth is, getting him off the island is trickier than we thought it would be. I really can't tell you much more than that."

Caty placed a hand on Jemma's knee as they sat in silence for a moment. She appreciated the gesture. "I'm sorry I kept this from you," she said, "and Haven. Have you heard from her lately? I don't recall seeing her or Addi at preschool either."

"Yeah, we had a playdate yesterday. She decided she wanted more 'mommy' time, so she pulled her out, um... I guess it was about a week ago."

Jemma wrinkled her nose. That was when Louie and Mackie started preschool... And she didn't remember a playdate being planned. "Did I miss a message?"

"She said she invited you but you couldn't come." Caty shrugged.

Jemma racked her brain. "I don't remember being invited, but I have had a lot going on."

"More popcorn!" Mackie roared in the other room. Jemma shifted, ready to stand.

"That's true." Caty squeezed Jemma's knee, keeping her there for a moment longer. "I'm here to help. If you need someone to watch the boys, or a listening ear—or a laugh." She winked and rose from the couch. Jemma followed her toward the family room. "And your boys have been doing great at preschool."

"Speaking of, has Louie used any energy?"

"No." Caty shrugged. "None at all. If I see he's starting to get worked up, I jump in and help him and the other child work through their issue. He's very receptive to help. As far as air, I haven't..."

They arrived at the doorway to see popcorn kernels dotting the space around the three children's heads like small, fluffy stars. A kernel flew into Mackie's open mouth. Another headed for Lily's but missed and bounced off her cheek. Laughter erupted. A wet, mushy piece of popcorn sprayed from Mackie's lips.

"Well, I *hadn't* seen it," Caty said, her eyes twinkling. "You've got one special kid."

"So do you," Jemma said as she watched Lily snatch a new kernel from the air and aim it at Louie's outstretched jaw. It bounced off his forehead, but it was the thought that counted. She didn't care that Louie was different. She accepted him. And that was one thing Jemma wanted for her children. To find friends who loved and supported them no matter their differences.

The way Caty supported her.

Red lipstick lined the rim of Margaret's wine glass as she lowered it. Sergeant Dominic Simmons sat across from her. "I didn't realize you liked Indian food."

"Oh, I like *all* food." The sergeant rubbed his abs, causing his shirt to ride up slightly. She bit her lip at the exposed patch of skin.

"You're saying you'll eat anything? Perhaps we should continue our date back at my place." She gave him a sly smile as she twirled her hair. Her eyes moved to the messenger bag he'd brought with him to the restaurant. She'd invited him out as soon as he got off work. No time to drop his laptop off at home. "I make a mean chocolate chip cookie. Even have some ice cream to place on top."

He raised an eyebrow. "I have an early morning tomorrow."

"You're welcome to stay the night." She widened her eyes slightly, pleading for him to agree. "You know my bed is comfortable." Flirting was easy when the man in front of her looked as fine as Dominic, with his broad shoulders and well-groomed silver hair.

And with the way he tilted his head and raised his dark eyebrow, taunting her. "Your guest bed, you mean."

"Gives us plenty of space to"—Margaret bit her lip—"stretch out..." She winked. She didn't like having other men in the bed she once shared with Skylar. She'd tried it once, and the month-long regret that hit was as deep as the chasm he'd left in her heart.

The sergeant released a chuckle. Perhaps Margaret wasn't as good at this flirting thing as she thought. "You do have a point there," he said as he rubbed the scruff on his chin. "As long as you promise not to keep me up *all* night. I suppose I can stop by for a bit."

It didn't take long for the bill to come. The sergeant paid for her portion, since she'd be covering dessert. She didn't mind his old-fashioned nature. It was one of the things that kept her coming back to him.

He offered his arm as they stood from the table. She slid her hand onto his brick-like bicep—another reason she kept calling.

"You're sure you won't get lost on the way to my house?" Margaret asked as he opened her car door for her. They'd met at the restaurant, and she wanted to make sure he didn't take a detour stop at home.

"I may need to grab some things first," he said.

Margaret placed a hand on his chest and leaned closer, standing on her tiptoes. "Are you sure we have time for that?" she whispered into his ear. "You're the one with an early meeting."

Dominic swallowed. "I suppose I could stop by my house in the morning."

She moaned. "I would like that very much." Dominic leaned in toward her as she slid into the driver's seat of her car. She didn't have time for distractions here. He seemed to understand as he headed toward his car. She waited until he started his before pulling out.

True to his word, Dominic followed her. His large white truck pulled into her driveway.

"Make yourself at home," she said as they entered. "I have some cookies already baked. Shouldn't take long to warm up."

"I'm sure it'll be worth the wait." He winked at her as he placed his bag and jacket on the table. A shiver rippled through Margaret.

No, I can't let him distract me. I'm on a mission tonight, she thought.

She opened the lid to her cookie jar, eyeing the pile of chocolate chip cookies before closing it. "Oh dear," she called to the other room. "I seem to have been mistaken."

Dominic entered the kitchen. "What's that?"

"My grandkids finished all the cookies. It won't take too long to make another batch."

He walked behind Margaret and wrapped his arms around her front. "I don't mind having a different kind of dessert."

Warmth flushed her cheeks. "Well then, I'm sure you'll love my famous fudge brownies. I have everything I need to make them."

He rubbed his large hands against her arms as he yawned. "I'm not sure I can stay awake long enough for that."

Margaret turned around in his arms, now standing face to face with his neck. She lifted herself up enough to brush her lips against his. The heat was instant, spreading through her body. She wanted to stay in his embrace but pulled away.

"I hope that was enough to wake you up," she said. "But I am craving something sweet—and don't you say you can be sweet. I already know that." She gave him a look to tell him to simmer down. "This really won't take long to prepare. You're welcome to take a little nap on my couch. You know, gain back some energy for later. I'll wake you when it's ready." Truth was, she couldn't focus on much other than the laptop of information sitting in her dining room.

Dominic smiled. His eyes were droopy but on fire. "Alright, I do have some emails to respond to. You can have it your way, like you always do. I know better than to argue; you'll make it worth it."

"That's right." Margaret placed her hand on his firm chest and let it linger before walking away to gather ingredients for baking.

Once she heard him sit on the couch, she pulled out the box mix she kept at the back of the pantry. She knew the sergeant wouldn't stay awake for long. With his early mornings and late work days, nine at night felt more like midnight. But still, she took her time getting the mixture ready. And promptly hid the box deep in the trash can.

As she placed the pan in the oven, a light snoring came from the other room. Her shoulders relaxed.

She quietly headed into the dining room. Dominic was spread across the couch, his laptop on his lap—open. Margaret's pulse quickened. His hand lingered on the keyboard.

She took a deep breath. She needed the information she was sure would be located on it. With light feet, she moved into the living room. She gently pulled on the laptop.

A loud snore escaped as his body moved. Margaret froze, waiting to see if he was stirring. She held onto the computer as he rolled toward the back of the couch, tucking his hands under his cheek. His snore resumed its usual pattern.

She sat on the floor and pulled the screen to face her. She didn't want to wander too far. If he woke up, he'd notice his laptop was missing. Margaret wasn't sure how she'd explain that.

He was still logged in. She released a quiet sigh of relief. The next obstacle was to find the security footage. Jerry had mentioned it was saved by R.E.I. on a server in the capitol.

She started by searching for "Public Safety Building" within his files. Pages of information populated. Scanning, none stood out as the one.

She tried "Stillfield Capitol" thinking perhaps she could find the server.

"Security Footage." Nothing.

"R.E.I. Stillfield." Also no results.

It was when she typed "Fire Anarchist" that a file popped out. She clicked on it. A message box opened, asking for fingerprint clearance.

She glanced at the man behind her. Dominic's back faced her. His hands were tucked against his face and the cushions.

She walked around the couch. Balancing the computer on the edge, she reached and pulled gently on one of Dominic's hands, hoping to slip it out without disturbing his rest.

This time, however, he did rouse. His eyes opened slightly. A smile spread across his face when he saw Margaret standing above him.

She quickly lowered the laptop to hide it. "Hello there, . No need to wake up quite yet. I was just missing your touch."

"I can give you more..." His words were slurred.

"No need for that yet. You can get another fifteen minutes in."

He yawned and nodded. His eyes closed once again. Margaret was relieved he hadn't woken more.

Once his breathing became deep, she pulled his hand and placed a finger upon the touchpad.

Access Granted.

Perfect. She moved to the table and looked through the new system. Each hit of the fire anarchist was listed in date order. At the bottom was March 13th.

She opened it, searching for a video file. Finally, she'd found it.

She held her breath as the video loaded.

A small raccoon dug through the trash. It sat up, its glowing eyes staring into the dark woods behind the building. Margaret leaned closer to the screen, trying to make out details on the black and white feed. The raccoon dropped something it was holding and scurried away, out of view of the camera.

From the other side of the back wall, a figure appeared. They were covered from head to toe in black but had a masculine form. The fire anarchist.

Movement from the couch diverted her attention for a moment. The sergeant had shifted in his sleep. She needed to finish this soon.

She fast forwarded the video, watching as the man opened the back door and slipped inside. Another figure followed behind him.

Margaret rewound and paused. The feed was blurry, and it was hard to distinguish the woman's features. There was no way to know for sure if it was her daughter.

As the woman approached the door, a spark lit from her shoulders and the footage blacked out. An Electric Disparate. This couldn't have been Jemma.

That was a fail; the video didn't give her much information. Margaret moved the mouse on the screen, seeing there were a few more minutes left of the footage.

The feed returned, now from the camera in the office hallway. Margaret released a breath. The footage had been edited, spliced together to follow the perpetrators.

A guard walked in through the hallway. Jerry. This must have been when the electricity went out. But then, where were the Disparate woman and hooded man?

Through the open blinds of her office window, Margaret saw movement. She paused the video once more. There, she saw the faint outline of a man, the side of his neck and face no longer hidden by a hood.

This was the man. The fire anarchist that'd been terrorizing Stillfield for the last few weeks. Something about him felt familiar, but she couldn't place what. But she knew it wasn't her son-in-law, as he'd been taken away already.

Someone he was working with? Still didn't feel right.

As she leaned closer, an email alert popped in the corner of the Sergeant's screen.

Public Safety Building: Fingerprint Analysis Results

Margaret's eyes flickered to Dominic. He was out. She clicked on the email notification.

Inside was a link to the Forensic Department. It let her enter without further security blocks, considering she'd already used the sergeant's fingerprint.

PSB: 3.13. 2 Results

She opened the file. On this page were two different fingerprints, likely lifted from the scene. The first was almost completely black, she wasn't sure why they even tried to run it. Underneath read:

Four Possible Matches. Identity: Benjamin Hodgerton

That wasn't possible. The man in the video wasn't Ben. Besides, he'd already been taken into custody. Someone was framing him. This man, this anarchist was to blame. He'd attacked four other buildings so far. Likely leaving the same trace at each. His fire left soot, making a clear fingerprint nearly impossible.

The other fingerprint was much clearer.

One Possible Match. Identity: Jemma Stillfield

Margaret sucked in a sharp breath. Her daughter's name.

She opened the results, not wanting to believe the words on the screen. She glanced from the print lifted at her office to the ones Jemma had done before starting her Analysis job. The pointer fingers were identical.

Jemma was involved in her office break-in. She'd been a part of stealing the letter and then placed it right in Dr. Paxton's hands. She'd been keeping her distance from Margaret the last few days, and now she understood why.

Her daughter was working with the fire anarchist.

An alarm from the kitchen went off, causing her to jump. The brownies were done.

Margaret needed to think. Her daughter was incriminated in a crime. She couldn't let her be taken from her boys as well. If she deleted the print from the break-in, someone would notice. They knew they lifted two separate prints.

However, if she deleted Jemma's original prints, someone would have to purposely look at her name to find that they were missing. And they wouldn't have a reason to do that if they never matched in the first place...

The alarm beeped once more. There was no time to debate her decision any longer. She found Jemma's original prints and clicked the option to erase.

Her heart pounded. She could be caught any second. The cursor rushed across the screen. Exiting the forensics website, stopping just long enough to refresh the results under Jemma's print.

Zero Matches in Database.

As she exited the other windows, the video footage filled the screen, still paused on the fire anarchist's side view. Margaret couldn't shake the familiar feeling, but she didn't have time to examine him closer. The snoring had stopped.

She pulled out her phone and snapped a picture of the anarchist before closing the footage to make it look as if she'd never been there.

She slipped the laptop into the sergeant's bag as he sat up, rubbing his eyes.

"How long was I out?" he asked.

"That's the brownie timer going off," she said. "You got in the perfect power nap. Woke up right in time for dessert."

He glanced around himself as if looking for something, but then his gaze returned to Margaret.

"Looking for your laptop?" she asked. "I put it away to give us extra room for some... fun." She gave him a wink.

He returned it. "I could really go for some dessert right now."

She put her phone in her pocket, determined to look closer at the fire anarchist later.

Right now, she needed to get the brownies out of the oven before they burned.

TWENTY-TWO

B en shivered. The cool breeze from an open window near his feet didn't help his shaking.

Window?

Ben gathered the strength to lift his head. He wasn't in the same white-walled lab as before. Instead, blue painted walls surrounded him in a half circle, closed by a straight steel wall opposite of where he lay. The wooden bed he was on squeaked as he raised slowly to a sitting position. A blanket, barely covering him, slid down to the brown floorboards.

The room had nods to a nautical theme. An old oar was mounted on the wall. The arched window mirrored the half circle design. Ben's ankle ached as he put pressure on it. The swelling had lessened, but it was sensitive to added weight.

Someone had changed him into a clean gray jumpsuit. He had no idea how long he'd been out.

He moved to the window opening. It was large enough to stick his head out, but his shoulders stopped at the bars. Which was for the best. Ben's head spun as moonlight drifted across small waves a good hundred feet below. The movement and distance caused Ben's stomach to drop. He looked to the side of the building: red and white stripes wrapped around the base of a lighthouse.

An escape from this height would be difficult to pull off.

He squeezed back into the room, leaning against the wall for balance as his body continued to shiver. On the steel wall was a rolling desk, the top of which was closed. Next to it was a door.

This was a very different prison than he was in before. That is, if it was a prison. Ben limped to the wall, testing the handle on the door.

Locked.

Of course.

The last memory he had was of the lab. A blue liquid being inserted into his bloodstream.

He lifted his arm. The sleeves of his new outfit were short, giving him a view of the bandage on his inner elbow.

He ripped it off. Dry blood dotted his purpled skin. Heat rose within his chest, anger for the way he was treated. Tested on. Given drugs he didn't approve. His list of grievances was growing.

The heat was quickly replaced with burning. But not the kind he was used to. An icy tomb crystallized around his heart, traveling upward. He fell to his knees, his head crashing into his palms as the same freezing pain as before frosted over his thoughts.

This time, instead of blacking out, the world became numb. The cold dispersed from his mind.

With heavy breathing, Ben lifted his arm once more. What did those monsters do to him?

As the cold dissipated, a throbbing came from his opposite shoulder. The gun wound. Disgust ran through his veins, bringing his thoughts to Buran. If he were here, the entire room would be frozen and not just his insides. He'd been wrong about *this* coworker. All along, it hadn't been Buran who framed him.

It was Oliver who'd left a knife in his back. The way he pretended to care as he ran to his bleeding body. Ben wanted to remove the bandage on his shoulder, to throw away everything these people had done to help him, but reopening a gunshot wound wasn't the best idea.

A scratching came from the ceiling, interrupting his thoughts. At first, he wasn't sure if the sound was real.

"Pssst," a voice from above whispered.

His body wanted to stay where it was, exhausted. But curiosity got the better of him.

"Pssst," it came again.

He followed the noise. A small hole fractured the middle of his ceiling, opened next to the light.

"Can you hear me?" The voice whispered a bit louder. "Is everything okay in there?"

Ben gathered the strength to stand. His muscles protested each step. From the hole, a blue eye looked down on him. A patch of blond bangs framed the top.

"Hello there, neighbor. Wow, you don't look okay," said the wide opened eye—or rather the hidden mouth it belonged to.

"Hi, uh, what are you doing in my ceiling?"

"I'm not exactly *in* your ceiling. I just cut through it so I'd have some company." She paused for a moment. "The last guy was pretty honored, but I can understand if you feel intimidated."

"No, no it's alright. I'm just not feeling well," Ben said as his body swayed. He grabbed the chair from the desk and dragged it to the middle of the room. Perhaps whoever this person was could help him understand what was going on. "Who are you and why are you spying on me?"

"I'm Quill. Professional spy extraordinaire, with all this view I have locked in the top of a lighthouse." She didn't use a number. "Been a resident on Lucky Island for ten years. Lived here for about a month."

So she was a prisoner like Ben. "Why are we here? What is the purpose of this place?" Ben couldn't recall seeing a lighthouse on the island. Somehow, it was hidden away from the docks and warehouses. But why?

"I imagine you're here to finish your recovery."

"My recovery?"

"Yes. I saw what happened a few minutes ago. Your reaction should become less and less severe over the next few days."

Ben began to shiver once more. Talking about what was done to him brought back his anger.

"Woah, breathe. Try to calm down. Your body needs more time before you'll feel normal."

"What does that even mean?" Ben growled, his fist clenching.

"They really don't tell anyone anything, do they?" Quill sighed. "Your body has been undergoing a transformation. Taking away your energy. That's why you're in a gray suit now. With how much you're shivering, I'd guess you used to make fire. Not anymore."

When you're no longer a Disparate, the blue coat had said. Had they truly found a way to take away a Disparate's power?

"Is that why you're here?" he asked.

"Not quite," Quill said, "but how about you tell me who you are before I start confessing my deep, dark secrets."

"I'm Ben." He wasn't sure how much to say. She'd brought up a good point that they didn't know each other. How could they trust each other? "I think I've been on Lucky Island a couple weeks. I'm not really sure how much time has passed." Or how long he'd been kept asleep while his body was given chemicals. A shiver rose through his core, causing him to shake uncontrollably.

"Are you alright?" Quill asked.

"I'm... fine," Ben said between each tremble.

An object touched his shoulder. His body jumped forward as he twisted. The blanket from the bed hung in the air.

"That was me," Quill said quickly as the blanket fell into a pile. "Didn't mean to startle you. Just thought you needed to warm up."

"So you've got air energy?" *Guess she hasn't been administered the same drug.* He retrieved the comforter and wrapped it around his shoulders.

"Kinda."

"Didn't look very 'kinda' to me."

"It's not always the easiest to use," Quill explained. "Happy is not a feeling I conjure often in this place."

"But you just did."

"Oh—wait!" Quill's voice sounded frantic. "I hope you don't think I saw your shaking as funny! I swear I was thinking of something else!"

Ben released a shaky chuckle. He didn't know this woman, but she sounded genuine.

But then again, so had 1198.

"What were you thinking about?" he asked. He was wary about trusting another inmate on the island, but he wanted to keep her talking.

"Promise not to think I'm silly?"

"I'm not sure I can make that promise."

Quill's face disappeared from the hole. "Well, okay then, Mister 'I'm fine.' Guess you won't get to find out."

"No, no," Ben said. "I was joking. If we're stuck in this place, we might as well get to know each other more."

Quill was silent. Her blue eye returned to its spot. "I was thinking about the guy I like."

Ben's face flushed. This was not the direction he expected the conversation to go. "So you have a crush? Was it the last Disparate in this room?"

"Oh no." Quill's face backed away from the hole far enough to shake. "That boy was too young for me."

"How young?" Ben's fear for Louie returned. The fact he hadn't seen children on the island yet had given him hope, but hearing there was a young boy here...

"He was a teenager. They didn't keep him here for very long. I believe the plan was to move him to a new place, although I can't imagine where." Her voice was filled with sadness.

A thought came into Ben's mind. "Did you catch his number?"

"His name's Chayse. But he's known as 1227."

The boy from the first lunch. "How long was he here?"

"Only a few days."

"*Why* was he here?" The room was silent as he waited for a response.

"The island pills weren't keeping him controlled anymore."

Ben thought about his outburst in the cafeteria. "That was because of me. I caused his reaction."

"You beat him? Made him so anxious he triggered a lightning storm?" Quill's voice was accusatory.

"What? No!" Ben said. "What do you mean?"

She took a deep breath. "He explained what happened to him before he was moved again. He mentioned yelling at lunch, and normally, that would get him reprimanded; it's happened before. But this time, the guard was angry and wouldn't stop."

Ben recalled the anger in Markus's face as he yanked Chayse from his seat. It was a stark difference to the look of surprise he had before he was consumed by flames. It lessened his guilt, knowing what a brute Markus was.

"Chayse wore a red suit, though," Ben realized. Had he been wrong about the meaning of the jumpsuits?

"Yeah. He's a Flame Disparate."

"But you said—"

"And an electric one, apparently. Not sure if this was the first time he'd burst, but it certainly was the first time he did in front of guards."

"But that's not possible."

The light in his room flickered off.

Ben sat in the dark. A small ray of moonlight shone through the window.

The light turned on again. Then off. Then on. A clap sounded above, in time with the alternating luminescence, as if working together to create its own musical show.

"What is going on?" Ben asked, his shaking decreasing with his distracted focus.

After a moment, the light remained on as the clapping ended.

"I needed to release some energy," Quill said. "Didn't mean to scare you, but two energies isn't as surprising as you may think."

Ben's eyes widened as he realized. "You floated the blanket... and you caused the light?"

"Yep."

"And you just show it off? Won't they take you away like they did Chayse?"

"Maybe. Maybe not. They already know about me, and I'm still here." In a soft voice, she added, "Might not be the worst thing to be taken somewhere else."

A wave of exhaustion washed over Ben. He wanted to continue this conversation with Quill, however, he was physically and emotionally drained. A sharp shudder caused his chair to squeal.

"Maybe you should lay down," Quill said. "We'll likely still be here in the morning."

The "likely" didn't sound convincing to Ben, but he didn't have much control over what would happen.

However, if Quill still had her abilities... No. The last time he trusted another Disparate didn't end well. He'd need to be sure of Quill before they tried anything.

A knock on the steel door echoed through the room as soon as Ben's head hit the thin pillow.

Who would be coming to see him at this time of night?

TWENTY-THREE

A few days later, Jemma set her purse on the counter after returning home from dropping the boys off at Caty's. As she turned around, she jumped. A spark of lightning shot out of her hands and into the plush carpet of her family room. A tall, muscular man stood next to the singed fibers.

"That was close," he said.

"Asher! What are you doing here?" Jemma rubbed her warm palms on her jeans as she caught her breath.

"You told me to come this morning, remember? Need to draw a map of the island. I know you're getting old, but not that old."

Jemma narrowed her eyes as she glared at him. "Breaking into my house was not what I meant. How *did* you get in?"

"Might want to double check your windows are closed before you leave next time. Besides, I've gotten pretty good at getting into places I'm locked out of."

Jemma shook her head. Louie had recently figured out how to open the windows on his own, and he and Mackie would play in the breeze for hours, Louie lifting an empty wrapper into the air and Mackie laughing as the breeze picked it up. If only they could perfect making it into the trashcan at the end of playtime.

Jemma motioned to her table. "I have supplies laid out here. Pencils for sketching and extra paper in case we need it. Not that you'll need it," Jemma said quickly, "at least not if you still draw as well as you used to."

Asher chuckled. "Looks like you started without me." He lifted a drawing of circle shaped people with lines for arms and legs.

"That was Mackie. He got into the supplies last night. But there's still plenty."

Asher stared at the picture. "This is a family picture, isn't it?" His voice was soft. "You're really missing Ben, aren't you?" He handed it to Jemma.

She hadn't looked too closely before. Mackie had drawn a family of four. The one for Jemma had long hair drawn across her frowning face. Louie's and Mackie's figures matched her sadness. Ben's person was drawn in the back, a space between the other three. Ben's face was empty. Before, Jemma thought it was Mackie's underdeveloped spatial awareness, but on closer inspection, she realized it was clearly done intentionally.

Tears welled in her eyes as she thought of her young child's pain. She understood what it was like to lose a father.

"We're gonna get him back." Asher placed a hand on her shoulder. "I promise."

"How can you promise something like that?" Jemma wiped away a tear. "As you said before—it's risky. It's dangerous. It's impossible."

"It is," he agreed. "But we're gonna do it anyway."

"Quick mind changing doesn't give me much confidence." She sat in a chair. No matter how deeply she wanted her husband back, the likelihood of it actually happening was slim.

"I'm not changing my mind," Asher insisted. "Look, I owe you an apology. When I said it was dangerous and risky, I was telling the truth. But that doesn't mean it was ever *impossible*."

"Then why did you distract everyone from it?"

At this question, Asher sat. "I wanted to make sure these Dissentients were for real. That they were truly in it no matter what. After what we pulled at the station, I think we've got a good chance."

"The news was a disaster." Jemma wasn't convinced that Asher was serious.

"It may have *looked* like a disaster," Asher raised a finger, "but one, we brought up possible problems with the pills and the possibility of Lucky Island still running on Republic television, and two"—another finger went up—"we didn't get arrested. Sounds like good potential for success to me. At least shows some innovation and thinking under pressure. Things could've gone much worse."

"I guess," Jemma said.

The lights above the table dimmed. Asher narrowed his eyes toward her. "That you?" he said.

She took a deep breath, the light returning to full brightness for a moment before it flickered on and off as she released a shaky breath.

"You know," Asher continued, "before we do anything, you need to get that under control. Don't need any accidents to happen *again*. What are you feeling right now?"

"I'm... nervous." Talking about her feelings wasn't something she was used to. With Ben, he'd look at her and be able to tell how she was feeling. Sometimes just his touch would calm her.

"Okay. Take that feeling and own it."

"What do you mean?"

"Instead of letting your nerves control you," he said, "you control them."

"Yeah," Jemma huffed, "sure. That sounds easy." She closed her eyes, her fingers tangling into her hair. How did she survive before Ben? Caty had brought up the dance. If that had been Jemma, that meant she'd been a Disparate much longer than a few weeks.

She glanced at Asher. He was looking around her home, his gaze stopping at a family picture her mother had gotten taken during her last campaign. Her mother's arms wrapped around Mackie and Louie, a smile on her wrinkling face.

Jemma couldn't imagine the thoughts that were going through Asher's mind. Then, her eyes landed on the silvery skin below his jawline. A gasp escaped. "I gave you your scar, didn't I?"

Asher laughed. "That's why we need to get you under control. Would rather not get a matching one. Not sure electricity jumping out of a socket will be as believable nowadays."

She let out a sigh and placed a hand to her head. "You told Mom it was from plugging in your game system."

"She was pretty gullible. But I also don't think she would've believed the truth. It was hard enough for her to have one child that was different." Asher's shoulders dropped. "Dad was always more understanding..."

"I didn't really believe I'd caused it either," Jemma admitted. "I'm so sorry."

"Ah, don't worry about it." Asher shrugged it off with a smile. "Now, back to you."

Jemma smiled. He was the one she talked to growing up. The only way her energy had been kept controlled for so long was thanks to him and his ability to read when she was anxious or worried. Then, when he was gone, she had to take on the role of caretaker for their mother. She had buried her feelings. The worst had happened to her; what else was there to stress about?

"I'm worried you're going to take off at any moment. I'm afraid we're never going to get Ben back. And I'm just waiting to get a call from Caty saying Louie's having an outburst. I'm tired. I'm lonely. And I don't know who I am anymore." Jemma hadn't expected to unload on Asher, but she was tired of presenting a confident facade. She took a deep, whimpering breath in and held it before releasing through her nose. She didn't want to start crying.

Asher placed a hand on her shoulder. "You're strong. I know you don't see it, and I know you don't even want to be, but you are. You have every right to your feelings. Don't try to hide them. Embrace them. Let yourself feel anxious, and scared, and worried. Acknowledge those feelings."

Jemma trusted Asher. A wave of fear and concern rushed over her. She gave her heart permission to beat faster.

"Good," Asher said. "Now, think about how your body is feeling."

Blood rushed through her body, as if it were running late to an appointment. The hair on her arms rose and tears wetted her cheeks. Jemma heard the buzz of electricity, unsure if it was all inside her head.

"Now, before you shock me, take a deep breath in through your nose. As you release through your mouth imagine those parts of you relaxing. As you do so, you're going to release your energy, but not all at once. Just imagine a small stream flowing through you, peacefully leaving your body through your fingertips. Direct that stream where you want it to go. Such as your light currents."

The front room brightened as Jemma followed Asher's instructions. She was doing it. Increasing the power of her home with her own natural gift.

The sound of popping disrupted her focus. Glass rained down on the siblings. As her concentration broke, the power in the room went out. She'd lost control again.

Asher laughed with the full force of his body. As he leaned over in the dark, the sun rays through the window silhouetted him. "I guess I should have asked how many watts your light bulbs could handle."

His joy was contagious. Jemma found herself chuckling at her mishap. But she had felt herself directing the flow of the stream. She had felt in control of the energy her body created, and although there were some bumps she'd need to refine, perhaps she could do it again.

A knock at her front door resounded through her quiet home. She looked at Asher and noticed the crease in his forehead.

"Don't worry, it's probably just a package delivery."

The knocking continued, becoming more frantic. Jemma had hoped if she ignored the door, whoever was there would leave. However, they did not give up.

"Jemma!" the voice on the other side shouted.

Asher's face paled.

"Go hide somewhere. I'll get her to leave." Jemma shooed Asher into the hallway. He'd have to find his own way through her house.

She opened her front door and stood face to face with her mother. Her crossed eyebrows and thin mouth, the corners of which pointed downward, gave Jemma pause as she pushed herself into the living room.

"Jemma Marigold Stillfield!" her mother declared. "You need to tell me what is going on right this instant."

Jemma could tell her mother was serious by the use of her full name; she didn't even bother to use her married surname.

"Mom, I—" She felt her mother's glare. She had never seen her so upset. "The boys started preschool, if that's what you're referring to."

Her harsh expression softened slightly. "That's nice to hear. I told you that would be good for them. But that's not what I'm here for." Her face hardened again. Of course that didn't work. "You need to come clean to me about what you were up to when I babysat a couple weeks ago. And why I saw you on the evening news Friday. Jemma, what is happening?"

She'd been avoiding this long enough. The fact it took a couple days for her mother to show up was surprising enough. If she was on Governor Dunn's side, Jemma needed to be careful about what information she gave away.

"I was helping a friend. The normal newscaster had to go out of town unexpectedly, and they needed someone to take her place. So she asked me." That wasn't exactly a lie, but either way, her mother didn't look like she bought it.

"Yes, I see, *Jennifer*. And what about a couple weeks ago?" her mother prodded.

"When I went to Ben's office? Like I said. I was trying to get his name cleared and get him home. Obviously that didn't work." Jemma saw her mother glancing at her right hand. Her fingers had been twitching. She hid her hands behind her back.

"Jemma, I have something to ask you. I need you to be honest with me. Please." Her voice was soft, the layers behind her pleading piercing into Jemma's soul. As much as they fought, their bond was unique.

She hadn't been avoiding seeing her mother again because she thought she was working for the wrong side. It was because she wouldn't be able to keep from telling her everything.

Her mother pulled out her phone and held it for Jemma to see. On the screen was a picture, clearly zoomed in. It was blurry and hard to make out.

Her mother continued, "Did you find my boy, Asher?" Her wide, tear-filled eyes met hers. "Were you with your brother?"

Jemma examined the picture again. It was from the break-in: a blurry outline of Asher's scar. She stayed quiet, unsure of what to say. A movement on her left turned her head as Asher stepped out from the shadow of the hallway.

Their mother's hands shot to her face, covering her mouth as she gasped. Her phone thudded on the carpeted ground.

"Hi, Mom."

*H*i, *Mom*, was all the deep, gruff voice needed to say. Margaret's world stopped the moment she had zoomed in on his scar in the picture she'd taken—her baby boy. She stood on her tippy toes as she hugged his neck. He may have grown a few inches since the last time she'd seen him, but he still had the same smoky scent. Asher stood still, his arms at his side.

Margaret finally let go and stepped back, allowing herself to see the full picture of her son—at least the details she could pick out with the dim light from the windows. His messy brown hair and emerald eyes reminded her of her husband. Asher had always resembled Skylar, but now that he was fully grown, he looked like his clone. Tears freely fell down her face. Jemma walked behind her and watched their interaction.

"Asher, how—" She tried to talk through sobs, but couldn't get the words to form. Asher shifted from his still pose by lifting his right hand to his left elbow, as if he was trying to cover himself.

Margaret got the feeling that he was uncomfortable. Her heart ached to think of what he may have been through these last seventeen years.

She composed herself enough to speak. "How are you here? Where have you been?"

Asher's face creased. His green eyes shifted slightly to the side and then back at her. "You know where I've been." He said each word slowly and thoughtfully, pausing slightly after each one. He pressed his lips together tightly after he finished speaking.

It was Margaret's turn to give a quizzical look. "What do you mean?"

"You know I've been on Lucky Island. You sent me there after Dad's death."

His words stung. None of what he said made sense to her.

"At the time, I couldn't blame you," Asher went on. "I thought I was dangerous. That I deserved to be sent away. I thought I started the fire that night. I was pretty upset at Dad about that stupid concert. When I heard he didn't make it out, I jumped to blaming myself. But I was just a kid." His voice was rough.

"You've been on Lucky Island?" Margaret asked, still in disbelief. How could he have been on Lucky Island all this time? Before the fire happened, while Skylar was the governor, he had worked hard to keep as many Disparates as he could off that island. That was why he had started Merrytime Clinic. And yet his own son had been taken to the island because of his death. Surely her husband was rolling in his grave.

Asher glared at her, his brows furrowed in anger. Margaret glanced at Jemma, who stood a few feet away, her face unreadable. Did her own daughter believe she sent Asher away? "I had no idea. If I did, I would have swum to that island myself and brought you home." Margaret tensed. "I need to know what happened. Who took you there? I've tried to find you all these years. I truly had no clue."

Asher's expression stayed tight. "I was stopped by Responders." Asher's face darkened. "They told me you didn't want to see me. I believed them. I thought I was the reason Dad was dead and Jemma was hurt. I couldn't blame you for not wanting to see me."

"I did everything I could to try and find you," Margaret said, tears welling in her eyes. Her son believed she didn't want him? *Never.* "I made flyers. Contacted newspapers. Wrote letters begging for you to come back home. I told Governor Dunn to keep looking."

"It's true." Jemma stepped closer. "We really didn't know. One private investigator said you might have ended up in Vasco, working in the factories there. Another thought your body was found in the outskirts of Preen."

"Private investigator?" Asher questioned.

Jemma nodded. "All we knew was that you ran away. Mom, you must've hired close to a dozen."

"More than that," Margaret admitted. She saw her son's eye twitch slightly. "You remember those 'me-cations' I would take every summer?" she asked her daughter.

Jemma nodded.

"Well," Margaret said, "I actually took those trips to check areas he might've been seen. Either following an investigators lead or reading about an unidentified body that was found. I can't even tell you how many I've seen, just wanting to know what happened to my boy."

"And I'm supposed to believe that?" Asher asked, his face scrunched. Like he'd do when he was a boy, trying to figure out a puzzle.

"After the fire, she was broken," Jemma jumped in. "She's still broken in many ways."

Years she'd like to forget. Hearing Jemma speak about her that way brought back the guilt Margaret harbored for her reaction.

Jemma continued, "For two years after Dad died and you disappeared, Mom couldn't get out of bed. She barely ate. The only thing that kept her going was trying to find you. And after a few months of hearing nothing, even that wasn't enough. I thought I was going to lose her too."

Jemma's gaze met Margaret's. It'd been wrong to put so much on Jemma's young shoulders. She was twelve and taking care of her own mother. Life wasn't supposed to be like that.

Then again, families weren't meant to be broken apart to begin with. Not in the way that seemed to be so common those days.

The memories of that time triggered a tear to roll down Jemma's cheek. Asher's gaze flicked between Jemma and Margaret as he listened.

"You don't understand," Jemma said. "The mom we grew up with died that night as well. But now, with Ben missing, I understand why."

Guilt seized Margaret's heart hearing her daughter talk about their past. A lump formed in her throat; she couldn't contain the heartache she felt. "I joined the Public Safety Committee because I never wanted another family to go through what we did. Not because I blamed you for the fire, but because I blamed myself. I felt like I'd failed you." Jemma turned her worried gaze toward Margaret while Asher looked at her in disbelief, his eyes welling with tears.

"You're serious, aren't you?" he questioned.

"As serious as a heart attack."

Asher smirked slightly. He'd use this phrase when he was younger, and Margaret reprimanded him for thinking heart attacks were funny. This time, she couldn't help but smile a bit with him.

His face hardened once more. "How do you explain the letter?"

Of course he knew about that. He was the one that'd stolen it from her office. "It's not what you think."

"Then explain," Jemma said. She folded her arms across her chest.

"Well..." Margaret paused to gather her thoughts. "There are things I've been looking into. Things that aren't ready to be exposed yet. Which, by the way, you've done now."

"Don't try and twist this on us," Jemma said.

Her words were like a punch to the gut, but Margaret understood where they came from. Being fully transparent was difficult for both of them; they'd grown used to doing things on their own.

"You're right. That's not what I'm trying to do. I'm working to stop Dr. Paxton's new initiatives."

Asher's eyes narrowed. "Then why keep it secret?"

"We're still looking into things," Margaret said. "The formula for Enertin has been changing the last couple of years. Which has resulted in the decrease of Disparate outbursts. However, it's also increased the severity of those that do occur."

Jemma nodded her head. "Yeah. I've noticed that." It seemed like she wanted to say more but didn't.

"So, what are you doing?" Asher asked. He still looked at her with distrust in his eyes. "And why don't you want anyone to know?"

"Not just anyone," Margaret said. "Dr. Paxton. When Tobias brought his concerns to her before, he always came back... well... different."

"How so?"

"He misses our coffee appointments, for one thing."

Jemma sighed. "You need to tell us everything," she said. "Missing coffee doesn't seem that drastic."

"We do more than drink coffee at these meetings. We discuss the families we've gone to see that have lost loved ones. We've learned the data put out from the Responders' cause of death are not fully accurate. Most families say the victim never missed taking Enertin. It's not like them."

"You've been conducting your own investigation?" Jemma's eyes widened.

"Yes. We've been trying to figure out what is going wrong and why it is happening." She turned to Asher. "I truly didn't know you were on Lucky Island. And I'm sorry you ever believed I did." Her heart ached at the thought that Asher ever trusted such a lie. She had truly failed as his mother.

"So was it *Dunn* that gave you that picture of me?" Asher asked. His eyes were narrow, still unsure about Tobias.

"Actually, no." Margaret wasn't sure how much detail to give. "I got it myself."

"How?" Jemma asked, her forehead creased and her voice laced with worry.

"If you must know, Dominic came over, and I hacked his computer."

Jemma's jaw dropped. "The sergeant?"

"Wait…" Asher gave her a squinted look. "What do you mean, 'came over'?"

"I'm a grown woman," Margaret said, standing tall. "I have my ways of getting information."

"Gross," Asher said. Jemma's face cringed.

Margaret shook her head. She didn't think further explanation would help. "It wasn't until this morning that I realized why the fire anarchist looked so familiar. After staring at my phone all night, it hit me. I grabbed Asher's Year Nine picture. The scars matched. And don't worry, the R.E.I. doesn't seem to know it's you. And, thanks to me, they also don't know that Jemma was involved." Her eyes connected with Asher's.

He hesitated for a moment, as if considering her words. Then, he closed the distance that had grown between them, wrapping his arms around her. She hugged him for the second time.

"I'm sorry," Asher said, his voice shaking. She sensed the weight of his apology had to do with more than questioning her actions with Dominic.

"It's okay, honey. I forgave you long ago." At that, Asher stood back, putting his hands on her shoulders and looking her in the face.

"For what?" Asher asked.

"Well, for everything. The fire. Running away, although it turns out that's not actually what happened. But the past doesn't matter anymore. What matters is that we are together now."

"No. I'm sorry I didn't believe you right away. I'm not sorry about the fire."

"What do you mean?" Margaret's insides fluttered, waiting for an explanation.

"I'm not sorry about the fire, because I didn't cause it. I'm not the reason Dad is dead. Governor Dunn is."

Margaret couldn't process his words. His claim that Tobias killed Skylar did not, would not, connect in her brain. It didn't seem possible to her. Yet, her son being on Lucky Island this whole time didn't either. If he was on the island, Tobias surely must have known and never told her.

She studied her daughter's face. Jemma's eyes were on her, her eyebrows pulled close together. She didn't seem startled by the news.

"I think I'm going to need to hear the full story," Margaret declared. "Oh, and Jemma, perhaps you can turn on a light?"

TWENTY-FOUR

The woods were dark as Ben ran through the trees, searching for the trail that would lead to his freedom. The ocean loomed in the distance. Black waves crashed onto a moonlit beach, on which three people stood: Jemma, Louie, and Mackie. He sprinted. His goal was in sight, and yet no matter how hard he raced, they never came nearer.

Markus appeared, blocking his path. Despite the burned and shriveled skin, Ben recognized the hatred in his eyes.

The guard's body erupted into flames, which filled the space around Ben. He was encapsulated in a new prison, one of heat and rage. Ben yelled, swatting at the blaze as it constricted around him, growing narrower and narrower with no escape.

He woke in a sweat. His heart pounded in his ears as he sat up on his narrow bed. He was still in the lighthouse cell, surrounded by reminders of the sea that kept him here, isolated on an island.

The knocking the previous night hadn't lasted for long. Whoever it was must've changed their mind after receiving no answer. Ben drifted into a world of nightmares shortly after.

"Good morning, Roomie," Quill's voice came from above. "Wasn't sure how late you were gonna stay asleep."

"Have you been watching me?" Ben evened his breathing as he glanced at the eye in his ceiling.

"You make me sound like some kind of stalker," Quill said. "I wasn't watching you, just peeking every once in a while to see if you were still breathing."

"Is that something to be concerned about?" He took another deep breath, reassuring himself that he was still alive.

"Well, yeah. Honestly, most people given EnertinX aren't strong enough to survive it. The ones that do have a reason to stay living." Quill paused, letting her statement sink in.

Ben was lucky to be alive. He shuddered. How much blood must this island hold?

"So," she continued, "what's your reason?"

The question was obvious to Ben. His family. He needed to stay alive for them.

"And don't say something like your loved ones back home," Quill continued, interrupting his thoughts. "We all have loved ones we want to get back to. That's not enough."

"So, then, what is?"

"Don't get me wrong, family is part of it, but not all of it. Perhaps you have a higher purpose? Or you just like to prove people wrong. You have a fighting spirit."

Ben shook his head. "I don't know about that. Any fight I have in me has only led to trouble."

"I wouldn't be so sure."

A sliding sound turned Ben's attention to the desk on the other side of the room. The rolling top had lifted, exposing the inside. On the desktop was a notebook and a pen.

Ben pulled the small chair to the desk—his body was still weak. The notebook's blue cover was worn, the pages filled with different hand-writing.

Dear Mom, one entry started. *Remember, I love you.*

Ben continued to flip through:

My dearest love....

I can't handle this much longer....

I miss you....

Be good for your mother....

Messages for people that were left behind. "Who wrote these?" Ben asked, already knowing the answer.

"Disparates like you."

"What happened to them?"

Quill sighed. "Well, they aren't in your room anymore, now are they?"

Ben thought for a moment. "Do you think they're dead? Was Chayse taken to die?"

"Chayse was different," Quill said, although her voice was hesitant. "He wasn't given EnertinX like most of the people in that notebook. Like I said before, not everyone survives this *cure.*"

These letters reminded Ben of Dogivan's last wish: for his son to know he was sorry. It wasn't right what happened. Ben wasn't okay with these last messages being left behind. "We need to get these to their families."

"There it is." Quill clapped.

"What?"

"Your fighting spirit. You're gonna make it out of here."

Ben looked back at the notebook. All the lives lost to time. He was going to make it out of here, if not for himself then for every Disparate that'd been abused and tested on. Treated as lab specimens instead of the people they were.

A knock came at the door, and this time, it opened. A woman with blond hair stepped into the room as a guard closed the door behind her. An ominous feeling entered with her.

"Hello, Benjamin Hodgerton. I'm Dr. Paxton, and I have a few questions for you."

The pen in front of Ben rose and landed on the paper. He quickly wrapped his hand around it, hoping Dr. Paxton hadn't noticed. He avoided glancing at the ceiling, not wanting to give Quill away.

"Dr. Paxton?" Ben said as the pen scribbled across the paper. "I'm not sure we've met."

The doctor chuckled. "We haven't; however, I've been watching you. And I'm fascinated by what I've learned. I hope I'm not interrupting anything," she said, nodding at the notebook that laid open in front of him.

"Not at all," Ben said as the pen stopped moving. *Don't trust her* was written on the page. He didn't understand the warning. He already knew better than to trust a doctor on the island. Ben closed it and turned toward Dr. Paxton.

She sat on the edge of his bed, a few feet from him. "I tried to stop by last night, but you had already gone to bed. I didn't want to disrupt your sleep, considering what your body is healing from."

"What your colleagues did to me," Ben spat out. He didn't care to play nice.

"Well, yes. You were pretty beat up after everything that happened. That earthquake came out of nowhere and caused quite the amount of damage. Honestly, it's a miracle you're still alive. That can't be said about *all* your fellow inpatients."

Was she referring to Mr. Dogivan, or were there others that died in the escape attempt? Ben's stomach clenched. This could be a mind game, he reminded himself. *Don't trust her.*

"How are Oliver and 1198 doing? They both seemed to be fine." He narrowed his eyes. Two could play this game.

"They... are," she said. She rubbed her fingertips together. "I understand it was a shock to see the two of them together. Oliver was the one who applied pressure to your wound to keep you from dying."

"He's also the reason I got shot in the first place. And why I'm on this island." Cold surrounded Ben's heart. Thinking about Oliver triggered his anger. The knife in his back was still fresh.

"Hmm," Dr. Paxton said. "If you'd like to make a formal complaint, that can be done. Then we will investigate any concerns you have further. To be truthful, I'm not much of a fan of Oliver either." She chuckled, as if laughing at an inside joke.

"Consider this a formal complaint," Ben said. He didn't expect anything to come from confiding in Dr. Paxton.

"Noted," she said. "On to the reason I'm here. Your treatment looks to have been successful. The fact you can talk about a weasel like Oliver without freezing was just the type of progress I hoped to see! Which brings us to a proposition I'd like to bring forward."

Ben wanted to be repulsed by her positive disposition, but as much as he tried to coil away, his thoughts told him to listen to what she had to say. No harm in listening, right?

"What kind of proposition?" he asked.

"Time for you to get off the island."

Her words hit him like a brick to his chest. She was offering him exactly what he wanted.

"What's the catch?" He looked at her warily.

Her face was smooth as she explained. "You are one of a handful of islanders that have successfully recovered from being a Disparate. I would like to invite you to join the team and share the good news with the rest of the Republics."

Ben thought of the notebook sitting on the desk. Full of letters of regret and last goodbyes. Written by Disparates who hadn't survived the new drug. And that notebook only represented those who made it to the lighthouse. Surely there were countless others that didn't survive past the rounds of shots.

"What about those who didn't survive?"

"What do you mean?" she narrowed her eyes.

"The Disparates that EnertinX didn't work for. Who died in the process."

Her eyes widened. "Oh, I believe you've been misinformed." Her fingers rubbed together once more.

Ben wanted to hear her explanation.

"This new drug has been in development for years, that is true. And it has been tested on other Disparates and been unsuccessful, but EnertinX didn't result in their deaths. Oh no. Their energy simply returned. We have been very thorough in making sure this medication is safe."

If this were true, EnertinX would usher in a new age. A generation where people wouldn't need to fear their emotions. Where they could be themselves with no repercussions, or at least none so deadly. It was the type of life he'd always dreamed of giving to Louie, and now, he was a part of doing it.

"So what would you need me to do?" Ben asked.

"Join my team." She rubbed her fingers. "Travel to the seven Republics to teach and educate members of the community on the effectiveness of EnertinX. Share how it's changed your life."

She was right. The cure had certainly changed his life. He wasn't sure if it was for the better. "And my family?"

"It may be difficult to bring them with us as we travel, but of course you will be able to be home with them when our schedule allows. I know your wife is buzzing for you to return."

Jemma was waiting for him. This was his opportunity to get back to her.

A light shock sparked on his good shoulder. His thoughts went to Quill. *Don't trust her.* "And what if I don't agree to join you?"

"If you decide this isn't the right fit for you, I understand." Dr. Paxton rubbed her hands together; a cold breeze had entered the small room. "We'd want to keep you here longer to make sure you continue your progress. If you choose to join our team, you would continue to receive regular check ups and care under my supervision."

Of course, join her or stay locked away. Those were his options.

"So," she asked, "what will it be?"

Pressure to decide washed over him, and yet in his mind, he knew his answer. "I'll do it."

A smile spread across her face. "Welcome to the team."

Margaret sat on the couch and watched in amazement as Jemma stood in the center of the room after replacing the broken light-bulbs. Her eyes were closed, concentrating.

"Focus on the energy within you," Asher told her. "You can use it to jumpstart the power in your walls."

"I'm not sure if this is going to work," Jemma said. She took a deep breath. As she released it, the light in the family room flickered on.

Margaret gasped. The light shut off, plunging the room into shadows.

"Try not to distract her," Asher said. "You're the one wanting the power on."

"I didn't realize why it was shut off to begin with." The fact her daughter was controlling electricity was a lot for her to wrap her mind around. She'd seen it on the security footage, thinking there was no way it'd been Jemma. But it was.

The girl she'd given birth to, rocked as a child, and raised into an adult with a family of her own. All this time she'd been a Disparate? Hiding her fears, and herself, from her mother.

Of course, Margaret couldn't blame her. After all the trauma she'd been through at such a young age, it was a wonder she was able to keep her struggle a secret at all.

"Why didn't you tell me?" Margaret asked as the lights turned on once more. This time, they stayed on as Jemma relaxed.

"I only learned myself a couple weeks ago." Jemma sat next to her mother on the couch.

"So you only recently developed your energy?"

"Well," Asher joined them, "only recently realized the true potential of it. She's been great at hiding and pushing her feelings away. That is, until she couldn't anymore and almost got herself into more trouble than she should've."

"What do you mean?" Margaret looked wide-eyed at her daughter.

Jemma shrugged and told her about the day Ben was taken and the poor streetlight outside the Responders office.

"Speaking of which"—Margaret's hurt at not being trusted returned—"why didn't you tell me he was taken to Lucky Island? Has he been there this entire time?"

"I didn't think you'd believe me." Jemma's words stung, but Margaret felt it was more than that.

"You didn't think I could handle it," she said. A part of her knew her daughter was right. All she had to do was look at the way her heart broke after Louie's burst a couple weeks ago.

Jemma was silent.

"Mom," Asher said, "there's something more we need to talk about."

"You wanted to tell me about Tobias." Margaret's pulse quickened. Asher nodded.

"If it's too much"—Jemma laid a hand on her knee—"we can always talk about this another day. Give the shock of Asher being back some time to settle."

"No." Margaret shook her head and patted Jemma's hand. "I'm not as fragile as you think. My boy has been kept from me all these years; I'm not about to let what he has to say go unheard." She turned toward Asher.

"Dunn"—he said the name with malice on his tongue—"was the one who started the fire. He's responsible for killing Dad."

"How do you know?" She wanted to believe her son was innocent, but the alternative truth hurt more than believing Skylar's death had been an accident.

"He came to the island multiple times. While I was there, I met someone who knows the governor well. Once she realized who I was, she told me what he'd done."

"Which was?" Margaret waited, still unsure of what to believe.

"Dunn told her that he started the fire. That he was to blame for me being on Lucky Island."

Margaret was confused. "But why would he tell anyone that?"

"I don't know," Asher said. "But I believe it."

Margaret wasn't sure if she should trust the word of her son—the son she hadn't seen in almost two decades. However, she had noticed certain irregularities when it came to Tobias. Moments of forgetfulness and flipping on certain issues. But was he truly capable of murdering her husband and hiding it from her all these years? And now working with her to uncover discrepancies in government reporting?

"I need to talk to Tobias," she said.

"You don't believe him?" Jemma asked, scooting away from her.

"It's not that I don't believe him." Margaret sighed. "It's a lot to take in. And it *is* hard to believe. But if it's true, then I need to talk to Tobias."

"He'll lie about it," Asher said. He clenched his fists together, smoke slithering between his fingers.

"And I'll see through his lie. We've become close friends over the years, and I trust who he is today. Perhaps there is more to the story than we know."

"Maybe"—Jemma placed a hand on Margaret's shoulder—"but be careful. If he's been hiding this secret, he won't like being called out."

Margaret nodded. She was confident Tobias wasn't dangerous, and yet she felt a pit settle on the bottom of her stomach.

"Wait," Asher said. "Don't confront him, at least not right away."

"Why?" Margaret asked.

Her children exchanged glances. Asher nodded at Jemma.

"We're going to rescue Ben," Jemma said.

"And," Asher jumped in, "confronting the governor about this would be a good distraction while we do it. But I'm not sure it's safe."

"I wouldn't worry about that," Margaret said. "I know Tobias well enough to pull information out of him. I'll be just fine." The idea of her children traveling to Lucky Island made her queasy. Surely there had to be a better way.

She turned toward Jemma, ready to suggest another plan; however, the twinkle of hope in her daughter's eyes stopped her. If Ben were truly on the island, it was for a reason. He wasn't likely to be released anytime soon, no matter what Dr. Paxton promised. Margaret knew better than to trust her. And Asher had experience on the island. If anyone would know how to operate a rescue, it would be him.

Margaret didn't like the idea, but her children were grown adults. It wasn't like she could ground them. And the fact they trusted her to help them in this small way made her want to prove to them that she could.

"Okay," Margaret agreed. "I'll wait until you leave to confront him. Hopefully it'll be enough of a distraction."

Jemma let out a breath. "Thank you, Mom."

TWENTY-FIVE

J emma stood on a small motorboat that belonged to Samay. He'd offered it for this mission, as long as they brought back some fish for the weekend special.

That was fine with the group. Having a reason to be on the water would benefit the mission in case something went wrong. A good alibi if Responders were to question them.

But certainly nothing would go wrong. Jemma reassured herself as she sat at the back of the boat, her hand on a fishing rod. Their plan was good. Asher's knowledge of the island layout helped them devise the best place to land and which path to take to get to the warehouse where Flame Disparates were kept. The idea of breaking into a large prison was daunting, but she needed to trust in the plan.

Aniyah groaned in her spot next to Jemma. The wind had started to pick up, tossing the boat side to side. Her hands clutched her stomach as she kept her eyes closed. The sea was not good to her.

Samay sat next to Jemma, his own rod in hand. She couldn't help but have her attention drawn to Buran and Asher at the steering wheel, deep in conversation. Likely going over the map once more, making sure they were headed in the right direction.

"Why don't you join them?" Samay said, noticing her gaze.

"Sure you don't mind?" Jemma asked.

Samay nodded. Jemma left the fishing to him and headed to the front of the boat.

The conversation between Asher and Buran seemed to wrap up as she arrived.

"How's the fishing going?" Asher asked.

Jemma shrugged. "Not so good. This weather seems to be keeping the fish away."

"Hmm, maybe I'll go try my hand at it," Asher said. "I haven't fished since before I was on the island." He left to go help Samay.

Jemma didn't mind. She had questions for Buran.

"Have you spoken to Calum?" she asked. She hadn't heard from him since their fight the other night.

Buran nodded. "He said he understands why he has to stay back. I know it's hard to not rescue everyone, but they'll have their turn."

"But he's not asking for everyone to be rescued," Jemma said. She understood Calum's hope and fear.

"Where do we stop?" Buran rebutted. "If we rescue his brother, do we also save Samay's niece? What about my cousin that was taken to the 'clinic' that we haven't heard from for over two years?"

Jemma was silent. She hadn't realized how much personal history each member of the Dissentients had with the island. What they were sacrificing in order for her to be reunited with Ben.

Buran sighed. "What we are doing will help them. It'll take some time, but eventually we will be reunited with our missing family members. Just right now, we can't afford the extra liability."

Waves crashed rhythmically onto the side of the boat. The waning moon above hid behind dark clouds, and the wind was heavy. Jemma hoped a storm wasn't rolling in. They were common on the ocean.

Samay shouted from the back of the boat. He'd caught something on the line. Buran glanced back briefly, longing in his eyes. "You catch a boot back there?"

"This one's alive," Samay yelled back.

Jemma recognized the look in Buran's eyes. He wanted in on the action. "I can take the wheel for a bit if you want to check it out."

"You know how to steer a boat?" Buran lifted an eyebrow.

"I've been on the water a time or two." Caty's family owned a boat, and they'd go sailing almost weekly during the summer, before kids. "Besides, you're close by if something goes wrong."

"True." Buran stepped back from the helm. He made sure Jemma was holding it comfortably before turning to admire Samay's catch.

Jemma kept the wheel steady as she watched the shadow-filled sea before her, searching the horizon for any view of land. Lucky Island was a few hours away, and they'd already been sailing for at least two. They shouldn't be far off.

A few minutes later, Samay approached from behind.

"My turn," he said and took over Jemma's position. He turned the wheel slightly. In the far distance was the outline of land.

Jemma's pulse raced. Her husband was on that island. They planned to dock on the west side, avoiding the normal boat routes.

"You're sure this half of the island is abandoned?" Samay asked.

Asher nodded. "I know it is."

As they neared, details of overgrown trees and a rocky shoreline came into view. There was no dock on this side, and even if there were, that'd be too obvious to use. Landing the boat would be tricky, but the trees and shelter of darkness would be a strong ally for them.

No one expected a group to infiltrate an island that was officially "decommissioned;" however, guards still roamed. Especially closer to the warehouses. Asher had explained they carried guns.

Samay steered the boat close to a cluster of rocks. "This may be as close as I can get."

"It's close enough," Buran said. "We should be able to walk the rest of the way to the beach."

"Don't forget the rubber waders," Samay said. "They'll be extra handy if someone's nerves pick up."

Buran looked at Jemma. "He makes a good point. Perhaps some breathing exercises first?"

Jemma took in a large breath and sighed it out. Asher gave her a smirk.

"Good." Buran nodded.

Samay stayed on the boat as the other four, dressed in rubber overalls, stepped into the water. The cold sea reached to Jemma's knees, heightening her awareness of the surroundings. She scanned the shoreline, looking for any signs of life. The wind had picked up and now rustled the leaves as they plodded through the cold, murky water.

Jemma rubbed her arms, more for reassurance than for warmth. Her hair was standing on edge. Waiting for something to go wrong.

"We need to head that way." Asher pointed to the north as they stepped out of the water, into a dark threshold of trees. The group of four followed him through the thick brush, leaves and broken tree branches snapping with each step.

Anticipation quickened within her. They were on their way to save Ben. Her husband would soon be in her arms. That knowledge kept her moving forward.

Asher slowed his pace. "We're nearing the warehouses. Guards should be changing nighttime shifts. Buran and Aniyah, you head toward the front of the warehouses, we'll take the back. Count how many you see and note where they're stationed. We'll rendezvous back here in twenty."

Buran nodded as he and Aniyah followed Asher's directions.

"How many guards should we expect?" Jemma asked.

"At this time of night, guards are likely in pairs. Keep an eye out; they may be patrolling. They tend to be stationary for five, then walk for five."

"How do you know all this?" His detailed knowledge of the guard patterns and numbers surprised Jemma, likely more information than they'd want their inmates to know.

"When you've been somewhere for so long, you start to pick up on things."

Jemma wanted to ask more, but Asher froze and placed a finger to his lips.

Through the trees, she heard muffled voices. She couldn't make out what they were saying, but one sounded more agitated than the other.

They inched closer.

Jemma stepped lightly, keeping her footsteps as silent as possible.

"...not Markus...no...I can't believe...really thought..." The angry male's volume continued to rise until they were close enough to hear it. "This mess never should have occurred in the first place. Should have learned from the fire last month."

The mention of fire made Jemma's stomach seize, as if a bomb settled in its pit, the trigger about to be pressed. She glanced at Asher. He seemed unsurprised by the revelation. It occurred to Jemma that *last month* he was still on the island. Or perhaps, he was in the middle of his escape.

"No one expected something like this," the second guard responded—a woman. "Patients take their medicine. It's designed to keep them hooked."

The man laughed. "Yeah. Great job it did."

Asher parted the branches of the bush in front of them to get a view of the guards. Jemma leaned and looked over his shoulder. Sure enough, a man with his back to them stood talking with a woman nearby. They both wore uniforms.

"At least we got the power back up and running a few days ago." The woman flashed a light across a large box on the ground. She turned, the light passing the bushes where Jemma and Asher hid. Jemma tucked herself lower to the ground.

"Took 'em long enough," said the man.

Jemma wanted to know more about the context of their conversation. Of course her husband would be drugged, but something more sinister seemed to be at play.

The wind picked up around them while a storm brewed inside of her. A sense of dread as she awaited the incoming tempest. She took a deep breath in through her nose, trying to settle the dark thoughts that raged through her mind.

She was stuck on an island in the middle of an ocean. And not just any island: Lucky Island. Guards stood only a few yards away from them; moonlight peeking through the clouds coruscated across their guns. One wrong move and they would be caught. Downed by the bullets that would pierce through the air.

"Hey," Asher whispered as he placed a hand on her shoulder. A shock jolted him away, revealing the energy that'd been building.

This was it. She needed to relieve this energy before it burst out uncontrollably. Jemma closed her eyes, trying to stay calm long enough to pick the target for her release. The power box. If she hit it, the guards would have to leave. And pitching the island into darkness should only aid in their mission, right? She wasn't sure, but she was running out of time.

She stretched her hands in front of her, imagining a snake slithering through her body as she directed her energy to hit behind the threats in front of them.

Asher's eyes widened. "The box?" he said in a hurried whisper. "Are you trying to kill them?"

Her focus faltered. He was right; if the box exploded, it could hurt the guards. She hadn't thought this through. However, the snake refused to stop. slithered out of her palms, aimed for her original destination.

In a split second, Asher's head whipped from her to the guards. He lunged forward, pushing Jemma's arms over as they both fell to the ground.

A loud, crinkling buzz erupted as the guards' screams reverberated throughout the trees.

Branches scratched against Jemma's face as she lay still, waiting for the aftermath of her outburst. Asher's body crushed hers, keeping her down. Her line of energy had skidded to the side when he'd tackled her. Were the guards still alive?

"Colleen!" the man shouted. "Are you okay?"

"My leg was hit, but other than that, I'm okay." They were both still alive.

"What was that? Did it come from the forest?" Jemma's heart paused at the man's question. She'd given their position away. They should run.

And yet—Asher didn't move. His weight kept her from escaping. She tried to push against him to no avail. "We need to go," she hissed at Asher.

He shook his head, bringing a finger to his lips.

"I think it was the power box," the woman guard, Colleen, said. "The incoming storm must have triggered it. Apparently the patch job wasn't as good as they thought."

Jemma narrowed her eyes at Asher. No way the guards were stupid enough to believe that.

The man sighed. "They need to bring real engineers here to do the work correctly."

Jemma was wrong. It didn't take much brains to patrol a secret island.

"They say they're working on it." Colleen groaned in pain. "I'm not sure I can walk. Can you head back to the barracks and grab the first aid kit?"

"What if it explodes again?" Although the voices were muffled, Jemma sensed the concern in his voice.

"Looks pretty dead to me. Power's probably out across the island again. Disparates are gonna be stuck in their rooms."

"Right," the man said. "I'll be right back."

As footsteps thudded away, Asher lifted himself off Jemma. He parted the branches once more, peering through the greenery. A smile lit his face as he stood. "Wait here." He motioned at Jemma, then, like a lion about to catch a mouse, he pounced out of the woods and headed toward the solitary guard.

Jemma gasped. She leaned forward to take Asher's spot at the gap in the brush. He sauntered forward, as if being shot wasn't a very real possibility right now. Perhaps he meant to finish this guard himself. The thought caused a chill to run through her.

"Asher?" Colleen said as he neared, surprise in her voice. "What are you doing back here?"

Her brother blocked most of her view of the guard, but Jemma could tell she was sitting on the ground holding her leg. Jemma waited for Asher to raise his arms and permit an inferno to escape. Instead, he lowered himself next to her, giving Jemma a full look at the woman's response to his presence.

Colleen's mouth gaped, her eyes wide. Yet from this distance, Jemma detected no fear in her body language toward Asher. In fact, she slapped his arm as he sat next to her.

"Hey, I'm here on a mission," he said as he rubbed where she'd hit. Jemma's reaction mirrored Colleen's. Her brother was sitting out in the open, talking with one of the guards he'd warned the Dissentients to watch out for. *They are ruthless and hateful and won't hesitate to hurt you.*

"What kind of mission?" Colleen asked.

"A rescue one." Asher leaned onto his knees. "Someone important."

Colleen nodded slowly. "I see. She's not here." Jemma barely made out her words as her voice lowered.

Asher's head twisted to face her. "Where is she?"

Colleen's voice dropped again, even softer this time. Jemma couldn't understand her over the rustling of the canopy above as the wind intensified.

If it didn't blow over, the storm might leave them stranded here. They needed to hurry.

Asher's face fell as his mouth moved. Colleen pointed her hand toward the northern part of the island. Had Asher asked about Ben? Although the friendliness of this guard was unexpected, she hoped it was a sign they could use her.

Colleen leaned into Asher, wrapping her arms around him. He returned her embrace. Heat rushed to Jemma's cheeks as the seconds ticked by.

Then, Asher lifted his head, looking behind Colleen. Jemma squinted to follow his gaze, but the foliage blocked her view. Asher let go and scurried on all fours toward Jemma. This time, instead of the lion, he looked to be the prey.

His breathing was deep as he emerged through the leaves, falling onto his stomach. Jemma ducked once more as a light illuminated her hiding spot, glaring through the shadows of the leaves.

"Is someone there?" the male guard shouted.

"Just an animal," Colleen said as the light lingered. "Probably seeking shelter before the storm hits. Not a good night to be out. Did you bring the kit?" The man must have turned away, as Asher and Jemma were once again consumed in darkness.

Jemma released her breath. She moved her attention to Asher. Her heart pounded in her chest. "Did your *friend* know where Ben is?" she whispered.

Asher, his body still plastered to the forest floor, nodded his head. "He's not here."

His words were like a knife plunging into her soul. Ben was their goal. He was their mission. "What do you mean? Where is he?"

Asher raised himself from the ground, wiping dirt from his hands. "He's in a lighthouse—on another island."

A drop of water from the canopy above fell on Jemma's cheek. The storm had arrived.

TWENTY-SIX

R ain sprinkled as Jemma and Asher retraced their steps.
"What if she's lying?" Jemma asked. They were headed to tell
the news to the rest of the group. She followed behind him.

"She's not."

"Maybe she wants us to go out in this storm." Wind directed soft
rain drops into Jemma's hair. It wouldn't stay this light for long.
"Have our boat capsize. That'd be an easy way to get rid of us all."

Asher whipped around to face her. "She wouldn't do that to me.
She's not that kind of person."

"She's a guard on Lucky Island!" Jemma didn't care that her voice
was rising. They should be far enough away for the storm to hide it.

"Who is?" Buran appeared on their path, Aniyah close behind.

Asher hardened. "Ben isn't here. He's on another island."

The new companions ' eyes widened at the same time. "What?"
Aniyah gasped.

"That might not be true," Jemma said. "He spoke to one of the
guards. I think she's lying."

"She's not!" Asher balled his hands into fists. "You're gonna have
to trust me on that."

"And why should I?" Jemma returned his glare. "*You* were the one that told us how dangerous the guards are."

They held their hostile stare, waiting for the other to break.

"She's right," Buran interrupted the wind-torn silence. "You aren't telling us everything. It makes it difficult to know what to believe."

Asher pursed his lips. "Fine."

Jemma crossed her arms.

"Her name is Colleen. Yes, she's a guard, but she's different from the others." His eyes darted to the side, as if thinking of how much to say.

Jemma wanted to know it all. "How so?"

"She cares about the people here," Asher explained. "Wants to make a change on this island."

"Ha." Aniyah let out an exasperated snicker. "Don't expect that to be successful anytime soon."

Asher turned his body so the four of them created a circle. "She helped me get out of here. I trust her with my life."

His escape. The details he'd been so careful not to reveal too much of. Was she the person he mentioned leaving behind?

"But how did you get off?" Buran asked. He looked as eager as Jemma felt to hear the truth.

"Everyone here thinks I'm dead." Asher rubbed his hand on his chin. "Except her. She sailed me off."

"She was your getaway driver." Buran looked at him curiously. "Huh. I didn't think anyone working on the island would have a conscience. You must have had quite the influence on her."

Jemma remembered the way Colleen's hug had lingered between them. "You care about her, and it seems like she cares about you as well."

Asher's cheeks reddened as thunder rumbled in the distance. "We need to get back to Samay. Especially if we want to make it to the lighthouse before this storm gets worse."

Jemma sat at the back of the boat as Asher directed Samay on where to find the second island. Buran stood next to them, his arms crossed. Water continued to fall onto the boat's awning, but they weren't ready to give up. Not yet. Besides, if they tried to return to the mainland now, they'd certainly be swallowed by the eyewall of the storm. The lighthouse island, on the other hand, was a short sail away.

"I haven't recovered from the first boat ride yet." Aniyah clutched the railing of the boat, ready to lean over any moment. "It was clear skies when we left. Not sure I would have agreed to come if I knew about this storm."

"I don't think any of us would've," Jemma said, noticing her sickly disposition.

"Even you?" she asked. "To be honest, I admire the loyalty you have for your husband. Someday I hope to find that kind of love."

"To the point you'd risk your own life to save theirs?"

"Better to risk and fail than to live the rest of your life wondering 'what if?'" Aniyah clutched her stomach and winced.

There seemed to be personal experience behind her words. They'd been working together for the last few weeks, yet Jemma didn't know much about the young woman next to her.

"How did you end up here?" Jemma asked. Buran and Calum had personal connections, both of their brothers being affected by the government's control of Disparates. Samay supposedly had a niece somewhere on the island. But she didn't know about Aniyah, with her hard exterior and short answers.

"I was needed for the mission..."

"No," Jemma explained, "I mean, how did you end up with Buran and the Dissentients?"

Aniyah raised an eyebrow at her. "Showing interest in someone else's problems rather than your own? Feels out of character for you."

Jemma's mouth fell open.

"Okay, that was a bit harsh," Aniyah said quickly. "I didn't mean it that way. I get why you're so worried about Ben."

"I didn't mean to ignore everyone else," Jemma said.

"When I'm hurt, I lash out," Aniyah continued. "It's kind of a defense mechanism to keep from falling into a pit."

"You have ground energy?" She wouldn't have guessed sadness to be the demon inside of Aniyah. If anything, she viewed her as icy.

"Samay found me when I was fifteen." Aniyah tugged her coat tighter around her body. "I was a runaway. Escaped the foster home that... wasn't a good place for me." Her face dropped. "I'd made my own bed at the bottom of a ditch. Didn't even realize what I'd done until he pulled me out. The section I'd been in was a good four feet deeper than the rest. He took me in, and he's been like a father to me ever since."

Jemma glanced at the helm. Samay's strong grip held the wheel. Past him was a dark, cloudy abyss of nothingness. Finding a second island in this weather seemed as likely as the storm deciding to pass over them.

"So you trust him," Jemma stated, eyeing Buran who was chatting with Samay. "Both of them?"

"I do. I was on Enertin when he found me. Likely would have been crushed by rocks if he didn't show up when he did. He and Buran have taught me how to handle my emotions when I get sad."

"By lashing out?" Jemma lifted a brow.

Aniyah let out a laugh. "Nope, that one's not on them. That came from my time in foster care. Had to present a tough front to keep the other kids from messing with me. Some habits are harder to break than others."

Jemma nodded, thinking about her own difficulties sharing her problems with others. She appreciated Aniyah's vulnerability. Perhaps she could trust her with some of her own. "You know, Ben and I haven't always had a strong relationship."

Aniyah narrowed her eyes.

"It's true," Jemma continued. "We fight. We argue. We have disagreements. There's been times when we've lashed out at each other. Okay, actually, I did most of that."

"Really?" Aniyah asked. "You?"

Jemma nodded. "Ben's the patient one. But turns out that's because of Enertin. Honestly, I'm worried I don't really know the man I've been married to for almost a decade."

"It's normal for people to change." Aniyah met Jemma's eyes. "Look at you. You're not the same timid Jemma from a few weeks ago. Conflict makes you stronger."

She was right. A month ago, Jemma didn't know how to admit she needed help. Now, she relied on people she didn't fully trust to save her family. Although, that trust was growing stronger the more she got to know the people around her.

"There! Up ahead!" Asher shouted from the front. Jemma perked up. Despite the dark storm clouds, wind, and rain, a darker mass of land broke across the horizon. Smaller than Lucky Island, and yet, more foreboding. There was no map or plan to use this time.

As they sailed closer, a long, tall object came into view. The lighthouse Colleen had spoken of. The top light was not shining. Wandering boats were not welcome here.

Samay navigated to a beach on the edge. The storm was good for one thing: the clouds covered the moon and stars. It not only made it difficult for them to see where they were headed, but it also made it nearly impossible for anyone at the top of the lighthouse to see them coming. Perhaps they did choose the right night for a rescue.

"So, what do we do now?" Jemma asked as they gathered in a circle.

"I think the fewer on this island the better." Asher glanced around the group. "Too many and we're more likely to be heard."

Buran nodded in agreement.

"How do we know no one is watching us now?" Aniyah's eyes darted to the trees on the edge of the sandy beach. Samay had landed the boat near a rocky cliff, but he couldn't find a spot that was fully hidden.

"No one's come out shooting yet," Asher said. "Seems like a good sign to me. From what Colleen said, this place isn't as guarded as Lucky Island. They don't keep many patients here."

"What is it used for?" Jemma's body shook. She'd tried not to let her mind wander. The reasons why researchers needed to put some Disparates on a separate island were numerous. Figuring out why Ben was moved could be vital to their next course of action.

"Colleen wasn't exactly sure. It's been used when a Disparate proved to be too much of a threat on Lucky." He hesitated. "It's also a place some have been moved to before being released back home..."

"Wait." Jemma's eyes widened. She couldn't imagine her Ben being any kind of threat. "Are you saying Dr. Paxton was telling the truth?" Wind whipped hair onto her face, but she didn't care. "That we didn't need to go on this mission to save him?"

"Even if she was telling the truth," Asher said. "They wouldn't let him leave without making sure there was no way he'd tell about the island."

"Is that how other people have been released?" Buran asked. "How could they guarantee they wouldn't say anything?"

Silence settled. No one wanted to say the dark suggestions that were likely going through their minds.

Jemma certainly didn't. She knew what it would take for her to stay quiet. A threat to her family. Her boys crossed her mind, staying at Caty's house that night. Was she putting them at risk by being here? If Ben went missing... would they become a target?

"Jemma," Asher said, looking at her, "hold onto that energy. We're gonna need it."

"Wait, so the two of us are going?" She looked around the boat, all heads nodding in agreement.

"You have the most to lose," Samay said. "So you'll work the hardest to make it happen."

Jemma took a steadying breath. "Isn't it usually advised against having those closest to the problem be involved?"

"Maybe in movies," Buran interjected. "However, in this situation, the deeper the emotions, the better."

Jemma hadn't thought about that. If it came down to a fight, energy was their best weapon. She breathed through her nose to keep her nerves from bursting before she'd need them.

Asher bobbed his head at the side of the boat. "You ready?"

Footprints filled with rain as they walked cautiously across the beach, heading for the cover of the tree canopy.

Jemma held her jacket over her head. "We should have brought umbrellas."

"Yeah, 'cause that would help us stay hidden."

"If they were black they would."

Asher laughed.

The sound warmed Jemma. They'd argued, but they'd also forgiven and returned to their sibling banter easily. She'd missed this.

There was a path within the forested area. Not well maintained, but the trodden-over foliage was clearly used on occasion. They followed it as it led toward their goal. As the lighthouse came into view, Asher put his arm out to stop her.

"There aren't guards outside right now, likely due to this storm, but I can guarantee they're inside."

"How many do you think there will be?"

"Not sure. No one is supposed to know about this place. They won't be expecting us to show up, but they still need someone to watch the Disparates here."

Jemma looked at the red door in their view. What awaited them behind it?

A rock hit its surface. She twisted to look at Asher, who was picking up a second rock. "What are you doing?" she whispered fiercely.

"Trying to see who comes to the door."

"Whoever's in there probably thinks it's the wind."

Asher threw another. "Guess we need to throw enough to get them to notice." He handed her a large rock.

"What happened to staying hidden?"

"They're gonna know we're here soon enough—might as well use the factor of surprise to our advantage while we can."

"And knocking at their door with rocks is surprising?"

Asher lowered his arm. "Perhaps not. Do you have a better idea?"

As she was thinking of something, the door creaked open. The siblings ducked, peering through the brush to see who was brave enough to face the storm.

"Nothin's here, as I said," a woman in a black uniform shouted to the room behind her. "Now stop fussin' and let me sleep." The door closed.

Asher looked at her with a gleam in his eye. "Sounds like there's two of them. Should be easy enough for us to handle. Are you ready to light things up?"

The smirk on his face was the same one he wore before executing a plan that was guaranteed to get him in trouble.

Now seemed like the best time to use it.

TWENTY-SEVEN

Tonight was the night, and Margaret was ready. Keeping herself from darting to Tobias's office the second after hearing Asher's claim took all the restraint she had. Thankfully, she only had to wait a few days, but in that time, her thoughts about Tobias and his inconsistencies heightened. Asher's story didn't seem so far-fetched anymore.

A chill was in the air as she arrived at the capitol building. This wasn't expected—then again, spring storms were unpredictable. She plastered a smile to her face as she waved at the guards.

"Busy day today?" she asked.

"You know it," the guard at the front said as he leaned back in his chair, tossing a ball into the air and catching it repeatedly. "Glad my shift is almost over. I'm ready to get home. Hopefully before this storm rolls in."

"Perhaps it will blow away?" Margaret stared out the window at the ominous clouds, her pulse racing. "Most do."

The guard shrugged. "Maybe. But I've got a feeling this one won't."

Margaret thought of her children, currently on a boat somewhere on the ocean.

She reminisced about the moments she'd spent here in the capital with Skylar. The late night dinners she'd packaged and shared with him;

their own special date. The times she brought the children for special "Dad" time. It wasn't much of a playground, but he made good use of his short breaks.

No.

She focused on her mission, thoughts running through her mind of how she would approach Tobias without revealing the truth about Asher.

"Mrs. Stillfield," the governor's newest receptionist proclaimed as Margaret approached her desk. There was no point in learning her name, as she'd be gone within the month. Tobias never was one who could keep a secretary. "I don't believe I see you on the schedule." She held a calendar in her hands, flipping through the pages.

"I'm not, but I'm sure Tobias has time to see me."

The young girl paused in her scurrying. Margaret presented herself with shoulders back, her confidence emitted through her stance. It worked. The receptionist pressed a button on the desk to unlock the governor's office doors.

"He has twenty minutes left of dinner," the girl said.

Margaret gave her a nod of thanks as she approached the doors.

She burst into his office, not pausing to knock. A ramen noodle ran down the governor's chin as a shocked expression painted his face.

"Oh! Maggie, hi." He slurped the noodle into his mouth. "What are you doing here?"

"I'm here because of a sensitive matter." She forced her face to change from angry to saddened. Seeing him now, in person, after letting Asher's truth settle in her brain, it was difficult not to immediately call him out. However, she needed to test the waters first. See how he reacted indirectly to the idea.

"What happened?" His forehead creased with what looked to be genuine worry.

"Another body was found in South Vasco. It sounds like it could be Asher's." She kept her face sullen as she watched his response. "It had been burnt in a house fire."

"Oh?" he said. "That is interesting. You don't know for sure if it's his. He could still be alive somewhere." He didn't look like he was lying.

"But he's most likely dead, right?" Margaret questioned.

Tobias's brows wrinkled, but he didn't respond.

"I can't handle looking at another dead body. Not again," she said as she shook her head.

"Again? Maggie, you know you don't have to go look at the bodies. You already have a sample of DNA on file. They can test it to see if yours is related."

"I know," she paused, "but I need to see for myself. I can't handle trusting saliva in a test tube to tell me if it's my boy or not." She watched his face for any sign of insecurity or distress. She saw none.

"I can see why you would feel that way, but it won't pan out. It wasn't Asher." He didn't expand further.

"How do you know?" Margaret was growing tired of playing this game. She was always a straight shooter; beating around the bush was agony for her. But if she shot too straight, it could make things worse. Clue him into the fact that Asher had found her. She decided she needed to take the plunge, hoping it wouldn't be too much. "Have you heard *anything* about my boy?" she asked.

Governor Dunn shook his head. Margaret noticed how deep his wrinkles had gotten with age. *Must reflect how deep his lies can run.*

"You know I want to find him too. That's what Skylar would want."

Her chest tightened at the mention of her late husband. *How would you know what he wanted,* she thought, but restrained herself from saying so. "That's true," she said instead. She didn't know this man in front of her like she thought she did. This conversation wasn't helping her figure out the truth. She needed a different tactic.

"I want to ask you about the other day," she said slowly, changing the subject. "I haven't heard from you since Friday's news."

"Ah yes. I can't believe the Peacocks beat the Roos. What an underdog victory!" He chuckled, recalling the sports report. Margaret looked at him strangely. All week, she had been expecting him to call or send a message or something about it—but she received nothing. Now he was acting like he didn't know what happened. That wasn't like him.

"No, I mean the special report with Dr. Paxton."

"Oh, was that Friday?" His face strained, as if trying to remember. "I don't believe I caught it. I watched the full news segment though, so not sure how it was missed. Oh well, how did she do? Hopefully she explained the next step of Initiative 67 well. It's going to help so many people."

Margaret stared at him blankly. "The letter was brought up. They almost showed it to the world."

Governor Dunn looked at Margaret, his forehead wrinkled. "What letter?"

Chills flowed through Margaret's body. Somehow, he didn't know about the news broadcast. He seemed genuinely supportive of the new initiative instead of wary of it like before. He would occasionally behave strangely, but never to this degree.

"Tobias, the letter you sent me. The one that was stolen in the break in. The one we needed to make sure Dr. Paxton never knew about. Well, now she knows."

"Oh, I saw Dr. Paxton Monday night. I'm not sure which letter you're talking about, but Dr. Paxton didn't seem bothered by it. Initiative 67 is great. EnertinX is wonderfully efficient. You should know; it's worked wonders for your son-in-law! He's even joined the marketing team."

Now it was Margaret's turn to look confused. Ben? She'd felt guilty after she learned Ben was on the island and that Jemma had been hiding it from her. Hearing he was a part of this new initiative made her stomach queasy. Especially after the government framed him for being the Fire Anarchist.

"I'm sure you're excited to have him home. Do you know when he'll arrive?"

"They're letting him off the island?" This all was news to Margaret. There had to be more.

"He's being released from Merrytime Clinic." Tobias's eyebrows creased together. "Hasn't Jemma mentioned it? What do you mean 'island'?"

Margaret hadn't meant to let "island" slip, but then again, she expected him to already be aware of Jemma's accusations. And yet he truly seemed oblivious.

"Right," she said, her mind on her children. If Ben was being moved off the island, then they wouldn't need to risk breaking him out. "I believe I need to check with Jemma on that." She stood from her chair and briskly left the governor's office, Tobias watching her leave. She caught the peculiar expression on his face as the doors closed behind her. She didn't care.

The wind had picked up since she'd been inside. As soon as she got to her car, she called her daughter.

She heard only one ring before the line went dead.

The wind caused the trees to bow, as if playing its part in Jemma and Asher's plan. The added chaos increased the feeling of dread in the air.

"You're gonna need to focus to hit it right." Asher had his hands on Jemma's arms, unafraid that her anxiety might spark at the wrong time.

"Will it catch?" Jemma asked, looking at the bark of the tree Asher held a flame to.

"Only one way to find out. You ready?"

Jemma nodded. They moved through the trees to the side of the building, where they had a good view of the door and a side window. A light fought to be seen through the storm.

Asher picked up a rock once more and tossed it through the window. Broken glass shattered around its impact. Shouting emanated from inside.

"It's just the storm!" This voice had to have come from the woman earlier.

"Can you knock out the inside light?" Asher asked once the other guards' screaming stopped.

"I can feel the electricity in the walls." Jemma followed the buzzing current until it met with multiple other lines, as if each were a train following its own route.

A generator.

"I'm still amazed it works like that." Asher faced his own hands toward the warmed tree. "We're gonna hit the two spots on the count of three. One... two..."

On his next count, Jemma let a small amount of her fears and worries flow through her and escape through her hand, pointing it toward the generator. It wouldn't need much, just one spark.

The power generator buzzed as a sizzling sounded from behind. She turned. Asher had caught the rain-drenched tree on fire, the blaze now consuming the branches at an alarmingly fast rate. Although they were a good ten feet away, the warmth from it thawed Jemma's frozen face.

Voices came from inside the lighthouse once more. "I'll check it out. It's only a power outage. Grab a flashlight. You'll be fine." The red door thrust open with the aid of the wind. The woman's face widened in the glow of the flames. "Holy crap! A tree's on fire!" She disappeared inside for a moment before stepping back out with a large extinguisher. She walked swiftly toward the flames.

Asher nodded his head at Jemma and mouthed "Now."

She focused her remaining store of anxiety on the tree. The worry for her children, for Louie. For this storm inching ever closer, likely waiting to strand them on this desolate island, making them sitting ducks. How her being caught would turn her children's world upside-down, thanks to her reckless abandonment.

An intense crack resounded through the rain and wind as electricity hit the tree like a lightning bolt. Limbs and splinters exploded in all directions. The guard, who'd been only a few feet away, now laid sprawled on her back. A branch laid across her body.

Asher grabbed Jemma's arm, tugging her toward the lighthouse door. They plowed through the opening, Asher stopping to fight against the wind to close the door.

"Ash..." Jemma said slowly as she faced the unseen guard from earlier. He held a flashlight in one hand, the shaky light illuminating the gun he held in his other one.

She raised her hands as Asher turned.

"N-no. Stop," the guard said. "Hands behind your back. I-I'll shoot."

Jemma obliged, lowering her arms. Asher, however, charged forward. In one swift move, he knocked the gun out of the guard's hand and wrapped his arms around his neck. The gun landed on the ground, a quick flash of light exploding as a shot rang out. Jemma jumped back, fearful that the gun had been aimed in the wrong direction.

The guard dropped the flashlight to the ground, the beam rolling as it illuminated the struggle. The guard clawed at Asher's forearms for a few seconds before his body became limp. Asher held on a little longer before laying his sleeping body on the ground.

Jemma's eyes widened. "What if he'd shot me?"

"If he was going to, he would have." Asher retrieved the flashlight from the ground as well as grabbing something from the guard's body. The jingling signified keys. "Besides, the sleep will do him good. Perhaps he will wake with a backbone."

"Shouldn't we grab the gun?" Jemma asked, eying the weapon on the ground.

Asher picked it up, removed the magazine, then tossed it against the wall. He placed the magazine of bullets in his pocket. "Who needs a gun when you're already a flame thrower?"

He made a good point. Jemma was dangerous enough without a trigger.

He searched around the room. There wasn't much. A table with some chairs, a small fridge, and a desk, which he now approached.

He flipped through the pages of a book. Jemma made out rows of writing, likely a ledger. Asher paused on a page, his eyes scanning across it until they stopped. His face fell.

"What is it?" Jemma took a step toward him.

"Oh," he said, his face straightening, "it's just that Ben's on the top floor." He rubbed his fingers against the page.

"Is that a problem?" Jemma's heart fluttered. *Ben is here. He's close.*

"No." Asher pursed his lips as he headed to the set of stairs on the side that spiraled to the next floor.

Jemma followed, surprise striking her at how different the second floor was from the one they'd just left. In fact, they didn't have access to the full room at all. A long steel wall cut the rest of it off from the stairwell.

They continued climbing higher, floor three... four... each with the matching wall and cell door. When they got to the fifth floor, the spiral staircase ended. Instead, a ladder led to the very top of the building. To the darkened light from which it got its name.

Asher approached the door, pulling out the keys he'd had the foresight to grab downstairs.

Jemma stood back. Waiting. Anticipation flooded her veins, causing them to shake. Her body longed to feel Ben's embrace. Her nerves wondered if she'd remember how to be held. But that didn't matter right now. Soon, she'd be back in his arms.

The door opened.

Jemma pushed her brother out of the way as she rushed into the room. "Ben!"

She froze.

The person in front of her wasn't her husband. In fact, it wasn't a *he* at all. A woman leapt from the bed she'd been sitting on and ran to the door, embracing Asher in the hug that Jemma had expected to receive from Ben just moments before.

Blond hair flew in the air as Asher twirled in a circle. The girl buried her head into his shoulder. For a moment, they seemed to be floating.

Jemma, however, was sinking, her legs shaking, threatening to bring her to the floor.

Asher sat the woman back on solid ground as she smiled at him. "What are you doing here?" she asked in a high-pitched voice, each syllable a knife in Jemma's chest.

This wasn't real.

This wasn't happening.

This woman wasn't Ben.

"I told you I wouldn't leave you here," Asher responded.

"Took you long enough to come back." The woman gave him a light punch to his arm.

Jemma's jaw dropped. Asher had assured them Ben would be here. That they would rescue him. Now it seemed his plan all along was focused on someone else. Her heart shattered as her brother's betrayal sank in. Turned out, the blood within their veins was thinner than the water they had crossed to get here.

"Quill, I want you to meet Jemma. My sister," he said as he walked toward her. A smile was plastered on his face. "And Jemma, this is Quill."

"Where is Ben?" Jemma narrowed her eyes.

Asher's smile faltered. "Look, I'm sorry. He's not here."

Breath caught in her throat. "What do you mean?"

"The ledger downstairs," Asher said. "It says he left this afternoon."

"But he's supposed to be here!" Jemma's voice rose as her heart beat in her ears. "*Colleen* said this is where he is, didn't she?"

Asher ran a hand through his hair. "Yeah, he was—"

"But clearly he's not!" Jemma yelled as she squeezed her fists. The flow of electricity from her nerves moments before quieted to the anger that overtook her body. "Was this the plan all along? Use the Dissentients so you could rescue your... your... *girlfriend*?" She didn't know the relationship between her brother and Quill, but she could surmise they were close.

Quill looked like a deer in the headlights as her gaze shot to Asher.

"Jem," Asher said, "that's not what happened."

Tears welled in Jemma's eyes. She didn't know what to believe. "Where is he, then? Where did they take Ben?"

Quill took a step forward. "He was here." Her voice was soft. "I met him."

"And why should I trust *you*?" Jemma crossed her arms.

Quill winced at the sharp tone. "Follow me." She headed toward the door. "I'll show you."

Jemma hesitated. What she wanted to see was her husband, but it was clear that wasn't happening. But proof that he was here, that this wasn't all an elaborate plan, might lessen the blow. And help them figure out *where* he was. She took a step toward the door as she wiped a tear from her cheek.

Twenty-Eight

Wind brushed past Ben's face as he stepped onto land. An ocean storm was coming, but that was behind him now. He was back in Stillfield. The last time he'd been on this dock, he'd gotten the burn that now marred his face. This time, he crossed the gangway with his head held high.

Dr. Paxton had explained the importance of their mission. Ben was part of a new time. A generation that would find healing from the emotions that haunted them. He would be remembered as a pioneer of the next decade.

It all sounded so grand and majestic. And yet, his stomach churned more with each step he took. His forehead wrinkled, his mind foggy as he entered the black car that was waiting at the end of the dock.

"We've made it," Dr. Paxton said from the seat next to him. "This is the start of our great mission. We're going to save the world."

Her confidence flooded his brain, bringing clarity once again. His head bobbed in agreement. This was going to be good. Surely, it had to be good.

And yet the pit was still there.

My Jemma,

I've missed you. I'm barely holding on. The thought of you is what propels me forward. The memory of your smiling face reminds me that I have something worth fighting for.

You. And Louie. And Mackie. The life we've built calls to me from across the sea. I know you're there, waiting for me. Wishing for me. Know I'm here wishing as well.

If somehow you get this letter, know I never gave up the hope of returning to you. Tell Louie and Mackie that I love them, no matter what. I will always love the family we've made. No ocean can change that.

I love you all ways, rightside-up or upside-down, next to you or across the sea.

Your Ben

Tears fell onto the page as Jemma finished reading. This notebook, filled with messages to loved ones from Disparates in dire circumstances. Ones that once lived in this small lighthouse room for a time before moving on. To where? There was no way of telling. And this last entry, Ben's letter, joined with the rest.

Asher placed a hand on her back. "He was here. And we *are* going to find him."

The lump in her throat prevented her from answering as she stared at his writing. Reading Ben's words, after weeks of worry and panic, not knowing where he was, only intensified her yearning. What kind of monsters would tear families apart this way?

Just above his declaration was a warning... *Don't trust her.* Maybe the *her* was who they needed to be wary of. This mystery woman causing damage and danger.

An alarm rang, diverting her attention from the page.

Asher's eyes widened. "The guard. He must have woken up. We need to go." He grabbed Quill's hand, whose face had paled to match the lightness of her hair.

Jemma grabbed the book of letters as they exited the room. They were on the fourth floor—the one Ben had spent the last few nights in—and headed toward the staircase. The shouting of voices from below urged them to head up, toward the top of the tower. It seemed there were more than two guards on the island after all.

They took the stairs two at a time. Jemma tried to keep pace with the pair in front of her. They stopped at the base of the ladder, Asher waving for Quill to climb first. As she ascended, he turned to Jemma.

"Your turn," he said.

"How are we going to escape from there?" she questioned. "Won't we be stuck?"

He bit his lip. "I have a plan. Trust me. I won't let you fall." He reached a hand to her. None of his fingers were twitching.

She hugged the notebook tight as she accepted his gesture. He pulled her hand to the ladder, and she climbed.

She emerged into the round, circular light room, Asher close behind. Windows surrounded the edge, holding strong against the intense storm outside. Lightning lit the sky on fire as thunder rumbled their bones.

The storm was upon them.

"This way." Asher headed toward a pane of glass with a handle. He pulled it open, letting the wind enter. The pages of the notebook ruffled as Jemma gripped it tighter.

She followed Asher and Quill as they headed out the doorway onto a narrow balcony. It didn't take much to avert her eyes from the distance below. She covered them with her free arm to keep the dust and debris from clouding her vision. Goosebumps crawled across her skin as they walked around the edge.

Asher stopped. "The boat is near the beach there." He pointed below. Lightning brightened the sky once more. Jemma peered over her arm. He was right.

But the lightning bolts weren't coming from the clouds. No, they were striking horizontally into the night. She focused on her heart rate. It was quickened, however, she used her energy downstairs. This lightning would take more energy than she currently had access to.

She looked at Quill. Her breathing was labored, her body shaking. A bolt of lightning escaped from her shoulder into the air.

Asher seemed to notice as well. He turned toward Quill. "Hey, breathe with me," he said. She took a shaky breath in. "Now out..."

The sky plunged into grayness once more.

"I can't do it," Quill said.

"Sure you can." Jemma stepped forward. "The lightning stopped. We'll figure a way out of this, right, Asher?"

Asher focused on Quill. "There's no other way out."

Banging echoed from inside. Through the shadows, Jemma saw the outline of a guard climbing into the light room. The glass was holding up against the wind, but she had a feeling a bullet would be too much for it.

"We need to hurry." Asher grabbed onto Quill's shoulders. "I know you don't think you can do this, but I believe in you. I wouldn't be here right now if it weren't for you. You saved me once, and I know you can do it again." He moved a hand to the back of Quill's head and pulled her face to his. A small spark lit in the night as their lips met. Asher didn't seem to care.

Jemma shuffled her feet, feeling like she was intruding on a private moment. An especially strong gust of wind caused her to grip the handle of the balcony railing.

Without breaking the kiss, Asher reached a hand to Jemma. Their feet were a foot off the metal flooring. This was his plan.

She needed to make a fast decision. Trust Asher, and this stranger Quill, with her life, or surrender to the guards behind her and be their next captive.

In his letter, Ben said she was worth fighting for. She wasn't going to be the one to give up. She gripped her brother's hand.

He pulled her to them as he broke the kiss. "You've got this now," he said to Quill as he wrapped his arm around Jemma, welcoming her into their hug, which had now turned into a group huddle as Quill wrapped an arm around her waist.

Quill's reddened lips now smiled as they floated over the railing. She closed her blue eyes.

Wind whipped at them, causing Jemma's hair to fly unconstrained, and yet they stayed suspended in the air.

With a soft sigh from Quill, the group fell. Not the way Jemma had expected to fall from six stories up, but as if she were going down a slide that'd been wrapped in silk.

A gunshot pierced through the storm that raged around them. They started to drop quicker, Quill's energy no longer surrounding them.

Jemma screamed as they plunged downward. She resisted the urge to let go, instead tightening her grip around her companions. Asher grunted. The wind had blown him into the side of the lighthouse. His back scratched down the stuccoed side. It slowed their fall.

Terror filled Quill's eyes. They were focused on the pain that riddled Asher's face.

Jemma shut her own and braced for impact. It came slower than she'd expected, as if they fell the last few feet in slow motion. The bushes at the base of the lighthouse softened their landing. Branches scratched at her arms and snagged on the fabric of her jacket.

After what felt like hours, but was more likely only a few seconds, Asher spoke. "Is everyone okay?" He sounded winded.

Jemma wiggled her arms. They responded. She tried her legs with equal success. "Other than some scratches, I think I'm alright."

"Me too," Quill said. She spoke softly. "Sorry I lost us."

"You came through at the end," Asher said as he climbed out of the bush. "I knew you would." The back of his shirt was ripped. Dark spots covered the fabric. If there'd been more light, Jemma was sure she'd see they were red. Asher reached both of his hands out, one for Quill and one for her. With a large heave, he pulled the two women out of the branches.

Jemma wiped leaves off herself as rain soothed her wounds. A loud bang echoed.

"Time to go." Asher headed toward the trees. Quill and Jemma followed.

Jemma didn't recognize the route they ran. They were no longer near the path they'd found earlier. Asher had spotted the boat at the top of the lighthouse. Jemma held onto hope that he knew the direction to go.

As they ran, the rain turned into hail. No longer soothing, it now beat on her lesions. She winced, her head feeling lighter with each step.

She wasn't sure how Asher continued on. Her chest was tight, begging for her to stop. As she gasped for air, a foreign object blew into her open mouth. She stopped, choking and coughing.

The two in front of her paused and turned. "Are you okay?" Quill asked, coming to Jemma's side, who was now bent over as she fought to clear her throat. Quill's hand patted her back, helping the object come loose.

Jemma spit a piece of bark into her hand. As she straightened, a dark figure emerged from the trees near Asher.

"Watch out," she rasped.

Asher whipped around, his hands up ready to fight. "Stop there!"

"Woah, woah, woah," Buran's familiar voice said. "It's just me."

Asher relaxed. "What are you doing off the boat?"

"We, uh... heard an alarm," Buran said.

Jemma nodded, but Asher didn't look like he believed him.

"Not buying it," Asher said. "What's the real reason?"

Buran let out a long breath. "Fine. You're right. We were thinking that the islands might house the warehouses for the medications."

Jemma's brows furrowed. "What?"

"The governor hasn't been listening to us," Buran explained. "The people aren't listening. If we don't do something more, and soon, things are going to get worse."

"So you were planning to do what, exactly?" Asher asked.

Buran's face darkened. "We need to get the Republics' attention. Disparates can't take Enertin if there's not enough to go around."

Jemma couldn't believe what she was hearing. All this time, she thought that they wanted to help her get Ben back... But in reality, they still had their own agenda.

Buran's eyes moved to Jemma—and then Quill. "Who's that?"

"This is Quill," Jemma said. "Ben wasn't here. She was instead."

Buran's face scrunched, taking in her words. "Where is he?"

"The mainland," Quill said.

Thunder cracked through the sky. "We need to get to cover," Asher said. "Is the boat far?"

"Just through these trees." Buran led the way.

The hail grew to the size of a ration coin. It lashed down with a fury as they burst out of the cover of the trees onto the beach. With each hit, Jemma ran faster. She threw herself over the edge of the boat, finally safe under the cover of the awning.

Buran, Asher, and Quill all matched Jemma's breathing. Bruises formed on her sore skin.

"That's not Ben," Samay observed from the helm, examining Quill with a critical eye. She somehow shrank smaller under his gaze.

"We missed him," Asher said. "He's off the island already."

Samay's eyes widened.

Waves crashed over the edge of the boat.

"It's not safe to sail," Samay shouted over a loud gust of wind.

Jemma crashed into the side railing. "I can see that."

"Guards are going to be searching for us." Asher grabbed onto the edge of the boat as it was tossed once again. "The island isn't very big. Where would we go?"

"Do you think you could sail to the other side of the island?" Quill asked. "I know of a cave. They brought me through it when they first brought me here. We can park inside."

Samay looked at the hungry sea as if calculating the risk. "It's the best option we have."

It took time for Jemma's eyes to adjust as they entered the cave. She shivered as Samay's fishing boat barely fit between the jagged, rough walls. It wasn't deep, but they tucked inside the back of it.

The boat stopped at the small, beach-like landing. They were protected from the wind outside, but the ocean continued to throw them around like a toy.

Aniyah was first to climb out of the boat, relieving her stomach as she fell onto the sand. No, not sand. Jemma stepped onto water-logged, torn carpeting. "What is this place?" she asked, looking at Quill.

"An old war bunker," she said. "Bombs created this island. They destroyed the land around, creating canals for the ocean to fill in as the water levels rose. This island, and others around, were once mountaintops."

Asher moved to a drier area, lighting a flame on his hand. In the dim glow, they saw the walls were metal. A door flickered in the flames. He pressed on the handle, but it didn't open.

"I wouldn't try to go in there." Quill placed a hand on Asher's arm. "It's risky enough hiding here; if you open that door you'll alert every guard on this island to our position."

"Maybe this isn't a good place to hide," Aniyah said, wiping her mouth.

"No one will think to look in here." Quill gathered driftwood, setting it in a circle on the ground. "This is used by the head scientist, and she's currently not here."

"Is she the one who took Ben?" Jemma asked as the group gathered around the growing fire pit. It reminded her of the warning. Whoever was the head scientist, Jemma knew she was dangerous.

Asher lifted his hand, but before any energy escaped, Samay stretched out his own. Flames escaped his palm and lit the pile of wood. "Thanks," he said, turning to Asher. "I needed to get that out."

"...No problem." Asher lowered his arms to his sides.

"So, is she the one Ben's with?" Jemma didn't want her question to be ignored.

Crackling from the new fire filled the silence before Quill spoke. "Yes. She took him back to the mainland."

Jemma took a deep breath. This was what they wanted. This was what they feared. "Who is she?"

"Dr. Paxton," Quill said.

"Wait." Jemma's heartbeat quickened. "*The* Dr. Paxton? As in, Elizabeth Paxton?" The woman she'd sat across from about two weeks prior. So Asher was right about her.

Quill nodded. "That's her. Ben's been *cured*. He agreed to go back to Stillfield and be one of the spokespeople for EnertinX."

That didn't sound like Ben. He didn't like having a spotlight on himself. But she really didn't know who Ben was without his medicine.

"So..." Buran jumped into the conversation. "Did you get to know Ben well?"

"He was my downstairs neighbor for a little while," Quill said. "I would talk to him through the ceiling."

"Did he ever mention why he was taken to the island in the first place?" Buran asked.

Jemma's stomach clenched. Of course he wanted that information. It was the reason they came here in the first place. It wasn't Ben he wanted, but rather the knowledge he had.

Quill narrowed her eyes at Buran. "Who are you people?"

"They go by Dissentients," Asher answered, "I've been working with them for the last couple weeks. They want to stop the new initiative, just like us. You can trust them."

Asher was so confident. So sure of the people Jemma introduced him too. And yet, Jemma had doubted them for so long. Even until this point, trusting them wasn't a matter of it being the right choice, but rather the only choice she had to reunite her family. Yet each plan they'd implemented had failed.

"He said he was in for a fire in his office." Quill rubbed her arms. "But I imagine what you really want to know is why he was framed."

"That would be nice," Buran said. "We think it might help with the whole save the world thing,"

"Well, he said that someone named 'Oliver' started the fire to cover up false alarms." Quill said.

"Oliver!" Buran and Jemma exclaimed at the same time.

"Oliver was Ben's best friend; surely he wasn't part of this," Jemma said.

"It wasn't only that... just the set up to get him here. I think it was really because..." Quill stopped and glanced around. Something that looked like guilt painted her face.

"Go on," Buran said.

"I think it was because of Asher. I helped him escape. He was the first to get out from under Dr. Paxton's claws. She did it to send him a message." Quill spoke directly to Asher. "She knows that Ben is your brother-in-law. She wanted you to know she's watching you. Wanted to get back at you."

Buran's shoulders sank with Jemma's hope.

They didn't have Ben.

What would be so important that a man's life was worth stealing?

The group gradually dispersed, heading to find dry spots to lay out. Quill and Asher lingered by the fire, talking in whispered tones. A laugh escaped Quill's lips, and Asher smiled.

Now was as good a time as any. Jemma rose from the hard ground and approached the couple.

"Hey, Jem Jam!" Asher greeted her. "I'm truly sorry that Ben's not here, I promise. I thought we'd be able to get him *and* Quill."

Although Jemma's chest was still hurt by the betrayal, she couldn't help but forgive him as she'd watched the joy the fire illuminated cross his face when he talked with Quill. "I understand."

"We'll find Ben," Quill said. "I'm sure of it!"

"You spent some time with him, correct?" Jemma asked. "Did he..."

"Talk about you? Oh yeah." Quill smiled. "He was as determined to get home to you as you seem to be about getting back to him."

Jemma nodded. Warmth filled her soul. Ben wanted to be home with her. Of course, she knew that, but hearing someone else confirm it created a new wave of longing.

"There's something else you want to ask, isn't there?" Asher said, studying her face.

"You have two powers." Jemma didn't know the proper way to discuss this.

Quill nodded.

"What is that like?"

"Not easy, I'll tell you that," Quill said. "Having to keep myself from feeling fear while at the same time not getting overly hyped up or excited about something? It's almost torture at times."

Jemma's thoughts went to Louie. He'd have a similar struggle throughout his life. "How do you do it?"

"Very carefully. I'd be happy to show you some techniques I've developed..." Quill yawned. It was getting late.

"You should get some sleep," Jemma said, eyeing Asher as he tried to hold in his own yawn. "Both of you. We have no idea what tomorrow will bring."

TWENTY-NINE

Margaret followed behind Tobias's black car. Homes built before the Rain of Fire—before the world erupted—flew past her side window. Wherever Tobias was headed, he was in a hurry. Trees blew sideways in the storm's wind, threatening to snap apart any second.

Tobias turned a corner. A few moments later, so did she. The old mall. Why would he be driving there?

She pulled into the driveway of a home nearby and waited as Tobias parked his car. He shuffled out the door and adjusted his gray blazer before heading inside the mall doors.

Margaret exited her own car. Trees in the parking lot of the mall would provide some coverage as she approached. She hoped the front doors were unlocked. If she was going to figure out what Tobias was up to, she'd need to see what was inside this mall.

As she neared the doors, she heard the squealing of wheels. She ducked behind a makeshift wall of old bushes, barely holding onto life. The wind whistled through the thin branches, sounding like a cry for the incoming rain.

A white van rounded the turn into the parking lot. Margaret peeked through the top of a branch as it parked. The mall doors squeaked as they opened. Tobias exited, staying under the mall's awning to avoid the full force of the increasing wind.

Dr. Elizabeth Paxton emerged from the van, holding the door open for... Ben?

Margaret rubbed her eyes as dirt flew into them. Tears washed the intrusion away, her vision clearing once more.

What she'd seen was real. Ben was at the mall, wearing a blue suit as if he were attending a special event.

Governor Dunn stood waiting. He smiled at Ben as he and Dr. Paxton joined him. "Welcome back! You're looking well." His voice was difficult to make out over the extra noise.

"Thank you, Governor," Ben responded.

Dr. Paxton smiled. "Time to go inside boys. It seems we're about to experience the eyewall of this storm. And we'll need to get some sleep before we depart tomorrow."

Margaret couldn't hold back a gasp, raising a hand to her mouth. *Depart tomorrow? What did that mean?*

As they entered the old building, Ben glanced to the side. Margaret ducked, pressing her back against the tree next to her. Her tailbone yelled at her for the maneuver, not happy with the speed of which it hit the ground. Had he heard her? Hopefully he'd think it was just the wind.

Margaret sat there, too stunned to move. Ben hadn't looked like himself in that blue suit, smiling at Tobias. To be honest, something looked off with him as well. Then there was Dr. Paxton. *She* looked like her usual pleased self.

Jemma hadn't answered Margaret's phone call earlier. It was too late to warn her about Ben. She was already worried her children would be caught, but it turned out they were putting themselves at risk for no reason. There was nothing she was able to do about that.

However, maybe there was something else she could do for them. Tobias acted strange, not like the man she knew. Following him once he left work seemed like the right thing to do at the time.

Seeing how comfortable her friend was greeting Dr. Paxton confirmed Margaret's suspicions that something sinister was going on. Tobias had been with her, interviewing families and reviewing paperwork for Disparates that passed on. The inconsistencies were there. And yet moments ago, he looked to be on the doctor's side. Maybe he was on it all along.

Margaret needed to message her daughter. She hoped they had made it off the island safely by now. She opened her phone and started writing a text. Before she finished, footsteps diverted her attention. Red heels stood a foot away. Margaret shoved her phone into her pocket, the message unfinished, and moved her gaze to the face in front of her.

"Hello there, Margaret," Dr. Paxton said, staring down at her with folded arms. "I don't believe you're on the guest list for our departure party."

Being back in the old part of Stillfield was surreal to Ben. It was strange being here after his own world had changed so much, let alone standing inside *this* mall. Ben scrunched his face. There was something important about this place... he couldn't quite recall what.

It wasn't as run down as he had thought. He'd been taught in school that before the nuclear war, this building was used to store and sell all kinds of goods. After the war, many survivors lived within these walls during the Crisis before the Republics were united. Then it was used as storage, until a Disparate outburst destroyed a good portion of it.

The ceiling was covered in fog-glassed diamonds, a nod to its once opulent status. Ben walked with Governor Dunn. Dr. Paxton had excused herself earlier to deal with some pressing business. They passed by what once must have been storefronts but were now covered with metal. It didn't look like a welcoming place.

"Fifteen years ago, this mall was destroyed in a tragic Disparate outburst." Governor Dunn spoke to Ben as if he were leading a full tour group. "It took the Disparate's life, as well as that of two others. At that time, Dr. Paxton and her team had recently developed the first Enertin pill. The introduction of that pill created a wave across the world. No longer were Disparates scared of losing control; they'd been given the control back."

They stopped in front of one of the stores. "This is where you'll be sleeping for the night," Governor Dunn said.

Ben glanced at him, panic rising in his chest. He'd finally been released from a locked, metal room. Was he truly being imprisoned once again?

The door opened, metal screeching as it revealed a set of bunk beds, two dressers and a wall covered in bookcases. A large man lay on the lower mattress, a book in his hands. He closed it as they entered. "Hey there, is this the roommate you were telling me about?" His voice was gruff.

Ben wouldn't be alone. This was different.

"This is Benjamin Hodgerton," Governor Dunn turned to him. "And this is Anthony Featherman, who you'll be rooming with for the next few weeks."

"Weeks?" Ben's face scrunched, trying to recall what he'd agreed to earlier that day. Dr. Paxton said he was going to change the world. He wanted to be a part of that. But he also wanted to be with his family.

"Yes," Governor Dunn continued, "we've had some scheduling difficulties with the Republic of Preen. Have to work around their harvest, of course. So it'll take a little longer than originally planned. But that's okay; it gives us the opportunity to spend extra time in the mountains."

"I need to be home with my family," Ben said. "How has Jemma been doing with me gone?" Governor Dunn was close friends with Margaret. Surely he understood how vital it was for Ben to be home. He second guessed his decision to agree to this, despite the threats from Dr. Paxton.

"She's well. So are your children." Governor Dunn's face wrinkled. "You are doing this for them, remember. This will create the future you want for them. The time apart is for her safety. But you'll see her, you can visit..." He sounded dazed, as if he were unsure about the words exiting his mouth.

"When?" Ben asked.

"What?" The governor tilted his head to the side.

"When will I see my wife?" A different type of fire spread through Ben's chest. One that filled him with anger. A heat he could no longer release.

"Oh, that." Governor Dunn pursed his lips. "I suppose that's a question for the doctor."

"Can I see her?" Ben was growing restless.

The governor nodded his head. "In the morning. For now, we all need to get some rest." He motioned toward the room.

Ben hesitated, not wanting to enter another cell.

"They don't lock this door," the man in the room, Anthony, said. Ben looked at him quizzically.

"That's true," Governor Dunn said. "Restrooms are that way," he continued, pointing down the hall where a sign with a toilet hung from the ceiling, "and you are welcome to come to the middle apartment if you need a snack. Other than that, there's not much else of interest here."

Reluctantly, Ben entered his room for the night. He waited after the governor shut the door, listening for a lock to slide into place. He heard none. After a moment, he checked the handle. The door opened slightly.

"I told you," Anthony said from his bed. "It's been quite the change. Since we're no longer a threat, no need to keep us locked up like animals."

"Were you on Lucky Island?" Something about this man felt familiar.

"Purple suit." He pumped a fist into the air. "Not as great as you might think. Turns out women don't care much for heights. At least, mine didn't."

Ben widened his eyes. "Wait. You're not *the* Anthony Featherman, are you?"

"I'm not sure what you mean."

"Sorry, I worked as a Watcher. Your story is infamous. A proposal to remember, that's for sure."

Anthony let out a huff. "If only my ex thought so."

"Oh..." An awkward silence fell. Ben's body yearned for him to lay down, it had to be past midnight by now. However, his mind was awake. He grabbed the door handle, wanting to open it and leave the room. To find a way home. He didn't understand why he couldn't return in the morning. For the first time in weeks, freedom was in his grasp.

"That door's not locked, but the other ones are," Anthony said. His eyes watched Ben.

"We're locked in the mall?"

"Yep. Checked earlier today. Not even the other rooms are open."

Ben's hope faltered. He was still a caged rat, placed in a larger maze. And Anthony had seen right through him. "Were you trying to leave?" Ben held his breath.

"Nah, I signed up for this. But you never know when you'll need an escape plan."

Ben wasn't the only one wary about this plan after all. Perhaps getting to know Anthony better would come in handy. Just in case.

The high-rise buildings of Stillfield reached into the sky as if they were paintbrushes coloring the clouds instead of the sun. Jemma knew it was an illusion. There was no way to create the beauty her soul yearned for. Only the heavens could provide that.

But men could take it away. Hide it behind dust, smoke, and nuclear fallout. Like the years after the Rain of Fire. Plunged into darkness, her ancestors waited, praying to see the sun once again.

Jemma had worked hard to create her own sunrise. To bring her family back together. But she was alone, despite the few group members who ushered her into Buran's car. Inside, she was empty, her heart covered by its own darkness. Her husband was gone.

Once the storm had ended last night, Samay insisted they head back. He needed to be home before the Saturday morning breakfast rush. There was no point in staying on the island. Not with Ben being somewhere on the mainland.

She entered the car with her shoulders slumped and eyes burning dry from crying. Asher and Quill were close behind. It was just bright enough for them to be wearing large-brimmed hats and sunglasses to hide their identities. Quill also wore the spare clothes they'd brought for Ben. Each glance at his favorite t-shirt was a reminder to Jemma of her failure. But she knew Quill's bright yellow jumpsuit would not have gone unnoticed among the Stillfield docks.

Jemma pulled her phone out. She had a missed call from her mother last night, but no voicemail accompanied it. She sent her a quick message to let her know she was safe. Then, she opened the text thread with Caty. She needed to check on her children.

> I'll be home in twenty minutes. Hope the boys stayed out of trouble last night.

Jemma's heart pounded as she waited for a reply. After a few moments, it arrived.

> Jemma! Thank goodness you're safe!! When I heard the storm roll in last night, I thought the worst. You better tell me everything!!

> The boys are doing great, don't worry about them. I can bring them home whenever you're ready.

A moment longer than it took for the first two messages to arrive, a third buzzed.

> Mackie is asking about a soccer game today? I told him he could stay here and play, but he said it's against their rivals and he needs to be there. I can tell him no, or even take him if it's easier.

Jemma sighed. She'd forgotten about his game. So much had changed for Mackie the past few weeks, whereas soccer was a constant through it all. In a couple more weeks, it would be his birthday. She wanted to do everything in her power to help keep him centered. Give him some kind of normal.

> Thank you so much for watching them. I can take him to his game. He needs his mom there.

> Okay. I can bring them to your house in thirty minutes.

> That would be perfect. Thanks so much.

The car ride was quiet as Buran made his way to Jemma's house. Once he pulled into the drive, he turned toward her. "We're gonna keep looking for Ben. I promise you we aren't giving up. I'm sure we'll figure out where he is soon."

Jemma nodded slowly. "I appreciate everything you've done to try."

Asher spoke from the back. "I shouldn't have insisted on stopping Initiative 67 first. It was a foolish idea."

Jemma didn't want to think about that right now. About how focusing on Ben sooner would have made their mission successful.

"Without you," she said, "going to the islands at all would've been impossible." She tried to take the sadness out of her voice, but knew she wasn't successful when she saw the way Asher hung his head low.

"I got to know Ben," Quill said. "He's not a quitter. I bet he's got another plan to get back to you already."

"Another plan?" Jemma looked at her.

"Yeah," Quill nodded. "He was given EnertinX and brought to the lighthouse because he tried to escape Lucky Island. He wanted to get back home. To be with you."

A glimmer of hope flickered in Jemma's chest. Ben hadn't given up on her. And she couldn't allow herself to give up now.

Before exiting the car, she turned to Asher and Quill. "You two might as well come into my house and get some rest. I imagine your other *home* will be a bit... soggy." She raised an eyebrow at Asher, thinking of how worn the treehouse roof had become.

"I suppose that's true." He grabbed his hat and put it on, making sure the brim covered his face. Quill followed his lead.

"You can use the couch, or the guest room down the hall," Jemma said as she gave a small tour of her home. "I need to leave with the boys once they get here, but you're welcome to stay as long as you need. I trust you won't try to take off with all the valuables I have lying around."

Asher laughed, looking at the toys spread around the house. "Yeah, you have so many. Any kid would love it here."

"Thank you for letting me stay," Quill said. "I'm not sure where else I could go."

"Do you have any family around?" Jemma asked.

A frantic knock at the door interrupted her answer. Caty must have arrived, although the urgency in the knock unsettled Jemma. She peered through the door peephole as Asher and Quill went into the hallway, heading toward the guestroom to keep from being seen.

"Wait," Jemma told them as she unlocked the door.

Her mother's wearied eyes met hers. "He's here," she said between heavy breaths. "Ben is on the mainland." She held her phone to show Jemma their text thread. A message draft waited.

Followed Tobias. Ben is here at

The message stopped abruptly. "Where is he?" Jemma asked, her hope rising once more.

Her mother, though, shook her head. "I don't know. I can't remember what happened last night. I don't even remember typing that message."

A sinking feeling once again washed over Jemma.

How could they be so close, and yet, so lost?

THIRTY

A sharp pain radiated through Margaret's head as she focused on last night. She clutched her hair while she rocked back and forth on Jemma's couch.

"You were going to confront Governor Dunn about the fire," Asher prompted. "Did you make it to the Capitol?"

Margaret shook her head. "I don't remember."

"How about we start by retracing your steps." Jemma placed a comforting hand on her back. "How did you end up here?"

"I got your message this morning," Margaret explained. "When I opened it and went to respond, I saw that I'd started a message already. I realized I couldn't send it to you that way, you'd be wanting to know more, but each time I tried to remember, I felt a jarring pain in my head. Almost as if a shock was reverberating through my mind."

The faces around her were creased with concern, including Quill, whom she'd been introduced to only moments before. The girl they saved in place of her son-in-law.

"Okay," Jemma said. "What about before you received my message?"

"I'd been asleep," Margaret said. "Your message woke me since my phone was still in my pocket. In fact, I'm pretty sure I'm wearing the same clothes as yesterday."

"That's definitely not like you..." Jemma tilted her head. "What *do* you remember?"

"I drove home and went to bed." She strained to recall something—anything—her head shaking. There had to be more.

"Drove home from where?" Asher asked.

Margaret pushed past the pain. "There were... worn doors. Older homes..." She groaned, falling into the back of the couch.

"That helps." Jemma rubbed her arm. "Gives us *something* to go off of."

"So you were in the old part of town," Asher said. "What would Governor Dunn go there for?"

Quill's eyes widened. "The old part of Stillfield? Like, the places that were built before the Rain of Fire?"

Margaret nodded. "If I remember correctly, I was somewhere in that vicinity. But that expands through the North and East Sectors. I could've been anywhere."

"It does, but I think I might know where Ben is." Quill leaned forward. "A place Disparates used to be taken to. Merrytime Clinic."

Clearly Quill had been through her own journey. Margaret's motherly heart ached for her, even though she'd just met her. Sure, Quill wasn't who she'd expected to see that morning, but Margaret wouldn't hold that against her.

Jemma shook her head. "No. He can't be there. No one even knows where it is."

This time, it was Margaret's turn to comfort her daughter. She placed a hand on Jemma's knee. "Let her finish."

Quill took a deep breath. "It's not as far away as everyone seems to think. It hasn't actually been used as a clinic in a long time. In fact, I'm pretty sure I was the only patient there for years."

Asher turned to her. "Wait, you stayed at the clinic?"

"Yeah." Quill nodded. "Since I was a little girl. My mom passed away when I was young, leaving just me and my dad. Honestly, I don't think he knew what to do as a single parent. Especially when I started to float toys to myself as a nine month old."

"You started that young?" Jemma's jaw dropped.

Margaret understood her surprise. She thought Louie starting at five was early. But having a baby using energy? With the emotions they cycle through?

"Yep. He was as surprised as you sound." Quill released a small laugh. "But I was young, and air energy wasn't too difficult to work around to keep me safe. Extra baby proofing seemed to do the trick. It wasn't until a couple years later when I shot a lightning bolt into the slide at the park that he realized I needed more help."

Margaret raised her eyebrows. This woman had more than one energy. She wasn't sure how it was possible.

"And then he sent you to Merrytime Clinic? When you were a toddler?" Anger dripped from Asher's voice. Margaret narrowed her eyes at him. Perhaps this was why he brought her back.

"I have two energies." She shrugged. "He didn't know what else to do. But he didn't let me go alone; he came with me. Lived in a little apartment in the middle of the clinic until I was eighteen. That's the home I remember. At least, until Dr. Paxton said she'd give me a college education. Instead, she sent me to the island."

"But you said you were the only one there." Margaret straightened. Her husband had worked so hard to make the clinic successful. Hearing how it wasn't used as he'd hoped made her nauseous. "Wasn't that suspicious?"

"Not at first," Quill explained. "It was a busy clinic for the first several years. Disparates came in and out regularly. I was ten when things started to change." She went quiet for a moment. "In fact, it was after your husband died."

Margaret sucked in a sharp breath. "What happened then?"

"Disparates gradually stopped coming." Quill lowered her head. "And those who were at the clinic long-term were moved. It wasn't always easy to get them to go. In fact, a couple of Disparates fought against it and destroyed half the building."

Asher's eyes widened. "But you were okay, right?"

"Yes," Quill said. "It was in the back part of the clinic away from where I lived."

"Wasn't your dad skeptical?" Jemma asked. Worry creased her face.

Margaret couldn't help but imagine the concern Jemma would have for her own children if the situation had happened to her.

"That's the thing about Dr. Paxton," Quill said. "She can be very persuasive. Unusually so. It was like she knew how to change his mind anytime she needed to. Like she has her own type of energy that manipulates thoughts."

The room filled with silence as Quill's accusations settled. Tobias came to Margaret's mind, how he always behaved differently after meeting with Dr. Paxton. So sure he could trust her. Then, a few weeks would go by, and he'd start to get wary once again. Until another meeting with the doctor.

"You said Ben was with her now?" Margaret asked. Is that who she had run into last night? Perhaps that was why she couldn't remember.

"He is." Quill bit her lip. "And I'm pretty sure they're at the clinic."

"But where is Merrytime Clinic?" Asher asked.

Jemma gasped. "Wait. I know where it is." All eyes turned to her. "In the older part of town, half of it was destroyed..."

"Oh!" Margaret exclaimed. She knew what her daughter was thinking. "The old mall."

The front door swung open as a little body ran into the room. "I'm home!" Mackie yelled. He stopped in his tracks when he realized they had visitors. Behind him, Louie entered. Caty stood at the door with her little one, whose name Margaret couldn't recall at the moment.

Surprise was written on Caty's face as she glanced from person to person. It seemed like she was looking for someone in particular. "Is this a bad time?"

"Not at all." Jemma stood and went to the door.

She whispered something to Caty, who gasped, placed a hand on Jemma's arm, then nodded. "I'll see you on Monday," she said before turning and heading toward the driveway.

Jemma closed the door as Mackie stared at Asher and Quill.

"Who are you?" he asked.

Margaret motioned to him and Louie for a hug. Mackie ran into her open arms.

Louie was more hesitant. "Who's that?" he pointed at Asher.

Asher squirmed in his seat.

"That's your uncle," Margaret said. "Uncle Asher."

Mackie started bouncing in her arms. "Uncle Asher! I thought he was lost."

"Yes." Jemma moved to the couch. "We found him. Remember I told you how he liked to steal my food?"

Louie answered from his spot near the couch, still not looking ready to join the group. "I remember that story."

"Hey," Asher . "Is that all you told them about me?"

"You also liked to draw!" Mackie said. "Like me!"

Asher grinned. "I saw some of your work. You've got talent, kid."

Mackie beamed. He ran to Asher and wrapped his arms around his side. Asher stiffened at first, then relaxed, and wrapped his free arm around Mackie.

Louie kept his distance. "What about her?" He motioned to Quill.

"That's a friend of ours," Jemma said. "And she's got something in common with you."

"What?" Louie asked.

Margaret was also intrigued. She thought Quill had two energies, neither of which was the same as Louie's.

"She has air energy," Jemma said, bopping a finger on Louie's nose. "Just like you."

"Like him?" Margaret wrinkled her face. "He has flame..."

"Yes, and air." Jemma shrugged. "And we are learning how to keep both in control, right Louie?"

Louie nodded and watched as Mackie gave Quill a high five.

Margaret wasn't sure how to process all the new information. Perhaps her head was still a bit blurry.

"Are you coming to my soccer game?" Mackie turned toward Jemma and asked.

Jemma's face fell. "Uh... I'm not sure..."

"I'll take you to your game," Margaret jumped in.

"You don't have to do that, Mom." Jemma ran a hand through her hair.

"I would very much like to," Margaret assured her. "I love watching my soccer star." She understood what Jemma's mission had been these last few weeks, and they were closer than ever before to finally finding Ben. Watching the boys was the best way Margaret could contribute.

"Really, Grandma?" Mackie's eyes twinkled as he ran over to her. "You're coming?"

"Yes, I'm taking you." Margaret nodded. "Your mommy has some things she needs to prepare."

Mackie wrinkled his face. "Like what?"

"Well"—Margaret tousled his brown hair—"your mommy needs to get everything ready so your daddy can come home."

"He's finally coming home?" Louie asked, joining Mackie next to her.

Margaret made eye contact with her daughter; she was pinching the skin at her throat, her brow creased. "Yes," Margaret said. "He will be home soon." She wanted Jemma to know her mother believed in her. She would find Ben, and she would bring him home.

Jemma cleared her throat. "It's true. Daddy's coming home."

"Now, go get ready for your game," Margaret said.

It didn't take more for Mackie to run to his room. "Today's gonna be the best day ever!" His shout echoed through the hall.

Margaret's chest tightened. She looked at Jemma, who already had her phone out, her fingers flying across the screen. Both of them understood what they needed to do.

They couldn't let this boy down.

Anthony's snores echoed through the space of the large ceiling above them. Ben didn't mind much—at least he wasn't alone. Besides, his thoughts kept him awake most of the night.

He wasn't free but rather imprisoned in a new way. Yet each time he thought about leaving, a sharp pain radiated through his mind.

This is right, he'd hear a voice say. *I'm helping change the world.*

He wasn't sure he believed that voice.

The door slid open. "Good morning." Governor Dunn's face popped through the opening. "Hope you slept well. Just wanted to let you know breakfast is ready. We're heading to the train station in an hour."

One hour and he'd be headed away from his family once again. The thought made his body tense.

"Mornin'," Anthony said mid-yawn. The bunk shook as he moved off the bed.

Ben followed his lead, climbing down the ladder and heading into the main hallway of the mall.

They stopped in front of a door with a pink frame in the middle of the mall. The old store doors were open, revealing a large studio apartment. On one side was a kitchen, platters of waffles and bacon lining the island. A large man had his back turned to Ben, standing over the sink. Opposite it was a large couch where two women relaxed with empty plates in their hands.

As Governor Dunn, Anthony, and Ben approached, the women straightened.

The governor motioned toward them. "I would like to introduce you to the other members of your tour group. Stacey"—a pink haired woman smiled at him—"and Robin." The older one waved. "And Johnson in the kitchen. The five of you will be an important part of our education plan for EnertinX. You'll be spending quite a bit of time together for the next six weeks."

Six weeks? The details of this mission continued to worsen. He wasn't expecting to wait another six weeks before going home to his family. No way. He needed to find a way out of this.

He looked around the apartment. Perhaps he could find a way to sneak out of here. They'd see him if he headed for the front doors, however...

Ben turned to Governor Dunn. "I need to use the restroom before we eat, if that's okay."

"Of course," the governor said. "Nature calls when nature calls."

Anthony seemed to give Ben a side-eye as he headed toward the doors, but that didn't stop him. There had to be a way out of this place.

He didn't get far after exiting the middle apartment before he ran into a familiar face.

Dr. Paxton brandished a smile on her face.

THIRTY-ONE

The Dissentients responded swiftly to Jemma's message, meeting at her house within fifteen minutes. Calum arrived first in his white truck with Samay and Aniyah. Then, Buran came behind him.

"You're sure the mall is where he is?" Buran asked, rolling down the window of his black car as he pulled into the driveway.

"It's the best lead we have." Jemma slid into the front seat.

Buran scratched his chin. "Hmm, if anything, maybe the medication is stored there—"

"Can we please focus on rescuing Ben first?" Jemma snapped.

"Right, sorry... we can figure out the rest of the plan later."

Asher closed the back door behind him and Quill. "He's gotta be. There's nowhere else for them to hide."

Buran drilled Quill on the layout of the mall as they headed to the old part of Stillfield. She answered his questions as best she could, Jemma's nerves heightening with each response.

"And the back was destroyed how?" he asked.

"That was where the ground energy Disparates slept," Quill explained. "They were some of the last to be moved from the clinic. I guess they heard a rumor that Lucky Island was being used again and the thought made them spiral. Too bad the rumor was true."

Jemma shook her head, thinking about the amount of pain and grief those Disparates must have felt to cause so much destruction.

"It's gonna be our best chance at getting into the mall unseen, though," Quill said.

Asher met her gaze. "We'll follow your lead."

Jemma turned back to the front window, noticing the mall a short distance away. Closer in front of them were some cones with caution tape surrounding a hole in the road. To the side of it, a pole was knocked over. Someone had crashed here. The flowers lying at the base of the pole told her it wasn't a good outcome.

She tried not to take it as a sign. They'd missed her husband twice already; surely now was their moment.

The organization rendezvoused at the back of the mall, hiding their cars within the trees. Together, they approached the building on foot.

The destruction laid before them was grander than Jemma had imagined. Minimal effort had been put into repairing the mess. More cones and caution tape lined a few edges of the chasm in front of them, while other spots were covered by wooden boards. Still, a gaping hole covered the parking lot and close to half of what once was Merrytime Clinic.

As they approached the ruins of the mall wing, Jemma stepped carefully over debris and broken glass. Toward the middle, the gaping hole sat, waiting to swallow any passersby that got too close. Jemma peeked over the side and saw metal racks and mattresses fallen to the bottom, covered in dirt. Her foot slipped, causing a large dirt ball to fall into the hole. Asher grabbed a hold of her arm as the dirt ball created a small cloud at the bottom of the canyon.

"Thanks," Jemma said to her brother.

"Try to be more careful, okay?" Asher chided. "Don't want to lose my sister already. I'm growing rather partial to her."

Jemma rolled her eyes at him but smiled.

They approached the part of the mall that was still standing. The edge that had once stood open from the Disparate quake was covered in strong steel. So they *had* repaired something. Jemma saw no door or way to enter from here. She looked at Quill.

"Over this way," Quill said as she climbed a pile of broken cement. The group followed. Between the broken pieces hung a large web. A black spider sat on it, waiting for unsuspecting prey. Jemma shuddered as she hurried past.

They walked around the side of the mall, where an old door sat. Asher tried the handle.

Locked.

"No worries, I've got this," Quill said as she pushed him aside. At the door, she closed her eyes, focusing with a smile on her face. The rest of the crew watched, every once in a while making eye contact with one another and shrugging. After several slow, agonizing minutes, the door clicked open.

"How did you do that?" Buran questioned, eyes wide.

"Lots of practice. Just used air to push the key gears into the right spot." Quill beamed.

"That's how she got us out of our rooms on the island," Asher confirmed. "Not ideal for a quick escape, but gets the job done."

They entered what looked to be a maintenance room. Multiple power boxes, each buzzing with the noise of electricity, lined the walls. Jemma covered her ears as her body tensed.

"You okay?" Asher asked.

"Can't you hear that?" Jemma shouted. "It's so loud in here."

Quill placed a hand on her back. "It's not as loud to them. Breathe. It'll help calm your own electricity and dampen the noise."

Jemma did as she said, catching her breath as they approached the inside door.

Buran motioned for everyone to stop. He walked to the door first and opened it slightly, checking that the coast was clear. He slipped out slowly then motioned for everyone else to follow. With his "okay" they did, entering into a large hallway that stretched in both directions.

Next to the maintenance room was a large store with glass doors. He motioned for everyone to enter. Once inside, the group of seven circled.

Buran turned to Quill. "Do you know where they'd be keeping Ben?"

She shook her head. "There's a lot of rooms in here."

"So how do we know which way to go?" Samay asked.

"I'm thinking we need to split up," Buran said. "Go in two different directions to cover more ground."

Jemma, Asher, Quill, and Buran formed one group, while Samay, Calum, and Aniyah were the other.

"There's an apartment in the middle of the mall," Quill said. "That's where I lived. Would also be a good place to meet up again, as we'll be walking around it."

"We have our radios. If you see anything, let the others know." Buran held his two-way radio to drill in the visual of his instruction.

The groups set off. Jemma moved slowly, staying hidden behind corners and other fixtures. She was at the back while Asher led the front with Quill's direction. Buran kept glancing at Jemma with encouraging eyes. She didn't need the encouragement. She was restraining herself from running ahead. She was more than ready to rescue Ben.

As they approached the other end of the mall Asher stopped and turned to the others, putting a finger to his lips. Jemma froze and listened. In the distance she heard voices.

Buran pulled out his radio and whispered into it. "Other end of mall. Hearing voices. Will investigate." Then clicked it off.

"We're almost there as well. Will approach slowly," Samay responded.

Jemma felt charged. She embraced that feeling but held it in. She needed to save it.

The voices became clearer as they neared the hallway turn. "...weeks is a long time."

Jemma froze. She knew that voice.

"I know it seems long, but I promise it'll go by quickly. What we are doing is bigger than a few more days."

Jemma also recognized this second one. Ben was speaking with Dr. Paxton around the corner. She wanted to keep moving, but Buran put out his hand to stop her.

"Not yet," he mouthed.

"I need to be with my family," Ben said. "Can't I share my story from Stillfield?"

"We plan on continuing our roll out through the Republic News." Dr. Paxton's voice was calm. "However, we will first need the Republic leaders to approve of EnertinX for the general population. That is where our campaign comes in. They know your story. The way you burned down your office." Jemma held in her protest.

This was a lie. Ben's office still stood.

The doctor continued. "Seeing how you've been rehabilitated will make them more confident in receiving the cure as well."

Jemma waited for Ben's response.

"Why do the governors need to take EnertinX?" Ben asked. Buran seemed to have been wondering the same thing, as his eyebrows raised at the question. Asher and Quill stayed pressed against the wall, trying not to move.

"Well, not all of them." Dr. Paxton laughed before her voice became serious. "But more than half. Then we can continue to push our plan to heal the rest of the Republics."

Jemma sensed a small buzz of electricity come from around the corner. As if a lightbulb was turned on. A quick jolt.

"You're right..." Ben said, sounding dazed. "This is right. I'll help however long you need me to."

"I'm glad to hear that," the doctor said. "Now, shall we join the others inside?"

Buran made eye contact with Asher and nodded.

It was time for them to act.

The doctor sounded pleased with Ben's decision, however something didn't sit right in his gut. He wanted to help the Republics, but this didn't seem like the right way.

It felt rushed and urgent, as if Dr. Paxton needed to get EnertinX approved sooner rather than later. Like time mattered to the process.

Otherwise, why couldn't Ben see his family before they left?

Governor Dunn stepped out of the apartment doors before they headed inside.

"Oh!" he exclaimed. "I wasn't expecting you both to be out here. I was just coming to check on our timing." He eyed Ben. "Have you had the opportunity to ask about the time restraints of the trip?"

Ben nodded. "It sounds like it's necessary." He winced as he tried to think of a different response.

Governor Dunn narrowed his eyes. "It is a long time, though, don't you think, Elizabeth? Ben has a wife and two young children. I'm sure we can come up with a plan where he isn't needed the entire time."

Dr. Paxton sighed. "Oh Tobias, why don't you trust me?" A small spark lit on the end of her finger, pointed at Governor Dunn.

It was probably his imagination, Ben decided. He was feeling a bit cloudy.

"You're right," the governor said. "I do trust you."

"Good, now shall we—" She stopped mid-sentence as a voice interrupted her.

"You really shouldn't." A tall man emerged from around the corner. Something about this man's brown hair and thin facial structure was familiar, but Ben couldn't put his finger on why.

"She's really not a trustworthy person," the man continued with a smirk on his face.

Dr. Paxton returned his smirk with one of her own. "Asher," she said warmly, "I've been wondering where you ended up. I thought for sure you took off running. That's what you do when you're in trouble, isn't it?"

"Asher?" Ben whispered to himself. The name was familiar, but there was no way…

"Yes, that's right," Dr. Paxton responded to Ben. "What an unconventional way to meet your brother-in-law. Thankfully, now that we've found him again, we can get him the help he needs."

"You're the one that needs help," Asher said defiantly, his stance strong. "You need to release Ben."

Ben pursed his lips. His brother-in-law was missing. Most likely dead. And yet the doctor claimed he was the man confronting her.

He did have Jemma's nose.

"Benjamin wants to stay to help others that were once like him," Dr. Paxton said. "Like you. The new shot is truly amazing. It's made him normal, and it can do the same for you. Right, Ben?"

She turned to face him. He went with his first thought. "Yes, EnertinX is amazing. I feel in control and so much better than I used to." His head throbbed, and he grabbed it. "I.... I miss my family. I want to be with them," he struggled to get out.

"You didn't want to test EnertinX on me while I was on Lucky Island." Asher held his hands at his sides, palms facing them.

"Wait, wait, wait." Governor Dunn looked bewildered as his head tossed back and forth. "You're Asher Stillfield? You were on the *island* all this time?"

Asher narrowed his eyes: a look of distrust. He said nothing to the governor.

"Look," Dr. Paxton said, "I understand things got messy. You had a good deal on the island. I still don't understand why you threw it out to risk an escape. Which, by the way, I'm fascinated to learn more about how you survived."

Asher spat on the ground. "I don't care to share story time right now."

"Very well," the doctor said. "But we're doing this the right way. Being a part of change. Disparates are dangerous to our society. We bring peace. And you can join us, Asher. Wipe your crimes away and start a new life. I'm sure Benjamin would love to get to know you better." She waved her hand at Ben, ushering him to step forward.

He followed her cues, unsure of what else to do. "Yeah, it'd be great to have you come with us." His thoughts went to Jemma. Her brother was alive.

"You would love to have me join you?" Asher asked.

"Yeah," Ben confirmed.

"All ways?" Asher asked.

Ben looked at him strangely. "Well... it's just a few weeks, not forever."

"No," Asher said, raising an eyebrow. "Would you *love* to have me join you *all ways*?"

Chills swept over Ben. Asher was sending him a message. A message from Jemma.

Dr. Paxton glared at Asher but didn't seem to catch what he meant.

How did Asher know their family saying? Ben threw that thought out of his mind. The "how" didn't matter as much as what his knowing it meant.

He was with Jemma.

"Yeah, *all* ways." Ben nodded slowly at Asher, hoping he could read the recognition in his eyes.

Asher shrugged. "I don't think I want to join your deluded group." Then he winked at Ben.

Jemma doesn't want me to go, he realized. *She wants me to stay.*

"What are you hoping to do here, Asher?" Dr. Paxton spoke. "I can tell you how this is going to go. I already have Responders on their way. They will happily escort you back to the island. I'm sure you've missed it. Although, I heard you've already visited it today. Your good friend, Colleen, told us all about it."

Asher's face paled at the mention of Colleen. Ben remembered the guard; she was one of the two that escorted him to his room the first night of his stay. She had seemed different from the others. He could see Asher's concern for her written across his face.

"What did you do to her?" he growled.

"Me?" Dr. Paxton placed a hand to her chest. "Why do you always assume it's me? I've been here this whole time, getting ready to kick off my Republic tour. She came forward herself."

Now, instead of showing concern, Asher's face turned to hurt. "Never mind, I'm not leaving without Ben."

"I still don't understand," Governor Dunn said. He'd been quietly watching the exchange. "Why was Asher on Lucky Island to begin with?"

"You don't need to concern yourself with that," Dr. Paxton said. A spark lifted off her fingers and connected with the governor's head. His worried expression calmed.

"Oh, right," he said.

Ben resisted showing his shock. Dr. Paxton was altering Governor Dunn's mind with a hit of electricity. And perhaps the governor wasn't the only one she'd been doing it to.

Footsteps came from behind. Ben twisted to see a woman he didn't fully recognize walking toward them.

Electricity flowed across her shoulders, light catching in the blue of her eyes.

THIRTY-TWO

J emma was surprised by how quickly Quill sprinted around the middle apartment to the other side of the mall. As the attention turned to her, Jemma moved through the shadows at the back of the hall to hide behind a pillar, leaving Buran at the corner.

She now had a view of her husband. The back of his head, at least. His hair had grown out in the last month. His face had a minimal amount of scruff on it. Not fresh, but as if he'd shaved in the past couple days.

And her heart tugged for him the same way it had the night she'd fallen in love. She needed to be near him. Have his arms wrapped around her. She'd get that—soon.

Quill stepped forward, keeping everyone's attention on her. She controlled her electricity as if it were clay, molding to her desires as the yellow lines danced across her collarbone, creating their own unique accessory.

"Quill?" Governor Dunn's shocked voice echoed through the mall.

Ben looked back at Asher, revealing the right side of his face. Jemma covered her mouth with her hand, catching her gasp. Although he was a distance away, she couldn't miss the red blotches that covered the side of his face. She didn't want to dwell on what had caused them.

Asher waved toward Jemma's hiding spot. She hoped the distraction of Quill would give them enough time for Ben to escape. Jemma's heart thumped in her chest as she waited for Ben to understand.

Ben looked at Asher, his face wrinkled. Then, his eyes swept over to meet Jemma's. The confusion immediately left, replaced by a brightness as his lips parted. He placed a hand to his mouth.

"Quill, honey." The doctor stepped toward Quill, unaware of what was happening behind her as Ben took his own step forward. Jemma breathed through her nose to level her nerves.

"I'd heard about your abduction," Dr. Paxton continued. "I was so very worried about you. I know your father was too."

"She was what?" The governor whipped his head to glare at the doctor. "I didn't—" His body twitched slightly, his expression calming. "I mean, I was so worried about you, darling. You know I just want to keep you safe."

Father? That was something Quill hadn't shared earlier. It was bizarre to Jemma to be meeting her this way. Especially with the years they'd known Governor Dunn. He'd always explained his daughter was off at school, unable to attend events with him. She never imagined that his daughter and Quill were one in the same.

"Well," Quill said, bouncing bolts of lightning back and forth between her hands, as if she was juggling a ball. "I didn't like being locked away in a tower. No matter how much you called me your princess, it didn't justify that." Her blue eyes glimmered in the light she generated around herself.

Ben inched closer to the side. The lights in the mall flickered. Jemma wondered if it was her or one of the other electrical Disparates in this room.

The door to the mall apartment opened and a stranger Jemma didn't recognize poked her head out the door. Her eyes grew wide as she took in the situation.

The distraction was enough to turn the doctor's attention to Ben.

Ben looked at her at the same time she caught him. He tried to run, but a bolt of light from the doctor's hand hit his head, causing him to stop in his tracks. His face scrunched with pain, his hands moving to his temple. Jemma sprang out of her hiding spot.

"I wouldn't get too close," Dr. Paxton warned. "The spark is still lighting his brain. Wouldn't want to cause it to hit the wrong spot. Might leave him unable to speak, or even think."

Jemma froze. The doctor was using electricity to control people. The same energy that Jemma had within her. The brain was a complex organ, not one to be messed with, and yet here was Dr. Paxton doing so without caution. Jemma's blood warmed as a current flowed through it. No one should have that power.

But I do, Jemma thought as she willed her energy to slow.

"Come on out, Stacey. This is a good example of why it's so important for Disparates to be healed." Dr. Paxton waved to the pink-haired woman to come out. She listened, followed by another woman and two men who looked equally confused and intrigued as they looked at Quill, mesmerized by her ability.

One of Quill's balls of electricity suspended in the air as she wiped her nose with the back of her hand. "Sorry, it's gotten awfully dusty inside here. Probably all the old ideals that have been stuck in these walls." She looked directly at Dr. Paxton as she said it. The doctor, however, did not look amused.

"Ben, why don't you come back and join me?" Dr. Paxton said. Ben turned to her, then looked at Jemma. She stared into his gray eyes, the stormy clouds that hid flecks of blue sea that were impossible to see at this distance.

"Jemma," he said to her. "I need to do this. It's important." He turned his back on her and headed toward Dr. Paxton, leaving Jemma behind with her thoughts.

I have the same power as the doctor. Her energy tingled at her finger-tips.

Pain scattered the thoughts in Ben's mind with each step he took toward Dr. Paxton.

We're changing the world.

Ben clutched his head. *No... Jemma's right there...*

I'm doing this for my family.

Then why am I walking away? His footsteps slowed, but the gap between him and the doctor continued to narrow. *This is the greater purpose I was made for.*

He let out a moan as an ache burned through his mind. As if the very act of changing his thoughts would cause his body, his world, to crumble. But it was worth it. For deep down, his gut knew the truth:

I was made for Jemma.

"It's time to stop this," Dr. Paxton said. "We have a train to catch. Those of you here are welcome to join us. However, if you'd rather do this the hard way, that can be arranged." She moved her coat back, revealing a gun on her side.

Heat flushed over Ben's back, coming from behind him—from Asher. He twisted out of the way as Dr. Paxton lifted her gun and fired. The bullet sliced past Ben.

The flames Asher had conjured dissipated into the air inches from their intended target—the doctor. As the smoke cleared, it revealed Asher's body lying on the hard tiled floor. Blood seeped from a hole in his chest. He didn't move.

Sweat scintillated across Dr. Paxton's face. "Such a waste."

"No!" Quill yelled. Bolts of electricity shot from her outstretched arms toward Asher. Ben dropped to the ground to escape being hit. Governor Dunn jumped toward the other four tour members while Dr. Paxton swept in the opposite direction. She turned the gun at Quill. "I'd rather not pull this trigger again. Washing away this memory from your father would be a challenge. But I'm up for it."

Governor Dunn looked at the doctor, his lips curled back.

A trail of ice shot from the shadows behind Asher, knocking Dr. Paxton's gun out of her grasp. It fell to the floor, covered in frost.

The doctor rubbed her hand. "There's more of you?"

"Many more." A light haired man emerged from the corner closest to where Asher's body lay. Wait—Ben knew him. Why was Buran here, now? Small crystals hung from his eyebrows.

"Maybe we should calm down. Let's talk about this?" Governor Dunn tried to intervene.

"Quiet you." Dr. Paxton silenced him. His face narrowed.

Ben's mouth dropped open. "Buran?"

"Hey Ben. I'd love to catch up, but I have some unfinished business first," he said, looking directly at the doctor.

Seizing her chance, Quill ran through the parted sea of Dr. Paxton and her minions, kneeling next to Asher's body.

Footsteps sounded from the front of the mall. Ben whipped around to see at least a dozen Responders marching toward them.

"Well, two can play that game," Dr. Paxton said.

Adding more guns to the fight made escaping this situation nearly impossible. "Tell them your plan," Ben said to Dr. Paxton. She raised an eyebrow at him. "If you tell them what you're doing," he continued, "they'll understand how important your work is."

Dr. Paxton gave a sly smile. She seemed to believe he was still on her side. "Oh Benjamin, of course you're right. We're going to heal the world of the hurt and pain caused by the hands of Disparates. Both purposely and accidentally. Buran Kuzmin, if your had this cure, he would still be here."

Buran looked at her disgustedly. "It's because of the pills he's not here. Don't you get it? The pills make Disparates more dangerous. This new drug may work short term, but it will never last, and when the Disparate's energy comes back, it will be stronger and more uncontrollable than ever."

The Responders were nearing. Ben's body shook. He tried to steady himself, but he quickly realized he wasn't the only one moving. The ground itself rumbled.

"Without medicine to suppress them, a Disparate can actually learn how to control their emotions, and their energy," Buran continued, unfazed by the Earth's sudden trembling.

"You don't understand," Dr. Paxton said. "If Disparates learn to control their energy, then who will control them?"

Her question caused Ben to pause.

"Just look at the fire anarchist," she continued. "He's been *controlling* his energy and attacking government buildings. Using his emotions to attack whomever he wants. Is that the type of power we should leave unrestrained?"

Dr. Paxton can't control Disparates, Ben realized. That was why she was so adamant about healing and curing the disease, even though she was a Disparate herself. The hypocrisy caused Ben's trembling to intensify.

"Where are you?" Dr. Paxton turned in circles, searching for someone. "There's more of you here."

More of who here? Ben thought.

The ground cracked open, creating a chasm between them and the incoming group of Responders. The Responders shook and fell, crawling away from the hole as their hands gripped their weapons.

Three figures moved into the light, coming from where Quill had emerged moments before. The figure in the middle had her arms stretched in front of her, sweat plastering her dark hair against her face. When she finished, her body dropped with her arms, and the two men caught her.

"Well then, if that's how you want to play, so be it," Dr. Paxton said. "Fix that inconvenience for me, Stacey dear." A spark flew out of her hand and hit Stacey's head.

Immediately, the shaking began again, but this time not as intense. Jemma ran to join Asher and Quill, falling to the floor and sliding the last few feet. The chasm in front of the Responders started to shrink. They stayed sprawled on the ground, trying to get away despite the fact the gap was narrowing.

"No!" Buran shot another steak of ice, aiming for Stacey. Before it reached her, Dr. Paxton sent a shock into the larger man next to her. He stood in front of Buran's ice, catching it with his own. A giant glacier formed a shield in front of the group, trapping Ben on the side with the doctor.

The man's eyes widened as he examined his creation. "I thought I couldn't do that anymore."

"Oh, don't worry," Dr. Paxton said, her voice echoing off the ice wall. "You can't. Your brain's been restructured so it doesn't produce energy on its own. That doesn't mean that part of your brain is gone, it's more like it's sleeping. I just happen to know how to wake it up. Temporarily, of course."

Jemma's attention moved to Aniyah. Her face was downcast after the effort it took to create the canyon. A tear fell down her cheek as she focused to keep the hole from being refilled. The shaking intensified with the effort of the two earth energies fighting against each other.

What did they have left? Asher was shot. Quill pressed on his wound as his chest heaved in shallow, uneven breaths. Buran's ice was stopped. Aniyah wouldn't last much longer before she had to give in, allowing the Responders to swarm the group. Samay and Calum held onto her, holding her up.

"Now, call your friends off," Dr. Paxton said, looking directly at Jemma. "Unless I need to practice this trick on Benjamin?"

The others in the mall seemed frozen in their current actions, as if they were waiting for her next move.

Jemma noticed Dr. Paxton's team as well. Governor Dunn stood dumbfounded as he watched the scene unfold. He was too much under the doctor's influence to do anything else. The girl she called Stacey held onto her head as the chasm continued to fill slowly; it seemed as if she was winning that war. The large, burly man stood by her, looking as dumbfounded as the governor as to what was happening.

Then there was Ben. He stood near the doctor, but his eyes met Jemma's. Concern swirled as they wrinkled. Did he truly believe the things the doctor was saying? Was he so easily controlled by the same energy that flowed through her? She had an idea, but it would only work if she could control her energy.

For Ben, she would do it. If only he would trust her.

Ben's head throbbed. He couldn't keep his eyes off her, just like the first time he saw her. The woman he married, the mother of his children. He thought his love for her had maxed with each life event they experienced together, and yet it continued to grow. In the mundane daily tasks. The arguments and discussions. In working through their problems. None of those things had been so trivial when he had her by his side. He thought he loved her then, but the way his heart swelled in this moment was something more.

He realized what he needed to do. "It's okay," he said to Jemma. "I want to go with Dr. Paxton. I want to be a part of her movement."

A pained look crossed Jemma's face.

"Let me go, please," he continued, his heart breaking. "It'll only be a few weeks. I'll come back to you. I'll *all ways* come back."

He needed to go with Dr. Paxton. She'd never let Jemma and the people she came with leave with him. He glanced at the Responders, who started to stand. He was her pawn, and if they fought it now, much worse would come than Ben being away from his family for a little more time. He didn't trust the doctor, but he couldn't risk Jemma.

"Ask your friend to stop. She looks exhausted. I'm sure the doctor would be willing to help them the way she's helped me."

Dr. Paxton smiled and nodded her head in agreement.

Jemma narrowed her eyes. "Aniyah, it's okay. You can stop," she said. The intense shaking lessened to a tremor. The canyon filled in. The Responders stayed where they were, watching to see how the events unfolded. Their confidence when they first entered the mall was now replaced with unease.

Jemma took a step toward Ben, the space between them lessening. As she neared, Ben noticed her hair rising. They were only a few feet away, easily bridged in just a moment.

"Tell the boys I love them and will see them soon." Speaking about his boys was almost too much for Ben. He held back his tears. Oh how his heart ached to hug them.

"You can tell them yourself," Jemma said. "I'm not leaving here without you."

Ben shook his head. "I'm needed..." He stopped, noticing the spark in Jemma's golden eyes. She knew what she was doing. With no apprehension, no second guessing. Ben needed to trust her.

"...at home," he finished his sentence.

Jemma smiled.

"Ugh!" Dr. Paxton shouted, moving her hand toward Ben. A flicker erupted from her fingers. Jemma wrapped herself around him, a shock emanating through their bodies as her arms encapsulated him.

She took the hit. Concern swept over Ben as streaks of lightning shot from their embrace around the top of the mall.

Wait... no. She didn't take the hit. This energy was coming from her. The small spark Dr. Paxton had sent to manipulate Ben's mind had been thrown off target, drawn away by the electricity Jemma generated, leaving a singed mark on the floor. It was tiny compared to the power from Jemma's body. This level of Disparate outburst would surely result in a level ten alert. Off the charts. Yet somehow Ben wasn't burned. Jemma controlled it enough to keep it away from consuming him.

The others, however, ducked to avoid being the next target. A spark grazed the governor's head, causing him to crash to the ground. The lights above shattered, glass raining upon the mass of people below. Screams joined the buzzing in the air.

With her own power, Jemma had saved him.

Her body glowed as it went limp in his arms.

THIRTY-THREE

Ben held onto Jemma as the lightning ceased. Jemma had generated electricity. He pushed her back. Her head lolled to the side, eyes closed.

"Jemma..." he pleaded. "Jemma, wake up." He cradled her in his arms, wiping the hair off her face. She wasn't breathing.

The scene around him swirled in panic. Arms slowly uncovered heads as people, who had thrown themselves to the ground during the outburst, peered around the mall. Safety lights flickered on, replacing the main sources that now lay as glass on the vinyl tiles. Although they were dimmer, they illuminated the blurs that moved around Ben as his tears wet Jemma's face.

"Stop there," Governor Dunn's voice echoed, a hand holding his singed hair. "Arrest the doctor."

Jemma's power had freed even him. But at what cost?

Ben pressed his lips to Jemma's, breathing life into her mouth. "Come on." He laid her on the ground.

Footsteps with the sound of rattling weapons approached the governor.

"Now, now," Dr. Paxton's voice rang. "I'm sure we can work this out."

Ben pressed on Jemma's chest in a steady rhythm.

"Don't even think about it," Quill said, turning toward the doctor. She rose to her feet. Asher lay below her, awake and holding the bottom of his shirt to his gunshot wound.

Ben had experience with the kind of pain that was likely burning through Asher. However, the pain he felt in this moment was more excruciating than any physical affliction. He bent to breathe in his wife's mouth. "Come back to me..."

As he pressed on her chest once more she gasped, sucking in air and trying to catch her breath. But her breathing didn't return to normal.

"I'm not sure what you mean," the doctor said, directing a spark toward the governor.

Quill reached with her own string of light, attracting the spark to her thread. She reeled it in.

A trigger sounded, causing Ben to pause his beats. A needle stuck out of Dr. Paxton's arm, having gone through her thick blue coat. Governor Dunn stood next to her, the doctor's tranquilizer in his hands. She immediately pulled out the dart and took a staggered step toward the governor. "You're... gonna regret... this," she said before collapsing to the ground.

"Ben."

He made eye contact with his wife. Although her breathing was light, she was doing it on her own.

"Jemma." This time his lips met hers for a kiss. Her small gasp made him stop, but only for a moment before he felt the edges of her mouth curl into a grin.

She was alive.

She was here.

She was in his arms.

"So how long have you known how to do that trick?" Ben asked, his face close to hers.

"This one with my lips?" She pressed against him once more. Static jumped as they met, adding a sensitivity to their touch.

He savored her taste a little longer before allowing her to move away again. "Yep. That spark right there."

"Turns out you don't know everything about me." Jemma gently brushed the burn scars on the side of his face.

Chills created goosebumps across his skin at her touch. "Good thing we have the rest of our lives for me to figure you out."

The smile she gave him warmed his soul more than his flame energy ever could.

The sun was bright on this warm spring day. Margaret found a grassy spot to sit on the sidelines of the soccer field. Mackie, dressed in his green uniform, ran to join his team, while Louie sat on the blanket she'd laid out.

"I'm bored," Louie said.

"We just got here." Margaret looked over her sunglasses at him. "Wait until your brother starts playing. Then you'll have something to watch."

He picked at some grass at the edge of the blanket. "Grandma?"

"Yes?"

"Where's my dad?" His face stayed downcast as he waited for her response.

Margaret wanted to shield him from the truth. Keep him protected. After Skylar died and Asher disappeared, she allowed herself to wallow in her sadness. Too much had been put on Jemma's shoulders. She'd tried since then to keep her problems to herself. But instead of lessening her daughter's burdens, she'd created distance between them. A length she'd been working on narrowing since this whole ordeal began.

She didn't want to add more lies to her relationship with Louie. "He's been away at a place with some people who think they are helping him." She chose her words carefully. After all, he was only six.

"That's what Mom said. Did they help him?" he asked.

"Not exactly." She took in a sharp breath. "Not everyone in this world has the same intentions. Even if they think what they're doing is right, that's not always the case."

"Mackie thinks there is gold at the end of a rainbow. I told him that's not true."

Margaret held in a laugh. "Well, rainbows might not lead to gold, but they do make the sky beautiful."

"So that makes it okay for him to be wrong?" Louie looked at her with his face scrunched.

"Not quite what I mean." Margaret pursed her lips. "What happens before a rainbow forms?"

"A storm?"

Margaret tapped his nose. "Exactly. Sometimes we go through bad storms in life just to get to the rainbow."

His face brightened. "Oh! So it's not about the gold!"

"Well, no." Margaret said. "The gold was never there."

"But *some* people think it is." Louie glanced at the field as Mackie's team got into their starting positions. "And they forget about the rainbow. We should talk about what's at the end of the storm."

"You make a good point." Margaret wrapped an arm around Louie and squeezed. It was time for her to focus on what waited for her at the end of a storm instead of searching for a pot of gold that didn't exist. There was beauty in the rainbows.

Her daughter was the brightest light she knew. She'd return un-harmed. And perhaps she would have found the pot of gold she'd been chasing. Maybe it was possible to have it all.

She deserved it after the raging storm she'd endured.

J emma walked as if in a haze, her hand intertwined in Ben's, hold-ing tight. It still didn't feel real. The soccer field was bright green, families sitting and clapping as another goal was scored, by Mackie

Ben cupped his free hand around his mouth. "Way to go, buddy!"

Mackie's attention turned away from his celebratory dance. "Daddy!"

"Dad?" Louie's voice came from the sidelines, following his brother's gaze. "Dad!" Louie's whole face beamed into a smile. He scrambled to his feet and joined Mackie as they raced to meet him. Louie floated the last few feet, as well as Mackie and some coolers nearby spectators had brought with them to the game.

Jemma's breathing paused, waiting for the worst to happen. For the crowd to see Louie using his energy. The reaction and fear that would trigger. She didn't have the energy to see more hate without breaking.

However, as the boys met Ben's embrace, the coolers dropped on the grass. The family they belonged to glanced at them with wrinkled brows and returned their attention to the game.

Ben looked at Jemma with wide eyes.

She shrugged, her shoulders relaxing. "You've missed a lot while you were gone."

"Clearly," he said.

Ben seemed like he didn't want to be the first to let go. He waited until the boys released him before standing.

A whistle blew. The game was over.

"Our team won!" Mackie shouted excitedly, jumping up and down.

"Why don't you go join their celebration?" Jemma said, watching as his team made a huddle.

Mackie looked at Ben, hesitant.

Ben rubbed the top of his head. "I'm not going anywhere."

Mackie smiled and ran to join his team.

Jemma caught sight of her mother at the edge of the field, folding her blanket. They made their way over to join her.

"I'm glad you're finally home," she said to Ben as she patted his arm. Jemma caught her eyes flicking to the burn on his face for a moment before resuming eye contact. "We've all missed you."

"I've missed you too." He gave her an embrace.

Her mother's eyes turned to Jemma. "And I'm glad you're okay. But where's your brother? Back at the house?"

"Asher's at the hospital," she said, her worry for him returning. "Quill and Governor Dunn are with him. He's stable for now."

Her mother's face paled. "Well, it seems you have it taken care of here. I'm going to head over there." She pulled out her keys.

"He'll be glad to see you," Jemma said, giving her mother a goodbye hug.

"Can we get ice cream?" Louie asked. Their tradition.

Jemma nodded. "Yes we can. Together, as a family."

Thirty-Four

Walking through *his* front door brought a new wave of relief to Ben. He was home. He pulled Jemma inside, having barely let go of her hand since they were reunited.

She didn't stop at the door but rather crashed against his chest. He winced; his shoulder was still sensitive.

"I'm sorry!" Jemma exclaimed. She placed her hand gently above where his wound was. The light pressure felt nice.

"It's okay." Ben tucked a strand of hair behind her ear. "I rather like you against me."

Her eyes twinkled before turning serious. "Do you think Asher will be okay?"

"If you want to head to the hospital with your mom, I'll understand."

"I just got you back." She wrapped her other arm around his middle and squeezed.

He tilted her chin to meet his gaze. "I'm not going anywhere. I promise."

As he leaned in for a kiss, the boys burst in from through the door, finally finishing gathering their shoes from the car. Which were promptly dropped to the floor.

"Daddy! I'm so glad you're home!" Mackie yelled. He slammed into Ben's side as Jemma took a step back.

"Now that's what I call a Mack Attack!" Ben knelt to his height and returned his hug. He noticed a mess on his face. "Great job on winning your game today! Did you eat any of the celebratory ice cream or just decide to wear it?"

Mackie laughed as he wiped his face. "You don't wear ice cream."

Louie was close behind him. "I'm hungry," he said.

"Really? You just had a treat." Ben raised an eyebrow. "I thought you had gotten taller; keep this up and you'll be taller than me!"

"Gotta keep his energy up," Jemma said.

Louie's eyes widened. "Yeah! So I can keep making fire, like you Dad!"

Ben's gaze locked with Jemma's. He didn't have any flame energy now, but wasn't sure it was the right time to explain.

Jemma seemed to understand that he wasn't ready to talk about it. "Why don't we go get you a snack?" She closed the door and ushered Louie toward the kitchen, standing on her toes for a light kiss as she passed by Ben. He wanted to wrap his fingers through her hair and keep her lips on his for a moment longer.

"Dad! Come see what I drew!" Mackie interrupted their moment, tugging on his arm.

"Of course." Ben smiled at Jemma as he was pulled away.

Mackie led him to the table covered in papers. He grabbed one that had four figures drawn on it. "That's me, and Mom, and Louie," he said pointing to one side of the paper. "And that's you." The last figure was drawn away from the rest; however, a heart in the middle connected them together. "To help you remember how much we love you!"

"Thank you," Ben said as he accepted the drawing. "I know exactly where this is going to go." He headed to the fridge and hung it up. Mackie beamed.

So did Ben. He was glad to be home.

Being in the hospital reminded Margaret of the time she'd spent here with twelve year old Jemma. But this time, it was Asher she walked down the pristine hallway for.

Tobias saw her as she approached, meeting her halfway. "He's not doing very well."

Margaret's heart stopped, her mouth dropping. Her baby boy.

"No, no," Tobias hurriedly said. "Not like that. Healthwise, he's doing great. They got the bullet and they've bandaged him up. It's just..."

As they neared, Margaret realized a person in uniform stood outside his door. She marched up to him. "Excuse me. You're blocking my son's room."

The man, who was a head taller than her, met her glare. "You need approval to enter." The badge on his chest read *R.E.I.*

"I'm his *mother*," Margaret said.

Tobias reached her side. "This is Margaret Stillfield, of the Public Safety Committee. She has approval."

The R.E.I. Responder nodded his head and stepped to the side, allowing them to enter.

Quill stood from the chair next to Asher and motioned for Margaret to take it. As she lowered herself, she noticed metal cuffs around Asher's wrists.

"Can you believe it?" he said, following her gaze. "You burn a few buildings on your quest to save the world, and this is the treatment you get." He pulled at the restraints, the metal clanging against the bed frame.

"I'll get this cleared up," Tobias spoke from near the door.

"I hope so." Asher winced as he lay back on the bed. "Otherwise, I'll take matters into my own hands."

"For now, you need to worry about healing." Margaret swiped his hair from his forehead.

"That's what I was telling him," Quill said.

A phone rang. "That's me," Tobias excused himself. "It's Buran. Hello? No, you can tell Calum we haven't heard anything about where Chayse is... The doctor's not being the most forthcoming with information..."

Margaret turned back to Asher, examining the bandage that wrapped from his right shoulder and around his left side. The middle was lightly stained red. "If he's not able to get you out of this," she whispered, placing her hand over his. The cold cuff brushed against her skin. "I will." She wasn't letting anyone take her son from her. Not again. Even if it meant risking herself.

"It's not going to be an easy transition," Tobias said into his phone, "but I'm sure, together, we can work out a system that will benefit all citizens."

Back in governor mode already. Margaret shook her head. He was right, though. The truth about Initiative 67, about Enertin, would be a lot to take in. The transition was unlikely to go smoothly knowing the six other Republic governors. It would take a lot of convincing.

But that was a worry for another day.

J emma sat on her bed. Alone. Like she'd been for the past month. She looked at Ben's side of the bed. Empty. The blankets untouched.

Her eyes scanned to the notebook of letters sitting on the bedside table, a reminder that not everyone made it off the islands alive.

The bedroom door squealed open and Ben's face came into view. "Did you miss me?" He locked the door behind him.

Jemma's pulse raised. He wasn't imaginary. He was here. "More than you know."

"Sorry, the boys wanted me to read three books tonight," he said. "I couldn't say no. I think Mackie may still be awake, but hopefully not for long."

She patted the empty space next to her. "Care to join me?"

Ben gave her a smirk. "I can't imagine anything I'd want to do more." He pulled his shirt over his head and plopped himself on the bed.

Jemma lay on his chest. She examined the dressing on his left shoulder. She was tempted to remove it, see how deep his wound went, but resisted.

He sighed, wrapping his arm tight around her. "I've missed this."

"Me causing your arm to go numb? Because I'm not moving from this spot. Ever."

Ben laughed at her attachment. She rubbed her hand across his cool chest, feeling the outlines of his bones that lay beneath the thin layer of skin. He'd lost some weight. She moved softly, lovingly, wanting to convey her feelings with her touch.

"Mmmm," he moaned. "If you keep that up, the only place I'll need you to move is a bit further south."

"Ben!" she responded, lifting her head to see the twinkle in his eye. He looked quite proud of himself; she was sure he thought his flirting was top shelf material. "We don't even know if the kids are fully asleep," she said. Not in a serious tone of voice, but rather a challenging one.

"Well, I guess you'll have to try and be quiet. If you think you're up for that."

Jemma thought about Ben's request. Her body was tired after staying up all night. However, the thought of having her husband to herself brought a second wind of energy. The type of energy she much preferred to release on her husband.

She moved her lips to meet his. As they touched, a shock erupted. Jemma jumped her head back, moving her hand to her mouth. "I'm so sorry," she said.

"Don't be." Ben laughed, moving a hand to cup under her chin. "I quite like the spark we have between us."

He pulled her mouth to his. Her lips had missed this movement. This spark had kept her going these last few weeks. This spark she never wanted to turn off.

End of Book One

ACKNOWLEDGEMENTS

This is the part where the author gets mushy. When "all is said and done" yet does an author ever truly say it all? How can they, when there are so many worlds to visit and characters to meet.

And I wouldn't be able to meet any of them without the support of my husband, Jeremy. Yeah, yeah, I'm acknowledging my husband. That might not be the most unique thing, but he most certainly is. Life would not be the same without him. I felt right alongside Jemma—if my husband were wrongfully taken away, I'd do whatever was in my power to bring him back.

Same goes for my alpha reader, critique partner, best friend: Kimberleigh Dixon. As I said in the dedication, this book wouldn't be in your hands now if it weren't for her. She got me into writing by recruiting me to be her alpha, and you should check out her fantasy book: Mapleshire: Secrets of Rose Manor.

Speaking of other authors, I was blessed to have some amazingly talented writers help me along the way, from my writing group, to my beta readers. Thank you A.M. Yeager, Haley Bono, and Jen Woodrum for sharing your insights and expertise to really shine this story. As well as a think you to Aleish for giving a reader's perspective. You all made the beta process run smoothly and I am eternally grateful for the time and effort you gave to my manuscript.

And an extra special thank you to my cover designer Benita Thompson, my artist EFA_finearts, my imprint designer Christy Boughan, and my editor Angela Morse. This beauty would be a lot less beautiful without your contributions. Thank you each for bringing my vision to life.

I would like to be cliché again and thank my parents and in-laws. First, my parents, Mark and Karen Ferrin, for their support and encouragement. I know they were surprised to learn their daughter was an author, yet I'm not so sure it was too surprising. I remember the nights at home when my mom would catch me reading in my bed with the lights off. She always warned me it was bad for my eyes, and yes, I do in fact wear glasses now. I think they really complete the author look.

And next my in-laws, Cliff and Kathy Morgan. My father-in-law is a huge reader and I appreciate his enthusiasm to read my work. Although the thought of having people I know read my book slightly terrifies me, I'm also excited to know I have people as supportive as you two on my side.

OH! The BIGGEST thank you goes to the most important people in my life, along with my husband. My four children. My babies. The ones that make me a mom. You've given me the experiences that have allowed this book to exist. You are the best things that have ever happened to me, as well as the hardest. Parenthood is messy. It's difficult. I'm nowhere near a perfect mother, but because of each of you parenthood is also beautiful, and joyous, and the best adventure of my life. Here I go crying again, and yet you each are used to your mom and her tears for you. I love you each so much.

Last, but not least, if you've made it this far—YOU! The reader! Thank you for taking the chance on a debut author. I hope you have found a piece of yourself within these pages, or maybe not but have been able to increase in empathy for others. That's the beautiful thing about the pages of a book. Being able to experience new thoughts and feelings from the perspective of someone new. I'm proud of you for going on this journey. And if you are struggling in your own life, know you aren't alone and help is always available. Reach out.

ABOUT THE AUTHOR

Holly D. Morgan is a wife and mother of four. She has a Bachelor's Degree in Elementary Education and taught fourth graders that they were mathematicians, scientists, historians, and writers. It wasn't until after she left teaching that she realized she, too, was a writer (with some motivation from a friend leading her to accept the call).

Although her short mystery stories have been published in anthologies, *One Spark* is her debut novel. She can be found typing away from her home in San Tan Valley, Arizona.

Follow along for updates:

Instagram: @hollydmorganbooks

Facebook: Author Holly D. Morgan

Website: https://hollydmorganbooks.company.site/

Milton Keynes UK
Ingram Content Group UK Ltd.
UKHW040215091024
449407UK00016BA/246/J